Mallory and the Trouble With Twins

MW01077753

**Look for these and other books
in the Baby-sitters Club series:**

Mallory and the Trouble With Twins
Ann M. Martin

AN
APPLE
PAPERBACK

SCHOLASTIC INC.
New York Toronto London Auckland Sydney

Cover art by Hodges Soileau

ISBN 0-590-43507-8

12 11 10 9 8 7 6 5 4 3   0 1 2 3 4/9

Printed in the U.S.A.   28

*This book is for
the Palladinos
and the Ameses,
especially Kathy.*

CHAPTER 1

"Kindergarten baby, stick your head in gravy! Wash it off with applesauce and show it to the Navy!" sang Nicky.

"Mommy, make him stop!" cried Claire.

"Nicholas Pike," said my mother, "this is supposed to be fun. We are going to Washington Mall, which you have been begging to do for weeks, and where, I might add, each of you kids is going to get a new pair of shoes. You do want new shoes, don't you?"

"Yes," said Nicky contritely.

"Then apologize to your sister. She doesn't like being called a kindergarten baby. You didn't like it either when you were her age."

"Sorry, Claire," said Nicky.

Mom didn't see it, because we were so jam-packed into our car, but Claire's response was to stick her tongue out at Nicky. So he silently mouthed "kindergarten baby" to her and she turned bright red. If I hadn't grabbed her then,

1

who knows what would have happened?

There are eight kids in my family. Nicky and Claire are just two of them, but they were having a big enough fight for all of us.

I am Mallory. I'm eleven and the oldest. Claire is five and the youngest. Between Claire and me are Margo, who's seven, Nicky, who's eight, Vanessa, who's nine, and the triplets, who are ten. The triplets are Adam, Byron, and Jordan, and they're identical. You would hardly know this, though, since they always wear different clothes and have such different personalities.

After I grabbed Claire, she calmed down. It was a good thing I was sitting between her and Nicky. I had put myself there on purpose. When it comes to kids — my brothers and sisters, or any others — I'm pretty smart. For instance, I had figured out the seating arrangement for our outing to the mall. (It takes awhile to drive there.) I had put Margo in the front seat with Mom and Dad, since she gets carsick sometimes and riding in the front is less bumpy. I had put the triplets in the way back, where they could be jerks without bothering anybody, especially Nicky, whom they are apt to tease mercilessly. And in the backseat, I had put Claire, me, Nicky, and Vanessa, in that order. Sitting between Claire and Nicky, I could break

2

up fights. And with Vanessa by the window, she could daydream or make up poems, lost in her own world, which is how she's happiest.

"There's the mall!" cried Margo, pointing. She had survived the trip without once saying she was going to barf.

"All *right!*" cried Nicky. "New shoes. I want sneakers, and they have to be Reeboks. Or Avias. Either one."

"Oh, you are so cool, Nick," said Adam sarcastically from the back.

"Shut up!"

"*You* shut up!"

"Mom, Nicky and Adam said 'shut up,' " announced Claire.

"I heard," said Mom dryly. (Poor Mom. Since Dad was driving, she got stuck handling the squabbling and complaining.) "And all I have to say is this: How badly does any of you want shoes?"

Us kids "shut up" right away. We didn't think Mom would *really* not buy shoes for us . . . but we couldn't be sure. Long car rides with eight children could drive anyone crazy. (I should point out, by the way, that our mother is not an ogre. She's just human. And half an hour of kindergarten baby and tattling was wearing on her nerves.)

Dad pulled into the entrance to Washington

Mall and found a parking space that was about three miles away from the nearest store. We hiked over to a boutique, walked through it, and were in . . . the mall.

I swear, the mall is another world. You are surrounded by stores and shops, and even better things: food stands, exhibits, a flower mart, and my personal favorite, the ear-piercing boutique. I hardly know where to look.

As badly as we wanted new shoes, my brothers and sisters and I also wanted to be turned loose to go exploring.

But, "Shoes first," said Dad.

So we went to Antoinette's Shoe Tree (what on earth *is* a shoe tree?) and each got what we needed — *not*, I might emphasize, what we *wanted*. For example, what I wanted were these extremely cool pink shoes with green trim. What I got were loafers.

"They're much more practical," said Mom. "They go with almost everything you own. And they'll last at least a year."

When you are a parent of eight children, you have to think of these things. But when you are an eleven-year-old who has to show up in school every day, you just want those cool pink shoes.

As soon as we'd gotten our shoes, Mom and Dad let us kids split up so we could explore

4

the mall for an hour. We had brought along spending money and were eager to, well, spend it. So the triplets went off by themselves, Nicky went off with Dad, Vanessa went off with Mom, and Claire and Margo begged to come with me.

"You do fun things," said Margo.

That was true. I check out all the stuff I'm not allowed to have yet, like glitter for my hair, makeup, and short skirts.

"Today," I announced, "we're going to watch people have their ears pierced."

"Goody," said Claire, and we set off.

The mall is huge, but I could find my way to the ear-piercing boutique blindfolded, so we reached it in under two minutes.

A girl my age was sitting on a stool, about to have a hole made in her right ear. I noticed that she already had one hole in each ear, and I immediately felt envious. I'm not allowed to have any holes in my ears, and this girl got to have three.

Claudia Kishi wanted three, also, but I didn't feel very sorry for her, since she already had two. Claudia is one of my friends in the Baby-sitters Club. What's the Baby-sitters Club? It's a business that my friends and I run. We baby-sit for people in Stoneybrook, Connecticut, where we live.

5

There are six of us in the club. The president is Kristy Thomas. She was the one who started the club. She started it last year with a bunch of her friends who are all thirteen now and in eighth grade. My best friend, Jessi Ramsey, and I are the two younger members of the club. (We're both eleven and in sixth grade.) What an interesting group we are. We're very different, but we get along really well.

Kristy, for instance, is loud and outgoing. And full of ideas. She's quite serious about running the club. She's small for her age and cares zero about her appearance. In fact, she almost always wears jeans, sneakers, a turtle-neck, and a sweater. She comes from a family of brothers, two older ones, and a little one, David Michael. Her mom, who was divorced, recently remarried a millionaire, so now Kristy lives in a mansion across town from her old house (and across town from the rest of us). She has a new little stepsister and stepbrother, Andrew and Karen, whom she loves to pieces. Kristy would not care one bit about having her ears pierced.

Mary Anne Spier, who is our club secretary and Kristy's best friend, couldn't be more different from Kristy. She's shy and sensitive and cries at just about anything. I think she's sentimental, too, which may explain why she's the first one of us to have a steady boyfriend. His name is Logan Bruno, and he and Mary Anne are perfect for each other. Mary Anne lives in the house next door to Kristy's old one, and across the street from Claudia. She lives with her dad and her kitten, Tigger. Her mom died a long time ago, when Mary Anne was very young. Mr. Spier used to be really strict with his daughter, but he's let up a lot lately. And since that happened, Mary Anne has taken more of an interest in her appearance. She wears clothes that are sort of preppy, but at the same time cool. I bet Mr. Spier would never let Mary Anne get her ears pierced, though.

Dawn Schafer is another good friend of Mary Anne's. In fact, I think Mary Anne has *two* best friends — Dawn and Kristy. Dawn is the club treasurer. Boy, is she different from anyone else in the club. She's a real individual. Dawn moved to Connecticut last year with her mom and her younger brother, Jeff. They moved all the way from California after her parents got divorced, and they picked Stoneybrook because Mrs. Schafer grew up here, or something like that. Dawn is so Californian that it's almost sad to see her transplanted to the East Coast. She's laid-back (but very organized and responsible), adores sunshine and warm weather, and even looks Californian, with incredibly long, pale blonde hair and sparkling blue eyes. Things haven't been easy for Dawn. There was the divorce, of course, and then, just recently, her brother moved back to California to live with Mr. Schafer because he hated Connecticut so much. But Dawn is not only an individual, she's a survivor. She'll get through this. Pierced ears? I don't know whether Dawn would want them. I'm sure she'd be allowed to have them, but she'd probably only get them if she were sure she wasn't going to look like every other thirteen-year-old around.

Now, let me get back to Claudia Kishi. She's the one who already has pierced ears, remember? Claud is the vice-president of the Baby-sitters Club and probably the trendiest, coolest kid in all of Stoneybrook Middle School. She's into art and makes some of her own clothes and jewelry — wild things, like socks on which she paints palm trees and coconuts; or gigantic, bright *papier-mâché* pins and bracelets. Whether she makes her clothes or buys them, they are totally cool, and you can count on Claudia to add her own personal touches. No matter what she wears, she looks great. That's because she's Japanese-American — beautiful and exotic with dark, almond-shaped eyes; long black hair that she styles in all different ways; and an absolutely clear complexion. It's unfortunate that Claud is a poor student, because her older sister, Janine, is a genius. Claudia's parents give her grief about this, but Mimi, her grandmother, never does. Mimi is just sweet and loving.

There are just two other members of the Baby-sitters Club: Jessi and me. Since we're young, we're called junior officers. Of all the kids in the club, I guess Jessi and I are most alike, except for some obvious differences that don't matter at all. For instance, I'm white and Jessi is black. And I have seven brothers and sisters, while Jessi has just one younger sister (Becca) and a baby brother (John Philip Ramsey, Jr., nicknamed Squirt). Beyond that, well, we're both the oldest in our families but think our parents treat us like babies. We both want pierced ears desperately but will probably get braces on our teeth instead, and we both wish we could wear trendier clothes and get decent haircuts. We love to read, too, especially horse stories — although I want to be a writer one day, while Jessi dreams of maybe being a ballet dancer. (She takes lessons and is very talented.) Most important, not long ago, we were both in need of a best friend, so we were very happy to find each other after the Ramseys moved to Stoneybrook.

Claire, Margo, and I stood watching the ear-piercing. I imagined Jessi and me sitting on the stools one day. (When, though? When we were seventy-two?)

A woman with one of those ear-piercing guns approached the girl on the stool. "One more in the right lobe, is that it?" she asked.

"Yes," said the girl.

Punch went the gun.

"Aughhh!" shrieked Claire.

The woman with the gun jumped a mile. The girl on the stool looked scared to death. And Margo said weakly, "I think I'm going to barf. She just got a *hole* punched in her *ear*."

"You are not going to barf. You are *not!*" I said firmly.

I grabbed my sisters by their hands, turned them around, and ran off, calling "Sorry!" over my shoulder to the woman and the girl.

I was *so* embarrassed. Little sisters. What pains they can be.

I'll be surprised if I live to see twelve.

CHAPTER 2

"Mallory! Hey, Mal!" Jessi Ramsey was running up the sidewalk to Claudia Kishi's house.

I'd been about to go inside for our meeting of the Baby-sitters Club, but now I stopped and waited for Jessi.

"Hi," I greeted her. I could tell she'd come straight from a ballet lesson. She was still wearing her leotard — she'd just thrown a shirt and jeans over it — and her hair was pulled back from her face the way it has to be during a dance class.

"Hi," Jessi replied breathlessly.

I opened the door to Claud's house and we went inside. Us club members spend an awful lot of time at the Kishis', since club meetings are held every Monday, Wednesday, and Friday afternoon from five-thirty until six, so we hardly ever bother to ring the doorbell.

11

"Hello, girls," said a soft voice.

Mimi, Claudia's grandmother, had entered the front hallway.

"Are we the last to arrive?" Jessi asked anxiously. Jessi has such a busy schedule (between ballet lessons and a regular, twice-weekly sitting job) that she's almost always the last to show up at the meetings. This makes her a little nervous, and I understand why. She and I are not only the youngest club members, but the newest, so we feel we have to be on our toes at all times.

"Yes, you are last ones," Mimi told us, "but not late. Not five-thirty yet." (Mimi had a stroke last summer, and it has affected her speech.)

"Thanks, Mimi!" I said.

Jessi and I raced upstairs, with Mimi calling after us, "You will find surprise in Claudia room."

Surprise? I hoped it wasn't Janine, Claudia's sister. She makes me crazy.

Jessi and I ran into Claud's bedroom and stopped short. We saw the surprise right away. It was Logan Bruno, Mary Anne's boyfriend. I don't think I mentioned earlier that Logan is a member of the Baby-sitters Club. He doesn't usually come to meetings, though, since he's

12

just an associate member, someone our club can call on to take a sitting job if none of the rest of us is free to take it.

I guess now would be a good time to stop and tell you how our club works, and I better go all the way back to the very beginning, when Kristy first got the idea for the club. That was over a year ago, before Kristy's mom was even thinking about marrying Watson Brewer, the millionaire.

What happened was this. Mrs. Thomas needed a sitter for David Michael, who was six at the time, but Kristy and her older brothers, Sam and Charlie, were all busy. So Mrs. Thomas got on the phone. Kristy watched her make call after call in search of a sitter, and while she watched, she thought what a waste of time this was for her mother. If only her mom could make one call and reach a bunch of sitters at once, she would find one much more quickly. That was when Kristy got the idea for the Baby-sitters Club. She and a few of her friends, she thought, could meet several times a week, and people could call them during the meetings and practically be guaranteed a sitter. One of the girls was bound to be free.

So Kristy got together with Mary Anne and

Claudia and a new friend of Claudia's, Stacey McGill. (I'll get back to Stacey later.) They made up fliers and began advertising their club, letting people know their meeting times and how to get in touch with them. They were in business!

The girls voted Kristy president of the Baby-sitters Club since it had been her idea, and since she's good at running things.

They made Claudia the vice-president. This is because Claudia has her own phone and personal, private phone number, so the meetings would always be held in her room. And she would probably get calls at nonmeeting times that she'd have to handle on her own.

Mary Anne was named the secretary, and she has a big job. She's neat and organized (and has nice handwriting), so the girls thought she would be good at keeping the club record book in order. The record book is where we write down our clients' phone numbers and addresses, keep track of the money we've earned (actually, that's the job of the treasurer), and most important, schedule our sitting jobs. Mary Anne has never once made a scheduling mistake.

Stacey McGill was the club's first treasurer. She kept track of the money earned and was also in charge of the club treasury. Each week, we pay dues into the treasury, and we use the money for two things: an occasional club party or sleepover, and supplies. The supplies are usually items for our Kid-Kits. Kid-Kits are another of Kristy's great ideas. Each of us has one. They're boxes we decorated and keep filled with our old games, toys, and books, as well as new things such as crayons or activity books or coloring books. Sometimes we bring them with us when we baby-sit. Kids really love them. And when the kids are happy, their parents are happy . . . and when parents are happy, they call us with more baby-sitting jobs!

Anyway, back to Stacey, the treasurer. Not long ago, Stacey had to move to New York City. Meanwhile, Dawn Schafer had arrived in Stoneybrook and joined the club. She'd been made an alternate officer, meaning she could take over the duties of anyone who might have to miss a meeting. When Stacey left, though, Dawn became the new treasurer. And then, because the club was so busy, the girls asked Jessi and me to join. They really needed help. We were named junior officers since we're only allowed to sit after school or on weekends (unless we're sitting at our own houses).

So who is Logan Bruno? Well, he and a friend of Kristy's, Shannon Kilbourne, are associate club members. As I said before, they don't come to meetings (usually). They're people we can call on in a real pinch — when none of the rest of us is free to take a job. Surprisingly, that does happen from time to time, and we hate to tell a parent that no one's available. So our associate members are very important.

And that's about it. The club is successful and fun, and Jessi and I are really glad we became members.

"Hi, you guys!" Mary Anne greeted us as we ran into Claud's bedroom. "Look who came to the meeting!"

Logan Bruno grinned at Jessi and me from his spot on the floor. I'm not very interested in boys yet, but I must admit that as they go, Logan is pretty cute. And he has this interesting southern accent. (He's from Louisville, Kentucky.)

"Hi," Jessi and I said shyly. We hadn't expected to see a boy. I was glad we looked halfway decent — and that we hadn't been running down the hall talking about underwear or deodorant or something.

"Okay, order! Order!" called Kristy. Kristy

conducts our club meetings in a businesslike way. She sits in Claud's director's chair wearing a visor, with a pencil stuck over her ear. "Any club business?" she asked as Jessi and I sat down on the floor — but not *too* near Logan.

"I have to collect dues," Dawn announced. She was sprawled on Claud's bed between Mary Anne and Claudia.

Us club members groaned but began searching our pockets or purses for money. (Logan didn't have to pay.) When Dawn had collected everything and stashed it safely in the treasury envelope, Kristy said, "Have you been keeping up with the club notebook?"

Uh-oh. I guess I forgot to tell about the notebook. It was *another* of Kristy's ideas, not to be confused with the record book. In the notebook, each of us club members is responsible for writing up every single job we go on. Then we're supposed to read the notebook once a week or so, just to keep track of what's going on with the families we sit for. It's pretty helpful — we write about sitting problems and how we solve them. That kind of thing. I like writing in the notebook, but most of the girls think it's a boring chore.

In answer to Kristy's question, the rest of us (except Logan) chorused, "Yes." She asks us about the notebook every Monday, and every Monday we tell her we've been reading it.

Club business was out of the way and we waited for the phone to ring. Sometimes we start gossiping about friends and school stuff while we wait, but with Logan there, I could tell that all of us, even Mary Anne and Logan, were a little uncomfortable.

Claudia took care of that by searching her desk drawers for a bag of pretzels she knew she'd hidden there. Claud is addicted to junk food and hides it all over her room. She has to hide it, since her parents don't approve of her bad habit. The rest of us like Claud's bad habit, though (well, Dawn refuses to eat things with sugar in them), and we eagerly dove into the bag. Wouldn't you know, as soon as our mouths were full — the phone rang.

We looked at each other in horror.

Logan, being a boy, swallowed his mouthful pretty quickly, and said, "I'll get it!"

But Kristy waved her arms at him. "No! No! Mmphh, mmphh, mmphh." After a moment, she swallowed, too, took a deep breath, and managed to say, "No. Our clients aren't used to a boy answering the phone. Not that there's anything wrong with it," she added quickly. "I just don't want to take someone by surprise."

The phone was on its fourth ring by then, so Kristy grabbed it. "Hello, Baby-sitters Club. . . . Yes? . . . Mrs. Arnold? . . . Oh, okay, I see. I'll get right back to you. 'Bye."

Kristy hung up and we all began laughing. We couldn't believe what had just happened. When we calmed down, Kristy said, "All right. That was Mrs. Arnold. You know, the mother of the twins?"

"The twins?" I repeated.

"Oh, I guess you haven't sat for them," said Kristy. "Actually, the club has only sat for them a couple of times. The Arnolds have twin daughters. They're seven. Marilyn and Carolyn — "

"Marilyn and Carolyn?!" exclaimed Logan.

"Don't tell me — they're identical," I guessed.

"Right down to the buckles on their shoes," agreed Kristy. "They're nice enough, though. I mean, they can't help how their mother dresses them — or what their names are. Anyway, Mrs. Arnold needs a steady sitter, someone who can take care of the twins two afternoons a week for the next couple of months."

"Wow," Logan said, and whistled through his teeth.

"Yeah. There's some sort of fund-raising project at Stoneybrook Elementary," Kristy went on. "That's where the twins go to school.

And Mrs. Arnold agreed to head it up. So she's going to be pretty busy, but only for the next eight weeks. She wants someone every Tuesday and Thursday afternoon from three-thirty till six. Mary Anne?"

Our secretary was already studying the appointment pages in the record book. "Boy," she said. "This is a tough one. Jessi, you're out, obviously."

"I better be out, too," said Claud. "There's a chance my art classes are going to switch to Thursdays."

"Okay," Mary Anne replied. "And Kristy, you've got several sitting jobs already lined up for Tuesdays and Thursdays. Hmmm."

After a lot of planning and discussion, I wound up with the job at the Arnolds'! I couldn't believe it. What luck! Sitting for twins would be fun. Plus, I'd be rich. I thought of all the earrings I would have been able to buy — if I'd had pierced ears.

I checked out Claud's ears. Hanging from them were little pairs of red sneakers. Cool! No one else was wearing earrings except Dawn. I could tell hers were clip-ons. They were big turquoise triangles. They were cool, too, I guess, but there was nothing like pierced ears. If only I could convince Mom and Dad. . . . And if only I could convince them to let me have my long, curly hair cut and styled. It looked like a rat's nest.

Oh, well. First things first. First I had to earn enough money for ear-piercing and hair-cutting. And in order to do that, I had to get started at the Arnolds'. I couldn't wait to begin.

CHAPTER 3

*D*ing-dong.

I stood nervously on the Arnolds' front stoop. A sitting job with a new client always reminds me of the first day of school. You have a vague idea what you're getting into, but you don't know the specifics. For instance, you know a little about who the kids are, you know you'll be responsible for them, but how will you get along with them? Will the kids like you? Will you like them? Will the kids be fun or will they misbehave? What will the parents be like?

I'd find out soon enough. I'd rung the bell, and now I could hear feet running toward the door.

I clutched my Kid-Kit and waited.

The door opened slowly and two faces peeked around it. The faces were so alike that it was as if I were seeing just one face and its reflection in a mirror.

22

"Hi," I said.

"Hi," replied two voices. They sounded uncertain.

The door opened the rest of the way, and before me stood Marilyn and Carolyn Arnold. Both girls were wearing blue kilts with straps that went over their shoulders, white blouses with lace edging the collars and sleeves, white knee socks, and black patent leather Mary Jane shoes. Their brown hair was cut in a bowl shape, framing their faces, and each twin had put on a blue headband with a blue bow on the side of it. Also, each wore a silver ring on the pinky finger of her right hand, and a beaded identification bracelet on her left wrist. The bracelets were the only difference between the twins. The beads on one bracelet spelled MARILYN. The beads on the other one spelled CAROLYN. I was glad I was wearing my glasses.

What a relief, I thought. As long as the girls wore their bracelets, I'd know who was who. I hoped they wouldn't take them off.

The girls were just looking at me, so I said, "I'm Mallory Pike, your baby-sitter. Can I come in?"

Marilyn and Carolyn stepped back and opened the door wider. I entered the Arnolds' house, still clutching my Kid-Kit.

"What's that?" asked one of the twins, pointing to the box.

I glanced at her bracelet. "It's a Kid-Kit, Carolyn," I replied.

Carolyn's face lit up. Why? Oh, she must have known about Kid-Kits from when other members of the Baby-sitters Club had sat at the Arnolds'.

"Do you like Kid-Kits?" I asked her. "This one has some good things in it. New coloring books and new sticker books."

"Oh, boy!" The twins jumped up and down excitedly.

"Mallory? Is that you?" called a voice from upstairs.

"Yes. Mrs. Arnold?"

"I'll be right there."

In a moment a fussy-looking woman came down the stairs. Do you know what I mean by fussy? I mean, everything about her was too much and too cute. She was wearing two necklaces, a pin, bracelets on each wrist, rings, earrings, and even an ankle bracelet. Her stockings were lacey, and she was, well, as Claud might have said, overly accessorized. Practically everything she wore had a bow attached. There were bows on her shoes, a bow on her belt, a bow in her hair, and a bow

24

at the neck of her blouse. Her sweater was beaded, and she hadn't forgotten to pin a fake rose to it. Whew! As for cute, her earrings were in the shape of ladybugs, one of her necklaces spelled her name — Linda — in gold script, her pin was in the shape of a mouse, and the bow in her hair was a ribbon with a print of tiny ducks all over it.

"Hi, Mallory, I'm Mrs. Arnold," said the twins' mother as she reached the bottom of the stairs. She held out her hand, and we shook in a businesslike way. "I'm sure you and the girls will get along fine. They'll show you where their toys are — "

"Mallory brought toys for *us!*" exclaimed one twin.

"Why, that's lovely. Well, good. I can see that the three of you are off to a happy start."

(Blechh.)

Mrs. Arnold showed me where the emergency phone numbers were posted, made sure I knew how to reach her at Stoneybrook Elementary, gave me a few quick instructions, reminded Marilyn to practice the piano for half an hour, and then kissed each of the twins. "Good-bye, loves," she said. "I'll see you in two and a half hours — at six-o'clock."

" 'Bye, Mommy!" chorused the girls.

Mrs. Arnold left in a fog of perfume. (That was another thing. She was wearing perfume, makeup, and nail polish. She'd probably painted her toenails, too.)

"Can we see what's in the Kid-Kit?" asked one of the twins as Mrs. Arnold started her car in the garage.

(A quick glance at the bracelet.) "Sure, Marilyn," I replied, and Marilyn beamed. The twins must really love Kid-Kits. I'd have to remember to bring mine with me each time I sat.

"Let's go to our room!" exclaimed . . . Carolyn. (Bracelet check.)

Well, I'd been prepared for identical twins and identical clothes, but not for two identical halves of a bedroom. That was how the girls' room looked, though. Again, it was as if someone had placed a huge mirror in the center of the room, and it was reflecting one side. On each side were beds covered with pink flowered spreads over white pleated dust ruffles. There were matching pillows. There were twin dressers, desks, and bookshelves. There were even two white rockers. Everything was arranged symmetrically. But what was most surprising were the toys — two of everything. Two identical stuffed bears, two Cabbage Patch dolls, two, two, two.

This was almost like a science fiction movie —

but I didn't say anything. Instead, I plopped myself down on the rug and opened the Kid-Kit.

"Okay, here you go," I said. "What do you guys like? I've got books to read and puzzles and jacks and those new coloring and sticker books."

"I like to read," said one twin. (Oh, it was Marilyn.)

"I like puzzles," said Carolyn.

I handed Carolyn a small jigsaw puzzle, and she immediately dumped it on the floor. Then I pulled out a handful of books.

"Let's see, Marilyn. Here's *Baby Island*. And here's *Charlie and the Great Glass Elevator*. Oh, here are three of the Paddington books."

"Paddington!" exclaimed both twins.

"We love him!" said Carolyn. She abandoned her puzzle and leaned over to look at *Paddington Abroad*, *Paddington Helps Out*, and *Paddington Marches On*.

In a flash, Carolyn had chosen *Paddington Marches On*, Marilyn had chosen *Paddington Abroad*, and each twin was lying on her bed with her legs crossed, reading happily.

"You guys are so cute!" I couldn't help exclaiming. "Look at you. I wish I had my camera. You look like bookends."

The twins exchanged a troubled glance.

27

"Boggle," Marilyn whispered across the room to Carolyn. (Or did Carolyn whisper to Marilyn? I couldn't read their bracelets.)

Carolyn nodded. Then the twins went back to their books.

But not for long.

"Oom-bah," said Carolyn a few minutes later, and the girls tossed the books aside and got to their feet.

With another sidelong glance at each other, they did the last thing I'd expected them to do. Very slowly, they removed their bracelets. They tossed them onto their beds. Then they ran around the room, jumping back and forth, darting from side to side.

"Hey, you guys!" I cried. "What are you doing?"

"Chad. Pom dover glop," said one.

"Huh?"

"*Now* tell us apart," said Marilyn-or-Carolyn.

"I can't," I replied helplessly. "You don't have your bracelets on."

"Do you like to baby-sit?"

"Sure."

"Well, you won't like to sit for *us*."

(What had gone wrong?)

The girls were still moving around. Since even their voices sounded alike, I couldn't tell who was talking. For all I knew, it was just one of them, and the other was keeping quiet.

Suddenly they ran downstairs.

I chased after them. When I reached the living room, I found only one twin.

"Okay, which one are you?" I asked.

Marilyn-or-Carolyn shrugged.

"You're not going to talk?"

Another shrug. Then, without warning, she stood up and darted out of the room. I ran after her, but not quite as fast (the twins are *quick!*) and found one of them at the kitchen table.

"Which one are *you*?" I asked.

"The same as before," was the cross reply.

I felt like saying, "Well, ex*cuse me!*" But instead I said, "Where's your sister?"

Shrug.

And then an idea came to me. I don't know where it came *from*, but it seemed like a good one. I took Marilyn-or-Carolyn by the hand, hauled her into the living room, sat her at the piano, and said, "Practice time."

Marilyn-or-Carolyn looked at me helplessly.

"Go ahead. Play," I urged her. "You *can* play, can't you?"

The twin scowled. "No," she said sullenly.

"Okay, Carolyn. Thank you very much. Now

please go find you sister and tell her it's time to practice."

So Carolyn did just that, and Marilyn began her playing. For exactly half an hour, I knew which twin was which. But when Marilyn stopped practicing, I was in trouble again.

I couldn't *wait* for Mrs. Arnold to come home.

CHAPTER 4

Sunday

Easy money, huh, Jessi?

Definitely, Mal.

This afternoon Jessi and I sat for my brothers and sisters and we hardly had to do a thing. Everyone was busy and as good as gold.

I think we were lucky. You know how awful rainy days can be, when everyone wants to go outside.

yeah, we were lucky. The kids entertained themselves inside.

We had time on our hands.

I know. But think of all the times my brothers and sisters have been real stinkers.

I'd rather not. I'd rather just think about the good time we had today....

31

Well, it sure was an easy sitting job. It was Sunday afternoon, and my parents had been invited to a reception. The reception was to be held indoors, which was lucky since it was pouring rain. And I mean, cats and dogs, streaming down the windows, rattling the gutters. That kind of rain. As Jessi pointed out in the club notebook, rainy days like this one can be a baby-sitting disaster if the only thing the kids want to do is go outside.

But — for once — every one of my brothers and sisters was busy and happy. The triplets were down in the rec room watching a movie that we'd rented for the weekend. Our entire family had watched it the night before, and now the triplets were watching it again. Personally, I don't see how they can do that. I can read a book over and over again, but there aren't too many movies I could watch twice in one weekend.

Nicky was upstairs in the room he shares with the triplets, working on a science-fair project. He was creating a solar system, and it wasn't easy. He had to find balls of various sizes to represent the planets, and then he had to figure out how to get them to revolve around the sun (a yellow tennis ball). It would keep him busy for hours.

Vanessa was in the bedroom she shares with me, writing poems. She keeps a fat notebook full of her poetry, and she said the rainy weather had inspired her, so she would be busy for hours, too. When Vanessa gets on a roll, she can write eight or ten long poems.

Finally Margo and Claire were upstairs in *their* room. They were playing Candy Land. Ordinarily, that causes endless arguments, and even a few tears, but they were also quiet.

"We're playing the best out of seven games," Margo informed Jessi and me when we stuck our heads in their room to make sure they were still alive.

The best of seven. That could take all day.

Jessi and I settled ourselves in the kitchen with cups of hot chocolate. (There is just nothing like hot chocolate on a rainy day, summer or winter.)

"Do you think we should split up?" Jessi asked me. "I'll sit upstairs, you sit downstairs — in case an argument breaks out or something. This seems too easy."

I smiled. "I really think everyone is okay. At the first sign of trouble, we'll separate. Right now, let's leave the kids alone and just relax."

Jessi didn't have a problem with that! We finished our hot chocolate, went into the living room, and sprawled on the rug.

"What would you do if you had a milllion dollars?" Jessi asked me.

"Get my ears pierced," I replied.

Jessi giggled. "Okay, after that, you'd still probably have, oh, about nine hundred thousand nine hundred and ninety bucks left. Then what would you do?"

"Get contacts. And get my hair cut and styled."

"And after *that?*"

"Pay the orthodonist *not* to give me braces."

Jessi couldn't stop laughing. "Then what?" she managed to say.

"Buy a nine-bedroom house for my family."

"So each of you kids could have your own room?"

"Exactly."

"Hmm. You'd really want separate rooms?"

"After sharing all our lives? Of course."

"Even the triplets?"

"Definitely. I mean, they spend a lot of time together, but they *are* different people. They have different interests and stuff. And sometimes they do get on each other's nerves."

"You know, it's funny. I've never had a bit of trouble telling the triplets apart," said Jessi. "Well, maybe a little when I first met them. But after that, never."

"Most people don't have any trouble," I

said. "Okay. What would *you* do with a million bucks?"

"Get my ears pierced," replied Jessi, and we both began laughing again.

"You know," I said, "I feel like a baby because Mom and Dad won't let me get my ears pierced or my hair cut or wear cool clothes. But when I think about it, maybe *they're* the babies. I mean, ear-piercing is safe if you have it done professionally. It isn't safe to have a friend do it with a needle and an ice cube, but — "

"Oh, EW! That is so disgusting! A needle and an ice cube!" cried Jessi. Then she calmed down. "But," she went on, "I don't think your parents — or mine — are babies. I know what you mean, but they must have good reasons for what they will and won't let us do."

"Whose side are you on?" I demanded, but I wasn't really angry.

Jessi smiled. "I'm just being diploma — Hey, look! Twins!"

I turned and saw Claire and Margo coming down the stairs hand in hand. Each was wearing a pair of pink sweat pants, a white turtleneck, and running shoes, with a pink bow in her hair.

"What happened to Candy Land?" I asked the girls.

"We got tired of it," Claire replied.

"*Claire* got tired of it," said Margo pointedly.

"Silly-billy-goo-goo," Claire said, and giggled. She's going through that five-year-old silly stage.

"So we decided to have a fashion show," Margo went on. "This is the first fashion of the year. It's the Terrific Twin outfit."

"Stunning," said Jessi.

"Superb," I added.

Claire turned around gracefully. Margo spun around and fell down.

Then they ran back upstairs.

"Gotta change," Claire yelled over her shoulder.

"New outfits coming up!" called Margo.

When they were out of earshot, Jessi said, "Remember how much fun it used to be to pretend you had a twin?"

"I guess," I answered slowly, trying to remember.

"Oh, Becca and I used to do it all the time. Once, we were wearing matching dresses and Mom took us shopping and we told everyone we were *really twins*. The only problem was, Becca and I are three years apart, and I've always been tall for my age, so I was, like, at least a whole head taller than Becca was. People must have thought we were crazy!"

I laughed. "I know Kristy and Karen" (Karen is Kristy's stepsister) "have a matching sister outfit that they get a kick out of wearing together. But I really don't remember ever pretending *I* was a twin. I do remember once, though, when our family was on vacation and Vanessa and I tried to convince people we were French. We said *oui* and *non* and spoke with an accent."

"Okay! Here we come again!" called Margo. "We're the fashion beauties. Close your eyes. When you open them, you'll see another new fashion."

Jessi and I obediently closed our eyes.

"What fashion will we be seeing?" asked Jessi while we waited.

We could hear whispering.

"You will be seeing Beach Fashion," replied Margo. "Now open your eyes."

We opened them. It was all we could do to keep from laughing. My sisters were wearing bathing suits, knee socks, some old high-heeled shoes of Mom's, and a ton of jewelry.

"Impressive," said Jessi.

"Smashing," I added.

The fashion show continued until Claire got tired of it and said, "Margo, let's play Candy Land, okay? Best out of seven."

The girls disappeared. Jessi and I made a

quick check on the rest of my brothers and sisters. Vanessa was murmuring to herself and writing in her notebook. Nicky was patiently revolving a Ping-Pong ball around the yellow tennis ball. The triplets were rewinding the movie, getting set to watch it one final time.

"All quiet on the western front," Jessi said to me as we returned to the living room.

I laughed. Jessi and I had both tried to read that book and had hated it, even though it was a classic and we knew we were supposed to like it.

"You know," I said suddenly, "I am so glad you moved to Stoneybrook. I think we make awfully good best friends."

"Definitely," agreed Jessi.

"But you know what would make my life perfect?" I asked.

"What?"

"Getting my ears pierced and looking more grown-up. Or at the very least, more human."

"Dream on," replied Jessi.

CHAPTER 5

Thursday

What pains! What rotten pains! Boy, you guys, we've had some tough baby-sitting charges before -- Jackie Rodowsky, the walking disaster; Betsy Sobak, the great practical joker; even my own brothers and sisters -- but these terrible twins are just the worst! If you have any idea how to handle them, please tell me, because I'm going crazy. No kidding.

Want to know what happened today? (Dumb question. This is the club notebook. I have to tell you what happened.) Okay, here goes. I'll start at the beginning, of course. Get prepared not to believe what you read, because I guarantee you won't. But I swear that every word is the truth.

Okay. I show up on the Arnolds' doorstep right on time, ready to start over again with the twins. I've remembered to bring the Kid-Kit....

39

Ding-dong!

I rang the Arnolds' bell, expecting to hear feet running toward the door.

Nothing.

After a moment, I rang the bell again.

"Marilyn? Carolyn?" I could hear Mrs. Arnold call. Silence. At last the door was flung open. "Hello, Mallory," said the twins' mother.

"Hi," I replied.

"Goodness, I don't know where the girls have gotten to. I'm sure they're here somewhere. I thought they would answer the door."

I stepped inside. Mrs. Arnold was patting the bow in her hair. I noticed that she was wearing three rings on that one hand — and nail polish, of course.

"Marilyn! Carolyn!" called Mrs. Arnold again. Then, "MARILYN! CAROLYN! I am going to count to three. If you're not here by then, you will be in big trouble. . . . One, two," (no twins yet) "two and a half, two and three quarters, I hope you like your bedroom because you'll be spending a lot of time there if — "

"Here we are! Here we are!"

Marilyn and Carolyn raced into the hallway. Inwardly, I sighed. They were dressed identically again. I guess I'd been hoping for . . . I don't know. But there they were — matching plaid dresses, white tights, black patent leather Mary Jane shoes, red ribbons in their hair, gold lockets, gold rings, pink nail polish, and (thank goodness) their name bracelets.

Mrs. Arnold took one look at her daughters and exclaimed, "Why, you switched bracelets again, you monkeys!" (How could she tell?) "Now switch them back. I hope you won't be teasing Mallory today."

Believe me, I hoped they wouldn't be teasing Mallory today, either.

The twins exchanged a disgusted look as they switched their bracelets, and I frantically checked them over for some sort of difference. Anything at all. A hole in somebody's tights, a chip in somebody's nail polish. Just something that would tell me which one was Marilyn and which one was Carolyn. But I could not find one difference.

"Well, good-bye, you monkeys," said Mrs. Arnold, adding a hat to her outfit. "I'll be back before you know it. Remember to practice for half an hour, Marilyn."

Mrs. Arnold left.

I stood anxiously in front of the twins. They stared at me. I held out the Kid-Kit as if it were both a shield and a peace offering.

"Kid-Kit?" I said. "You never did read those Paddington books. And I added some new puzzles, Carolyn."

"Go-blit?" said . . . Marilyn.

"Der. Blum snider,"was Carolyn's response.

And with that, the bracelets were off, tossed carelessly onto a couch in the living room.

Oh, no, I thought. But all I said was, "The least you two could do is speak English."

"Okay," replied one twin. "Let's play hide-and-seek."

"Well . . . all right." How bad could hide-and-seek be?

"We'll hide, you seek!" cried the other twin. "Stand in the hallway, cover your eyes, and count to one hundred."

"Okay." I covered my eyes and listened to the twins run off.

As they went, I thought I heard one whisper to the other, "In-bro duggan, tosh?"

"Tosh," was the answer.

I began to count. I counted out loud. I had learned to do that long ago, playing hide-and-seek with my brothers and sisters, who would accuse me of cheating and skipping numbers if I counted silently and then came looking for them before they'd found a hiding place. ". . . Twenty-three, twenty-four," I continued. (I *hate* counting to a hundred.) ". . . Ninety-seven, ninety-eight, ninety-nine, one hundred! Ready or not, here I come!"

The Arnolds' house was quiet, and I wondered if the girls were hiding outdoors. We should have made some hiding rules before we began the game. Oh, well. Too late now. Besides, I hadn't heard any doors open or close.

I began to search the house. I felt funny, as if I were invading the Arnolds' privacy, so I stuck to the kitchen and living room and dining room at first. They aren't personal, like bedrooms are.

I found one twin behind a full-length curtain in the dining room. (I could see her shoes sticking out.) "Found you!" I cried, pulling the curtain aside. "Come on and help me look for your sister."

Marilyn-or-Carolyn trailed behind me into the kitchen. "You must know all the good hiding places," I said to her. "Where should we look?"

A shrug. "I don't want to look. You're the seeker. You look. Can I have a snack? We didn't have one after school."

"Okay." Quickly I set out some juice and graham crackers. "You stay right here," I told

Marilyn-or-Carolyn. "I'll be back when I find your sister." I left the kitchen, searched the den, returned to the kitchen — and found only some graham cracker crumbs and an empty paper cup. The snack was gone and so was the twin who'd eaten it. Oh, brother.

I kept searching and came across the other twin under one of the beds in the girls' room. "Found you!" I cried.

"Can I have a snack?" asked Marilyn-or-Carolyn.

"Sure." I set her up in the kitchen with juice and graham crackers. "Now where is your sister?" I wondered.

"Isn't she hiding?"

"Yes, but I already found her once."

"Oh." Marilyn-or-Carolyn tried to hide a smile. "My sister is sneaky. I bet she hid again. She does that sometimes."

"Well, I better find her." I left the room. Of course when I returned, the snack and the twin were gone again. I should have known better.

I finally found a twin squished behind a couch in the living room, and she said, "Took you long enough. . . . Can I have a snack?"

"You've already had one," I replied.

"No, I didn't."

"Well, I gave out two snacks."

"Then you gave both of them to my sister."

"Sorry. If I knew which of you was which, that wouldn't have happened."

Marilyn-or-Carolyn scowled. Then she said, "Okay, I'm Carolyn. Now can I have a snack?"

I almost gave in, but I decided to be firm instead. Maybe that was my problem with the twins. Maybe I hadn't let them know who was boss. Besides, how could I be sure this twin was really Carolyn and she hadn't had a snack yet? I was beginning to see what the twins could do. Maybe this twin had already had two snacks and wanted a third.

"Nope. No snack," I told Marilyn-or-Carolyn. "There are two of you and I gave out two snacks. That's it. No more."

"No more? No *fair!*"

"It's very fair. Two twins, two snacks. I think you guys just fooled your*selves.*"

"Gummy grog!" shouted Marilyn-or-Carolyn.

A moment later, her sister ran into the room. "What?"

"Colley-moss. Der blum tiding poffer-tot."

"Hanky? No gibble dandy."

What was going on? The girls were using their twin talk so much I didn't have a clue.

Well, I was sorry I made them angry. Too bad. They had tried to trick me. Oh, all right, they *had* tricked me.

For the next hour or so, Marilyn and Carolyn chattered away in their twin talk. They ignored me. But at five-thirty they couldn't ignore me. That was when I said, "Time to practice, Marilyn."

"Which one of us is Marilyn?" asked one twin.

"Oh. So you *can* speak English," I replied.

" 'Course we can. . . . Which one of us is Marilyn?"

"The one of you who hasn't practiced yet, and who has only half an hour *to* practice before her mother comes home. If she doesn't start playing the piano *now*, I'll have to tell her mother she didn't get all her practice time in."

Reluctantly, one twin sat down at the piano. While Marilyn played, I tried to talk to Carolyn, but Carolyn would have nothing to do with me. She took *Paddington Marches On* out of the Kid-Kit, opened it, and both girls ignored me again until their mother returned.

CHAPTER 6

saturday

Well excuse me for living but waht
is it whith these twins? Today was my
frist time babbysitting for them and mal
I see waht you mean. They are very big
pians. They triked me and they even got
me in trueble. I have never goten in
trouble siting befor. At laest your frist
job at the arnolds started of okay. Mine
didn't even get of to a good start. It
got of to a bad start and grew worse. mal
I bet you cant' waite for mrs. arnolds
job to be over....

Finally. Somebody besides me had to sit for the twins and got to see what terrors they were. I think Kristy had sat for them once quite awhile ago. And Mary Anne, too. But no one else. And no one had sat for them recently.

I was almost glad when Claudia had her bad experience with the Arnold girls. Not that I wanted her in trouble. I didn't. Not at all. It was just that, until Claud sat for the twins, I'd been worried that I wasn't a very good sitter. Like, maybe I didn't have enough control or whatever. But when I read Claud's notebook entry and saw that she'd had trouble, too, I realized the Arnold girls simply *were* trouble. They were twin trouble. Double trouble. Us baby-sitters were fine.

Anyway, Claudia took her Kid-Kit with her to the Arnolds' that Saturday morning. She'd learned, from reading my entries in the club notebook, that the twins like the Kid-Kits, so she went prepared.

Claud's job was to be longer than my afternoon jobs. She was taking care of the twins from ten in the morning until three in the afternoon while their parents went to an antique car show in Stamford. Poor Claud. Five hours with the twins. At least there were special things to keep the girls busy.

"Marilyn's piano lesson is at eleven-thirty," Mrs. Arnold told Claud. "Her carpool will arrive at eleven o'clock. She's going to be in a recital next week, and today is a special rehearsal and lesson. It'll last an hour and a half. She'll be dropped off here around one-thirty. While Marilyn's gone, Carolyn should work on her project for the science fair. Carolyn just loves science, don't you, dear?"

Claudia looked doubtfully at the twins in their red flared skirts, blue sweaters, white turtlenecks, and Mary Janes. The girls were pretty, Claud thought, and they were dressed nicely (even if they *were* a little dressed up for a Saturday morning), but somehow they had the look of terrors about them. They were scowling and didn't appear to love *any*thing, including science and piano-playing.

"Don't you love science, dear?" Mrs. Arnold repeated.

Carolyn shrugged.

"Tell Claudia what your project is called," Mrs. Arnold went on.

"The World of Electricity," replied Carolyn.

Mrs. Arnold beamed.

Claudia tried to smile back, but found it difficult. Instead, she took a look at the twins. Like I had done, she tried to find some difference between them, while they were still wearing their bracelets. (She was pretty sure they were planning to take the bracelets off as soon as their parents left.) She thought she noticed some differences in their faces, but it was hard to tell, and she didn't want the girls to think she was staring. And their clothes were impeccable. Not a scuff or a tear anywhere.

"Well, we should be on our way," said Mrs. Arnold. She showed Claud the emergency numbers and told her what she could fix for lunch after Marilyn returned from her lesson. Then she went on, "You're ready for your lesson, aren't you, Marilyn?"

Marilyn smiled sweetly. She showed her mother that her piano books were stacked on the bench in the front hallway.

"And Carolyn, you have everything you need for your project?"

"Yup."

"All right. Then we'll be off."

Mr. and Mrs. Arnold left. Before they had even backed the car down the driveway, Carolyn turned to Marilyn and said, "Snuff bat crawding fowser. Der blem, tosh?"

"Tosh," answered her sister.

Sensing what was coming, Claud said, "I guess this is the part where you guys take your bracelets off and try to confuse me, right?"

The twins hesitated, and for just a moment, Claud thought they might leave the bracelets on, just to spite her (which was what she was hoping for).

But no such luck.

"That's right!" cried Carolyn.

In a flash, the bracelets were off and twin talk was in full swing.

"You two just go ahead and play," Claud told them. "I don't care if you don't want me to be able to tell you apart." (Boy, is Claudia a cool one.) "Anyway, I'll be able to tell you apart at eleven."

"How come?" one twin couldn't help asking.

"Because at eleven, Marilyn will leave for the music school. Carolyn will be the one who stays to work on her project."

The twins looked at her. More twin talk followed.

"Well," said Claud, "I've got a good mystery to read. If you guys are just going to talk to each other, I'm going to read. You can look in the Kid-Kit, if you want."

So for the next hour, Claud read and the twins ignored her and played together. At eleven, Claud said, "Okay, Marilyn. Your ride will be here any minute. Why don't you get your books? Carolyn and I will wait outside with you."

51

"Okay!" One twin bounced to her feet and gathered up the piano books.

At last Claud knew which girl was which. She and Carolyn followed Marilyn outside and sat on the front stoop with her. Five minutes later, a car slowed down in front of the Arnolds'house, and the driver honked the horn.

"There's Mr. Bischoff," said Marilyn. "He's going to bring me home, too. See you later!" She ran across the lawn.

"Okay, Carolyn," said Claud to the remaining twin. "We better go inside so you can get to work on The World of Electricity." (Although what Claud knows about the world of electricity you could fit on the head of a pin.)

Carolyn went into the rec room. She opened a door and slid a display out of a closet.

"What are you going to do to your project today?" asked Claudia.

"Just fix the letters on the display and then read. I have to find out more about some experiments I could show the kids. Here are my books."

Claudia felt relieved. Not only did she know which twin was which (at least until one-thirty), but she wasn't going to have to work on The World of Electricity. She went back to her mystery while Carolyn fooled around with the display.

At eleven-thirty, the phone rang.

"I'll get it!" said Claud. She dashed into the kitchen and picked up the receiver. "Hello, Arnolds' residence."

"Yes, hello. Mrs. Arnold?"

"No, I'm afraid Mrs. Arnold can't come to the phone." (Us baby-sitters know never to say that the parents aren't home.) "This is Claudia Kishi. May I help you?"

"Well . . . perhaps. I'm Margaret Cohen. I teach piano at the music school. I've got a very tone-deaf Arnold twin here, so I'm wondering where Marilyn is."

It took Claud a moment to figure out what Ms. Cohen meant. Then she sputtered, "You mean *Carolyn's* there? The girls switched! I don't believe it!"

"Is there any way to, um, switch them back?" suggested Ms. Cohen. "I really need to work with Marilyn today."

"Well, I'm sorry. I can't bring Marilyn over. I — I can't drive yet," replied Claud. "Has Mr. Bischoff left already?"

"Yes, I'm afraid he has."

"Oh." Claudia was fuming, but she tried not to show it. "I'm sorry," she said again. "I guess Carolyn will just have to stay there until one o'clock. Do you mind keeping her?"

"Nooo. . . . But, well, I'll have to speak to

Mrs. Arnold about this. Will you please tell her to call me?"

"Of course," replied Claudia.

When she'd hung up the phone, she peeped into the rec room. Marilyn was reading a comic book. She hid it quickly when Claudia walked noisily into the room. She picked up one of the science books instead.

"You can stop pretending now, *Marilyn*," said Claudia.

Marilyn at least had the grace to blush and look embarrassed.

"That was Ms. Cohen on the phone. She is not pleased that you skipped this rehearsal. . . . Don't you like playing the piano, Marilyn?"

Marilyn looked surprised by the question. "I like it," she assured Claudia. "And Carolyn likes science. Really. We just wanted to play a trick."

"Well, you did that, all right. I think you also got yourselves into trouble. Ms. Cohen is upset, you're missing an important rehearsal, and Carolyn is wasting time she could be spending on The World of Electricity. Now, I can't punish you," Claud went on. "That's not part of my job. But I can make sure I can tell you guys apart for the rest of the afternoon."

Marilyn widened her eyes. "You can? How?"

"Like this." Claud took a Magic Marker out

of the Kid-Kit. Before Marilyn knew what was happening, Claud had drawn a happy face on the back of Marilyn's right hand. She knew it would wash off eventually. (Of course, when Carolyn returned later, she immediately drew a face on *her* hand, but it didn't look like Claud's, so Claud could still tell the girls apart.)

That was the only good thing about the day. When the Arnolds came home later, Claudia had to tell them about the mix-up, and they were not happy.

"I'm disappointed in both of you," said Mrs. Arnold to the twins.

"We know it must be tempting to play tricks and jokes," added Mr. Arnold, "but you have to choose the right times for them. A time when Marilyn misses a piano rehearsal is not a good time."

"And Claudia," Mrs. Arnold continued, "I must admit that I'm a bit surprised at you. We trusted you to be in charge of our daughters. We understand that it's difficult to tell them apart when their bracelets are off. Still . . . you were supposed to be responsible for them while we were out."

"I know," Claud replied, and she could feel her face burning. (This was *so* unfair!) "I'm very sorry. I'll understand if you don't want me to sit for you again. Or if you don't want anyone from our club to sit for you again, either." She hated to add that last part, but felt she had to.

"Oh, no, no," said Mrs. Arnold quickly. "Nothing like that will be necessary."

(Darn.)

Claud wondered if the Arnolds had been having trouble getting sitters lately, but of course she didn't say anything. She just offered *not* to take the Arnolds' money (they gave it to her anyway) and got out of there as fast as she could.

Malory, you can have the twines, was the last line in Claudia's notebook entry.

CHAPTER 7

Well, that was very kind of Claudia, but I didn't want the twines. They were making my life miserable. I dreaded Tuesdays and Thursdays. I dreaded them so much that sometimes I would forget, for a moment or two, about wanting pierced ears and a decent haircut. I even considered asking Kristy if I could quit the job at the Arnolds'. But I knew I couldn't do that. Couldn't ask Kristy, I mean. That would be as good as asking to be kicked out of the club. As far as I knew, no one in the club had ever backed out of a job she was signed up for just because the kids were difficult. And certainly, no one had ever been kicked out of the club.

There was something I could do, though, and that was discuss the problem of the twins with my friends at the next club meeting. I'd been writing about them in the notebook, so everyone was aware of what was going on.

Maybe Kristy or one of the other more experienced sitters would have some suggestions for me. The problem was worth bringing up.

Monday. Five-thirty. The members of the Baby-sitters Club had gathered in Claud's room. It was a typical scene.

Our president, dressed in jeans, a white turtleneck, a pink-and-blue sweater, and new running shoes, was sitting in Claudia's director's chair. Her visor was in place, and a Connecticut Bank and Trust pencil was stuck over her ear. She was looking in the record book and exclaiming over how much money we'd been earning lately.

Claudia was lying on her bed with one leg propped up on a pillow. She'd broken that leg a few months earlier and every now and then, especially if rain was on the way, her leg would give her some trouble. She looked absolutely great, though, pillow or no pillow. Her long hair was fixed in about a million braids which were pulled back and held in place behind her head with a column of puffy ponytail holders. She was wearing a T-shirt she'd painted herself, tight blue pants that ended just past her knees, push-down socks, and no shoes. From her ears dangled small baskets of fruit. She'd made those, I knew. She'd found the baskets and the fruits at a store that sells miniatures and dollhouse furniture. Claudia amazes me.

Sitting next to Claud on the bed were Mary Anne and Dawn. I might add that they were sitting fairly gingerly, like they thought that if they so much as moved, they would break Claud's leg all over again, which couldn't have been further from the truth. (Claud wasn't in *that* much pain.) Mary Anne was wearing a short plum-colored skirt over a plum-and-white-striped body suit. The legs of the body suit stopped just above her ankles, and she'd tucked the bottoms into her socks. I don't know where her shoes were. She'd taken them off. The neat thing about her outfit was that she was wearing white suspenders with her skirt. I immediately decided to use some of my hard-earned Arnold money to buy suspenders. And maybe a pair of push-down socks like Claud's. Or, if I became rich, to copy Dawn Schafer's entire outfit.

Dawn was wearing this cool oversized (*really* oversized) blue shirt. One of the coolest things about it was that it was green inside, so that when she turned the collar down and rolled the sleeves up, you could see these nice touches of green at her neck and wrists. She was wearing a green skirt — and clogs. I'd never seen a person actually wearing clogs, just photos of people in Sweden. Dawn was the only kid in school who could get away with wearing them. She is so self-possessed.

Then there were Jessi and me. We were sitting on the floor and we truly *looked* like we were in the sixth grade, as opposed to Claudia, Dawn, and Mary Anne, who might have been able to pass for high school students. Jessi and I looked dull, dull, dull. We were both wearing jeans. Jessi was wearing a T-shirt that said YOU ARE LOOKING AT PERFECTION. And she was wearing running shoes. But no interesting jewelry or anything else. Same with me. I was just wearing jeans, a plain white shirt, and running shoes. Yawn.

Kristy called the meeting to order. After we'd sworn that we'd been reading the notebook regularly, and after Dawn had collected the weekly dues, Kristy said, "Any problems? Anything to discuss?"

My hand shot up, and I didn't even wait for Kristy to nod to me. I just blurted out, "The Arnold twins are a major problem."

"I'll say," agreed Claud. She sat up and stuck some pillows behind her so she wouldn't have to be flat on her back while she tried to make her point. "That job Saturday was the pits." (Since we'd been keeping up with the notebook, we all knew what she was talking about.) "I have never been so humiliated," Claud went on. "Those girls got me in trouble. No parent has ever scolded me in front of the kids I've just sat for. The girls purposely made a big mess of things. And *why?* That's what I can't figure out."

"Me neither," I spoke up.

"No offense, Mal," added Claud, "and I *really mean* no offense, but I have to admit that I went to that job on Saturday thinking that maybe, just *maybe*, there was some sort of problem with you and the Arnolds. You know, that they were okay kids, but somehow the three of you just weren't hitting it off. In other words, that — that, um, *you* were the problem." Claud blushed.

"Don't worry about it," I said, even though I was a little hurt. "I was wondering the same thing myself. But after what happened to you on Saturday, I realized that wasn't true. The thing is," I went on, looking around at the rest of the club members, "we have problem clients. And, to quote Mom, I'm at my wit's end. I just don't know what to do about the twins."

The phone rang then, and a couple more times, too, so for awhile we were busy scheduling jobs. When we were done, Kristy said, "Mal, we've read your notebook entries, so we have a pretty good idea what's going on, but tell us again anyway. Maybe you'll think of things you didn't mention in the notebook."

"Okay," I said, and drew in a deep breath. I looked around and realized I had the complete attention of everyone in the room, which made me slightly nervous. I wanted to sound articulate. And I did *not* want to sound like a big baby, like someone who'd just run up against an annoying problem she didn't feel like handling.

"The twins," I began slowly, "*seem* like nice girls. They're always beautifully dressed, well, sometimes sort of over-dressed, but then their mother is, too. I think they're smart. Marilyn is an excellent piano player. She's been taking lessons since she was four. And Carolyn loves science. They both like to read, and I bet they do pretty well in school. Anyway, they must be smart to have invented their twin talk."

"Twin talk?" Dawn repeated.

"Yeah. You know, their private language," I explained, and Dawn nodded. "They can just babble away in it. Think how hard it is to learn a different language, like French or Spanish."

"*Tell* me about it," said Claud, rolling her eyes. She absolutely hates foreign languages, even Japanese, which Mimi sometimes tries to teach her.

"Well, if that's hard," I went on, "think how

difficult it must be to *invent* a language."

"But you know something?" said Claud, "I'm not sure the twin talk is a real language. I mean, I think Marilyn and Carolyn have made up a few secret words, but when they sit around going, 'Moobay donner slats impartu frund?' or something, I'm *positive* they just want us to *think* they have this secret twin talk. They don't understand each other any more than we understand them."

"But why?" I asked. "Why do they do that? And why do they take off their bracelets and confuse me when they're playing hide-and-seek, and try to get extra snacks and stuff? I don't get it. They're mean, and I was never mean to them."

"Maybe those are just things identical twins *do*," said Mary Anne doubtfully.

"I don't know," I replied. "The triplets are identical and they don't do stuff like that. Not even to people who can't tell them apart. And there are *three* of them. I mean, sure, they've played a few tricks, like switching places in school when there's a substitute teacher, but *all* kids try to trick substitutes. It's, like, a law."

Everyone laughed. And then the phone rang twice. Mary Anne scheduled a job for herself, and one for Kristy.

When things calmed down, Kristy said, "I

don't know that there's much you can do about the twins, Mal. It sounds like you're being the best sitter you can be, and they're just brats. You'll have to finish up your job with them, but after that, I won't expect anyone" (Kristy looked around the room at all us club members) "to feel she has to take a job at the Arnolds'. If Mrs. Arnold calls again, we'll just tell her we're busy. I don't like doing that, but I think we'll have to. Or we'll ask Logan or Shannon if one of them wants to brave twin trouble."

I nodded. "Okay. I guess you're right. But if anybody gets an idea about how to handle Marilyn and Carolyn, please tell it to me. . . . Boy, it's too bad they're so rotten. They're really cute little kids. Even their identical clothes are cute. There's just something . . . sweet . . . about seeing those lookalikes. I bet people stop them on the street to tell them how adorable they are."

"Nobody would ever stop me on the street to tell me I'm adorable," said Kristy.

"Me neither," added Jessi.

"Maybe they would stop me," I said, "if I didn't look like such a nerd."

"You don't look like a nerd," said Claud quickly.

"Thanks," I replied, "but yes I do. I wouldn't if I had pierced ears and a better haircut, though. I'd look at least twelve, not nerdy, and adorable."

Dawn smiled. "What would you do to your hair?" she asked me.

"I'm not sure. Cut it short, I think, so it wouldn't be such a wild tangle of curls."

"I want pierced ears and decent hair, too," spoke up Jessi.

"I want one more hole in my right ear." (That was Claud, of course.)

"And I want to get back to business," said Kristy.

And just as she said that, the phone rang. Kristy gave us a look that said, "See? We *are* here to do business, you guys."

But the caller was Stacey McGill, our former treasurer. Claud began shrieking, and begged to speak to her first. Then Dawn, Mary Anne, and even Kristy chatted with her.

Jessi and I grinned. Club meetings are great, especially when something fun like this happens. But part of me was disappointed. I hadn't gotten any suggestions on how to work with the troublesome twins — and I would have to face them again the very next afternoon.

CHAPTER 8

Tuesday

To quote Claudia, "Oh, my lord!" What a day today was. I sat for the twins again, and they were their usual pill—y selves -- at first. Then something happened that changed our relationship. I wouldn't say we're best friends now, but I think we're going to get along better. You know that saying, "Fight fire with fire"? Well, that's what I did today, and the twins and I ended up talking and really having fun. (Funny, but I owe it all to my brothers, and they don't even know it.)

It started when the twins began speaking in their twin talk the second their mother left, and barely said a word to me in English. I couldn't stand it!...

Tuesday afternoon. I turned up at the Arnolds' at the regular time. Mrs. Arnold flurried out the door in a blur of jewelry, nail polish, and accessories. I heard the car door slam in the garage, and she was off.

I was sitting on the floor in the living room, the Kid-Kit opened in front of me. I was looking hopefully at the twins.

Marilyn and Carolyn, dressed in blue sailor dresses, red hair ribbons, white tights, and their Mary Janes, took off their bracelets, dangled them rudely in front of me, and dropped them on the floor.

"Good," I said. "Why should today be different from any other day? I think it would confuse me terribly if I could tell you two apart."

I don't know what kind of answer I was expecting from them. Maybe no answer. That was just something to say, something rude because the girls were rude and I was feeling cross.

"Poopah-key," said one twin in a voice as cross as mine had been.

I sighed. I deserved that. "Look," I said, rummaging around in the Kid-Kit. "Here's a sticker book. Oh, and Carolyn, I brought you a book about electricity. I borrowed it from

Adam. He's one of my brothers."

The girls remained standing.

"Do you want to look at the book?" I asked.

I was sure one of the girls was going to reply, "Which one of us is Carolyn?" Instead, the answer was, "Tibble van carmin."

That was a first. The girls usually spoke English in the beginning of the afternoon, or if I asked them a question. This was the first time they had completely ignored me. Well, they weren't *ignoring* me, but they might as well have been. They were ignoring me in twin talk.

"How about puzzles?" I asked.

"Zoo mat," replied one twin. But at least the girls sat down then.

"Chutes and Ladders?" I tried. "Dominoes?"

"Perring du summerflat, tosh?" asked one.

"Du mitter-mott," replied the other.

"Okay. Go ahead. Have fun," I said to the girls. I pulled my copy of *Dicey's Song*, by Cynthia Voigt, out of my purse, sat on the couch, and began to read. The twins pawed through the Kid-Kit, babbling to each other.

After about ten minutes, one of them stood up and said, "Mallory, can I have an ice-cream sandwich? We have a box of them in our freezer."

My first reaction was to say, "Oh, thank

goodness you're speaking English again." But I didn't jump in with that answer, which I knew the twins were expecting. Out of the blue a very different kind of answer came to me, and somehow I knew that it was exactly the right thing to try. I didn't have anything to lose, and it might be kind of fun. At any rate, I could give the twins a taste of their own medicine. Fighting fire with fire.

I answered the question in pig Latin. "At's-thay ine-fay ith-way ee-may."

Marilyn-or-Carolyn looked stunned. "What?" she said.

"Oh-gay on-hay. I-hay on't-day are-cay."

The twins glanced at each other in confusion. The other one spoke up warily. "What are you saying?" she asked.

"I'm-hay aying-say at-thay oo-yay an-cay ave-hay a-hay ack-snay. O-say an-cay our-yay ister-say."

"I can't understand you!" cried Marilyn-or-Carolyn in frustration.

I smiled. "Oo-tay ad-bay."

"But can I have an ice-cream sandwich?"

"Ure-shay. Ine-fay ith-way ee-may."

The twin stamped her foot. Was she getting ready to throw a tantrum? I decided I didn't care if she was.

"I want an ice-cream sandwich!" she cried.

"Me too!" cried her twin.

"Ood-gay. Oh-gay on-hay. Ut-whay are-hay oo-yay aiting-way or-fay?"

"Talk to us!" demanded the twin.

"I-hay am-hay alking-tay oo-tay oo-yay. Oo-yay ust-jay on't-day understand-hay ee-may." I was speaking as fast as I could, which made the pig Latin sound even odder.

"Talk in English! Talk right!" yelled the foot-stamper.

I gave in. "You two haven't been speaking to *me* in English," I pointed out.

"Malvern toppit samway," said Marilyn-or-Carolyn.

"Ut's-whay is-thay? Ore-may in-tway alk-tay?"

"Are you going to talk like that all after-noon?" asked one of the girls angrily.

"Nope," I replied. "Only as long as you and your sister talk in *your* language. When you stop, I'll stop."

"Maybe we don't want to stop," said Marilyn-or-Carolyn.

"Aybe-may I-hay on't-day either-hay," I answered.

"Okay, okay, okay. We'll stop."

"Good," I said. "But now you know how it feels when you leave someone out of a conversation. Or when you're rude to her."

The twins scowled but didn't apologize. Finally one said, "What language were you talking in?"

"Pig Latin," I told her.

"Pig Latin?" The girls couldn't help smiling.

I nodded. "I could teach it to you. Anyone can learn it. My brothers taught it to me. They talk in it sometimes when they need a private language. Of course," I went on, "you've got a language of your own, so you probably don't need pig Latin."

"Oh, yes! Yes, we do!" cried one twin.

And that was when I decided that Claudia was probably right: twin talk wasn't much of a language at all, except for a few words the girls had made up. If it was, they wouldn't be so eager to learn pig Latin.

"I'll teach you pig Latin on two conditions," I said to the twins.

"What?" they replied. Instantly, they were on their guard.

"One, that you put your bracelets on — and on *right*. I'll just have to trust that you do it right. But I really want to be able to tell you apart. And two, that after I teach you pig Latin, you stop using your own language around me, because I don't like it. Is that a deal?"

The twins whispered to each other. Then one said, "If you ask for two things, then we want two things, too. We want to learn pig Latin, *and* we want the ice-cream sandwiches."

"Fair enough," I replied. "Put your bracelets on and follow me into the kitchen."

The girls did so. They sat at the table while I took three ice-cream sandwiches out of the freezer. Then I joined them. I passed out the sandwiches. As we were unwrapping them, I said, "Thank you for putting the bracelets back on. I appreciate that."

"Do you really want to be able to tell us apart?" asked . . . Marilyn. (Bracelet check.) "We are *so* tired of looking alike."

"Yes. I really do. There must be *some* difference between you. Something besides the bracelets."

"We-ell," said Carolyn slowly, "there is one thing."

"Are you going to *tell* her?" spoke up Marilyn, sounding worried.

Carolyn nodded. "It's all right. She said she really wants to know. . . . Okay?"

Marilyn nodded.

"Look very, very closely at our faces," said Carolyn.

"Look at our cheeks," Marilyn added.

I stared and stared. At last I saw a tiny mole on Carolyn's left cheek, under her eye. Marilyn had a mole, too, under her right eye. "The moles?" I asked.

The girls nodded. "It's the only difference between us that's really easy to see," Carolyn told me.

"Thank you," I replied. "Now I'll keep my part of the bargain and teach you pig Latin. It's really simple. All you do is take the sound at the beginning of a word, drop it, say the rest of the word, and follow it up with that sound plus 'ay.' Like, 'Marilyn' would be 'Arilyn-may'. Or 'Carolyn' would be 'Arolyn-cay.' Or 'table' would be — "

"Able-tay!" cried Marilyn.

"Right!" I said. "Good. Now here's a harder one. What would 'twin' be?"

The girls frowned. "Win-tay?" guessed Carolyn.

I shook my head. "For a word like 'twin,' you take the whole sound at the beginning of the word — not just the first letter — and move it around. So 'twin' would be 'in-tway.' "

"What if a word begins with a vowel?" asked Marilyn. "With 'a' or 'e' or 'i' or 'o' or 'u.' Then what? What would 'apple' be? 'Apple-ay'?"

"Nope. That's the only other rule you have to learn. When a word begins with a vowel, you stick an 'h' in there. 'Apple' would be 'apple-hay.' Or 'island would be 'island-hay.' "

"Oh! Cool!" exclaimed Marilyn.

"Easy!" said Carolyn.

And the rest of the afternoon was a dream. The girls didn't use any twin talk, and they didn't switch their bracelets.

Then Mrs. Arnold came home and asked me the last question I would have expected to hear.

"The twins' eighth birthday is coming up," she began. "They're going to have a big party. I was wondering if you and two of your friends would want to help at the party. You know, organize games, keep an eye on the kids. Do the girls in your club ever do that kind of thing?"

"Well, yes," I replied. "Not very often, but we have helped at parties."

I couldn't believe she would hire other club members after what had happened with Claudia. But Saturday seemed forgotten. "When will the party be?" I asked.

Mrs. Arnold told me, and I took down all the information — how long the party was supposed to last, how many kids had been invited, etc.

"I'll tell the girls about it at our club meeting

tomorrow, and then I'll call to let you know if we can do it, okay?"

Mrs. Arnold nodded. She seemed pleased.

So did the girls.

When I left, they called, "Ood-gay eye-bay!" instead of "Snod peer," which was what they had shouted the last time I'd left their house.

CHAPTER 9

Sunday

Today was pretty interesting. I thought it was going to be just another afternoon sitting job at my house, but I guess by now I should know better. There isn't any such thing as just another sitting job -- not with Karen, Andrew, and David Michael. Oh, nothing bad happened, but something surprising did. You never know what to expect from little kids. I guess the important thing to remember is that a kid is not just a kid. A kid is a person -- a human being -- who happens to be shorter and younger than an adult.

Anyway, the afternoon started off quietly. Hannie and Linny Papadakis came over to play with Karen and David Michael, while I tried to help Andrew memorize lines for this program he's going to be in at his preschool....

Kristy has said so herself: Her favorite sitting charges of all are David Michael, Andrew, and Karen. Well, I wouldn't expect anything different. After all, they're her little brother, stepbrother, and stepsister. Plus, they are awfully cute and fun. If I didn't have so many brothers and sisters of my own, Kristy's brothers and sister might be my favorite sitting charges, too.

Kristy was sitting because her two older brothers were out somewhere, and her parents had gone to another estate sale. That seems to be Mr. and Mrs. Brewer's new hobby. An estate sale is like a very, very, very fancy yard sale. At an estate sale, the contents of a whole house are being sold, so instead of walking around someone's front yard, looking at chipped plates and falling-apart couches, you walk through someone's house, looking at all their furniture and valuable stuff. The big difference between a yard sale and an estate sale is how much everything costs. At a yard sale, you could probably get a lamp for two, maybe three, dollars. At an estate sale, things are in good condition and sometimes cost an awful lot of money.

Kristy's mom and stepfather have started

going to estate sales to find interesting things for their house and yard. Once, they came back with a birdbath. Another time, they found a chandelier. And another time, they got this big lampshade, that looks like it's made of stained glass. Kristy thinks the things they find are weird. I think they're fun. At any rate, the Brewers had gone off in search of wall sconces (whatever those are), and Kristy was left in charge.

Andrew and Karen only live with their father part-time — every other weekend, every other holiday, and for two weeks each summer. The rest of the time, they live with their mom and stepfather, who are also in Stoneybrook. Believe me, Kristy really looks forward to the weekends with Karen and Andrew. She loves them to bits — which I think makes David Michael a little jealous, since he's so close to their ages. (She loves David Michael, too, of course.)

When Mr. and Mrs. Brewer had left, the three kids immediately began telling Kristy what they wanted to do that afternoon.

"I want to play with Hannie," Karen announced.

Hannie Papadakis is Karen's best friend when Karen is at her father's house. Hannie lives across the street and a couple of houses down. Her older brother, Linny, is David Michael's friend.

"And I want to play with Linny," added David Michael.

"How about you, Andrew? What do you want to do?" Kristy asked.

"Daddy said I have to work on my part for the program."

"The program?" Kristy repeated. "Oh, right. At school."

Andrew's entire preschool class was planning a program for the parents. Andrew did not want to be in it. He's terribly shy. But every kid was supposed to be involved, so Andrew had some lines to learn. He was playing a roller-skating bear (on pretend skates) in a circus skit — and he wasn't happy about it.

"Okay, Andrew," said Kristy, "I'll help you with your lines. Karen, why don't you call Hannie and Linny and invite them over?"

"Goody!" exclaimed Karen. "Thanks, Kristy."

Kristy took Andrew into the den to work on his lines. She chose the den because it's a smallish room and very cozy. She thought it might help Andrew to feel more comfortable.

Andrew stood in the middle of the room,

and Kristy sat on the couch, holding the paper that Andrew's teacher had sent home with him. On it were the lines for the skating bears skit. Andrew's lines were highlighted in yellow.

"All right," said Kristy. "Let's see. It says here that the ringmaster — "

"Jason is the ringmaster," Andrew interrupted.

"Okay, that Jason the ringmaster says, 'And now, all the way from Europe, here are the famous skating bears!' "

"Right," said Andrew. "Then I'm supposed to stand up and say, 'I am . . . I am' . . . um . . . Kristy, I forget what I'm supposed to say, and anyway I don't want to say it. I don't want to stand up and talk at *all*."

"I know you don't," Kristy replied gently, "but you have to. That's your job. You know how your daddy and mommy both have jobs and go to work?"

"Yeah."

"And my mother and your stepfather have jobs and go to work?"

"Yeah."

"Well, I have jobs, too. My jobs are babysitting and going to school. Going to school is also a job for Charlie, Sam, David Michael,

Karen, and you. And part of *your* job is to be in this program."

"But I don't want to be in it," replied Andrew, and his lower lip began to quiver. "I don't want everyone looking at me and listening to me."

"But you know what they'll probably be thinking while they're doing that?"

"What?"

"They'll probably be thinking, What a good bear that Andrew makes. He knows his lines so well. I bet he worked very hard."

"What if I forget my lines? Then what will they be thinking?"

"They'll be thinking, Oh, too bad. He forgot his lines. Well, that happens sometimes. He *still* looks like a very nice, smart boy."

Andrew didn't seem convinced, so Kristy only worked with him for a few minutes. Then she let him go to his room. He said he wanted to be alone.

"Karen!" Kristy called. "David Michael! Where are you guys?"

Kristy had heard the doorbell ring while she was talking to Andrew, so she assumed the Papadakises had come over. Sure enough, she found Linny and David Michael on the back patio reading Basho-Man comics. Then she went to Karen's room, where she found the girls. They were dressed as twins!

"Look!" cried Karen. "Look what Hannie got! It's a dress exactly like ours!" Karen was wearing her sister-outfit dress that Kristy's grandmother had given her and Kristy the previous Christmas.

"My mommy bought it for me," Hannie spoke up, "and as soon as I saw it, I said, 'That's just like Karen's dress.' So I wore it over as a surprise."

"And we both have on white tights," added Karen, "and our shoes almost match." The girls were wearing Mary Janes, but Hannie's had two straps each, while Karen's had just one.

"Are we twins?" asked Hannie, putting her arm around Karen.

Kristy smiled. The girls couldn't have looked less like twins. Karen is blonde-haired, blue-eyed, and thin, while Hannie is dark-haired, dark-eyed, and stocky, but Kristy said, "You look just like twins."

The girls beamed.

"Let's do something twins do!" cried Karen. "Let's . . . let's . . ."

Kristy left the girls deciding what to do. She had an idea of her own. She went to her room and found *her* matching dress. She took off her jeans and turtleneck and put the dress on.

"Whoa," she whispered. "This thing's *tight*." Kristy is the shortest kid in her grade at Stoneybrook Middle School, but she must have been growing. The thought made her happy.

She barely managed to zip up the dress. Then she found a pair of white stockings and looked for some black shoes. She didn't have Mary Janes, of course, but she found some black flats and slipped into them.

She smiled at herself in her mirror. Then she returned to Karen's room.

"Hi, you guys!" she said.

Karen and Hannie turned to look at their "triplet."

"What do you think?" asked Kristy, pleased with her idea.

"I — " Karen began. "It's — " She gave Hannie an odd look. At last she said, "I think — I think we're tired of being twins."

"Yeah," agreed Hannie.

"You are?" said Kristy.

The girls nodded. "I think I'll change," added Karen.

"Then I will, too," said Kristy.

Kristy left the girls and put her jeans on again. She checked on Andrew, whom she found muttering his skating-bear lines in his room. Kristy smiled. Andrew was afraid and shy, but if he *had* to perform, he wanted to do it well. Kristy was proud of him.

She tiptoed away from his room and ran into Karen and Hannie, who were heading downstairs. Karen was no longer wearing her twin dress.

Interesting, Kristy wrote in the club notebook. *Jessi said girls this age like to pretend they're twins, but Karen said they got tired of the game.*

I thought about that for a long time after I read Kristy's notebook entry. I thought about some of the things Marilyn and Carolyn had said to me. I thought about what Jessi had said — that it's fun to *pretend* you have a twin, someone who looks just like you.

Then I thought about me. I remembered the time a year ago when I had bought this very cool floppy bow for my hair. Vanessa liked it so much that two days later, she bought one, too. I was so angry. Whenever Vanessa wore her bow to school, I wouldn't wear mine. I wanted to be the only one with that bow. I wanted to be an individual — like Dawn. Dawn

84

never follows the crowd. She insists on being unique, on being *herself*.

I thought of all these things, and suddenly something clicked. I had an idea about the troublesome twins. And I had an idea about how I might help them make a little change in their lives . . . or maybe a big change.

CHAPTER 10

Saturday

Wow! Some birthday party!!

So what did you think about the twins, Dawn?

I think they're brats, Mary Anne.

Oh, but they aren't. I've got them all figured out.

You're prejudiced, Mal. You've been sitting for them.

No, honest. I have figured out the trouble with the twins. But, look, you guys, we better start back at the beginning and describe this sitting job. Over to you, Dawn.

Well, the beginning is that Mallory and Mary Anne and I were the three sitters who ended up helping out at the Arnold twins' birthday party....

And *I*, Mallory, think the party turned out to be fun. Well, maybe not fun exactly, because it was work, and there were some bad moments with the twins. On the other hand, any party is exciting, and there were also some good moments with the twins. The thing is, only the twins and I knew that they were good moments. . . . Hmm, like I said before, I better start at the beginning.

The birthday party was supposed to go from one o'clock to three o'clock on Saturday afternoon. Mrs. Arnold asked us sitters to work from twelve to four so we could help prepare for the party beforehand and clean up afterward.

Mary Anne and Dawn walked over to my house, picked me up, and then the three of us walked to the Arnolds'. We arrived at ten minutes to twelve, which pleased Mr. and Mrs. Arnold.

"Happy birthday, Marilyn! Happy birthday, Carolyn!" I exclaimed as soon as I saw the twins. I'd gotten pretty good at telling them apart, even without their bracelets. Once I'd learned to look for the mole, I found other differences between the girls. For instance, Marilyn's nose is just slightly more rounded than Carolyn's. And Carolyn's cheeks are fuller than Marilyn's. But those are just physical differences. As I came to know the girls better — as they *let* me know them better — I found personality differences, too. After all, they *are* two different people, not Marilyn-or-Carolyn, so they're as different as any two sisters, or even any two strangers.

"Hi, Mallory!" cried the twins. They were bouncing up and down with excitement, still in their pajamas (matching, of course). They were not going to get dressed until just before the party started.

I introduced Dawn to the girls and their parents, and then Mary Anne said hello to everyone.

After that we got down to work.

"Let's see," Mrs. Arnold said. "Dawn, you're the tallest. Why don't you help Mr. Arnold put up the crepe paper in the dining room? Mary Anne, you can help the girls blow up balloons. And Mallory, you can fill the goody bags and then give me a hand in the kitchen."

"Okay," I replied.

Mrs. Arnold showed me into the living room, where an assembly line had been set up on the floor — fifteen paper bags with clown faces on them, fifteen packages of neat-looking barrettes (apparently, all the guests were going to be girls), fifteen sets of Magic Markers, fifteen tiny clip-on koala bears, fifteen candy bars, and fifteen beaded necklaces.

Boy, goody bags had certainly improved since I last got one. When we were little, didn't goody bags just have, oh, peanuts and a pencil and maybe a plastic ring in them?

I stuffed the bags neatly and stacked them on a chair in the living room. Then I helped Mrs. Arnold set out paper plates and cups and napkins, and fill candy baskets for the table. After that, we put the finishing touches on the twins' birthday cake. I wrote HAPPY BIRTHDAY, MARILYN AND CAROLYN in pink frosting. Believe me, this was not easy. But Mrs. Arnold thought the cake looked fine.

"It's perfect," she said. "Now let me think. Mallory, could you help the girls dress, please? I've laid their clothes out on their beds."

"Sure," I replied. "Marilyn, Carolyn!" I called. "Time to get dressed."

The girls and I went upstairs.

"Your mom said she laid your clothes out," I told them on the way.

No response.

Now what? I wondered.

We entered the girls' room. There on the beds were two absolutely beautiful dresses. They were white with pink ribbon running in rows from the neck to the waistline, and with lace at the collar, the edges of the sleeves, and all around the bottom.

"Those are gorgeous!" I exclaimed as soon as I saw them. "Are they new?"

"Yes," replied Carolyn shortly.

She and Marilyn looked at each other, looked at the dresses, then looked at each other again.

I decided to take a chance. "Gosh," I said, trying to sound casual, "you guys probably don't like having to dress the same all the time. I'm not sure I'd like it."

The twins' eyes widened in surprise. Then Marilyn said slowly, almost as if she were afraid to say it, "It's funny. Last year we *loved* wearing the same dresses. This year, it just doesn't seem like fun anymore. Hardly anyone knows whether I'm Marilyn or Carolyn. No one even cares."

"It's like we're one person instead of two," Carolyn added.

A-ha!

"Maybe you could dress differently today," I suggested. "One of you could wear your sailor dress. That would be good for a birthday party."

Carolyn's face lit up at the thought, but then she said, "No. We have to wear what Mommy says."

So on went the two white dresses — and

two pairs of pink tights, two pairs of Mary Janes, two gold lockets, two pink hair ribbons, and the name bracelets.

No sooner were the girls dressed, than the doorbell rang.

"They're here!" cried Marilyn. "The kids are here!"

The twins made a dash for the front door. Standing on the stoop outside were three dressed-up little girls. Each was holding two identical presents.

"Come on in!" said Mr. Arnold heartily. And the girls stepped into the living room. They put their presents in two piles on the couch.

For the next fifteen minutes, the doorbell kept ringing and guests kept arriving. Each one came with two gifts which were placed on the two piles. When all the children had arrived and Mary Anne and Dawn were organizing them for pin-the-tail-on-the-donkey, I secretly added my own gifts to the piles. I slipped them underneath the other presents.

Marilyn and Carolyn had seemed a little upset while they were getting dressed, but they were just fine during the games. All the girls liked pin-the-tail-on-the-donkey. Marilyn and Carolyn giggled and shrieked as they and their guests wandered blindly around the rec room, groping for the donkey poster. By the time everyone had had a turn, there were tails tacked up all over the rec room. The winner was the one who had pinned the tail on the donkey's nose. The twins were hysterical.

After the prize had been awarded, the kids played musical chairs (twice, Carolyn fell on the floor), and then they had a peanut hunt. When the hunt was over, Mrs. Arnold said, "Time for presents!"

The kids began cheering. The guests were as excited as the birthday girls were.

Marilyn and Carolyn sat down on the floor in the living room and their father set one stack of gifts beside each girl. The twins reached for the presents at the very top of the stacks. They were wrapped in Winnie-the-Pooh paper and were from a pigtailed girl named Jane. Marilyn and Carolyn tore off the wrapping. In each box was a small Raggedy Ann doll.

"Thank you," the twins said at the same time, and set the dolls on the floor.

They opened the next packages — two Barbie dolls. Then two stuffed elephants, then matching necklaces. Two, two, two. Each twin kept tossing her presents onto the floor, and growing crosser-looking by the second, although the guests kept exclaiming, "Aw, isn't that cute?" or "Oh, can I play with that?"

At last, the only presents left were mine. They were not the same size or shape. They were wrapped in different paper. The twins looked intrigued.

"Is this a mistake?" asked Carolyn.

"Who are they from?" asked Marilyn.

"Me," I replied. "Go on. Open them."

So they did. I'd picked out a tiny pin in the shape of a piano for Marilyn, and a book of simple science experiments for Carolyn.

"Boy, thanks!" cried the girls enthusiastically. They absolutely beamed at me.

But their smiles didn't last long. Mrs. Arnold wanted to take some pictures. She took the twins standing together holding hands. She took them cradling their new Raggedy Anns with the party guests grouped behind them. She took them sitting next to their piles of identical gifts. The girls were always together, always doing the same things.

It was no wonder that by cake time, the twins' faces were identical thunderclouds. They were sitting at one end of the decorated dining room table, the cake between them.

"Now lean over and blow out the candles," instructed Mrs. Arnold, her camera poised.

Two angry faces blew out the candles, then turned toward the camera.

Click!

The camera caught me in the background. I was trying to smile, but I'll bet my face looked pretty strange. I felt terrible for the twins. How awful to have no identity, to be just Marilyn-or-Carolyn, a cute lookalike twin.

As I walked home from the party later that day, I knew that my idea had been right. The girls didn't want to look identical. They might have enjoyed it when they were younger, but now they wanted to be individuals, just the way Dawn does — just the way almost everybody does — and I planned to do something about it.

CHAPTER 11

The next time I sat for Marilyn and Carolyn Arnold was on Tuesday, three days after their birthday party. The girls were waiting for me when I arrived. They were sitting side by side on the front stoop. In their matching yellow jumpsuits and white T-shirts they looked like gateposts marking the entrance to the house. When I was still only halfway up the walk, though, I noticed one difference between them. Marilyn was wearing the piano pin I'd given her.

"Hi, Mallory! Hi, Mallory!" the twins cried as I approached. They jumped up and ran to me, throwing their arms around my waist.

What a welcome.

"Hi, you guys!" I replied with a smile.

"We couldn't wait for you to get here," said Carolyn, taking one of my hands.

"You want to play with our new toys?"

asked Marilyn, taking my other hand.

The twins led me inside, where the three of us were greeted by Mrs. Arnold. As soon as she left, we went upstairs to their bedroom so I could look at their gifts. (A good project, since I'd forgotten to bring the Kid-Kit.) I'd seen the gifts the girls had received at the party, of course, but I hadn't seen the ones from their parents or relatives.

"These are from Aunt Elaine and Uncle Frank," said Carolyn, holding up two sticks. Attached to the ends of each was a long rope that fell beneath the stick in a loop.

"What are they?" I asked.

"Jump sticks," answered Carolyn. "See?" She put one of them down, held onto either end of the other, the stick poised in front of her at waist level, and made the rope circle up over her body. Jump, jump, jump. It was like a skipping rope, except that you held onto the stick instead of the ends of the rope.

"Neat!" I said. "But that looks like a better outdoor toy than an indoor one."

Carolyn obediently set the stick on the floor.

"Mommy and Daddy gave us these," spoke up Marilyn. She was pointing to two brass doll beds. Each had been placed at the foot of the girls' own beds.

"Boy," I said, "I never had anything like those." We aren't poor, but with eight kids in your family, you don't get duplicate copies of brass doll beds. You don't even get one brass doll bed.

"Now," said Carolyn, "you have to come downstairs to see our biggest presents."

Biggest presents? The doll beds weren't enough?

The twins took my hands again and led me to the rec room. There, on the floor, were two dollhouses. Pretty impressive ones, I might add.

"Look," said Marilyn. She ran to one house and pressed a button. Lights came on in each room! You should have seen those houses. They were decorated with everything from furniture (naturally) to teeny-tiny books and teeny-tiny plates of food. In each attic were a Christmas tree, a wreath, and garlands of greens, so the houses could be decorated for Christmas.

I was speechless.

But I was even more speechless after Marilyn said, "Guess what our best presents are."

"The dollhouses," I replied immediately.

"Nope," said Marilyn. "The piano pin and the science book."

"*My* presents?!" I exclaimed. "You're kidding! How come?" But already I knew the answer. I just hadn't realized how strong the girls' feelings about individuality were.

"Because . . . because," Marilyn said, giving her sister a sidelong glance, "they were different."

"And they were meant just for us, "added Carolyn. "I mean, you know, a piano for Marilyn because of her lessons, and the book for me because of the science fair."

"It seems like you know us," said Marilyn. "Is — is that silly?"

"Of course not," I answered seriously. "It isn't silly at all. Did I tell you that three of my brothers are triplets?"

"No! They are?" exclaimed Carolyn.

"Yup. And our family never treats them like they're all one person. I think maybe that's because there are so many kids in our family. There wouldn't be any point in treating three of them like one person, and the rest of us like five different people."

"So," said Marilyn, "you mean your brothers don't dress alike?"

"Nope," I said.

"Or have three of everything?"

"Nope. Unless they want three of something that isn't too expensive."

The twins looked thoughtful. "How come," Carolyn ventured after a moment, "you thought it was so neat that Marilyn and I *are* lookalikes and have all the same things?" I must have appeared sort of blank because she went on, "Remember that first day you sat for us?" I nodded. "Well, in the very beginning you tried to tell us apart, but then . . . then you were just like everyone else. You said, oh, how cute we were in our matching outfits and stuff. We decided we weren't going to be nice to any baby-sitters anymore."

So *that* had been my mistake.

"I'm sorry," I apologized. "Really I am. But you *were* cute. I didn't mean that I didn't care who you were. I just meant you were cute."

"Then we're sorry, too," said Carolyn. "We didn't understand."

"Yeah, we're sorry, too," added her sister.

I smiled. "You know, I've been thinking. Would you like to talk to your mother about how you feel? I'd help you." Please say yes, I begged silently. This was my plan and I wanted it to work.

"Talk to our mother about . . . what?" asked Marilyn.

The twins looked mystified.

I had thought it was obvious. "About *you* two. About letting you be individuals, separate people. Marilyn, if you could wear any kind of clothes you wanted, what would they look like?" I asked.

"More grown up," was her answer. "Like skirts without straps and stuff."

"Carolyn, how about you?"

"More cool," she said immediately. "Push-down socks and zipper jeans and barrettes with ribbons on them."

"You see?" I went on. "You guys like different things. It isn't just that you don't want to dress the same anymore, you also want to dress like *you*. You are two different girls and you have different tastes. Just like my sisters and I have different tastes."

"And you'd help us talk to our mother?" asked Marilyn.

I nodded. "How about it?"

"Yes!" cried the girls.

Talking to the twins' mother had seemed like a good idea when I'd first thought of it — but by the time Mrs. Arnold came home, I was a wreck. What right did I have, I wondered, butting into another family's business?

I had promised the girls I would help them talk, though, so as soon as Mrs. Arnold had paid me, I drew in a deep breath and said,

"Um, I was wondering. Could Marilyn and Carolyn and I talk to you?"

"Of course," replied Mrs. Arnold. "Is there a problem?" She began to look worried.

"Well, yes," I answered. "Not a baby-sitting problem, but . . ."

"Let's sit down," suggested Mrs. Arnold.

We stepped into the living room. I sat on the couch with one twin on either side of me. Mrs. Arnold sat across from us in an armchair.

I cleared my throat. I wasn't sure where to begin. At last I said, "Mrs. Arnold, did you know that three of my brothers are triplets?" I asked.

Before she could answer, Marilyn jumped into the conversation: "And they don't have to wear name bracelets!"

"No," said Carolyn. "They dress differently. Everyone can tell Mallory's brothers apart."

"Even though they're identical," I added.

"Yes?" said Mrs. Arnold, frowning.

"Well, the thing is," I went on, "I think Marilyn and Carolyn would like to be — "

"Different," spoke up Marilyn. "But we look alike and dress alike, so everyone treats us like one person — the same person."

"And we aren't one person, Mommy!" said Carolyn desperately. "We're *two*. Only no one knows it. At school, the kids call both of us 'Marilyn-or-Carolyn.' "

I cringed, remembering that that was how *I* used to think of the girls.

"We hate it!" added Marilyn.

"The girls do look sweet in their matching outfits," I said, "but," I added quickly as Carolyn poked me in the ribs, "they've told me they think they're old enough to choose their own clothes. They have different tastes."

"If we went to school *look*ing different," said Marilyn, "maybe the kids would get to know who we are."

Oh, good line, I thought as Mrs. Arnold melted before our very eyes.

"Girls," she said, "I never realized. . . . You're so adorable in your matching outfits. And it's so easy to lay out the same clothes for you every day and to buy two of everything. Plus, when you were little you liked looking identical, didn't you?"

"Yes, but we're not babies anymore," said Carolyn. "We can choose our own clothes every day. Honest."

"And if you let us come shopping with you," said Marilyn, "we could pick out the kinds of things we each like."

The twins looked hopefully at their mother.

"Of course you can come shopping with me."

"Can I grow my hair out?" asked Marilyn.

"Can I get mine cut?" asked Carolyn.

"Oh, you two," said Mrs. Arnold with a little gasp, and for a moment I was afraid she was going to cry. "I feel terrible. I always assumed that since your father and I liked the way you look, *you* liked the way you look."

"Well, we used to," Carolyn admitted.

"But not anymore," added her sister.

"Mallory," said Mrs. Arnold, "thank you. I know it wasn't easy for you to bring this to my attention."

"It wasn't," I said with a smile, "but I really like Marilyn and Carolyn. I'm glad this worked out."

"Mallory," whispered Carolyn, nudging me.

"Oh, right," I said. "There's one more thing."

"Yes?" said Mrs. Arnold.

"Mommy," Carolyn began, "you know the money we got for our birthday? Well, if you say it's okay, we want to spend it on new clothes."

"That's okay," agreed Mrs. Arnold quickly. "It's your money."

"Great," I spoke up. "Could I take them

shopping on Thursday? You could drop us off downtown on your way to the school and pick us up afterward."

"Please?" begged the twins.

"It's a date," said Mrs. Arnold.

The girls cheered.

And I walked home that afternoon feeling as if I were on air.

CHAPTER 12

By the time I reached my own house, not only did I feel as if I were on air, but I'd come up with another idea. (I was getting like Kristy Thomas, with all my ideas.) Anyway, the talk with Mrs. Arnold had gone awfully well. So it had occurred to me that I should probably try talking to my own parents. If I really wanted pierced ears and decent hair, maybe I should tell them so, instead of moping around, dropping hints about how unattractive and babyish I thought I was. Mrs. Arnold had given in to an awful lot, and the twins were barely eight years old. Imagine what my parents might agree to for someone who was closer to twelve than eleven.

As soon as I walked through our front door I ran up to my room, hoping Vanessa wouldn't be there. She wasn't. Good. There was about a half an hour before dinner, and I needed peace to plan my strategy. I wanted to talk to

Mom and Dad right after dinner, and I figured I would *need* a good strategy.

It never hurts to be prepared, especially with Mom and Dad. As the parents of eight children, they know every trick in the book — because one or the other of us kids has pulled every trick in the book at least once. My parents can tell a real stomachache from a fake one. They know when someone is eating and when someone is just moving food around on the plate. And I'm pretty sure they have eyes in the backs of their heads — under their hair or something — because without even turning around, they can see a kid who's trying to sneak something upstairs. Maybe they are wizards.

After twenty minutes, the ideal plan of attack came to me: bargaining. I am very good at bargaining. Once, I went to a flea market and saw this really neat old jewelry box. The price tag said $7.50, but I bargained with the guy who was selling it and bought it for $4.75. The man was asking for more than the box was worth, so first I offered *less* than it was worth (only a dollar) and finally we agreed to $4.75, which was a pretty fair price.

Yes, I thought, bargaining just might work.

Dinner that night was a typical Pike meal. Nicky tortured Claire by telling her that in first grade she would get six hours of homework each night and her gym teacher would be Mr. Berlenbach, who would make everyone play touch football whether they wanted to or not.

"That's not true!" cried Claire.

Nicky put his hands over his ears and began humming loudly. "Hmm, hmm-hmm, hmm-hmm. I ca-an't hear you! Hmm, hmm-hmm, hmm-hmm."

Then Adam stuck two straws up his nose and announced that he was a walrus, at which point I said, "Mother, that is revolting." (It couldn't hurt to get on her good side before our talk.)

"It certainly is," she agreed. "Everyone, calm down and behave."

"Everyone?" echoed Margo. "Even Daddy?"

"No, Daddy is behaving himself quite nicely," said my father.

We all laughed. But that didn't stop Jordan from very quietly singing the most disgusting song he knows: "Great big globs of greasy grimy gopher guts, little birdies' dirty feet — "

He stopped abruptly when I kicked him under the table. Margo was turning green, and I didn't want dinner to wind up being such a disaster that Mom and Dad would be too fed up for a talk.

Things calmed down. Margo's face returned to its normal color. We finished our meal. I helpfully volunteered to clean up the kitchen, and I even made coffee for Mom and Dad. I brought it to them in the living room, where they were unwinding.

"Oh, Mallory, you're a lifesaver," said Mom.

"Thanks, honey," added Dad.

"You're welcome. . . . Um, could I talk to you about something?"(Hadn't I said almost the same thing to Mrs. Arnold just a couple of hours earlier?)

My parents glanced at each other, and in that one glance, I could see that they had figured out everything. Their eyes were saying, "Oh, so that's why she was so helpful during dinner, and then cleaned up the kitchen and made coffee for us."

I think they really are wizards.

Wizards or not, I had to go on with my talk. I mean, I'd already said I wanted to talk to them, so I'd better get started.

"Mom, Dad," I began, "I'm — I'm eleven years old. Soon I'll be twelve."

"And after that you'll be a teenager," said Dad, groaning slightly.

"Exactly!" I exclaimed. "I'm not a kid anymore. But I feel like one. I have this dumb hair, and my clothes are sort of, well, babyish.

108

They're *nice*," I added diplomatically, "but they're young. And I would really like to get my ears pierced." (I had purposely decided not to say, "Half the girls in my class have pierced ears," because then one of my parents would have said, "If half the girls in your class were going to jump off a cliff, would you do that, too?") "I would also like to get contact lenses," I went on. "That's all I want — a haircut, pierced ears, contact lenses, and a brand-new wardrobe." (If I got permission for a haircut, I'd be lucky. But that's how bargaining works.)

"What?" cried my mother with a gasp. "You want *what?*"

"A haircut, pierced ears, contact lenses, and a new wardrobe."

My parents just stared at me. This must have been one trick they hadn't encountered. I decided to try another.

I hung my head. "I'm such a baby," I moaned. "I'm a freak."

"Oh, honey, you are not," said Mom sympathetically.

"You are also not old enough to get contact lenses," added Dad.

"And I'm afraid we can't afford a new wardrobe for you," said my mother. "Do you have any idea how much that would cost?"

I did, but I didn't say so. The wardrobe was one of my bargaining chips. It was something I wasn't expecting at all, so I could easily give it up.

"No," I replied. "How much?"

"A lot," said Dad.

"Oh." I hung my head again.

"I don't see why you couldn't get your hair cut, though," said Mom. "Could you pay for half of it with your baby-sitting money?"

"Sure!" I cried.

"All right. Then you may get your hair cut. On one condition."

"What?" I asked.

"That you don't go to that place where you'll come out with a green mohawk. I want you to go to the salon downtown."

"Deal." (That was no sacrifice. I'd wanted to go to the salon, anyway.)

I paused, thinking. I'd given up the wardrobe and the contacts, but I'd gotten the haircut. What about the pierced ears? "What about piercing my ears?" I asked, and suddenly I forgot about bargaining and tricks. "Please, please, please, please, *please* can I get them pierced? I really want to. Earrings look so pretty, and I promise I won't get more than one hole in each ear, or wear anything weird like, you know, snake fangs. I'll just wear little gold dots, or maybe gold hoops, but tiny ones. Please could I have my ears pierced?"

Another look was exchanged between Mom and Dad, but I couldn't tell what this one meant.

At last Mom said, "I was twelve when I got my ears pierced. You're pretty close to twelve." She turned to Dad. "What do you think?"

"I suppose it's all right — if it's all right with you."

"It's all right with me on three conditions," replied Mom.

Three conditions this time? I guess my wizard parents know how to bargain, too.

"What are the three conditions?" I asked.

"One," Mom answered, "that you pay for the piercing and the earrings yourself."

"Okay," I said.

"Two, that you do everything you're told to prevent infected ears — put alcohol on them, don't change your earrings right away. *Every*thing."

"Okay."

"And, three, that you *don't* stick to tiny gold earrings. What's the fun of having pierced ears if you can't wear snake fangs every now and then?"

I laughed. "Oh, thanks, you guys! Thank you so much! This is great! I understand about the contacts and the wardrobe. Really. But would it be okay if I spent my baby-sitting money on clothes sometimes?"

"Of course," said Mom. "Just be sensible."

"Oh, I will! I will! Wow! Thanks again. This is awesome! I have to call Jessi and give her the news."

I ran down to the kitchen phone. Jordan and Byron were there making ice-cream sandwiches out of graham crackers and frozen yogurt. (There is no such thing as privacy at my house.) I leaned against the counter and dialed Jessi's number.

Jessi answered the phone herself.

"Hi, it's me," I said in a rush, "and guess what. My parents said I could get my hair cut and my ears pierced."

"You are kidding!"

"Nope. It's the truth. I just had a talk with them."

From across the kitchen I heard Byron say, "Ooh, big deal. Pierced ears."

"SHHH!" I said. "No, not you, Jessi. Byron. My brothers are being pains. And pigs."

"Yeah, piggy-pains," said Jordan, and he and Byron began to laugh uncontrollably.

"Would you please go somewhere else? . . . No, I don't mean you, Jessi. The piggy-pains."

112

My brothers finally left, and Jessi and I got down to serious business.

"What are you going to do to your hair?" asked Jessi.

"I'm not sure. It's so curly. Maybe something short would be good. Short and fluffy. But not too short. Oh, I don't know."

"Boy," said Jessi, "if you get your hair cut and your ears pierced, I'll really stick out. I'll look like such a baby at club meetings.

"You don't look like a baby *now*," I said honestly.

"Well, I'd still like to get my hair cut and my ears pierced. Just like you."

"Talk to your parents," I suggested. "It worked for me. But be sure you don't say you want those things because I'm getting them. If you do — "

"I know, I know," Jessi interrupted. "Then my parents will say, 'And if Mallory jumped off a cliff, would you do that, too?' "

We both laughed.

"They must learn that at Parent School," said Jessi.

Jessi and I stayed on the phone until we both remembered we had homework to do. Then we got off in a hurry. But for the rest of the evening, the only thing I could really think about was The New Mallory Pike.

CHAPTER 13

Shopping Day!

I was as excited as the twins were. I couldn't wait to go downtown with them. I just knew we were going to have a totally super time. Not only was it going to be fun, but I couldn't wait to see what sorts of things the twins would actually buy. How different would they look? Marilyn had said she wanted to look more grown-up, and Carolyn had said she wanted to look more cool, but that didn't tell me much. The afternoon just might be full of surprises. Also, I had brought along some of my own spending money, in case I saw something that was perfect for The (Soon-to-Be) New Mallory Pike.

Well, the afternoon *was* full of surprises (and fun), and I got my first surprise as soon as I reached the Arnolds' house. The twins were waiting for me outside again — and they were *not* dressed in matching outfits. They were wearing clothes that their mother had bought and that I knew the twins didn't particularly like, but at least the clothes didn't match. The funny thing was that just by wearing non-identical outfits, the girls suddenly seemed less like twins. Their hair and faces were the same as ever, of course, but getting them out of those matching outfits made a world of difference. They looked more like two little girls than two peas in a pod.

"Oh, boy! Shopping time!" cried Carolyn as I approached.

"We can't wait!" added Marilyn.

"Neither can I," I replied as the twins threw themselves at me. "Gosh, you two look great!"

"We got to wear different clothes as soon as you talked to Mommy," Carolyn told me excitedly.

"We wore different pajamas to bed that night," said Marilyn, "and different clothes to school yesterday, and these clothes to school today."

"And you know what?" Carolyn went on.

"What?" I said.

"Right away, the kids at school tried to tell us apart."

"That's great!" I exclaimed. I took each twin by the hand and we walked up the Arnolds' front path.

"Yeah," agreed Marilyn."Most of the time, they get us wrong, but they haven't called us 'Marilyn-or-Carolyn' for two whole days!"

I led the excited twins inside, where Mrs. Arnold greeted us with a big smile and immediately bustled us down the stairs and right out the garage door and into the car.

"Sorry for the rush," she apologized, "but I've got a lot to do today. Girls, you have your money, don't you?"

"Yes," they replied. They had managed to grab their (identical) pocketbooks as their mother whisked us to the car.

"Good. Then we're on our way."

Ten minutes later, Mrs. Arnold was driving slowly through Stoneybrook's downtown, caught in a small traffic jam. "How about if I let you out up there, by Bellair's?" she asked.

"Perfect," I said.

Bellair's is a department store. It would be a good place to begin our shopping.

"And why don't I pick you up in front of Bellair's in two hours?"

"Okay. We'll be waiting right by that mailbox," I replied, pointing.

Marilyn and Carolyn said good-bye to their mother, leaning over the back of the front seat to plant kisses on her cheek. Then they tumbled out of the car like puppies, and made a dash for the entrance to Bellair's.

I ran after them. "Hey, you guys!" I called breathlessly. "We have to stick together. No running off. I wouldn't want to lose you."

The girls slowed down.

"Okay, what department should we go to first?" I asked.

"Girls' clothing," said Marilyn and Carolyn in one voice, and I realized then that no matter how much the girls wanted to appear different from each other, there were some almost uncanny likenesses about them. They often spoke as one, or picked up on each other's thoughts as they told a story. I wondered whether they could read each other's minds.

"Girls' clothing," I repeated. I checked the store directory. "Second floor," I announced. "Let's go."

"Goody, there's the escalator," said Carolyn. "I just love escalators."

We rode to the second floor and found the girls' clothing department.

"We have a plan," Marilyn told me.

"Yeah," said Carolyn. "Clothes are expensive, and we have *pretty* much birthday money, but not a *lot*."

"So we want to be very careful today,"

Marilyn went on. "We want to see what we like at a lot of stores — "

"And how much the things cost," cut in Carolyn.

" — and then we'll decide what to buy and go back and get them."

"That makes sense to me," I told the girls.

So we began looking.

At Bellair's, Marilyn tried on a beautiful pink mohair sweater. I guess she really did want to look more grown-up. Then she checked the price tag.

"A hundred and thirty-five dollars!" she cried.

The sweater went back on the shelf.

Carolyn looked at a neat white sweat shirt with a glittering yellow moon and two stars on the front. "Oh, cool!" she exclaimed. "And I think I can afford it, but I better wait."

Both girls looked at shoes (loafers for Marilyn, high-top sneakers for Carolyn) and immediately realized that any shoes were out of the question. Too expensive. They bypassed the nightgown rack, the underwear table, and a couple of racks of dresses that looked like the stuff their mother would have chosen for them. Then they stopped and looked at pants. I realized I'd never seen them in pants and hoped they could afford them.

118

"Nice corduroys," said Marilyn.

"Cool jeans," said Carolyn.

Then in the same breath, they added, "We'll come back."

They had pretty much exhausted the girls' clothing department by that time, so I said, "How about going to the Merry-Go-Round? You could probably find some great accessories there."

"What are excorceries?" Marilyn wanted to know.

"Accessories," I repeated. "They're little things to add to an outfit, like jewelry or barrettes or hair ribbons or cute socks."

I could tell by the looks on the girls' faces that the Merry-Go-Round would be our next stop. So we left Bellair's.

The twins fell in love with the Merry-Go-Round, and I couldn't blame them. I'm sort of in love with it myself. The three of us wandered around the store for at least fifteen minutes, calling out things like, "Ooh, look at this unicorn pin," or "Hey, cool, these barrettes are sparkly!" or "Here are knee socks with rows of hearts on them."

Marilyn and Carolyn did their careful looking and planning, but I made a purchase. Two, actually. I couldn't help myself. I found earrings that were perfect for me — and for Jessi.

119

They were tiny studs in the shape of open books. Since we like to read so much, I bought a pair for each of us. Best friends, I thought, should have matching earrings. We wouldn't always have to wear them together, but they'd be nice to own. And Jessi's pair would be a just-because-you're-my-best-friend present. Guess what, though? Both pairs were *pierced*. That's how certain I was that Jessi would be given permission to have her ears pierced, too.

After the Merry-Go-Round, the twins and I went to a sport shop. There the girls priced socks and shirts, and I bought . . . blue push-down socks! I would have to stop buying things, though, or I'd never be able to pay for the ear-piercing and half of my haircut.

"You guys," I said, as we left the sport shop, "we have to meet your mom in a little less than an hour, so I think you better decide what you want to buy, and then go back and get the things. Are you ready to do that?"

"Yes," said Marilyn.

"I think so," said Carolyn.

"Do you need to do some figuring?" I asked them. They looked like they were frantically trying to add prices in their heads. I could practically see their eyeballs whirling around from the effort. "There's a bench. Let's sit down," I suggested.

We sat down and I pulled a pad of paper out of my purse. After much discussion and scribbling and adding and subtracting, we went back to Bellair's.

"Clothes first," said Marilyn. "They're more important than excorceries."

In the girls' clothing department Carolyn tried on the "cool jeans" she had seen. "They're a little expensive, but I can wear them with almost all of my shirts and blouses and sweaters," she said sensibly.

Marilyn tried on the corduroys and didn't like them. "I'm more used to skirts and dresses," she admitted. "I don't want any more baby dresses or things with straps, though. I saw a cute pink jeans skirt. Maybe I should try that on. It was grown-up."

Twenty minutes later, we left Bellair's. Marilyn was carrying a bag with the jeans skirt and a ruffly white blouse in it. She had forked over at least three quarters of her money for them, but looked quite pleased and proud. Carolyn was carrying a bag with the jeans and the moon-and-stars sweat shirt in it. The grins on both girls' faces were at least a mile wide.

We went back to the Merry-Go-Round. Marilyn bought the knee socks with the hearts on them ("I'm tired of tights," she explained) and a pair of pink barrettes.

121

The barrettes were important because the girls had made a decision about their hair. "If Mommy won't let me get my hair cut right away," said Carolyn, "at least we can wear our hair differently."

"I'm going to pull mine back with barrettes," said Marilyn.

"And I'll wear a headband," added Carolyn, who found one she liked at the Merry-Go-Round.

Our last stop was the sport shop. Marilyn was out of money, but Carolyn bought some push-down socks like the ones I'd gotten, except that they were yellow, to match her new sweat shirt.

As we left the sport shop, the girls turned satisfied faces toward me.

"All our money is gone," commented Marilyn, "but we don't care."

"Yeah, we are so lucky," said her sister. "And from now on, when Mommy goes shopping, we'll go with her. We'll never have to wear yucky clothes again."

Don't count on it, I thought, knowing how mothers can be. But Mrs. Arnold *was* going to try to be understanding. I was pretty sure of it.

I looked at my watch. "Ten minutes until

your mother will be back," I said. "What do you want to do?"

"Oh, please," began Carolyn, "could we go to the ladies' lounge in Bellair's and put our new clothes on? Please? Then we could surprise Mommy when we meet her."

I didn't see why not, so we returned to Bellair's and told a sales clerk what we wanted to do. The clerk cut the price tags off of the clothes, and Marilyn and Carolyn did a quick change in the lounge. Then we dashed outside to the mailbox.

No Mrs. Arnold yet. I took a moment to really look at the twins. With their new hairdos, they appeared more different than ever. And, I thought, they seemed to have changed from the terrible, troublesome twins into two sunny little girls whom I could tell apart even when they "matched." I thought back to when I began sitting for them and wondered how I could ever *not* have been able to tell Marilyn from Carolyn. And I remembered what terrors they'd been and how I'd dreaded Tuesday and Thursday afternoons. Now I looked forward to them — but my steady job would be over soon. I hoped Mrs. Arnold would need me to sit sometimes in the future. I'd take care of the troublesome twins any day!

A few minutes later, Mrs. Arnold's car pulled to a stop by the mailbox, and the twins and I scrambled inside. I wish I'd had a camera to capture the expressions on Mrs. Arnold's face when she saw Marilyn and Carolyn. First she looked, well, almost horrified . . . then amazed . . . and finally pleased. I think she liked her daughters' new appearances, but they would take some getting used to.

I knew that the Arnolds, all of them, were going to be just fine.

CHAPTER 14

"Guess what, guess what, guess what!"

"What?" I cried. Jessi's voice was at the other end of our phone, and I had never, and I mean *never*, heard it so excited.

"My parents said I can get my ears pierced!"

"Oh, wow! That is awesome!" I screeched. "Now we can go together!"

At the next meeting of the Baby-sitters Club, Jessi and I told the other girls our news.

Claudia started to laugh. "You won't believe this," she said. "It must be ear-piercing season in Stoneybrook! I just got permission to have another hole pierced in one of my ears!"

"You're kidding!" I cried. "Then we should all have them done at the same time. Where are you going to have your ear done?"

"I'm not sure. . . ."

"Hey," said Kristy, "I've got an idea."

(Naturally.)

"We haven't had a club party in awhile.

Instead of one, how about if we pay Charlie to drive us out to Washington Mall next Saturday. You three could have your ears pierced at that boutique, and then we could shop and eat lunch and stuff. You want to?''

Of course we did.

"Gosh," said Claud, suddenly looking almost sad, "it's too bad Stacey's not here. She would *love* this. She'd probably have another hole pierced in one of her ears, too."

"Why don't you call her?" suggested Kristy in a gentler-than-usual tone. "At least tell her what we're going to do. I bet she'd want to know. Oh, but, um, well, why don't you call her *after* the meeting so you don't tie up the line?" (The old Kristy again.)

"Okay," agreed Claud glumly. Then she brightened. "Hey, Kristy, Mary Anne, Dawn — are you guys going to ask if you can have your ears pierced, too? You should. It would be fun."

"No way!" exclaimed Kristy. And Mary Anne shook her head. (Dawn shook hers, too, but she looked a little uncertain.)

"My father won't let me," explained Mary Anne, "but we'll definitely come with you," she assured us.

"Yeah. We wouldn't miss it for the world!" said Dawn.

126

* * *

Five days later, Charlie Thomas was dropping us off at an entrance to Washington Mall. It was eleven o'clock in the morning. "See you at three!" he called as he drove off.

Jessi, Dawn, Mary Anne, Claudia, Kristy, and I practically ran inside. I was so excited that my heart was pounding, and I could hear its beat in my ears.

"What should we do first?" asked Kristy when we were in the center of the mall, surrounded by the stores and restaurants and exhibits.

What were we going to do *first?* Weren't we heading straight for the ear-piercing boutique? I'd waited more than eleven years for this moment. We weren't going to postpone it . . . were we?

I gave Kristy a tortured glance, and she laughed. "Just kidding. Of course we're going to do ears first. Come on, everybody."

We headed for the boutique. On the way, Jessi grabbed my hand.

"I'm getting scared," she said.

"Don't be. I mean, try not to be. I think it's going to be fine. You know, they freeze your ears with this spray before they pierce them, so you don't feel anything. Well, you feel the punch, but it doesn't hurt — "

I stopped. The more I said, the worse Jessi looked.

Claudia noticed her then and exclaimed, "Cheer up! This is fun. We're going malling, you guys. We've never done this as a club!"

Malling. It had a nice ring to it.

Thirty seconds later, the six of us were gathered around the ear-piercing boutique. We were looking at the display of earrings.

"May I help you?" asked a young woman. She was wearing a name tag that read "Sue," and I was relieved to see that it wasn't the same woman Claire had scared to death when she'd screamed, watching the ear-piercing with Margo and me.

My friends looked at me, so I stepped forward. I was feeling pretty calm. I usually am calm. In fact, the more there is to be nervous about, the calmer I become.

"I want to get my ears pierced, please," I told Sue, "and so does she," (I pointed to Jessi), "and she wants one more hole in one ear," I added, indicating Claudia.

"Very good." Sue smiled. "Choose your earrings first. We suggest the simple gold studs, no large hoops or anything fancy."

"Okay," I said.

Jessi and I chose tiny gold balls and Claudia produced an earring she already owned, which

Sue said she could use after it had been sterilized.

"All right. Who's first?" Sue wanted to know.

My friends were grinning. Somebody nudged me forward. "Go on, Mal," said Dawn. "Ear-piercing was your idea."

I hopped onto the stool. In a few minutes, my ears would be pierced. I would look so, so cool. I didn't care what the piercing would feel like.

Sue took a pen and made a tiny mark on each of my earlobes. "Do those look even to you?" she asked. "If they do, that's where I'll make the holes."

I leaned over and examined the marks in a mirror on the counter.

"Perfect," I said.

Then, *spray!* Sue blasted my right ear with something cold. And *punch.* She came at me with that gun, an earring loaded into it like a bullet. *Spray* again. *Punch* again. "All done!" said Sue. The gun had pierced my ears and put the earrings in all at once.

I looked in the mirror. I couldn't believe it. There were my ears, shining with actual ear-rings! I had done it! I felt incredibly cool.

"Who's next?" asked Sue as I slid off the stool.

I was sure Claud would hop onto the stool, since Jessi looked like a nervous wreck while Claud seemed to be your basic cool cucumber. But Claud pushed Jessi forward. I guess she thought it would be better for Jessi to get it over with, so she could stop feeling so nervous.

Reluctantly, Jessi climbed onto the stool and Sue marked her ears. "Hold my hand," she whispered to me, sounding extremely embarrassed.

No problem. I gripped her hand. Jessi squeezed her eyes shut.

Spray, punch! Spray, punch!

Jessi hadn't moved. Her eyes were still closed.

"It's over," I told her.

"You're kidding," she replied. She opened her eyes. "That was nothing!"

"Look at yourself in the mirror," said Sue.

Jessi looked — and grinned.

"Pretty sexy," Mary Anne teased her.

"Okay, Claud, you're on," said Kristy.

Ever so casually, Claudia climbed onto the stool. Sue marked a second spot on one of her ears.

"That looks fine," said Claudia breathily. She folded her hands and sat back. She might have been in a restaurant, waiting for someone to come take her order.

Spray! Punch!

"Thanks!" said Claud brightly. She jumped up — then started to slump to the floor.

Kristy and Dawn caught her arms and eased her back onto the stool.

"Put your head between your legs," Sue instructed her briskly.

Claud did as she was told. After a moment, she raised her head.

"Feel better?" asked Sue.

Claudia nodded sheepishly. "I think I can walk now."

"Okay, but just a sec," said Sue. "I have to give all three of you a few instructions on caring for your ears over the next few weeks."

She talked to us about cleaning the holes with alcohol, and not changing the earrings, and turning the posts. Then we paid Sue and left.

"I am so, so embarrassed. I can't believe I almost passed out," wailed Claudia. At the same time Dawn cried, "Wait! I changed my mind. I want my ears pierced after all. I've got to call my mom!"

The next few moments were sort of confusing. Mary Anne sat down on a bench with Claud and tried to make her feel better. Kristy dashed off with Dawn to look for a pay phone, and Jessi and I kept trying to find mirrors or windows in which we could admire our ears.

Five minutes later, Jessi, Dawn, and Kristy gathered at the bench.

"My mom gave me permission!" cried Dawn. "And guess what. She said I could get *two* holes in each ear!"

So we returned to Sue.

Spray, punch, punch! Spray, punch, punch!

When we finally left the ear-piercing boutique for good, we went malling. First, we sort of window-shopped to see what was what. Those of us who had just had our ears pierced were pretty low on money, though.

Then we ate lunch at Burger King. "Lunch is being paid for out of the club treasury," Kristy announced, "since we're malling instead of having a party or a sleepover."

After lunch, we made the rounds of the stores again. Kristy and Mary Anne kept ducking into little shops and making secret purchases. They wouldn't tell the rest of us what they were buying.

We went to the Music Cellar and checked out the new tapes.

Finally, about half an hour before Charlie was supposed to pick us up, we parked ourselves outside of Donut Delite and spied on the cute boys working inside. I have to admit that this was fascinating to Claudia, Dawn,

Mary Anne, and even Kristy, but that Jessi and I couldn't stop looking at our ears in store windows.

Today, I decided, I had taken the first big step toward becoming The New Mallory Pike.

CHAPTER 15

"Order, please!" called Kristy Thomas. It was time for another Monday meeting.

Three weeks and two days had gone by since the Baby-sitters Club's ear-piercing adventure. My steady job with the Arnolds had ended — but already I had sat for the twins twice more, and a weekend job was lined up.

And two days ago, on a red-letter Saturday, a couple of very important things had happened to me, The New Mallory Pike. I had changed my earrings for the first time, and (ta-dah) I had gotten my hair cut!

I have to admit that I looked pretty good, even with my glasses. And even with the revolting braces the orthodontist had put on my teeth a few days earlier.

Jessi had gone with me to the hairdresser. When I entered the salon, I still didn't know exactly what I wanted done. Luckily Amber, the woman who was going to cut my hair, was very understanding.

"I'll show you some pictures," she said. "See what you like. Then I'll tell you if I can do it to your hair."

Jessi and I looked through a book filled with photos of hairstyles. I pointed out four to Amber before she said, "Now *that's* one your hair is perfect for. See how wavy that style is? It's all natural. No perm or anything. When we cut your hair, your curls will relax into those waves."

So here I was, sitting in Claudia's room with my pierced ears (I was wearing the open books I'd bought at the Merry-Go-Round), my fluffy, short hair (which showed off my ears nicely), and, well, my braces. (I tried not to think about the braces too much.)

Kristy was perched in the director's chair, wearing her visor. "Order," she called again.

The rest of us quieted down.

"Well, let's see," Kristy began.

Well, let's see? Our president never opens meetings that way. She always knows just what to say, just what she wants to accomplish. But at the moment, she sounded sort of vague.

"Um," Kristy went on. "Oh, yeah. Has everyone read the notebook?"

"Yes," answered the rest of us in bored voices.

"Well, um. . . . Oh, Dawn, how's the treasury?"

"Still a little low since we went malling, but we have enough to pay Charlie to drive you to and from meetings this week, and after I've collected today's dues" (everyone groaned) "and next Monday's, we'll be okay again."

The six of us fished around for dues money, which we handed to Dawn. She counted it, made a notation on a page in the record book, and placed the money in the treasury envelope.

"Okay, well, oh, yeah," said Kristy. "Any business to discuss?" (It was as if she'd just thought of it. You'd never know she asks us that question at the beginning of absolutely every club meeting.)

I half-raised my hand (how kindergarten of me) and said, "Kristy, is everything all right with you?"

"Oh, sure. Why?"

"I don't know."

"Well, I'm fine."

"Okay."

Kristy paused. "Darn it!" she finally exclaimed. "I can't stand it any longer. Mary Anne, it's time for — "

Ring, ring. I couldn't believe it. The phone! And just when Kristy was about to . . . to do whatever it was she wanted to do.

Claudia took the call, while Mary Anne flipped through the pages in the record book to check the appointment calendar. When Claud hung up, she said, "That was Mrs. Arnold. She needs a sitter for the twins next Thursday afternoon."

"Let's see," said Mary Anne. "Gosh, three of us are free. Kristy, Dawn, and me."

"Hey, Mal," said Dawn, "how *are* the twins these days? I know you ended up liking them, but . . ."

"Oh, you wouldn't believe them," I replied. "They're completely different. Mrs. Arnold finally let Carolyn get her hair cut. It's really cute, shorter than mine. And Marilyn is growing hers out. They never dress the same anymore, and *everyone* can tell them apart, so they're much happier. Whichever one of you gets the job next Thursday will be really surprised. And pleased," I added. "They are not troublesome twins anymore."

After a lot of discussion, Dawn took the job. Then Kristy said, "Okay. Now — "

Ring, ring!

"Aughh!" cried Kristy.

Three more job calls came in, one right after the other.

We are just too popular.

"*Now*," Kristy tried again, "Mary Anne and I have some surprises."

"Surprises?" repeated Jessi and I at the same time. (Then we had to hook pinkies and say "jinx.")

"Yup." Kristy smiled secretively. "Okay, Mary Anne."

Mary Anne, who was sitting on the end of Claudia's bed, reached down to the floor and hauled up a tote bag. Out of it, she pulled four small boxes. She handed one to Dawn, one to Claudia, one to Jessi, and one to me.

"These are from Kristy and me," she said. "They're presents in honor of the fact that you guys can now change your earrings."

"Oh, wow!" Jessi and Dawn and I exclaimed. "That was so nice of you! Thanks!"

But Claudia started to laugh. "What a coincidence! Wait, don't open them yet." She slid off the bed, opened a drawer in her desk, and removed three small tissue-wrapped packages, one for Dawn, one for Jessi, and one for me.

Well, we had all guessed that the presents were earrings, of course, so I said, "Hold it!

One more!'' and gave Jessi a box containing her pair of book earrings. "I'm sorry I don't have anything for you two," I said to Claud and Dawn, "but I got these before I knew you were going to get your ears pierced, too." I'd brought the earrings along, planning to give them to Jessi after the meeting.

Claud, Dawn, Jessi, and I began opening our presents. We opened the ones from Kristy and Mary Anne first.

"These are the things we kept buying at the mall that day," Kristy informed us. Her eyes were shining.

Well, you've never heard such squealing. The earrings had been chosen very carefully, and we were all thrilled. Dawn had been given two pairs, studs in the shape of California (her home state) and others that were gold loops with oranges hanging from them. California oranges, I guess. Claud's earrings looked like artists' palettes, Jessi's were ballet shoes, and mine were horses, since I like to read about them.

"Thank you, thank you!" we kept saying.

Then we opened Claud's earrings. "I made them myself," she announced.

Even if she hadn't said so, we all would have known. And we began laughing nonstop.

Claud had collected little charms and strung together these wild bunches of miniature Coke cans, eyeglasses, forks, animals, you name it, and added feathers and beads.

We put them on immediately, crowding around Claudia's mirror for a look.

"Don't worry," said Claud. "I made a pair for myself. Oh, and all the posts are hypoallergenic."

"Boy, I sure wish *I* had pierced ears," said Mary Anne wistfully.

"How about the next best thing?" asked Claudia. She produced two more packages — one for Mary Anne, one for Kristy. They were earrings like the others Claud had made, but they were for nonpierced ears. Kristy and Mary Anne beamed.

"Whoa, it's six o'clock," said Kristy suddenly, and the meeting broke up, the six of us still calling thank you to one another.

Not until Jessi and I were outside and walking down the Kishis' driveway did I say, "Hey, Jessi, you didn't open — "

"I know," she interrupted me. "For some reason, I wanted to do it in private." She pulled my present out of her purse, and we stopped while she tore the paper off the box. "Ooh," she breathed as she peered inside, "books. Just like yours." She paused. "So we can be twins?" she asked.

We both laughed, thinking of Marilyn and Carolyn.

"No," I replied. "Best friends."

"Oh. Best friends," Jessi repeated, and gave me a big hug.

Then we headed for our homes.

About the Author

ANN M. MARTIN did *a lot* of baby-sitting when she was growing up in Princeton, New Jersey. Now her favorite baby-sitting charge is her cat, Mouse, who lives with her in her Manhattan apartment.

Ann Martin's Apple Paperbacks are *Bummer Summer, Inside Out, Stage Fright, Me and Katie (the Pest)*, and all the other books in the Baby-sitters Club series.

She is a former editor of books for children, and was graduated from Smith College. She likes ice cream, the beach, and *I Love Lucy*; and she hates to cook.

Look for #22

JESSI RAMSEY, PET-SITTER

Claudia hung up the phone and looked up from some notes she'd been making. She found the rest of us staring at her.

"Well?" said Kristy.

"Well, the Mancusis need a pet-sitter," Claudia began.

"A *pet*-sitter?" Kristy practically jumped down Claud's throat. "How could you even *think* about another pet-sitting job?"

"Another one?" I asked.

"Yeah," said Kristy. "The very first job I got when we started the club — my first job offer at our first official meeting — was for two Saint Bernard dogs, and it was a disaster."

"But Kristy," protested Claudia, "if the Mancusis can't find a pet-sitter, they'll have to cancel their dream vacation."

Kristy sighed. "All right. Suppose one of us was crazy enough to *want* to pet-sit — don't the Mancusis need someone everyday?"

143

"Well . . . well, um," I began, "my ballet school is closed next week, remember? So I'm available. For the whole week. I could take care of the Mancusis' pets. I mean, if they want me to."

"Perfect!" exclaimed Claud. She called Mrs. Mancusi back, as promised. As you can probably imagine, Mrs. Mancusi was delighted to have a sitter. She asked to speak to me. After thanking me several times, she said, "When could you come by? My husband and I will have to show you how to care for the animals. There are quite a lot of them, you know."

After some discussion, we decided on Friday evening, right after supper. Since the Mancusis live near my house, I knew that would be okay with my parents.

I hung up the phone. "Gosh, the Mancusis sure are going to pay me well."

"They better," Kristy replied. "I don't think Claud told you exactly how many pets they have. There are three dogs, five cats, some birds and hamsters, two guinea pigs, a snake, lots of fish, and a bunch of rabbits and turtles."

I gulped. What had I gotten myself into?

**Here's some news about other books
in The Baby-sitters Club series
by Ann M. Martin**

#1 Kristy's Great Idea

Kristy thinks the Baby-sitters Club is a great idea. She and her friends Claudia, Stacey, and Mary Anne all love taking care of kids. But nobody counted on crank calls, wild pets, and uncontrollable two-year-olds! Having a Baby-sitters Club isn't easy, but Kristy and her friends won't give up till they get it right!

#2 Claudia and the Phantom Phone Calls

Claudia has been getting some mysterious phone calls when she's out baby-sitting. Could they be from the Phantom Jewel Thief who's operating in the area? Claudia has always liked *reading* mysteries, but she doesn't like it when they *happen* to her!

#3 The Truth About Stacey

The truth about Stacey is her parents want to find a miracle cure for her diabetes. They're making Stacey's life so hard! The other Baby-sitters are busy fighting the Baby-sitters Agency. How can they help Stacey and save the club, too?

#4 Mary Anne Saves the Day

Mary Anne's never been a leader of the Baby-sitters Club. Now there's a big fight among the four friends. It's bad enough when Mary Anne has to eat at the lunch table all alone. But when she has to baby-sit a sick child with no help from her friends — it's time to take charge!

#5 Dawn and the Impossible Three

Poor Dawn! It's not easy being the newest member of the Baby-sitters Club. She's got three impossible kids to take care of. And Kristy thinks things were better *without* Dawn around. It'll take a lot of work to make things run smoothly again, but Dawn's up to the challenge!

#6 Kristy's Big Day

It's a big day for Kristy, all right — she's a bridesmaid in her mother's wedding! And if that's not enough, she and the other Baby-sitters Club members have *fourteen* wedding-guest kids to take care of. Only the Baby-sitters Club could cope with this one!

146

#7 Claudia and Mean Janine

This summer the Baby-sitters Club is starting a play group in the neighborhood. Claudia can't wait for it to begin — it'll give her some time away from her mean big sister. But then her grandmother has a stroke . . . and the whole summer changes.

#8 Boy-Crazy Stacey

Who needs baby-sitting when there are boys around? Stacey and Mary Anne are mother's helpers at the Jersey shore, and Stacey's mind is on hunky lifeguard Scott. Mary Anne's doing the work of two baby-sitters . . . but how can she tell Stacey that Scott's too old, without breaking Stacey's heart?

#9 The Ghost at Dawn's House

Creaking stairs, noises behind the wall, a secret passage — there must be a ghost at Dawn's house! The Baby-sitters find themselves and one of their charges wrapped up in a mystery. Will they be able to solve it?

#10 Logan Likes Mary Anne!

Quiet, shy Mary Anne has been growing up lately . . . and the Baby-sitters aren't the only ones who've noticed. Logan Bruno likes Mary Anne! He has a dreamy southern accent, he's awfully cute — and he wants to join the Baby-sitters Club. Life in the club has never been this complicated — or this fun!

#11 Kristy and the Snobs

The kids in Kristy's new neighborhood aren't very friendly. In fact they're . . . well, snobs. They laugh at everything — even Kristy's poor old collie, Louie. Kristy's fighting mad. But if anyone can beat a Snob attack, it's the Baby-sitters club. And that's just what they're going to do!

#12 Claudia and the New Girl

Claudia really likes Ashley, the new girl at school. Ashley's the only one who takes Claudia seriously. Soon, Claudia's spending so much time with Ashley that she doesn't have time for baby-sitting — or her old friends. And they don't like it one bit!

#13 Good-bye Stacey, Good-bye

There are lots of tears when the Baby-sitters hear the news: Stacey and her family are moving back to New York. The club members can't think of a special enough way to send Stacey off. They want to give her much more than a party. But how do you say good-bye to your best friend?

#14 Hello, Mallory

Mallory Pike has always been good at baby-sitting her younger brothers and sisters. But is she good enough to join the Baby-sitters Club? The club members go overboard giving Mallory baby-sitting tests. Mallory's getting pretty fed up. . . . Maybe she'll just start a baby-sitting business of her own!

#15 Little Miss Stoneybrook . . . and Dawn

Mrs. Pike wants Dawn to help prepare Margo and Claire for the Little Miss Stoneybrook contest. And Dawn wants her charges to win! The only trouble is . . . Kristy, Mary Anne, and Claudia are helping Karen, Myriah, and Charlotte enter the contest, too. And nobody's sure where the competition is fiercer: at the pageant — or at the Baby-sitters Club!

149

#16 *Jessi's Secret Language*

Jessi had a hard time fitting in to Stoneybrook. But things got a lot better once she became a member of the Baby-sitters Club! Now Jessi has her biggest challenge yet — baby-sitting for a deaf boy. And in order to communicate with him, Jessi must learn his secret language.

#17 *Mary Anne's Bad-Luck Mystery*

Mary Anne finds a note in her mailbox. *"Wear this bad-luck charm,"* it says, *"OR ELSE."* Mary Anne's got to do what the note says. But who sent the charm? And why did they send it to Mary Anne? If the Baby-sitters don't solve this mystery soon, their bad luck might never stop!

#18 *Stacey's Mistake*

Stacey's so excited! She's invited her friends from the Baby-sitters Club down to New York City for a long weekend. But what a mistake! The Baby-sitters are *way* out of place in the big city. Does this mean Stacey can't be the Baby-sitters' friend anymore?

150

#19 *Claudia and the Bad Joke*

Claudia's not worried when she hears she has to baby-sit for Betsy, a great practical joker. How much trouble could a little girl cause? *Plenty* . . . and now Claudia might even quit the club. It's time for the Baby-sitters to teach Betsy a lesson. The joke war is on!

#20 *Kristy and the Walking Disaster*

Kristy's little brother and sister want to play on a softball team, so Kristy starts a ragtag team of her own. With Jackie Rodowsky, the Walking Disaster, playing for them, Kristy's Krushers aren't world champions. But nobody beats them when it comes to team spirit!

#22 *Jessi Ramsey, Pet-sitter*

Jessi's always liked animals. So when the Mancusis need an emergency pet-sitter, she quickly takes the job. But what has Jessi gotten herself into? There are animals *all over* the Mancusis' house! This is going to be one sitting job Jessi will never forget!

by Ann M. Martin

The Baby-sitters' business is booming! And that gets Stacey, Kristy, Claudia, and the rest of The Baby-sitters Club members in all kinds of adventures...at school, with boys, and, of course, baby-sitting!

**Something new and exciting happens in every Baby-sitters Club book.
Collect and read them all!**

More titles... ➤

THE BABY-SITTERS CLUB®

titles continued...

☐	MG42501-3	#28	Welcome Back, Stacey!	$2.95
☐	MG42500-5	#29	Mallory and the Mystery Diary	$2.95
☐	MG42498-X	#30	Mary Anne and the Great Romance	$2.95
☐	MG42497-1	#31	Dawn's Wicked Stepsister	$2.95
☐	MG42496-3	#32	Kristy and the Secret of Susan	$2.95
☐	MG42495-5	#33	Claudia and the Great Search	$2.95
☐	MG42494-7	#34	Mary Anne and Too Many Boys	$2.95
☐	MG42508-0	#35	Stacey and the Mystery of Stoneybrook	$2.95
☐	MG43565-5	#36	Jessi's Baby-sitter	$2.95
☐	MG43566-3	#37	Dawn and the Older Boy	$2.95
☐	MG43567-1	#38	Kristy's Mystery Admirer	$2.95
☐	MG41588-3		Baby-sitters on Board! Super Special #1	$2.95
☐	MG42419-X		Baby-sitters' Summer Vacation Super Special #2	$2.95
☐	MG42499-8		Baby-sitters' Winter Vacation Super Special #3	$3.50
☐	MG42493-9		Baby-sitters' Island Adventure Super Special #4	$3.50
☐	MG43745-3		The Baby-sitters Club 1990-91 Student Planner and Date Book	$7.95
☐	MG43744-5		The Baby-sitters Club 1991 Calendar	$8.95
☐	MG43803-4		The Baby-sitters Club Notebook	$1.95

Available wherever you buy books...or use this order form.

Scholastic Inc., P.O. Box 7502, 2931 E. McCarty Street, Jefferson City, MO 65102

Please send me the books I have checked above. I am enclosing $_____
(please add $2.00 to cover shipping and handling). Send check or money order — no cash or C.O.D.s please.

Name _____

Address _____

City _____ State/Zip_____

Please allow four to six weeks for delivery. Offer good in the U.S. only. Sorry, mail orders are not available to residents of Canada. Prices subject to change.

BSC390

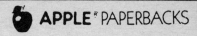

Jessi Ramsey, Pet-sitter

**Look for these and other books
in the Baby-sitters Club series:**

Jessi Ramsey, Pet-sitter
Ann M. Martin

AN
APPLE
PAPERBACK

SCHOLASTIC INC.
New York Toronto London Auckland Sydney

Cover art by Hodges Soileau

ISBN 0-590-43658-9

12 11 10 9 8 7 6 5 4 3 2   9/8 0 1 2 3 4/9

Printed in the U.S.A.

*This book is for my friends
Nicole, Anna, Rebecca,
Katie, and Alison*

CHAPTER 1

"Meow, meow, meow. Purr, purr."

I leaned over the edge of my bed and peered down at the floor.

"Pet me," said a small voice.

It wasn't a talking animal. It was my sister, Becca, pretending she was a cat.

I patted the top of her head but said, "Becca, I really have to do my homework."

"Then how come you're lying on your bed?" asked Becca, getting to her feet.

"Because this is a comfortable way to work."

"You're supposed to sit at your desk."

This is true. My parents believe that homework magically gets done better if you're sitting up than if you're lying down.

I sighed. Then I changed the subject, which usually distracts Becca. "Why are you a cat tonight?" I asked her.

She shrugged. "I'm trying all the animals. It's fun to pretend."

1

The night before, Becca had been a dog, the night before that, a horse.

"Well, kitty, let me finish my work," I said.

"Meow," replied Becca, who dropped to her hands and knees and crawled into the hallway.

Becca is eight and has a big imagination. If she weren't so shy, she'd probably make a really terrific actress, but she has awful stage fright.

I do not have stage fright, which is lucky since I'm a ballet dancer and have to perform in front of audiences all the time.

I guess I should stop and introduce myself. I am Jessi Ramsey, and I'm eleven and in sixth grade. "Jessi" is short for "Jessica." (And "Becca" is short for "Rebecca," as if you couldn't have guessed.) Becca and I live with our parents and our baby brother, Squirt. Squirt's real name is John Philip Ramsey, Jr. When he was born, he was so tiny that the nurses in the hospital started calling him Squirt. Now his nickname seems sort of funny. Well, it always has been funny, but it seems especially funny since Squirt, who has just learned to walk, is now the size of most other babies his age.

Anyway, as I said before, I'm a ballet dancer. I've been taking dance classes for years. My ballet school is in Stamford, which isn't too far from Stoneybrook, Connecticut, where my

2

family and I live. We haven't lived here long, though. We moved to Connecticut from New Jersey just a few months ago when my dad was offered a job he couldn't turn down.

Oh, something else about my family — we're black. Actually, that's much more important than I'm making it sound. You know what? It wasn't so important when we were living in Oakley, New Jersey. Our old neighborhood was mixed black and white, and so was my ballet school and my regular school. But believe it or not, we are one of the few black families in all of Stoneybrook. In fact, I'm the only black student in my whole grade. When we first moved here, some people weren't very nice to us. Some were even mean. But things have settled down and are getting better. Becca and I are making friends. Actually, I have a lot more friends than Becca does. There are two reasons for this: one, I'm not shy; two, I belong to the Baby-sitters Club. (More about that later.)

My mother is wonderful and so is my father. We're a very close family. Mama, Daddy, Becca, Squirt, and me. No pets. We've never had a pet, although Becca apparently wishes we had one. (Sometimes I do, too, for that matter.)

In case you're wondering what the Baby-sitters Club is, let me tell you about it. It's very important to me because that's where I found most of my friends. The club is really a business, a sitting business. It was started by Kristy Thomas, who's the president. There are six of us in the club. We sit for kids in our neighborhoods, and we get lots of jobs and have lots of fun.

My best friend in Stoneybrook is Mallory Pike. Mal and I have a lot of classes together at Stoneybrook Middle School. And Mal is the one who got me into the Baby-sitters Club. The girls needed another member and ended up taking both of us. We were just getting to be friends then — and now that we've been in the club together for awhile, we're best friends. (I have another best friend in Oakley — my cousin Keisha.)

Anyway, the people in the club are Mallory, Kristy, me, plus Claudia Kishi, Mary Anne Spier, and Dawn Schafer. Two people who are sort of part of the club but who don't come to our meetings are our associate members, Logan Bruno and Shannon Kilbourne. (I'll tell you more about them later.) It's funny that us six club members work so well together, because boy, are we different. We have different personalities, different tastes, different looks, and different kinds of families.

4

Kristy Thomas, our president, is . . . well, talk about not shy. Kristy is direct and outgoing. Sometimes she can be loud and bossy. But basically she's really nice. And she's always full of ideas. Kristy is thirteen and in eighth grade. (So are all the club members, except Mal and me.) She has this long brown hair and is pretty, but doesn't pay much attention to her looks. I mean, she never bothers with makeup, and she always wears jeans, a turtleneck, a sweater, and sneakers. Kristy's family is sort of interesting. Her parents are divorced, and for the longest time, Kristy lived with just her mom, her two older brothers, Sam and Charlie (they're in high school), and her little brother, David Michael, who's seven now. But when her mom met this millionaire, Watson Brewer, and got remarried, things sure changed for Kristy. For one thing, Watson moved Kristy's family into his mansion, which is on the other side of Stoneybrook. Kristy used to live next door to Mary Anne Spier and across the street from Claudia Kishi. Now she's in a new neighborhood. For another thing, Kristy acquired a little stepsister and stepbrother — Watson's children from his first marriage. Karen is six and Andrew is four. Although it took Kristy some time to adjust to her new life, she sure loves Karen and Andrew. They're among her favorite baby-sitting charges. Kristy's family has two pets — an adorable puppy named Shannon and a fat old cat named Boo-Boo.

The vice-president of the Baby-sitters Club is Claudia Kishi, and she is totally cool. I think she's the coolest person I know. (I mean, except for movie stars or people like that.) Claud is just awesome-looking. She's Japanese-American and has gorgeous, *long*, jet-black hair; dark, almond-shaped eyes; and a clear complexion. Really. She could be on TV as the "after" part of a pimple medicine commercial. Claud loves art, Nancy Drew mysteries, and junk food, and she hates school. She's smart, but she's a terrible student. (Unfortunately, her older sister, Janine, is a genius, which makes Claudia's grades look even worse.) Claudia also loves fashion, and you should see her clothes. They are amazing, always wild. Like, she'll wear a miniskirt, black tights, push-down socks, high-top sneakers, a shirt she's painted or decorated herself, and big earrings she's made. Her hair might be pulled into a ponytail and held in place with not one but six or seven puffy ponytail holders, a row of them cascading down her hair. I'm always fascinated by Claudia. Claud lives with Janine, her parents, and her grandmother, Mimi. The Kishis don't have any pets.

Mary Anne Spier is the club secretary. She lives across the street from Claudia. And, until Kristy's family moved, she lived next door to the Thomases. Mary Anne and Kristy are best friends, and have been pretty much for life. (Dawn is Mary Anne's other best friend.) I've always thought this was interesting, since Mary Anne and Kristy are not alike at all. Mary Anne is shy and quiet and, well, sort of romantic. (She's the only club member who has a steady boyfriend. And guess who he is — Logan Bruno, one of our associate members!) Mary Anne is also a good listener and a patient person. Her mom died years ago, so Mary Anne's father raised her, and for the longest time, he was strict with her. Boy, was he strict. I didn't know Mary Anne then, but I've heard that Mr. Spier made all these rules, and there was practically nothing she was allowed to do. Lately, Mr. Spier has relaxed, though. He won't let Mary Anne get her ears pierced, but at least she can go out with Logan sometimes, and she can choose her own clothes. Since she's been allowed to do that, she's started dressing *much* better — not as wildly as Claudia, but she cares about how she looks, unlike Kristy. Mary Anne's family is just her and her dad and her gray kitten, Tigger.

Dawn Schafer is the treasurer of the Baby-sitters Club. I like Dawn. She's neat. Dawn is neither loud like Kristy nor shy like Mary Anne. She's an individual. She'd never go along with something just because other people were doing it. And she always sticks up for what she believes in. Dawn is basically a California girl. She moved to Connecticut about a year ago, but she still longs for warm weather and she loves health food. She even *looks* like a California girl with her white-blonde hair and her sparkling blue eyes. Although you'd never know it, Dawn has been through some tough times lately. When she moved here, she came with her mother and her younger brother, Jeff — her parents had just gotten divorced. Mrs. Schafer wanted to live in Stoneybrook because she'd grown up here, but that put three thousand miles between Dawn's mother and Dawn's father. As if the divorce and the move weren't enough, Jeff finally decided he couldn't handle the East Coast and moved back to California, so now Dawn's family is cracked in two, like a broken plate. But Dawn seems to be handling things okay. Luckily, she has her best friend (Mary Anne), and she and her mother are *extremely* close. Just so you know, the Schafers live in a neat old farmhouse that has a secret passage (honest), and they don't have any pets.

Then there's Mallory. Mallory Pike and I are the club's two junior officers. All that means is that we're too young to baby-sit at night unless we're sitting for our own brothers and sisters. Speaking of brothers and sisters, Mal has *seven* of them. She comes from the biggest family I know. Apart from that, and apart from the fact that Mal is white and I'm black, we're probably more alike than any two other club members. We both love to read books, especially horse stories, we both enjoy writing (but Mal enjoys it more than I do), we both wear glasses (mine are only for reading), and we both think our parents treat us kind of like babies. However, there was a recent breakthrough in which we convinced our parents to let us get our ears pierced! After that, Mal was even allowed to have her hair cut decently, but I'm still working on that angle. Neither of us is sure what we want to be when we grow the rest of the way up. I *might* want to be a professional dancer and Mal *might* want to be an author or an author/illustrator, but we figure we have time to decide these things. Right now, we're just happy being eleven-year-old baby-sitters.

Oh, one other similarity between Mal and me. Neither of us has a pet. I don't know if Mal wants one — she's never mentioned it —

but I bet her brothers and sisters do. Just like Becca.

"Hiss, hiss."

Becca was in my doorway. She was lying on her stomach.

"Now what are you?" I asked.

"I'll give you a hint." Becca flicked her tongue out of her mouth.

"Ew, ew!" I cried. "You're a snake. Slither away from me!"

Giggling, Becca did as she was told.

I went back to my homework, but I couldn't concentrate. Not because of Becca, but because of next week. I was going to have next week off. Well, sort of. Ordinarily, my afternoons are busy. When school is out, I go either to a ballet class or to my steady sitting job. My steady job is for Matt and Haley Braddock, two really great kids. But next week, my ballet school would be closed and the Braddocks were going on a vacation — even though school was in session. So, except for school and meetings of the Baby-sitters Club, I would be free, free, free! What would I do with all those spare hours? I wondered. Easy. I could put in extra practice time, I could read. The possibilities were endless!

CHAPTER 2

"Hi! Hi, you guys! Sorry I'm late." I rushed breathlessly into the Wednesday meeting of the Baby-sitters Club.

"You're not late," said Kristy, our president. "You're just the last one here."

"As always," I added.

"Well, don't worry about it. But it *is* five-thirty and time to begin." Kristy sounded very businesslike.

Mallory patted the floor next to her, so I shoved aside some of Claudia's art materials and sat down. We always sit on the floor. And Dawn, Mary Anne, and Claudia always sit on Claudia's bed. Guess where Kristy sits—in a director's chair, wearing a visor, as if she were the queen or something.

Club meetings are held in Claudia Kishi's room. This is because she's the only one of us who has a phone in her bedroom, and her own personal, private phone number, which makes it easy for our clients to reach us.

Hmmm. . . . I think I better stop right here, before I get ahead of myself. I'll tell you how the club got started and how it works; then the meeting won't sound so confusing.

The club began with Kristy, as I said before. She got the idea for it over a year ago. That was when she and her mom and brothers were still living across the street from Claudia, and her mother was just starting to date Watson Brewer. Usually, when Mrs. Thomas wasn't going to be around, Kristy or Sam or Charlie would take care of David Michael. But one day when Mrs. Thomas announced that she was going to need a sitter, neither Kristy nor one of her older brothers was free. So Mrs. Thomas got on the phone and began calling around for another sitter. Kristy watched her mom make one call after another. And as she watched, that mind of hers was clicking away, thinking that Mrs. Thomas sure could save time if she could make one call and reach several sitters at once. And that was when Kristy got the idea for the Baby-sitters Club!

She talked to Mary Anne and Claudia, Claudia talked to Stacey McGill, a new friend of hers, and the four of them formed the club. (I'll tell you more about Stacey in a minute.)

12

The girls decided that they'd meet three times a week in Claudia's room (because of the phone). They'd advertise their club in the local paper and around the neighborhood, saying that four reliable sitters could be reached every Monday, Wednesday, and Friday afternoon from five-thirty until six.

Well, Kristy's great idea worked! Right away, the girls started getting jobs. People really liked them. In fact, the club was so successful that when Dawn moved to Stoneybrook and wanted to join, the girls needed her. And later, when Stacey McGill had to move back to New York City, they needed to replace her. (Stacey's move, by the way, was unfortunate, because in the short time the McGills lived in Stoney-brook, she and Claudia became best friends. Now they really miss each other.) Anyway, Mal and I joined the club to help fill the hole left by Stacey, and Shannon Kilbourne and Logan Bruno were made associate members. That means that they don't come to meetings, but if a job is offered that the rest of us can't take, we call one of them to see if they're interested. They're our backups. Believe it or not, we do have to call them every now and then.

Each person in the club holds a special

position or office. There are the associate members, Shannon and Logan, and there are the junior officers, Mal and me. The other positions are more important. (I'm not putting the rest of us down or anything. This is just the truth.)

As president, Kristy is responsible for running the meetings, getting good ideas, and, well, just being in charge, I guess. Considering that president is the most important office of all, Kristy doesn't do a lot of work. I mean, not compared to what the other girls do. But then, the club *was* her idea, so I think she deserves to be its president.

Claudia Kishi, our vice-president, doesn't really have a lot to do, either, but the rest of us invade her room three times a week and tie up her phone line. Plus, a lot of our clients forget when our meetings are held and call at other times with sitting jobs. Claud has to handle those calls. I think she deserves to be vice-president.

As secretary, Mary Anne Spier is probably the hardest-working officer. She's in charge of the record book, which is where we keep track of all club information: our clients' addresses and phone numbers, the money in the treasury (well, that's really Dawn's department), and most importantly, the appointment calendar.

Poor Mary Anne has to keep track of everybody's schedules (my ballet lessons, Claud's art classes, dentist appointments, etc.) *and* all of our baby-sitting jobs. When a call comes in, it's up to Mary Anne to see who's free. Mary Anne is neat and careful and hasn't made a scheduling mistake yet.

This is a miracle.

Dawn, our treasurer, is responsible for collecting dues from us club members every Monday, and for keeping enough money in the treasury so that we can pay Charlie, Kristy's oldest brother, to drive her to and from meetings, since she lives so far away now. The money is spent on other things, too, but we make sure we always have enough for Charlie. What else is the money spent on? Well, fun things, like food for club slumber parties. Also new materials for Kid-Kits.

I guess I haven't told you about Kid-Kits yet. They were one of Kristy's ideas. A Kid-Kit is a box (we each have one) that's been decorated and filled with our old toys and books and games, as well as a few new items such as crayons or sticker books. We bring them with us on some of our jobs and kids love them. The kits make us very popular baby-sitters! Anyway, every now and then we

15

need treasury money to buy new crayons or something for the kits.

The last thing you need to know about is our club notebook. The notebook is like a diary. In it, each of us sitters has to write up every single job she goes on. Then we're supposed to read it once a week to find out what's been going on. Even though most of us don't like writing in the notebook, I have to admit that it's helpful. When I read it, I find out what's happening with the kids our club sits for, and also about baby-sitting problems and how they were handled. (The club notebook was Kristy's idea, of course.)

"Order, order!" Kristy was saying.

I had just settled myself on the floor.

"Wait a sec," Claudia interrupted. "Doesn't anyone want something to eat?"

Remember I said Claudia likes junk food? Well, that may have been an understatement. Claud *loves* junk food. She loves it so much that her parents have told her to stop eating so much of it. But Claud can't. She buys it anyway and then hides it in her room. At the moment, she's got a bag of potato chips under her bed, a package of licorice sticks in a drawer of her jewelry box, and a bag of M&M's in the pencil case in her notebook. She's very generous with it. She offers it around at the beginning of each meeting since we're starved by this time of day. And we eat up. (Well, sometimes Dawn doesn't since she's so into health food, but she *will* eat crackers or pretzels.)

"Ahem," said Kristy.

"Oh, come on. You know you'll eat something if I get it out," Claudia told her. Claudia usually stands up to Kristy.

"All right." Kristy sounded as cross as a bear, but this didn't prevent her from eating a handful of M&M's.

When the candy had been passed around, Kristy said, "*Now* are we ready?"

(She sure can be bossy.)

"Ready, Ms. Thomas," Claudia replied in a high, squeaky voice.

Everyone laughed, even Kristy.

We talked about some club business, and then the phone began to ring. The first call was from Mrs. Newton. She's the mother of Jamie and Lucy, two of the club's favorite sitting charges. Mary Anne scheduled Dawn for the job. Then the phone rang twice more. Jobs for Mal and Mary Anne. I was sort of relieved that so far, none of the jobs had been for next week. I was still looking forward to my week off.

Ring, ring.

Another call.

Claudia answered the phone. She listened for a moment and then began to look confused. "Mrs. Mancusi?" she said.

Kristy glanced up from the notebook, which she'd been reading. "Mrs. Mancusi?" she whispered to the rest of us. "She doesn't have any kids."

We listened to Claud's end of the conversation, but all she would say were things like, "Mm-hmm," and "Oh, I see," and "Yes, that's too bad." Then, after a long pause, she said, "Well, this is sort of unusual, but let me talk to the other girls and see what they say. Someone will call you back in about five minutes. . . . Yes. . . . Okay. . . . Okay, 'bye."

Claudia hung up the phone and looked up from some notes she'd been making. She found the rest of us staring at her.

"Well?" said Kristy.

"Well, the Mancusis need a pet-sitter," Claudia began.

"A *pet*-sitter?" Kristy practically jumped down Claud's throat.

"Yeah, let me explain," Claud rushed on. "They're going on vacation next week. They've had this really nice vacation planned for months now. And you know all those animals they have?"

"Their house is a zoo," Mary Anne spoke up.

"I know," Claud replied. "All I could hear in the background was barking and squawking and chirping."

"What's the point?" asked Kristy rudely.

"Sheesh," said Claud. "Give me a minute. The *point* is that the Mancusis had a pet-sitter all lined up and he just called and canceled."

"That is *so* irresponsible," commented Mallory.

"I know," agreed Claud. "Now the Mancusis can't take their vacation, not unless they find a pet-sitter."

"Oh, but Claudia," wailed Kristy, "how could you even *think* about another pet-sitting job?"

"Another one?" I asked.

"Yeah," said Kristy. "The very first job I got when we started the club — my first job offer at our first official meeting — was for two Saint Bernard dogs, and it was a disaster."

I couldn't help giggling. "It was?" I said. "What happened?"

"Oh, you name it. The dogs, Pinky and Buffy, were sweet, but they were big and gallumphing and they liked making mischief. What an afternoon that was! Anyway, I swore we would never pet-sit again."

19

"But Kristy," protested Claudia, "if the Mancusis can't find a pet-sitter, they'll have to cancel their dream vacation."

Kristy sighed. "All right. Suppose one of us was crazy enough to *want* to pet-sit — don't the Mancusis need someone every day?"

"Yes, for a few hours every day next week, plus the weekend before and the weekend after. They're leaving this Saturday and returning Sunday, a week later."

"Well, that kills it," said Kristy. "I don't want any of my sitters tied up for a week."

At that, I heard Dawn mutter something that sounded like . . . well, it didn't sound nice. And I saw her poke Mary Anne, who mouthed "bossy" to her. Then Mal whispered to me, "Who does Kristy think she is? The queen?"

All of which gave me the courage to say (nervously), "Um, you know how the Braddocks are going away?"

"Yes?" replied the other club members, turning toward me.

"Well . . . well, um, my ballet school is closed next week, too. Remember? So I'm available. For the whole week. I could take care of the Mancusis' pets. I mean, if they want me to." (So much for my week of freedom.)

"Perfect!" exclaimed Claud. "I'll call them right now."

"Not so fast!" interrupted Kristy. "I haven't given my permission yet."

"Your per*miss*ion?" cried the rest of us.

Kristy must have realized she'd gone too far then. Her face turned bright red.

"Listen, just because *you* had a bad pet-sitting experience — " Dawn began.

"I know, I know. I'm sorry." Kristy turned toward me. "Go ahead," she said. "You may take the job."

"Thank you."

Claud called Mrs. Mancusi back, as promised. As you can probably imagine, Mrs. Mancusi was delighted to have a sitter. She asked to speak to me. After thanking me several times, she said, "When could you come by? My husband and I will have to show you how to care for the animals. There are quite a lot of them, you know."

After some discussion, we decided on Friday evening, right after supper. It was the only time the Mancusis and I were all free. Since the Mancusis live near my house, I knew that would be okay with my parents.

I hung up the phone. "Gosh, the Mancusis sure are going to pay me well."

"They better," Kristy replied. "I don't think Claud told you exactly how many pets they have. There are three dogs, five cats, some birds and hamsters, two guinea pigs, a snake, lots of fish, and a bunch of rabbits and turtles."

I gulped. What had I gotten myself into?

CHAPTER 3

As soon as I saw Mr. and Mrs. Mancusi, I realized I knew them — and they knew me. They're always out walking their dogs, and I'm often out walking Squirt in his stroller, or baby-sitting for some little kids. The Mancusis and I wave and smile at each other. Until I met them, I just didn't know their names, or that beside their dogs they owned a small zoo.

This is what I heard when I rang their doorbell: *Yip-yip, meow, mew, chirp, cheep, squawk, squeak, woof-woof-woof.*

By the way, I am a pretty good speller and every now and then my teacher gives me a list of really hard words to learn to spell and use in sentences. On the last list was the word *cacophony.* It means a jolting, nonharmonious mixture of sounds. Well, those animal voices at the Mancusis' were not jolting, but they sure were nonharmonious and they sure were a mixture.

23

The door opened. There was Mrs. Mancusi's pleasant face. "Oh! It's *you!*" she exclaimed, just as I said, "Oh! The dogwalker!"

"Come on in." Smiling, Mrs. Mancusi held the door open for me.

I stepped inside and the cacophony grew louder.

"SHH! SHH!" said Mrs. Mancusi urgently. "Sit. . . . Sit, Cheryl."

A Great Dane sat down obediently. Soon the barking stopped. Then the birds quieted down.

Mrs. Mancusi smiled at me. "So you're Jessi," she said. "I've seen you around a lot lately."

"We moved here a few months ago," I told her, not mentioning that, in general, the neighbors hadn't been too . . . talkative.

Mrs. Mancusi nodded. "Is that your brother I see you with sometimes?" she asked. (A bird swooped into the room and landed on her shoulder while a white kitten tottered to her ankles and began twining himself around them.)

"Yes," I answered. "That's Squirt. Well, his real name is John Philip Ramsey, Junior. I have a sister, too. Becca. She's eight. But," I added, "we don't have any pets."

Mrs. Mancusi looked fondly at her animals. "I guess that makes us even," she said. "My husband and I don't have any children, but we have plenty of pets. Well, I should start — "

At that moment, Mr. Mancusi strode into the front hall. After more introductions, his wife said, "I was just about to have Jessi meet the animals."

Mr. Mancusi nodded. "Let's start with the dogs. I guess you've already seen Cheryl," he said, patting the Great Dane.

"Right," I replied. I pulled a pad of paper and a pencil out of my purse so I could take notes.

But Mr. Mancusi stopped me. "Don't bother," he said. "Everything is written down. We'll show you where in a minute. Just give the animals a chance to get to know you. In fact," he went on, "why don't you talk to each one? That would help them to feel more secure with you."

"Talk to them?" I repeated.

"Sure. Say anything you want. Let them hear the sound of your voice."

I felt like a real jerk, but I patted the top of Cheryl's head (which is softer than it looks) and said, "Hi, Cheryl. I'm Jessi. I'm going to walk you and take care of you next week."

Cheryl look at me with her huge eyes — and yawned.

We all laughed. "I guess I'm not very impressive," I said.

On the floor in the living room lay an apricot-colored poodle.

"That's Pooh Bear," said Mrs. Mancusi. "Believe it or not, she's harder to walk than Cheryl. Cheryl is big but obedient. Pooh Bear is small but devilish."

I knelt down and patted Pooh Bear's curly fur. "Nice girl," I said. (Pooh Bear stared at me.) "Nice girl . . . Um, I'm Jessi. We're going to take walks next week." Then I added in a whisper, "I hope you'll behave."

The Mancusis' third dog is a golden retriever named Jacques. Jacques was napping in the kitchen. He tiredly stuck his paw in my lap when I sat down next to him, but he barely opened his eyes.

"Now Jacques," began Mr. Mancusi, "is only a year old. Still pretty much a puppy. He tries hard to behave, but if Pooh Bear acts up, he can't help following her lead."

"Right," I said. I tried to think of something creative to say to Jacques, but finally just told him I was looking forward to walking him.

"All right. Cats next," said Mrs. Mancusi, picking up the kitten. "This little fluffball is Powder. He's just two and a half months old. But don't worry. He knows how to take care of himself. Also, his mother is here."

26

"Hi, Powder," I said, putting my face up to his soft fur.

Then Mrs. Mancusi set Powder on the ground and we went on a cat-hunt, in search of the other four. Here's who we found: Crosby, an orange tiger cat who can fetch like a dog; Ling-Ling, a Siamese cat with a *very* loud voice; Tom, a patchy gray cat with a wicked temper; and Rosie, Powder's mother.

Next we went into the Mancusis' den, where there were several large bird cages holding parakeets, cockatoos, and macaws.

"Awk?" said one bird as we entered the room. "Where's the beef? Where's the beef? Where's the beef?"

Mr. Mancusi laughed. "That's Frank," he said. "He used to watch a lot of TV. I mean, before we got him." I must have looked astonished, because he went on, "It's natural for some birds to imitate what they hear. Frank can say other things, too, can't you, Frank?"

Frank blinked his eyes but remained silent.

"See, he isn't really trained," added Mr. Mancusi. "He only talks when he feels like it."

Mrs. Mancusi removed the bird that had landed on her shoulder earlier and placed him in one of the cages. "Often, we leave the cages open," she told me, "and let the birds fly around the house. I'd suggest it for next week, but most people don't feel comfortable trying to get the birds back in the cages, so maybe that's not such a good idea."

It certainly didn't sound like a good one to me.

I started to leave the den, but Mr. Mancusi was looking at me, so I peered into the bird cages and spoke to Frank and his friends.

In the kitchen were a cage full of hamsters and a much bigger cage, almost a pen, that contained two guinea pigs. I looked in at the hamsters first.

"They're nocturnal," said Mrs. Mancusi. "They're up all night and asleep all day. You should see them in the daytime. They sleep in a big pile in the middle of the cage."

I smiled. Then I looked at the guinea pigs. They were pretty interesting, too. They were big, bigger than the hamsters, and they were sniffing around their cage. Every so often one of them would let out a whistle.

"The guinea pigs are Lucy and Ricky. You know, from the *I Love Lucy* show," said Mr. Mancusi. "They shouldn't be any trouble, and they *love* to be taken out of their cage for exercise."

"Okay," I said, thinking that Lucy and Ricky looked like fun.

We left the kitchen and walked toward a sun porch. The job, I decided, was going to be big but manageable. I could handle it.

Then I met the reptiles.

The aquarium full of turtles wasn't *too* bad. I don't love turtles, but I don't mind them.

What was bad was Barney.

Barney is a snake. He's very small and he isn't poisonous, but he's still a snake. A wriggling, scaly, tongue-flicking snake.

Thank goodness the Mancusis didn't ask me to touch Barney or take him out of his cage. All they said was I'd have to feed him. Well, I could do that. Even if I did have to feed him the insects and earthworms that the Mancusis had a supply of. I'd just try to wear oven mitts. Or maybe I could stand ten feet away from his cage and throw the worms in.

"Nice Barney. Good Barney," I whispered when the Mancusis stopped and waited for me to talk to him. "You don't hurt me — and I'll stay away from you."

Next the Mancusis showed me their fish (about a million of them), and their rabbits (Fluffer-Nut, Cindy, Toto, and Robert). And after *that*, they took me back to the kitchen, where they had posted lists of instructions for caring for each type of animal, plus everything I'd need to feed and exercise them — food

29

dishes, chow (several kinds), leashes, etc. I would be going to their house twice a day. Early in the morning to walk the dogs and feed the dogs and cats, and after school to walk the dogs again and to feed all the animals.

When I said good-night to the Mancusis I felt slightly overwhelmed but confident. The job was a big one, but I'd met the animals, and I'd seen the lists of instructions. They were very clear. If the animals would just behave, everything would be fine . . . probably.

Saturday was my test. The Mancusis left late in the morning. By the middle of the afternoon, Cheryl, Pooh Bear, and Jacques would be ready for a walk. After that, the entire zoo would need feeding. So at three o'clock I headed for the Mancusis' with the key to their front door. I let myself in (the cacophony began immediately), managed to put leashes on the dogs, and took them for a nice, long walk. The walk went fine except for when Pooh Bear spotted a squirrel. For just a moment, the dogs were taking *me* on a walk instead of the other way around. But the squirrel disappeared, the dogs calmed down, and we returned to the Mancusis' safely.

When the dog's leashes had been hung up, I played with the cats and the guinea pigs. I let the rabbits out for awhile. Then it was feeding time. Dog chow in the dog dishes, cat chow in the cat dishes, fish food in the tank, rabbit food in the hutch, guinea pig food in the guinea pig cage, bird food in the bird cages, turtle food in the aquarium, hamster food in the hamster cage, and finally it was time for . . . Barney.

I looked in his cage. There he was, sort of twined around a rock. He wasn't moving, but his eyes were open. I think he was looking at me. I found a spatula in the kitchen, used it to slide the lid of Barney's cage back, and then, quick as a wink, I dropped his food inside and shoved the lid closed.

Barney never moved.

Well, that was easy, I thought as I made a final check on all the animals. A lot of them were eating. But the hamsters were sound asleep. They were all sleeping in a pile, just like Mrs. Mancusi had said they would do, except for one very fat hamster. He lay curled in a corner by himself. What was wrong? Was he some sort of outcast? I decided not to worry, since the Mancusis hadn't said anything about him.

I found my house key and got ready to go. My first afternoon as a pet-sitter had been a success, I decided.

CHAPTER 4

Sundae

Oh, my lord waht a day. I babbysat for Jamie newton and he invinted Nina marshal over to play. That was fine but I thoght it would be fun for the kids to see all the ani022als over at the Me Mar makusees or however you spell it. So I took them over but Jamie was afriad of the ginny pigs so we took the kids and the dogs on a walk but we ran into Chewey and you now waht that means -- trouble.

Well, it was trouble, as Claudia said, but it wasn't too bad. I mean, I'm sure we've all been in worse trouble.

Anyway, on Sunday afternoon when I was about to head back to the Mancusis', Claudia was baby-sitting for Jamie Newton. Jamie is four, and one of the club's favorite clients. Kristy, Mary Anne, and Claudia were sitting for him long before there even *was* a Baby-sitters Club. Now Jamie has an eight-month-old sister, Lucy, but Claud was only in charge of Jamie that day. His parents were going visiting, and they were taking Lucy with them.

When Claudia arrived at the Newtons', she found an overexcited Jamie. He was bouncing around, singing songs, making noises, and annoying everybody — which is not like Jamie.

"I don't know where he got all this energy," said Mrs. Newton tiredly. "I hope you don't mind, but I told him he could invite Nina Marshall to play. Maybe they'll run off some of Jamie's energy. Anyway, Nina is on her way over."

"Oh, that's fine," said Claud, who has sat for Nina and her little sister Eleanor many times.

The Newtons left then, and Claudia took Jamie outside to wait for Nina.

"Miss Mary Mack, Mack, Mack," sang Jamie, jumping along the front walk in time to his song, "all dressed in black, black, black, with silver buttons, buttons, buttons, all down her back, back, back. She jumped so high, high, high," (Jamie's jumping became even bouncier at that part) "she touched the sky, sky, sky, and didn't come back, back, back, till the Fourth of July, ly, ly!"

Lord, thought Claudia, I have hardly ever seen Jamie so wound up.

Unfortunately, Jamie didn't calm down much when Nina arrived. Claudia suggested a game of catch — and in record time, an argument broke out.

"If you miss the ball, you have to give up your turn," announced Jamie.

"Do not!" cried Nina indignantly.

"Do too!"

"Do not!"

"Whoa!" said Claudia, taking the ball from Jamie. "I think that's enough catch. Let's find something else to do today."

"Miss Mary Mack, Mack, Mack — " began Jamie.

Claudia didn't want to listen to the song

again. She racked her brain for some kind of diversion — and had an idea. "Hey, you guys," she said excitedly, "how would you like to go to a place where you can see lots of animals?"

"The *zoo?*" exclaimed Nina.

"Almost," Claud replied. "*Do* you want to see some animals?"

"Yes!" cried Jamie and Nina.

"Okay," said Claud. "Nina, I'm just going to call your parents and tell them where we're going. Then we can be on our way."

Fifteen minutes later the Mancusis'doorbell was ringing. I had arrived to do the afternoon feeding and walking. As you can imagine, I was surprised. Who would be ringing their bell? Somebody who didn't know they were on vacation, I decided.

I peeked out the front windows before I went ahead and opened the door. And standing on the stoop were Claud, Jamie Newton, and Nina Marshall! I let them in right away.

"Hi, you guys!" I exclaimed.

"Hi," replied Claud. "I hope we're not bothering you."

"Nope. I just got here. I'm getting ready to walk the dogs."

"Oh," said Claudia. "Well, if it isn't too much trouble, could Jamie and Nina look at the animals? We're sort of on a field trip."

I giggled. "Sure. I'll show you around."

But I didn't have to do much showing at first. Pooh Bear was lolling on the floor in the front hall, and then Rosie wandered in, followed by Powder, who was batting his mother's tail.

Jamie and Nina began patting Pooh Bear and Rosie and trying to cuddle Powder. When the animals' patience wore out, I took Jamie and Nina by the hand and walked them to the bird cages. Frank very obligingly called out, "Where's the beef? Where's the beef?" and then, "Two, two, two mints in one!"

"Gosh," said Jamie, "I know a song you'd like, Frank." He sang Miss Mary Mack to him. "See?" he went on. "Miss Mary Mack, Mack, Mack. It's kind of like 'Two, two, two mints in one!'"

Next I showed the kids the rabbits and then the guinea pigs.

"We can take the guinea pigs out — " I started to say.

But Jamie let loose a shriek. "NO! NO! Don't take them out!"

"Hey," said Claud, wrapping Jamie in her arms, "don't worry. We won't take them out. What's wrong?"

36

"They're beasties!" Jamie cried. "They come from outer space. I saw them on TV."

"Oh Jamie," Claud said gently. "They aren't beasties. There's no such — "

"*Beast*ies?" exclaimed Nina.

"Yes," said Jamie. "They're mean and awful. They bite people and then they take over the world."

"WAHHH!" wailed Nina. "I want to go home!"

I nudged Claudia. "Listen," I said, "I have to walk the dogs now anyway. Why don't you and Jamie and Nina come with me?"

"Good idea," agreed Claudia.

Jamie and Nina calmed down as they watched me put the leashes on Pooh Bear, Jacques, and Cheryl.

"Can Nina and I walk a dog?" asked Jamie.

"I'd really like to let you," I told him, "But the dogs are my responsibility. The Mancusis think *I'm* caring for them, so I better walk them. I'll bet you've never seen one person walk three dogs at the same time."

"No," agreed Jamie, as I locked the front door behind us. He and Nina watched, wide-eyed, as I took the leashes in my right hand and the dogs practically pulled me to the sidewalk.

37

Claud laughed, I laughed, and Jamie and Nina shrieked with delight.

The beasties were forgotten.

"I'll walk you back to your neighborhood," I told Claudia.

"You mean *Cheryl* will walk us back to our neighborhood," said Claud with a grin.

Cheryl was trying hard to be obedient, but she's so big that even when she walked, Jamie and Nina had to run to keep up with her.

"Actually," I told Claudia, "Pooh Bear is the problem. She's the feisty one. And when she gets feisty, Jacques gets feisty."

"Well, so far so good," Claud replied.

And everything was still okay by the time we reached Claudia's house. Just a few more houses and Jamie would be home again.

That was when Chewbacca showed up.

Who is Chewbacca? He's the Perkinses' black Labrador retriever. The Perkinses are the family who moved into Kristy Thomas' old house, across the street from Claudia. We sit for them a lot, since they have three kids — Myriah, Gabbie, and Laura. But guess what? It's harder to take care of Chewy by himself than to take care of all three girls together. Chewy isn't mean; don't get me wrong. He's just mischievous. Like Cheryl, he's big and lovable, but he gets into things. You can almost hear him thinking, Let's see. *Now* what can I do? Chewy finds things, hides things, chases things. And when you walk him, you never know what might catch his eye — a falling leaf, a butterfly — and cause him to go on a doggie rampage.

"Uh-oh, Chewy's loose!" said Claudia.

"Go home, Chewy! Go on home!" I coaxed him. I pointed to the Perkinses' house (as if Chewy would know what that meant).

Jamie added, "Shoo! Shoo!"

Chewy grinned at us and then pranced right up to the Mancusis' dogs. He just made himself part of the bunch, even though he wasn't on a leash.

"Well, now what?" I said as we walked along. Cheryl and Jacques and Pooh Bear didn't seem the least bit upset — but what would I do with Chewy when we got back to the Mancusis'? . . . And what would happen if Chewy saw something that set him off?

"Turn around," suggested Claudia. "Let's walk Chewy back to his house."

Jamie, Nina, Claudia, Pooh Bear, Jacques, Cheryl, and I turned around and headed for the Perkinses'. But Chewy didn't come with us. He sat on the sidewalk and waited for us to come back to him.

"He is just too smart," remarked Jamie.

I rang the Perkinses' bell, hoping someone would go get Chewy, but nobody answered.

"I guess he'll just have to walk with us," I finally said.

We rejoined Chewy and set off. Chewy bunched up with the dogs again as if he'd been walking with them all his life.

"Oh, no! There's a squirrel!" Claudia cried softly. "Now what?"

Chewy looked at the squirrel. The squirrel looked at Chewy.

Pooh Bear looked at the squirrel. The squirrel looked at Pooh Bear. Then it ran up a tree.

Nothing.

The rest of the walk was like that. A leaf drifted to the ground in front of the dogs. "Uh-oh," said Nina. But nothing happened. A chipmunk darted across the sidewalk. We all held our breaths, sure that Chewy or Pooh Bear or maybe Jacques was going to go off his (or her) rocker. But the dogs were incredibly well-behaved. It was as if they were trying to drive us crazy with their good behavior.

We circled around Claudia's neighborhood and finally reached the Perkinses' again. This time they were home and glad to see Chewy. We left him there, and then Claud took Jamie and Nina home, and I returned to the Mancusis' with the dogs. I played with the cats and guinea pigs and rabbits, and I fed the animals. In the hamster cage, the fat one was still curled in a separate corner. I wondered if I should be worried about him. When I stroked him with my finger, he didn't even wake up. I decided to keep my eye on him.

CHAPTER 5

On Monday afternoon I raced to the Mancusis', gave the dogs a whirlwind walk, played with the animals, fed them, and then raced to Claudia's for a club meeting. I just made it.

When I reached Claudia's room, Kristy was already in the director's chair, visor in place, the club notebook in her lap. But it was only 5:28. Two more minutes until the meeting would officially begin. Dawn hadn't arrived yet. (For once I wasn't the last to arrive!) Claudia was frantically trying to read the last two pages of *The Clue of the Velvet Mask*, a Nancy Drew mystery. Mary Anne was examining her hair for split ends, and Mallory was blowing a gigantic bubble with strawberry gum.

I joined Mal on the floor.

"Hi," I said.

Mal just waved, since she was concentrating on her bubble.

"Hi, Jessi," said Claudia and Mary Anne.

But Kristy was engrossed in the notebook and didn't say anything. When Dawn came in, she snapped to attention, though.

"Order, please!" she called. "Come to order."

Reluctantly, Claudia put her book down. "Just one *paragraph* to go," she said.

"Well, nothing ever happens in the last paragraph," remarked Mary Anne. "The author just tells you which mystery Nancy's going to solve next."

"That's true."

"ORDER!" shouted Kristy.

Boy, was I glad I was already *in* order.

"Sheesh," said Claud.

Kristy ignored her. "Ahem," she said. "Dawn, how's the treasury?"

"It'll be great after I collect dues," replied Dawn.

Groan, groan, groan. Every Monday Dawn collects dues, and every Monday we groan about having to give her money. It's not as if it's any big surprise. But the same thing —

"Please pay attention!" barked Kristy.

My head snapped up. What was this? School?

I glanced at Mallory who mouthed, "Boss-lady" to me and nodded toward Kristy. Then I had to try not to laugh.

"All right," Kristy went on, "has everyone been reading the notebook?"

"Yes," we chorused. We *always* keep up with it.

"Okay," said Kristy. "If you're really reading it — "

"We are!" Claud exploded. "Sheesh, Kristy, what's with you lately? You're bossier than ever."

For a moment, Kristy softened. "Sorry," she said. "It's just that Charlie suddenly thinks he's the big shot of the world. Next year he'll be in college, you know. So he bosses Sam and David Michael and me around nonstop." Kristy paused. Then her face hardened into her "I am the president" look.

"But," she went on, "I *am* the president, which gives me the right to boss you club members around."

"Excuse me," said Claudia in an odd voice, and I wondered what was coming, "but as president just what else *do* you do — besides get ideas, which any of us could do."

"Oh, yeah?" said Kristy.

"Yeah."

"Well, what brilliant ideas have you had?"

"I believe," Mary Anne spoke up, "that Claudia was the one who designed the alphabet blocks that say The Baby-sitters Club. That's

44

our logo and we use it on every flier we give out."

"Thank you, Mary Anne," said Claudia. "And I believe that Mary Anne figured out who sent her the bad-luck charm, which was the first step in solving that mystery a while ago."

"And Mallory — " I began.

"Okay, okay, okay," said Kristy.

But the other girls weren't finished.

"I," said Dawn, "would like to know, Kristy, just what it is — "

Ring, ring.

We were so engrossed in what Dawn was saying that we didn't all dive for the phone as usual.

Ring, ring.

Finally Mary Anne answered it. She arranged a job for Mallory. Then the phone rang two more times. When *those* jobs had been set up, we looked expectantly at Dawn. (Well, Kristy didn't. She was glaring at us — all of us.)

Dawn picked up right where she'd left off. " — just what it is you do besides boss us around and get great ideas."

"I run the meetings."

"Big deal," said Claudia.

"Well, what do *you* do, Ms. Vice-President?" asked Kristy hotly.

"Besides donating my room and my phone to you three times a week," Claudia replied, "I have to take all those calls that come in when we're not meeting. And there are quite a few of them. You know that."

"And," spoke up Dawn, "*I* have to keep track of the money, collect dues every week — which isn't always easy — and be in charge of remembering to pay your brother, and of buying things for the Kid-Kits."

"*I*," said Mary Anne, "probably have the most complicated job of anybody." (No one disagreed with her.) "I have to schedule *every single* job any of us goes on. I have to keep track of our schedules, of our clients, their addresses, and how many kids are in their families. It is a huge job."

"And we do these jobs *in addition* to getting ideas," pointed out Dawn.

There was a moment of silence. Then Mary Anne said, "Okay. We have a problem. But I've got an idea. I suggest — "

"We do *not* have a problem," Kristy interrupted her. "Trust me, we don't. All you guys need to do is calm down and you'll see that things are actually in control." Kristy paused. When none of us said anything, she went on, "Okay, now I have a really important idea.

Forget this other stuff. To make sure that each of you is reading the notebook once a week, I'm going to draw up a checklist. Every Monday, in order to show me you've been keeping up with the notebook, you'll initial a box on the chart."

"*What?!*" exclaimed Claudia.

Dawn and Mary Anne gasped.

Mallory and I glanced at each other. We hadn't been saying much. We didn't want to get involved in a club fight. Since we're the newest and youngest members, we try to stay out of arguments. It's hard to know whose side to be on. We don't want to step on any toes. And the easiest way to do that is to keep our mouths shut.

But the other girls *wanted* us to take sides.

"Jessi, what do you think?" asked Claudia. "Mallory?"

I hesitated. "About the chart?" I finally said.

"Yes, about the chart."

"Well, um, I — I mean . . ." I looked at Mal.

"See," Mal began, "um, it — I . . ."

Claudia was thoroughly annoyed. "Forget it," she snapped.

"Kristy, there is absolutely no reason to make a checklist for us," said Dawn. "There's not even any reason to *ask* us if we've been reading the notebook. We always keep up with it. Each one of us. Don't we say yes every time you ask us about it?"

The argument was interrupted by several more job calls. But as soon as Mary Anne had made the arrangements, the club members went right back to their discussion.

"There's no need for the checklist," Dawn said again.

"Don't you trust us?" Mary Anne wanted to know.

Kristy sighed. "Of course I trust you. The checklist will just, well, prove to me that I can trust you. Plus, I won't have to ask you about reading the notebook anymore."

"But can't you *just trust* us?" said Mary Anne.

Kristy opened her mouth to answer the question, but Dawn spoke up instead.

"You know," she said, changing the subject, "personally, I am tired of having to collect dues on Mondays. Everyone groans and complains and makes me feel about *this* big." Dawn held her fingers a couple of inches apart.

"We don't mean to complain — " I started to tell Dawn.

But Claudia cut in with, "Well, *I'm* pretty tired of getting those job calls all the time. You know, some people don't even try to remember when our meetings are. Mrs. Barrett hardly ever calls during meetings. She calls at nine o'clock on a Sunday night, or on a Tuesday afternoon, or — worst of all — at eight-thirty on a Saturday morning."

"And I," said Mary Anne, "am especially tired of scheduling. I'm tired of keeping track of dentist appointments and ballet lessons — "

"Sorry," I apologized again. (I am really wonderful at apologizing.)

"Oh, it's not your fault, Jessi. Everyone has things that need scheduling. In fact, that's the problem. I'm up to my ears in lessons and classes and dental visits. I've been doing this job for over a year now, and I'm just tired of it. That's all there is to it."

"What are you guys saying?" Kristy asked her friends.

"That I don't like scheduling," Mary Anne replied.

"And I don't like collecting dues," said Dawn.

"And I don't like all the phone calls," added Claudia.

I looked at Mal. Why didn't Kristy speak up? What did she not like about being president? Finally it occurred to me — nothing. There was nothing she didn't like be- cause . . . because her job was pretty easy and fun. Conducting meetings, being in charge, getting ideas. Kristy sure had the easy job. (Mal and I did, too, but we had been *made* junior officers with hardly any club responsibilities. We hadn't had a say in the matter.)

I think we were all relieved when the meeting broke up. Well, I know Mal and I were, but it was hard to tell about the others. They left the meeting absolutely silently. Not a word was spoken.

Mal and I stood around on the sidewalk in front of the Kishis' until the other girls left. As soon as Mary Anne had disappeared into her house across the street, I said, "Whoa. Some meeting. What do you think, Mal?"

"I think," she replied, "that this is not a good sign. I also think that you and I might be asked to take sides soon."

"Probably," I agreed, "but it's going to be very important that we stay neutral. No taking sides at all."

CHAPTER 6

Tuesday

Oh, wow. I don't have words to describe what happened today. I could write down awful, disgusting, gross, shivery, blechh, but even those words don't say it all. I better just explain what happened. See, I was baby-sitting for Myriah and Gabbie Perkins, and I decided to take them over to the Mancusis' to visit the animals. I knew Claudia had done that with Jamie and Nina, and I thought it was a good idea. (How did I know Claudia had done that? Because I read the notebook, Kristy, that's how.) So I walked the girls over to the Mancusis'....

51

Mary Anne just loves sitting for the Perkinses. Remember them? They're the owners of Chewy; they're the family who moved into Kristy's house after the Thomases left it for Watson's mansion. The three Perkins girls are Myriah, who's five and a half, Gabbie Ann, who's two and a half, and Laura, the baby. Laura is so little that we usually don't take care of her, just Myriah and Gabbie. Right now, Laura pretty much goes wherever her mother goes.

Myriah and Gabbie are fun and us sitters like them a lot. The girls enjoy adventures and trying new things, which was why Mary Anne thought they'd like the trip to the Mancusis'. And they did like it. The awful-disgusting-gross-shivery-blechh thing had nothing to do with the girls. In fact, Mary Anne was the one who caused it. Myriah helped to solve it.

I better back up a little here. Okay, at about four o'clock on Tuesday afternoon I returned to the Mancusis' after walking the dogs, and found the phone ringing.

"Hello, Mancusi residence," I said breathlessly as I picked up the phone.

"Hi, Jessi, it's Mary Anne."

Mary Anne was calling to find out if she

could bring Myriah and Gabbie over. I told her yes, of course, and about twenty minutes later they showed up.

"Oh, boy! Aminals!" cried Gabbie. Her blonde hair was fixed in two ponytails that bobbed up and down as she made a dash for the Mancusis' kitchen.

"All kinds!" added Myriah. Myriah's hair was pulled back into one long ponytail that reached halfway down her back. She followed her sister.

The girls began exploring the house. The cats and dogs weren't too interesting to them since they've got one of each at their house — Chewy, and their cat, R.C. But the other animals fascinated them.

I showed them Barney. I showed them Lucy and Ricky. I explained everything I could think of to them. We moved on.

"These are — "

"Easter bunnies!" supplied Gabbie, as we looked in at Fluffer-Nut, Robert, Toto, and Cindy.

"You can hold them," I said. "The rabbits like to have a chance to get out of their hutch."

So Myriah held Toto, and Gabbie held Fluffer-Nut. For a few minutes, the girls had a giggle-fest. I looked around for Mary Anne.

When I didn't see her, I was relieved instead of worried. I didn't want to talk about Kristy or our club problems with her.

Soon the girls grew tired of the rabbits, so we put them back.

"Now these," I told Gabbie and Myriah, "are hamsters. Since they're sleeping, we won't disturb them. But see how fat that hamster's face is?" I pointed to one on top of the pile of hamsters. It was not the fat hamster. He was still off by himself in that corner of the cage. He seemed to have made a sort of nest. No, I pointed to one of the other hamsters.

"He looks like he has the mumps!" said Myriah.

"He does, doesn't he? But his fat cheeks are really — "

"AUGHHH!"

The scream came from the direction of the sun porch.

"Mary Anne?" I called.

"AUGHHH!" was her reply.

I put the lid back on the hamster cage, took Myriah and Gabbie by their hands, and ran with them to the sun porch.

A truly horrible sight met our eyes. We saw Barney's cage and the lid to Barney's cage — but no Barney.

"Mary Anne, what on earth happened?" I cried.

"Barney's loose!" was her response. "The *snake* is *loose!*"

Mary Anne and I got the same idea at the same time. We jumped up on one of the big porch chairs, the way people do when they've just seen a mouse.

Myriah and Gabbie looked at us as if we were crazy.

"What are you *do*ing?" exclaimed Myriah. "Barney's just a little snake. He can't hurt you. Besides, he could probably slither right up onto that chair. You can't escape him that way."

"Oh, EW!" shrieked Mary Anne.

"How did Barney get loose?" I asked her.

"Well, I'm not sure, but I think he just crawled out of his cage, or slithered out or whatever sn-snakes do. I — I mean, he did it after I forgot to put the lid back on his cage. I took it off so I could get a closer look at him, and then I heard someone saying, "Where's the beef? Where's the beef?" so I left to see who it was. And then I found the birds, and *then* I remembered Barney, and when I came back to replace the lid on his cage, he was gone. I am *so* sorry, Jessi."

"Oh . . ." I cried.

"Shouldn't we *find* Barney?" asked Myriah sensibly. "Before he gets too far away?"

"I guess so." I couldn't believe I was going to have to search for a snake. I couldn't think of anything stupider than searching for something you didn't want to find — or anything grosser than searching for a flicking tongue and a long, scaly body.

But it had to be done, and done fast.

"Let's split up," I suggested. "Barney probably couldn't have gotten upstairs, so we don't need to search there. Mary Anne, you and Gabbie look in the back rooms on this floor. Myriah and I will look in the front rooms."

"Okay," agreed Mary Anne, and we set off.

The search was a nightmare. Well, it was for Mary Anne and me. For Myriah and Gabbie it was like playing hide-and-seek with an animal. The odd thing was, I was so afraid of Barney that I was *less* worried about *not* finding him and having to tell the Mancusis he was lost than I was that we *would* find him. I went looking gingerly under chairs and tables and couches, always terrified that I'd come face to face with Barney and his flicking tongue.

But after twenty minutes of searching, there was no sign of Barney. And we'd been through every room on the first floor.

"Uh-oh," I said, as the four of us met in the hallway. "Now what? How am I going to tell the Mancusis that Barney is missing?"

"Long distance. It's the next best thing to being there!" called Frank from his cage.

We began to laugh, but then I said, "This is serious. We have to find Barney."

"Yeah," said Mary Anne. "Boy, am I sorry, Jessi. If — if you have to tell the Mancusis that . . . you know . . . I'll help you."

"Hey!" said Myriah suddenly. "I just thought of something. We're learning about animals in school, and Barney is a snake and snakes are reptiles and reptiles are cold-blooded. If I had cold blood, I'd want to warm up."

"Could Barney have gotten outside?" I said nervously. "Maybe he wanted sunshine. We might never find him outdoors, though."

"Well, let's look," said Mary Anne.

So we did. And we hadn't looked for long when Mary Anne let out another shriek.

"Where is he?" I cried, since I knew that was what her scream had meant.

"Here," she yelled. "On the back porch."

I ran around to the porch and there was Barney, napping peacefully in a patch of sunshine.

"You were right," I whispered to Myriah. "Thank you." Then I added, "How are we going to get him back in his cage, Mary Anne?"

Mary Anne looked thoughtful. "I have an idea," she said. "Do the Mancusis have a spare aquarium somewhere?"

I wasn't sure. We checked around and found one in the garage. It was empty but clean.

"Okay," said Mary Anne, "what we're going to do is put this aquarium over Barney. I'll — I'll do it, since I was the one who let him loose."

I didn't argue. The four of us returned to the porch, and Mary Anne crept up behind Barney, holding the overturned aquarium. She paused several feet from him. "I hope he doesn't wake up," she said.

Boy, I hoped he didn't, either.

Mary Anne tiptoed a few steps closer, then a few more steps closer. When she was about a foot away from him, she lowered the aquarium. Barney woke up — but not until the aquarium was in place.

"Now," said Mary Anne, "we slide a piece of really stiff cardboard under Barney. Then we carry him inside and dump him in his own cage. This is my spider-catching method. See, I don't like spiders, and I also don't like to squish them, so when I find one in the house, I trap it under a cup or a glass and take it outside."

Well, Mary Anne's suggestion was a good one. I found a piece of cardboard in a stack of newspapers the Mancusis were going to throw away. Mary Anne carefully slid it under Barney, the two of us carried him inside, Myriah opened his cage for us — and we dumped him in. I think Barney was relieved to be at home again.

Believe me, *I* was relieved to have him home. But if I'd known what was going to happen at our club meeting the next day, I would have thought that a snake on the loose was nothing at all.

CHAPTER 7

The Wednesday club meeting started off like most others, except that I actually arrived early! It was one of the first times ever. My work at the Mancusis' had gone quickly that day, and the dogs had behaved themselves, so I had reached Claudia's fifteen minutes before the meeting was to begin. I had even beaten Kristy.

"Hi, Claud!" I said when I entered her room.

"Hi, Jessi."

Claudia sounded sort of glum, but I didn't ask her about it. Her gloominess probably had something to do with the Kristy problem, and I wanted to stay out of that. So all I said was, "Neat shirt."

Claudia was wearing another of her great outfits. This one consisted of an oversized, short-sleeved cotton shirt with gigantic leaves printed all over it, green leggings — the same green as the leaves on her shirt — bright yellow push-down socks, her purple high-tops, and

60

in her hair a headband with a gigantic purple bow attached to one side.

Claud is so, so cool . . . especially compared to me. I was also wearing an oversized shirt — a white sweat shirt with ballet shoes on the front — but with it I was just wearing jeans and regular socks and regular sneakers. And honestly, I would have to do something about my hair soon. It looks okay when it's pulled back, I guess, but I want it to look special.

I sat down on the floor. Since no one else had arrived, I guess I could have sat on the bed, but Mallory and I just don't feel comfortable doing that. We're the youngest and we belong on the floor. Period.

I was about to ask Claud if she'd printed the leaves on her shirt herself, when Dawn burst into the room.

"Hi, you guys!" she said cheerfully. She tossed her long hair over one shoulder.

"Hi," replied Claudia. "You're in a good mood."

"I'm thinking positive," Dawn informed us. "Maybe it'll help the meeting along. . . . I mean, I *know* it will help the meeting. This meeting," she went on, "is going to be wonderful. There aren't going to be any prob . . ."

Dawn's voice trailed off as Kristy strode into club headquarters. Without so much as a word, she crossed the room to Claudia's bulletin board, pulled out a few thumbtacks, and posted a piece of paper right over a bunch of photographs of Claudia and Stacey.

Kristy turned to us and smiled. "There!" she announced proudly, as if she had just achieved world peace.

"There what?" said Claudia darkly.

"There's the checklist. I made it last night. It took forev — "

"And you put it up over my *pictures?!*" exclaimed Claudia. "Not on your life. Those are pictures of Stacey and me before she moved away." Claudia marched to the bulletin board and took the checklist down. She gave it back to Kristy. "Find another place for this, Ms. Bossy."

"Sheesh, I'm *sorry*, Claud," said Kristy. "I didn't know those picture were so important to you."

"Well, they are."

Personally, I thought Claud was overreacting a little. I guess Kristy thought so, too. The next thing I knew, she was tacking the checklist up over the photos again.

Claudia yanked it off.

Kristy put it back up.

Claudia yanked it off again. This time, the

checklist ripped. From one side hung a wrinkled strip.

Mallory and Mary Anne arrived just in time to hear Kristy let out a shriek and Claudia yell, "Leave this thing *off!* I don't want it on my bulletin board. I don't care how long it took you to make it!"

"Girls?" The gentle voice of Mimi, Claudia's grandmother, floated up the stairs. "Everything is okay?" (Mimi had a stroke last summer and it affected her speech. Sometimes her words get mixed up or come out funny.)

"YES!" Claudia shouted back, and I knew she didn't mean to sound cross. She lowered her voice. "Everything's fine, Mimi. Sorry about the yelling."

"That okay. No problem."

Claudia and Kristy were standing nose-to-nose by Claud's desk. They were both holding onto the checklist, and I could tell that neither planned to give it up. Not easily, anyway.

The rest of us were just gaping at them — Mallory and Mary Anne from the doorway, Dawn from the bed, and I from the floor.

"You," said Claudia to Kristy in a low voice, "are not the boss of this club."

Kristy looked surprised. Even I felt a little surprised. I don't think Kristy had meant to be bossy. She was just overexcited about her checklist.

But Kristy retorted, "I am the *president* of this club."

"Then," said Claudia, "it's time for new elections."

"*New* elections?" Kristy and Mallory and I squeaked.

"Yes," said a voice from the doorway. "New elections." It was Mary Anne.

Claudia and Kristy were so taken aback that they both let go of the checklist. It fell to the floor, forgotten.

Everyone turned to look at Mary Anne.

And then Mallory spoke up. Even though she's only a junior officer of the club, she's known for having a cool head in tough situations. So she took charge. "Everybody sit down," she said quietly. "In your regular seats. We have some things to straighten out. And we better calm down in case the phone rings."

As if Mal were psychic, the phone did ring then. We managed to schedule a job for the Barrett kids. By the time that was done, we had settled into our places. Kristy, in the director's chair, had even put her visor on.

"Okay," she began, "a motion has been made for . . . for . . ."

"New elections," supplied Claudia.

"All right. I'll consider the idea," said Kristy.

"No way," said Dawn, who, since the checklist war, had barely said a word. "You can't just consider the idea. Elections are our right. I *demand* new elections."

"Me too," said Mary Anne.

"Me too," said Claudia.

Mallory and I exchanged a worried glance. We were certain to be asked our opinion soon. And we were still trying to remain neutral.

Sure enough, Kristy looked down at Mal and me. I cringed. I knew she wanted us on her side. If we were, then the club would be divided three against three.

"Mallory, Jessi, what do you two think about the elections?" Kristy asked.

It would have been awfully nice to side with Kristy. Siding with the president is always nice. But I just couldn't. I didn't want to get involved in a club fight. I knew Mal didn't, either.

Since Mal wasn't speaking, I finally said, "What do we think about the elections?"

"Yes," said Kristy sharply.

"I . . . Well, I . . ." I shrugged. Then I looked helplessly at Mal.

"I — That's how . . . um . . ." was all Mallory managed to say.

"Do you want them?" Mary Anne asked us.

65

"Not that your positions would change, but you'd be voting."

Mallory and I did some more stammering. I think both of us felt that elections were a good idea, but neither of us wanted to admit it. Furthermore, a new worry was already creeping into my worry-laden mind. *How* would Mal and I vote in an election? If we voted to keep Kristy president, all the other club members would hate us. If we voted Kristy out, Kristy would hate us, and whether she was the president or the secretary, the club was still hers because she had dreamed it up and started it.

"Jessi? Mallory?" said Kristy again. We didn't even bother to answer, and suddenly Kristy threw down the pencil she'd been holding and exclaimed, "Okay, okay, okay. We'll have an election." I guess she could tell that no one was on her side. Jessi and I might not have been on the *other* side, but we weren't on hers, either.

"Good," said Claudia. "Well, we're ready."

"Not *now!*" cried Kristy as the phone rang.

We scheduled three jobs, and then Kristy went on, "I don't want to waste one of our regular meetings on elections. Besides, people call all the time during meetings."

"They call plenty of other times, too," Claud couldn't resist saying.

"Whatever," said Kristy. "Anyway, I'm calling a special meeting for the elections. Saturday afternoon at four o'clock. *This* meeting is adjourned."

"Whew," I said to Mallory when we were safely outside. "I don't like the sound of this."

"Me neither," agreed Mallory. "Not at all."

CHAPTER 8

On Thursday, I had help at the Mancusis'. Mallory came over so we could discuss the election problem, and Becca came over so she could play with the animals. The night before, she'd been so excited about the trip to the Mancusis' that she practically couldn't sleep. Nevertheless, she was a big help that afternoon, and so was Mallory.

Becca and I reached the Mancusis' about fifteen minutes before Mal did. I wanted to walk the dogs before I began feeding the animals, so we would have to wait for Mal to arrive. I used the time to introduce Becca to the animals.

"Come on," I said to her. "Come see the birds. You'll love them."

"Just a sec," replied Becca. She was lying on the floor, playing with Ling-Ling and Crosby, who were enjoying every second of her attention.

When Becca finally got to her feet, I led her back to Frank. I was just about to say, "This is Frank. Listen to what he can do," when Frank said, "The quicker picker-upper! The quicker picker-upper!"

Becca began to giggle. "That's great! How'd he learn to do that?"

"Watched too much TV, I guess. Like some people I know," I teased my sister.

"Oh, Jessi," replied Becca, but she was smiling.

"Try saying, 'Where's the beef?' " I suggested.

"Me?"

I nodded.

"Okay." Becca stood directly in front of Frank and said clearly, "Where's the beef? Where's the beef?"

"Long distance," replied Frank.

Becca and I laughed so hard that we didn't hear Mallory ring the doorbell until she was leaning on it for the third time.

"Oh! That's Mal!" I cried. "I'll be right back, Becca."

I dashed to the door and let Mal in.

"What took you so long?" she asked cheerfully. (Mal is usually cheerful.) "I rang three times."

I explained about Frank, and then, of course,

I had to show him to her. I led her back to Becca and the birds, and Becca promptly said, "Hi, Mallory. Listen to this. Hey, Frank, where's the beef? Where's the beef?"

"The quicker picker-upper!" Frank answered.

When we had stopped laughing, I said, "Come on, you guys. We've got to walk the dogs. Cheryl looks sort of desperate."

I took the leashes from the hooks and before I could even call the dogs, they came bounding into the kitchen.

"Okay, you guys. Ready for a walk?" I asked. (Dumb question. They were *dying* for a walk.)

I snapped their leashes on and they pulled me to the front door. "Come on!" I called to Becca and Mallory, who were still talking to Frank. "The dogs can't wait!"

Becca and Mallory clattered after me. As we ran through the doorway and down the steps, Mal asked, "Can we help you walk them? We could each take one leash."

"Thanks," I replied, "but I better do it myself. Besides, they're used to being walked together. You can hold onto them while I lock the door, though."

So Mallory took the leashes from me while I locked the Mancusis' door. Then she handed them back, and we set off down the street —

at a fast pace, thanks to Cheryl and her very long legs.

"Keep your eye on Pooh Bear," I told Becca and Mal. "She's the troublemaker."

"The little one?" exclaimed Becca.

"Yup," I said. "For instance, up ahead is . . . Oh, no, it's a cat! For a moment I thought it was just a squirrel, but a cat's worse. Pooh Bear might — OOF!"

Pooh Bear had spotted the cat, who was sunning itself at the end of a driveway. She jerked forward with a little bark, straining at the leash. Jacques spotted the cat next, and then Cheryl, although Cheryl doesn't care about cats. Anyway, the cat heard the barking, woke up, saw the dogs, and fled down the driveway.

"*Hold* it, you guys!" I yelled to the dogs. Pooh Bear and Jacques were practically dragging me down the street. Cheryl, too. She always likes a good run.

"We'll help you, Jessi!" I heard my sister cry. A few moments later, she and Mallory grabbed me around the waist. They pulled back so hard that the dogs stopped short, and all of us — dogs, Mal, Becca, and I — fell to the ground. When us humans began to laugh, the dogs started licking our faces.

It took several minutes to sort ourselves out

and stop laughing, but finally we were on our feet and walking again. Things went smoothly after that.

"I never knew dog-walking was so hard," commented Becca.

"It's only hard when you're walking Pooh Bear, Jacques, and Cheryl," I told her. "And when they're in the mood for cat-chasing."

We returned to the Mancusis' and I let the dogs inside and hung their leashes up. "Okay," I said, "feeding time."

"Puh-*lease* can I feed some of the animals?" begged Becca. "Even though it's your job? I'll be really good and careful."

"We-ell . . . okay," I said, relenting. "You have to follow instructions exactly, though, okay?"

"Yes, yes, yes! Okay!" Becca was so excited she began jumping up and down.

"All right. You can feed the guinea pigs, the rabbits, and the cats. Let me show you what to do."

I gave Becca instructions, and then Mal came with me while I fed the other animals. I started with the dogs because they absolutely cannot wait, and they are gigantic pains when they're hungry.

"Well," said Mallory, as I spooned dog food

into Cheryl's dish, "What do you think about the elections?"

I groaned. "Please. Do we have to talk about them?"

"I think we better."

"I know. You're right. I was just trying to . . . I don't know what. Oh well. Hey, Mal, you're not thinking of quitting, are you?" The idea had just occurred to me and it was an awful one, but if Mal and I refused to take sides, would we feel forced to quit the club?

"Thinking of quitting?!" exclaimed Mal. "No way. No one's going to get rid of me *that* easily. . . . But the meetings *are* pretty uncomfortable."

"I'll say," I agreed.

"And how are we going to vote Saturday?" wondered Mallory.

"Well, I guess," I began slowly. "Let me think. Okay, there are four offices — president, vice-president, secretary, and treasurer. And you and I are going to remain junior officers, so it'll be the same four girls running for the same four offices."

"Right," agreed Mallory.

I finished feeding the dogs, rinsed off the spoon I'd used, changed the water in their bowls, and moved onto the bird cages.

"Yesterday I was thinking," I told Mallory, "that if we vote Kristy out of her office — if we make her secretary or something — she'll be mad at us, which won't be good. I mean, I'll always think of the club as hers, whether she's president or not, because it was her idea and she started it. And I don't want her mad at us. On the other hand, if we vote for Kristy for president, all the other girls will be mad at us, and that won't be good, either. It almost doesn't matter how we vote for Mary Anne and Dawn and Claudia, but where Kristy is concerned, we lose either way."

"Wait a sec," Mal cut in. "Won't the voting be secret?"

"It should be, but even if it is, everyone will figure out who voted for whom. People always do."

"Oh, brother," said Mallory. "You're right. *And* I just thought of something even worse. If enough feelings are hurt by the voting, the club could *break up*. It really could. Then what?"

"I don't know," I said, heading for the hamster cage. "I hadn't even thought of that."

Mal and I peered in at the hamsters.

"Do they always sleep in a pile?" asked Mallory.

"Pretty much," I replied. "Except for that one. I pointed to the one in the corner. "He sleeps by himself, and you know, I think he's fatter than he was a few days ago. I'm getting worried about him."

"Well, at least he's eating," said Mal.

"Maybe he's gotten too fat to move," I kidded, but I didn't try to smile at my joke. I was too worried. I was worried about the hamster, and worried about our special Saturday meeting.

Mal and Becca and I finished feeding the animals and changing their water. Becca played with the cats again and then it was time to leave.

"Good-bye, Cheryl! Good-bye, Ling-Ling!" Becca called. " 'Bye, Barney!' 'Bye, Fluffer-Nut!' 'Bye, Frank!' "

"Awk!" squawked Frank. "Tiny little tea leaves!"

CHAPTER 9

Thursday

I always look forward to sitting for
Jackie Rodowsky, our walking disaster,
even though he's more of a challenge than
almost any other kid I can think of.
Today was a challenge as usual, but it was
a different kind of challenge. Jackie's having
a tough time -- and I tried to help him
with his problem. I'm not sure I did,
though. In fact, I think I might have
been bossing him around. I mean, I guess
I was bossing him. Have I always done
that? Or is it just lately? Well, anyway,
Jackie was nice about it.

Kristy *might* have been bossing Jackie around? I'll say she bossed him! The good thing is that I think she learned something from Jackie. Let me start back at the beginning of the afternoon, though, when Kristy first arrived at the Rodowskys'.

Ding-dong.

"Rowf! Rowf-rowf!" Bo, the Rodowskys' dog, skidded to a halt at the door and waited for someone to come open it so he could see who was on the other side. A moment later, the door was opened by Jackie himself.

"Hi, Kristy," he said gloomily.

"Good afternoon, Eeyore," Kristy replied with a smile.

"Huh?" said Jackie.

"You look like Eeyore. You know, the sad donkey from *Winnie-the-Pooh*."

"Oh."

"What's wrong?"

"I'll tell you later. Come on in."

Kristy stepped inside. She took a good look at Jackie's sad face. He's got this shock of red hair and a faceful of freckles. When he grins, you can see that he's missing teeth (he's only seven), so he looks a little like Alfred E. Neuman from *Mad* magazine. You know,

"What, me worry?" But not that day. Jackie wasn't smiling.

"My brothers are at their lessons," Jackie informed Kristy, "Dad's at work, and Mom's going to a meeting."

Kristy nodded. That often happens. Jackie doesn't take any lessons because he's too accident-prone. He's our walking disaster. When Jackie's around, things just seem to happen. Vases fall, dishes break, earrings disappear. Things happen to Jackie, too. *He* falls or breaks things or loses things. Which is why he doesn't take lessons anymore. He tried to, but there were too many accidents when he was around.

Mrs. Rodowsky came downstairs then, and Kristy greeted her and listened to her instructions for the afternoon. Then Mrs. Rodowsky kissed Jackie good-bye and left.

"So," said Kristy, "what's up, Jackie? You look like you have a big problem."

Jackie nodded. "Yeah. I do."

"Do you want to tell me about it? I don't know if I could help, but I might have a couple of suggestions."

"Well," Jackie answered, "I could tell you, I guess. That won't hurt anything."

"Shoot," said Kristy.

Jackie heaved a huge sigh.

"Wait, let's make ourselves comfortable." Kristy led Jackie into the rec room and they settled themselves on the couch, Bo between them.

"Okay," said Kristy.

"All right. See, in my class," Jackie began, "our teacher said we were going to have elections." (Elections? thought Kristy.) "There are all kinds of neat things you can run for — blackboard-washer, messenger, roll-taker."

"Sounds like fun," said Kristy.

Jackie nodded. "That's what I thought. I wanted to run for the job of taking care of Snowball. He's our rabbit. That sounded like the funnest job of all." Jackie stopped talking and stroked Bo behind his ears.

"But?" Kristy prompted him.

"But there's no way I'm going to win."

"How come?"

" 'Cause I'm running against Adrienne Garvey. Adrienne is . . . is . . ." Jackie paused, thinking. "Well, she never erases holes into her workbook pages, and she never gets dirty, even in art class. And she always finishes her work on time. And she never forgets her lunch or trips or spills or *any*thing!"

"Ms. Perfect?" Kristy suggested.

"*Yes*," said Jackie vehemently. "And all the

other kids will vote for her. I just know it. They don't like Adrienne very much, but they know she'll do a good job. She'll never forget Snowball, and she'll keep his cage neat and stuff."

"What about you?"

"Me?" replied Jackie. "You mean, what kind of job would I do?"

Kristy nodded.

"Just as good as Adrienne!" Jackie cried. "Honest. I take good care of Bo, don't I, Bo?" (Bo whined happily.) "But, see, Bo's not mine. I mean, not just mine. He belongs to my brothers *and* me, so I don't take care of him everyday. And Snowball wouldn't be mine, either. He belongs to the whole class. But if I got the job, he would *feel* like mine since I would be the only one taking care of him. And I know I could do a good job. I know it."

"Then prove it to the kids in your class," said Kristy. "Show them that you'll be as neat and as responsible as Adrienne. Maybe even neater."

"And responsibler?"

Kristy smiled. "That, too."

"But how am I going to show them that?" wondered Jackie.

"Well, let's think it over."

"I — I could be neat myself," said Jackie after a few moments, sitting up straighter.

"That's a good start."

"And I could try to keep my workbook neat. And my desk neat."

"Even better."

Jackie paused, frowning.

"Do you think you can do those things?" asked Kristy.

" 'Course I can!" To prove his point, Jackie jumped to his feet. "Watch me neaten up," he cried, and then added, "I did this once before, for a wedding. . . . Okay, buttons first." Jackie's shirt was buttoned wrong, so that on top an extra button stuck up under his chin, and on the bottom one shirttail trailed an inch or two below the other.

Jackie unfastened the first button — and it came off in his hands.

"Uh-oh," he said, but his usual cheerfulness was returning. "Um, Kristy, if you could . . . whoops." Another button came off.

"Here," said Kristy, "let me do that for you."

"No," said Jackie, "I have to learn to —"

Too late. Kristy was already unbuttoning and rebuttoning Jackie's shirt. "There you go," she said. "Now the next thing I think you should do is start a campaign—you know, slogans, speeches, that sort of thing."

"But *I*," Jackie replied, "think I should practice filling Bo's dish neatly. It's almost time to feed him anyway."

"Well," said Kristy reluctantly, "okay." She was thinking that she really wanted to help Jackie win the election for the job of Snowball-Feeder. But she was also thinking that Jackie plus a bag of dog food equals big trouble. However, if Jackie believed that feeding Bo would help him, then Kristy would go along with his idea.

"Where's Bo's food?" Kristy asked.

"It's — Oh, I just remembered. We used up a bag yesterday. We have to start a new one. Mom keeps them in the basement."

Kristy cringed. Jackie was going to carry a bag of dog food from the basement up to the rec room and then up to the kitchen? "Be careful," she called after him.

Jackie disappeared into the basement. A moment later, Kristy heard his feet on the stairs. "I'm coming!" Jackie announced. "And I'm being careful!"

Jackie reached the rec room safely.

He grinned at Kristy.

He headed up the stairs to the kitchen.

Halfway there, the bottom of the bag gave

out. Dog food cascaded down the stairs into the rec room.

Jackie looked at Kristy in horror. Then he smacked his forehead with the heel of his hand. "I did it again!" he exclaimed. His face began to crumple.

"Oh, Jackie," said Kristy, eyeing the mess. "Don't cry. It wasn't your fault." She wanted to reach out and give him a hug, but a sea of kibbles lay between them.

Jackie stood miserably on the steps. "I *know* it wasn't my fault," he cried.

"It couldn't have been," agreed Kristy. "The glue on the bottom of the bag must have come undone."

"But that's just it!" Jackie replied. "Don't you see? It came undone while *I* was holding it. Not Mom. Not Dad. Not my brothers. Not the man at the grocery store. Me. I'm bad luck. Maybe that's why the kids at school don't want me feeding Snowball."

"Then make the kids forget about your bad luck," suggested Kristy.

"How?"

"Campaigning. I'll help you with it as soon as we put this food into another bag."

"All right," said Jackie, but he didn't sound very enthusiastic.

Kristy found a garbage bag and the two of

them swept the kibbles into it. When nothing was left on the stairs but kibble dust, Kristy got out the Dustbuster.

"Let me do that," said Jackie.

"No, *I'll* do it." Kristy wasn't about to let Jackie touch an appliance. "Okay," she said a few minutes later, as she switched the Dustbuster off, "let's plan your campaign."

Jackie found a pencil and a pad of paper. He and Kristy sat down on the couch again, but Jackie immediately got up.

"Forgot to feed Bo," he said. "See? I am responsible. I remember to take care of animals." He ran upstairs, fed Bo, and returned to the couch without a single accident.

"All right," said Kristy, "now what I think you should do—"

"Kristy?" Jackie interrupted. "Can I tell you something?"

"Sure."

"I like you, but you're an awful bossy babysitter. You buttoned my shirt when I wanted to do it myself, you wouldn't let me vacuum up the mess I made, and now you're going to plan my campaign for — Whoops."

Jackie had dropped his pencil into a heating grate. He and Kristy had to scramble around in order to get it out. In the excitement, Jackie forgot about what he'd said to Kristy. But Kristy didn't. It was all she could think of later as she helped Jackie with his campaign — and tried very hard not to be too bossy.

Was she really a bossy person?

CHAPTER 10

I was scared to go to the Friday meeting of the Baby-sitters Club.

Isn't that silly? I really was afraid, though, so while I was at the Mancusis' feeding the animals and worrying about the hamster, I phoned Mal.

"Hi," I said. "It's me."

"Hi, Jessi. Where are you?"

"At the Mancusis'. I'm almost done, though. Um, I was wondering. You want me to come by your house so we can walk to the meeting together?"

"Are you scared, too?"

Now this is what I love about Mallory. I suppose it's why we're best friends. We know each other inside out, and we're always honest with each other. Mal knew I was scared. And she admitted that she was scared. She could easily just have said, "Are you scared?" but she said, "Are you scared, *too*?" which is very important.

"Yeah, I am," I told her.

"Well, *please* stop by. I'd feel much better."

So of course I stopped by. Mallory and I walked to Claudia's with our arms linked, as if we could fend off arguments and yelling and hurt feelings that way.

We had to unlink our arms at the Kishis' front door, though. It was the only way to get inside.

Mimi greeted us in the hallway.

"Who's here?" I asked her.

I must have looked scared because she answered, "All others. But do not worry, Jessi. I know plobrems will . . . will work out."

I nodded. "Thanks, Mimi."

Mal and I climbed the stairs as slowly and as miserably as if we were going to our own funerals. We walked down the hallway. I heard only silence. I threw a puzzled glance back to Mallory, who shrugged.

A few more seconds and I was standing in Claudia's doorway. Well, there was the reason for the silence. Everyone was present all right, but no one was talking — not to Kristy, not to each other.

Mary Anne was sitting stiffly on the end of

Claudia's bed. She was gazing at the ceiling; her eyes looked teary.

Claudia, at the other end of her bed, was leafing silently through one of her sketchbooks.

Dawn was seated between Mary Anne and Claudia, and her long hair was falling across her face, almost as if she hoped to hide from everyone by not being able to see them.

And Kristy, well, Kristy looked like she always looks. She was poised in the director's chair, her visor in place, a pencil over one ear. I couldn't read the expression on her face, though.

Oops, I thought, as I paused in the doorway. If I stand here too long, Kristy will say, "What's with you guys? Are you going to stand there all day? Come on in so we can get started."

But Kristy didn't say a word. She just glanced at Mal and me and gave us a little smile. So we crept into Claudia's room and settled ourselves on the floor.

Kristy waited another minute until the digital clock on Claud's desk read 5:30. That minute was the longest one of my life. I was dying to whisper something to Mal like, "This room feels like a morgue," or, "Calm down, everybody. You're too cheerful. You're going to get out of control." But I couldn't. For one thing, in all that silence, everyone would have heard what I said. For another, I think the girls kind of *wanted* to feel bad, and I wasn't about to be responsible for cheering them up.

"Order," said Kristy as the numbers on the clock switched from 5:29 to 5:30.

Everyone already was in order.

"Well, um, is there any club business?" asked Kristy.

No one said a word. No one even moved.

Since it wasn't Monday, there were no dues to be collected, and Kristy didn't need to ask if we'd read the notebook. (Not that she'd bring it up. I had a feeling "notebook" was going to be a dirty word for awhile.)

Kristy cleared her throat. "Well," she said in this falsely cheerful voice, "any snacks, Claud?"

Silently Claudia reached behind the pillows on her bed and pulled out a bag of Doritos and a bag of popcorn. She passed the Doritos to Dawn and the popcorn to Kristy. The bags circled the room in opposite directions. No one reached into the bags. No one took so much as a kernel of popcorn, not even Kristy, who had asked about food in the first place.

I guess that had just been something for Kristy to say, that she wasn't really hungry.

And that was when I realized that she — our president, our queen — was as uncomfortable as the rest of us were.

Ring, ring.

Thank heavens. A phone call. I had never been more relieved to hear that sound. Like robots, Dawn answered the phone and Mary Anne scheduled a job for Claudia with the Marshall girls.

Ring, ring.

Another call came in. Then another and another.

At about 5:50, the phone stopped ringing, and Kristy, looking more uncomfortable than ever, said, "All right. I — I have a few things to say about the elections tomorrow."

"We're still going to have them, aren't we?" asked Claudia.

"Of course. But I wanted to figure out a way to avoid ties in the voting. This is what I came up with. First of all, Jessi and Mallory, you'll be voting, as you know."

We nodded.

"There are two reasons for that," Kristy continued. "One, you're club members, so you *should* vote. Two, we need five people voting in order to prevent a lot of ties. I know that sounds confusing, but you'll see what I mean in a few minutes."

90

"Okay," Mal and I said at the same time.

"Next, the voting will be secret. I'll make up ballots with boxes by our names. All we'll have to do is write X's in the boxes. I don't think we can get much more secret than that."

Stony silence greeted Kristy. I frowned. Wasn't anyone else relieved to hear what she'd just said?

Kristy continued anyway. "The last thing," she said, "is that, you, Mary Anne, you, Claudia, you, Dawn, and I—the four of us—will be able to vote in the election for each office except the one we hold. In other words, I can vote in the elections for vice-president, secretary, and treasurer, but not president. The reason for this is that without me, for instance, five people will be choosing from among four people for president. A tie is possible, but not likely. I think we'll avoid a lot of revotes this way."

"Anything else?" asked Dawn from behind her hair.

"No, that about covers it."

"I'll say it does," snapped Claudia.

"What's that supposed to mean?" Kristy replied.

Yeah, I wondered. What *is* that supposed to mean?

"Can I answer?" spoke up Mary Anne. Her

voice was wobbling ever so slightly.

"Be my guest," said Claudia.

Mary Anne drew in a deep breath, probably to control her voice. "Kristy," she began, "have you ever heard of a democracy?"

Sensing an argument, Kristy replied sarcastically, "Why, no. I never have. What is a democracy, Mary Anne?"

Mary Anne tried hard to ignore the tone of Kristy's voice. "In a democracy," she said, "everyone has a say — "

"Which is why we're holding elections," Kristy interrupted, "and why we're all voting in them."

"I don't believe it," Dawn muttered. "She did it again."

"Kristy, would you listen to Mary Anne, please?" said Claudia.

Kristy rolled her eyes. Then she turned her gaze on Mary Anne and waited.

"In a democracy," Mary Anne began again, "everyone has a say in running the country. This club should be a democracy, too, Kristy, and the members should have a say in running things. In other words, you should have consulted us about the voting — about the ballots and the way the elections will be run."

Kristy blushed. I really thought she was going to apologize, but Dawn cut her off.

"But *nooooo*," Dawn said sarcastically. "You just barge ahead and do whatever seems right to you. You, you, you. You never think of what other people might want or feel."

It is not a good idea to make absolute statements like that — you *never*, *no one* does, *everybody* does. I have learned this the hard way. If I say to my mother, "But Mama, *everyone* is wearing them," she'll reply, "*Every*one? Your grandfather? Squirt?" You know, that sort of thing.

So naturally Kristy pounced on the "you never think" part of what Dawn had said. "I *never* think of other people? What about when Claudia broke her leg and wanted to quit the club. Didn't I help her through that? I even helped her figure out what was wrong. And what about — "

"But Kristy," said Mary Anne in a small voice, "so many times you just don't think. You just don't . . . " Mary Anne's wavery voice finally broke and she burst into tears.

Dawn jumped to her feet. "Oh, that is nice, Kristy. That is really nice. Now look what you did."

"Look what *I* did?! I didn't do that! Mary Anne cries all the time. She does it by herself."

Dawn didn't answer. She walked out of Claudia's room in a huff.

"Be back here at four o'clock tomorrow," Kristy shouted after her. She looked at the rest of us. "You, too," she added. "This meeting is adjourned."

Mary Anne didn't move from her place on the bed, and Claud edged toward her, looking sympathetic. Mallory and I waited for Kristy to leave. Then we left, too. We walked slowly down the stairs.

When we were outside, I said, "Well, was the meeting as bad as you thought it would be?"

"Yup," replied Mallory. "How about you?"

"Worse. It was worse. Do you have a good feeling about tomorrow?"

"Not really. Do you?"

"No. Well, 'bye, Mal."

"'Bye, Jessi."

On Saturday morning I woke up with butterflies in my stomach. I felt just like I do on
the morning of a dance recital. Nervous, nervous, nervous. What on earth would happen at
the special meeting that afternoon? I lay in bed
and worried.

It was funny. I'd only been living in Stoneybrook, Connecticut, for a few months, but the
Baby-sitters Club had become extremely important to me. Maybe that was because it was
the first place here, besides Mallory's house,
where I'd felt completely accepted; where I'd
felt it truly didn't matter that I'm black.

If the club were to break up — if the girls
were to get so mad at each other that they
decided not to continue it — what would happen? I knew I'd still have Mallory, and I knew
I'd still be friendly with the other girls, but it
wouldn't be the same. Not to mention that I

love baby-sitting and I'd miss all the jobs I get through the club.

I heaved a deep sigh, trying to make the butterflies in my stomach calm down. I rolled over. At last I sat up. Maybe, I thought, if I stay in bed I can make time stop, and four o'clock will never arrive. Unfortunately, I'm too old to believe in things like that anymore.

I got out of bed, put some clothes on, and went downstairs. But I didn't go into the kitchen for breakfast. Instead, I checked my watch, decided it wasn't too early for a phone call, and dialed Mallory's number.

I sprawled on the couch in the den.

"Hello?" said a small voice on the other end of the phone.

"Hi . . . Claire?" (The voice sounded like Mallory's five-year-old-sister.)

"Yeah. Is this Jessi?"

"Yup. How are you?"

"Fine. I lost a tooth! And guess what — after *I* lost it, the *Tooth Fairy* lost it."

"She did? How do you know?"

"'Cause I found some money under my pillow and I found the tooth on the floor. The Tooth Fairy must have dropped it after she left the money."

I managed not to laugh. "I guess even the

Tooth Fairy makes mistakes," I said to Claire. "Listen, can I talk to Mallory, please?"

"Sure," answered Claire. "Mallory-silly-billy-goo-goo! Phone for you!"

A few moments later, I heard Mallory's voice. "Hello?"

"Hi, it's me."

"Hi, Jessi. How long did you have to talk to Claire?"

"Just for a few minutes."

"That's good. She's in one of her silly moods, in case you couldn't tell."

I laughed. Then, "So," I said, "are you ready for this afternoon?"

"I hope so."

"What do you think is going to happen?"

"You know, I really don't have any idea."

"Do you know who you're going to vote for?" I asked.

"I've been trying not to think about it," Mal told me. "And I tried so hard that I really haven't thought about it, and now I don't know who to vote for."

"Oh. I just don't know who to vote for, period."

Mal sighed.

I sighed.

"Well," I said finally, "I better get going. I

have a lot to do before the meeting. The Mancusis come home tomorrow, so today I want to make sure everything is perfect at their house. I've got to walk the dogs and feed the animals as usual, but I also want to clean out some of the cages, change the litter in the cats' box, that sort of thing."

"Okay. Will you come by for me again this afternoon? It'd be nice to walk to the meeting together," said Mallory.

"Sure," I replied. "I'll see you around quarter to four."

We said good-bye and hung up, and then I wandered into the kitchen, where I found my mother and Squirt. "'Morning," I said.

"'Morning, honey."

"Where are Daddy and Becca?"

"Your father went into the office for the morning, and Becca's gone over to Charlotte's house."

I nodded. I sat down in front of Squirt's high chair and made faces at him. "Mama?" I said after awhile.

My mother looked up from the recipe card she was reading. "Yes, honey? Aren't you going to eat breakfast this morning? Everyone else has eaten already."

"I'll eat," I replied, "but I have to ask you about something first."

Mama could tell it was important. She sat down next to me at the table. "What is it, honey?"

As best I could, I explained to her what was going on in the Baby-sitters Club. I told her everything — how Kristy can be bossy sometimes, that the other girls are upset, and what might happen at the elections that afternoon.

"Go-bler?" said Squirt from his high chair. He was playing with a set of plastic keys and two red rings.

"Jessi," said Mama, "I think you want me to tell you how to vote, don't you?"

"Well, yes," I answered. "I mean, even just a hint or something."

"But I can't give you answers. You have to make up your own mind. I will give you one piece of advice, though."

"Okay."

"Vote for the person you honestly think is best suited for each office. Don't worry about anything else."

"All right. Thanks, Mama."

I ate my breakfast, feeling somewhat let down. My mother always has the answers. Why couldn't she tell me who to vote for? But I knew there was no point in asking her again. I would just have to figure things out for myself, and I would have plenty of time to think while I worked at the Mancusis'.

The first thing I did was walk Pooh Bear, Cheryl, and Jacques. It was late morning and the dogs were frantic to get outside. I snapped their leashes on and led them to the front door. As soon as it was opened a crack, Pooh Bear pushed her way through. The dogs tried to bound across the front lawn while I was still trying to lock the Mancusis' door.

"Hold on!" I yelled.

I locked the door, and the dogs pulled me to the street. We took a wild walk, racing past people, bicycles, and mailboxes. At last the dogs slowed down, and I relaxed a little.

I decided to think about the elections. I would consider one office at a time, starting with treasurer. Dawn, I thought, made a good treasurer. She always collected our dues, she always remembered to pay Charlie, she always let us know when the treasury was getting low. But if she didn't like the job, then . . . well, Claudia certainly couldn't be treasurer. She's terrible at math. Mary Anne's okay at it, but she was so good as secretary. That left Kristy. Somehow, I just couldn't see her as treasurer of the Baby-sitters club.

This isn't getting me anywhere, I thought as I walked the dogs back to the Mancusis'.

I decided to try a different office. Vice-president. Claudia really was the perfect vice-president, what with her own phone and her own phone number. But, okay, she was tired of the job. So let's see. Kristy could be our vice-president, but how was she going to answer all the calls that come in at nonmeeting times? She couldn't. Not unless we moved club headquarters to her house. Maybe she could ask her mother and stepfather for her own phone. . . . That sounded like an awful lot of trouble to go to, just to switch offices in the club.

I couldn't solve that problem, so I put the election dilemma aside while I tended to the animals. I let the dogs back in the house and fed them. Then I changed their water. They ate quickly (and messily) and ran off. I cleaned up their area of the kitchen.

Then I moved on to the cats. Since they were in the living room, sleeping, I cleaned up their dishes and placemats first. I set their food out. I cleaned their litter box, found the Mancusis' Dustbuster, and vacuumed up the stray kitty litter that was strewn across the floor.

I worked very hard. I took care of the birds

and the bird cage, the rabbits and their hutch, and the fish and aquarium.

Time for the hamsters. I leaned over and peered into their cage. The fat one in the corner suddenly woke up and looked back at me with bright eyes.

"Why are you all alone?" I asked him. I stuck my finger in the cage, intending to stroke the hamster, but he lunged for me. I pulled my hand back just in time. "Whoa! What's wrong with you?" I exclaimed. I paused. I realized I had just said, "What's wrong with you?" A cold feeling washed over me. Something *was* wrong with the hamster. Maybe he had broken a bone. Maybe that's why he didn't want to be with the others and why he was bad-tempered.

Whatever was wrong had been wrong all week. It had been wrong since the Mancusis left, maybe even before that. The Mancusis hadn't noticed for some reason, but I had. I'd noticed right away. Why hadn't I done anything about it? What would the Mancusis think if they came back and I pointed out the hamster, saying he'd been sick or hurt all week, and then admitted that I hadn't done anything for him? That certainly wasn't very responsible. If I were baby-sitting and one of the kids got sick or broke a bone, I'd call his parents or his doctor or an ambulance. Well, I certainly wasn't going to call the Mancusis long distance about a maybe-sick hamster . . . but I could take the hamster to the vet.

I grabbed the phone and dialed my number. My mother answered.

"Mama!" I cried. "One of the hamsters is very sick. He sleeps in the corner by himself, and he's getting fatter and fatter, and just now he almost bit me. I think he might have a broken bone. Anyway, I noticed something was wrong last weekend and I don't know why I didn't do anything, but I didn't, and — "

"Jessi, honey, slow down," Mama broke in. "What do you want to do?"

"Take the hamster to the vet. Can you drive me?"

"Of course. Bring the address of the vet with you. And give me a few minutes to get Squirt ready. Your father's still at work. Oh, and please be careful with the hamster, especially since he's biting."

"Okay," I replied, calming down a little. "Thanks, Mama. You know which house is the Mancusis', don't you?"

Mama said she did, so we got off the phone. I was just about to figure out how we were going to take the hamster to the vet, when something occurred to me. I looked at my watch. Two-thirty. The special meeting of the Baby-sitters Club was supposed to start in an hour and a half.

I would never make it.

CHAPTER 12

I couldn't worry about the meeting, not just then, anyway. I had to get the hamster ready for the trip to the vet. What could I carry him in? I ran into the Mancusis' garage and found a stack of cardboard boxes. Among them was a shoe box. Perfect, I thought.

I filled the shoe box with shavings and carried it inside. Then I had to figure out how to get the hamster into the shoe box. I didn't want to touch him in case he was hurting. Finally I cleaned out an empty dog-food can, made sure there were no rough edges, placed some treats in it, put it in the hamster cage right next to the fat hamster — and he crawled in! Then I moved the can into the box. We were all set.

The hamster crawled back out of the can and quickly settled down in the box. He didn't try to get out. Even so, I punched some holes in the lid of the box, planning to bring it with me. You never know what might happen, so it's always best to be prepared.

Beep, beep.

That must be Mama, I thought.

I grabbed the box and my jacket and went outside, being careful not to jostle the box. The Mancusis' house key was in my pocket. I remembered to lock their front door.

"Thanks, Mama!" I cried, as I slid into the front seat of her car.

Behind me, Squirt was strapped into his car seat. He was babbling away.

"Let's see this little guy," said Mama.

I removed the lid and held out the box.

"He seems quiet," commented Mama, "but — "

"He's been just like this all week," I interrupted her.

"Okay, then. We better be on our way. Where's the Mancusis' vet?"

I gave her the address. Then I sat back. I felt relieved just to be doing something.

"Broo-broo-broo-broo," sang Squirt as we drove along.

We pulled into the parking lot of the veterinary offices, and I put the lid back on the box. No telling what we would find when we got inside. Well, it was a good thing I did. The waiting room was a madhouse. Mama stepped out of the car carrying Squirt and a bunch of

106

his toys, and I stepped out with the hamster in the box. When I opened the door to the vet's office I was surprised. I'd never been to a vet because we've never had a pet, so I don't know what I thought the waiting room would be like, but . . .

For starters, it was noisy. Most of the people were sitting there with dogs or cats. The cats were safely in carrying cases, except for a Siamese on a leash. And they were fairly quiet, but two cats — the Siamese and a tabby cat — were yowling loudly. And plenty of the dogs were barking; the little ones with high, sharp yips, the big ones with deep rowfs.

Squirt looked around, taking in the people and animals, and listening to the noise, and his lower lip began to tremble.

Mama patted him on the back. It's okay, Mr. Squirt," she said. "It's just a lot of — "

Suddenly my mother let out a shriek. She pointed at something across the room. I looked and saw it, too.

It was a snake. And not just a little garter snake like Barney, either. Some great big kind of snake was draped around the neck of a boy who looked as if he were about fourteen years old.

"Oh, my . . ." my mother started to say.

She looked like she might faint, so I tried to

figure out how to catch both her and Squirt without squishing the hamster, if she did.

But she didn't. Thank goodness.

And from across the room the boy said politely, "Don't worry. He's just a boa constrictor. He's not poisonous or anything. Sorry he scared you."

My mother smiled at him, but headed for seats as far from the boy as possible. She sat Squirt safely in her lap. "All right, honey," she said to me, "you better go tell the receptionist about your hamster and explain why you don't have an appointment."

"Okay." I carried the hamster across the waiting room, skirting around the boy with the snake, and stepped up to the desk. I placed the box on the desk and opened it.

"Yes?" said the receptionist.

"Hi," I began. "My name is Jessi Ramsey. I'm pet-sitting for the Mancusis this week and one of their hamsters is sick."

"Oh, the Mancusis," said the woman. She seemed to remember the name. I realized that with all their animals, they must have to go to the vet fairly often. "What seems to be the trouble?"

"Well, it's just that he doesn't sleep with the other hamsters and he's very bad-tempered."

I edged the box forward and the woman peered in at the hamster.

"Fat, isn't he?" she commented.

"Yes," I replied. "In fact, he's fatter than he was a week ago. I think maybe he's in pain. Something just doesn't seem right."

The woman nodded. "Okay. If you're worried, it's better to have things checked out. I have to tell you, though, that because you don't have an appointment, and because this isn't an emergency, you might have a long wait. It's hard to tell. There are five doctors in today, which is a lot, but there are also a lot of animals waiting."

"That's okay," I told her. "Just as long as he gets checked." I started to stroke the hamster's head before I replaced the lid on the box, but thought better of it. Then I made my way back to Mama.

I was beginning to feel awfully nervous. I checked my watch. Two forty-five. A quarter to three. Our special meeting would start in a little over an hour. Could I possibly make it? Was there any way?

I sat down next to Mama and tried hard not to bite my nails.

Then Squirt leaned over from his place on Mama's lap and said, "Pockita?" which is his way of asking to play patty-cake. We played patty-cake until a girl about Becca's age came into the waiting room with her father. She was holding a kitten, and she headed for the empty seats next to Mama. Her father spoke to the receptionist.

"What an adorable kitten," said my mother as the girl settled herself in a seat.

Immediately the girl stood up again. "Her name is Igga-Bogga," she said. She offered Igga-Bogga to us, and Mama and I took turns holding her, while Squirt patted her.

Igga-Bogga was skinny. And she was pure white, not a patch or a stripe or even a hair of another color anywhere. If she were my cat, I would have named her Misty or Clouds or Creampuff.

I was about to mention those names to the girl, when she spoke up again. "Guess what. It's so sad. Igga-Bogga is deaf."

"Deaf!" I cried.

The girl nodded. "That happens sometimes with white cats."

Her father joined us and he and Mama began talking about white cats being deaf. I looked at my watch. Three-ten. Less than an hour until the special meeting. What could I do? The hamster was my responsibility, my sitting responsibility. If I were baby-sitting on a weekday afternoon and the parents didn't come home and I had a club meeting to go to — well, I'd just have to miss the meeting, wouldn't I? Sitting responsibilities come first. So right now, a sick hamster came first.

I knew I was right, yet I started tapping my fingers and jiggling my feet. Oh, I *hate* being late and missing events I'm supposed to go to, and I *especially* hate upsetting Kristy.

"Miss Ramsey?" It was the receptionist.

My head snapped up. "Yes," I said. "I'm right here."

I picked up the hamster and his box and got to my feet. Next to me, Mama gathered up Squirt and his toys.

I checked my watch for the umpteenth time. Three-thirty! How did it get to be three-thirty? I would have to call Kristy as soon as I could safely step out of the doctor's office.

A nurse led Mama and Squirt and me through a doorway, down a corridor, and into an examining room.

"Hi, there. I'm Doctor West," said a friendly looking man wearing a white lab coat. He stuck his hand out.

Mama and I shook it, and I introduced us.

"So you've got one of the Mancusi pets here?" said Dr. West when the introductions were over. "Let me take a look."

While Dr. West examined the hamster, I ducked into the waiting room to use the pay phone I'd seen there. First I called Kristy.

". . . so I'm not going to be able to make the meeting," I finished up after I'd told her the story. "I'm really sorry."

"No problem," Kristy replied easily. "You did the right thing."

"I did?" I said. "Even though it's a hamster?"

"The hamster is your sitting charge," said Kristy. "Pets, kids, it doesn't matter. You're being responsible. That's what matters."

"Thanks, Kristy."

"Listen, I'll call the others and tell them the meeting has been postponed. We'll try to arrange it for eleven o'clock tomorrow morning, but call me tonight to check on the time."

"Okay," I said. "Thanks again, Kristy."

I hung up the phone, then dropped in another coin and called Mal to explain why I wouldn't be stopping by her house to pick her up.

When that was done, I returned to Dr. West's office. I found him and my mother grinning.

"What?" I said. "Why are you smiling?"

"Because," answered Mama, "your hamster isn't a he, he's a she. And *she* is pregnant!"

"I'd say she's going to have her babies within the next twenty-four hours," added Dr. West.

112

"You were lucky you didn't touch her today. A pregnant hamster should not be handled." Dr. West instructed me to transfer the other hamsters to a separate cage so the mother could be alone with her babies after giving birth. "And don't handle her at all," he said again. "A pregnant hamster is very delicate. Put her back in her cage by lowering the box inside it and letting her crawl out."

"Okay," I replied. Then I thanked Dr. West.

I rode back to the Mancusis' in high spirits. "Just think," I said to Mama. "The hamster is a girl, not a boy, and she's going to have babies! I'll have to give her a name. I want to be able to call her something."

Mama dropped me off and Squirt waved to me from the car window."

"Good-bye!" I called. " 'Bye, Squirt. Thank you for helping me, Mama. I'll be home as soon as I walk the dogs again and do the afternoon chores."

Mama beeped the horn as she drove down the street.

I ran to the Mancusis' garage before I did anything else. There I found the aquarium we had used to capture Barney. I poured shavings into it and added some food and a spare water bottle, and gently moved the hamsters into it. Then, even more gently, I set the shoe box in the old cage and let the pregnant hamster crawl out.

"What should I call you?" I asked aloud as she settled into her nest in the corner of the cage. "Maybe Suzanne. I always liked that name. . . . No. Suzanne is dumb for a hamster. Chipper? Nah, too cute. And it sounds like a boy's name. Sandy? You are sand-colored. Nah, that's boring. After lots of thinking, I decided to call her Misty, which is what I would name a white kitten if I had one. The hamster wasn't anywhere near white, but I decided that didn't matter. Misty was a good name.

I went home feeling excited. When I came back in the morning, Misty would be a mother!

CHAPTER 13

Sunday morning I woke up super-early. I had a lot to do at the Mancusis' before I left for Claudia's. I had to walk the dogs, feed the dogs and cats, and finish the chores I had begun the day before. And of course I wanted to check on Misty and her babies.

I ran straight for Misty as soon as I'd closed the Mancusis' door behind me. When I reached the kitchen, though, I slowed down and tiptoed inside. I peeked into Misty's cage.

Nothing.

Just Misty and her nest and a pile of shavings.

"Oh, you didn't have them yet," I said, feeling disappointed. I began to wonder if Dr. West had been wrong. Then what? Well, the Mancusis would be home in the afternoon. I would tell them the story and let them decide what to do. At least Misty had been to a doctor.

Besides, worrywart, I told myself, Dr. West said the babies would be born in the next twenty-four hours. There were about seven more hours to go until the twenty-four were up.

So I left Misty to herself, walked the dogs, fed them and the cats, finished the cleaning, and then . . . took off for our special club meeting. I dropped by Mallory's house on the way, since we were still planning to arrive at Claudia's together.

Mallory was waiting on her porch steps. "Hi!" she called when she spotted me.

"Hi," I replied.

Mallory ran across her front lawn. "Did the hamster have her babies yet?" she asked breathlessly. (I'd told Mal everything the night before.)

I shook my head. "Not yet. I wish she had. I wanted her to have them before the Mancusis get back."

"Maybe we could check on her after the meeting," suggested Mal.

"Oh! That's a good idea. We could *all* come."

Mal made a face at the thought, but the only thing she said was, "Do you know who you're going to vote for?"

I nodded my head slowly. "I think so. I probably won't know for sure until I'm actually voting, but right now I *think* I know."

"Funny," said Mal. "I feel the same way. . . .

Should we say who we're going to vote for?"

"No," I replied. "Better not. We should go ahead with what we've planned on. If we say anything, we might change each other's minds."

"Okay."

A few more minutes and Mal and I had reached the Kishis' house. We looked at each other.

"Dum da-dum dum," sang Mal ominously.

I laughed — or tried to.

Mal opened the door. We went inside and straight up to Claud's room. Kristy was already there, busily sorting through some slips of paper.

"Hi, you guys," Claud greeted us.

"Hi," we replied, settling into our places on the floor.

"What — " Claud started to say, but she was interrupted by the arrival of Mary Anne and Dawn, both looking a little sleepy.

When everyone was sitting in her usual spot, Kristy surprised us by beginning the meeting with, "Tell us about the hamster, Jessi."

I jerked to attention. I'd been preparing for the voting. Now I had to switch gears. "Well," I said, "this is good news. The hamster isn't sick — "

"Oh, that's wonderful!" cried Dawn. "So it was a false alarm?"

117

"Not exactly," I answered. "The hamster turns out to be a she. By the way, I'm calling her Misty for the time being. And Misty is . . . " (I looked at Mal, dragging out the suspense.)

"Yes?" shrieked Mary Anne.

" . . . Going to have babies!" I exclaimed. "Probably lots of them. Doctor West said hamsters usually give birth to six to twelve young. Those were his exact words. And it should happen any minute now, because yesterday afternoon he said it would happen within the next twenty-four hours."

"That is so exciting!" squealed Dawn.

"Babies!" exclaimed Mary Anne.

"Lots of them!" added Claudia.

"The Mancusis will be thrilled!" cried Kristy.

For a moment, I felt as if I were in a regular club meeting, back before we had started fighting all the time. Then Kristy said, "When the meeting is over, maybe we could go to the Mancusis' and see how Misty is doing." (Mal elbowed me.) "But right now," she went on, "we have a job to do."

I watched the faces of the other club members turn from happy and expectant to worried and uncertain.

Kristy organized the pile of papers before her into a neat stack. "Now," she said, "I've made those special ballots, just like I said I would. Each piece of paper is headed with the name of one of the offices. Below that are the names of the four officers. All you have to do is make an X in the box by the name of the person you'd like to see in the office. Okay?"

The rest of us nodded our heads.

"Great," said Kristy. "Let's start with treasurer." She handed blank ballots to Mary Anne, Claudia, Mal, and me, and then gave one to herself.

"Everyone votes except Dawn," she reminded us.

Mary Anne raised her hand. "Uh, Kristy," she said timidly, "I'm — I'm really sorry, but I have to say something about that."

"Yeah?" replied Kristy.

"Well, it's just — it's just that, for instance, Dawn might not want to be the treasurer anymore, but maybe she's got a good idea about who the new treasurer should be. Who would know that better than Dawn? I understand what you said about ties, but I think we should *all* get to vote. If there's a tie, we'll have a revote. If we have to have too many revotes, then we'll think about letting only five people vote. But we should vote with six first."

I have to hand it to both Kristy and Mary

Anne. Kristy listened to Mary Anne's suggestion and took it seriously, and Mary Anne didn't cry.

"Okay," said Kristy, "let's vote on what Mary Anne said. Nothing fancy, just a show of hands. All those in favor of letting everyone vote in the elections, raise your hand."

Five hands went up. (Guess which one didn't?)

"Great. I guess we're all voting," said Kristy. "Luckily, I made extra ballots, in case of mistakes, so we're ready."

Kristy handed a ballot to Dawn. Then she gave each of us a blue ballpoint pen.

I looked at my ballot, my heart pounding. TREASURER was written across the top. Below it were the names Kristy, Claudia, Mary Anne, and Dawn. A box had been drawn to the left of each name.

I paused for a moment, but I knew what I was going to do. I picked up the pen and made an X next to Dawn's name. She was the best treasurer I could think of. But I was pretty sure she was going to kill me when she found out what I'd done (*if* she found out). The business of elections had started because the girls were tired of their old jobs and wanted a change. Well, too bad. I couldn't help that. Dawn was my choice for treasurer.

I glanced around Claudia's room and tried to measure the tension in the air. Funny, but there didn't seem to be much of it. The club members were busy voting, that was true, but more than that, no one was arguing. I think we were relieved that election day had finally come, no matter what it would bring.

When everyone had voted, we folded our papers in quarters and gave them back to Kristy, who carefully put them in a pile. Then she handed out the ballots for secretary, a few minutes later the ones for vice-president, and last of all, the ones for president. Each time, I voted quickly, knowing just what I had to do.

After the ballots for the office of president had been collected, Kristy said, "Let me just take a fast look through the ballots. If I see a lot of problems, I'll ask you guys to help me count."

Kristy picked up the ballots for treasurer and glanced at them.

"Hmm," she said.

She looked at the ballots for secretary.

"Huh," she said.

She looked at the ballots for vice-president.

"Well," she said,

And then she looked at the ballots for president.

She burst out laughing.

"What *is* it?" cried Claudia.

"You will not believe this," Kristy told us. "I hardly believe it myself."

"But?" Dawn prompted her.

"But we unanimously voted ourselves back into our old offices! We all voted for Dawn for treasurer — even Dawn did. We all voted for Mary Anne for secretary — even Mary Anne did. And so on. You guys even voted for me for president."

There was a moment of silence. Then every single one of us began to laugh. Dawn laughed so hard she cried. Kristy laughed so hard I thought she was going to fall out of the director's chair. And all the time we were laughing I was thinking. Now I understand what Mama meant when I asked her to tell me how to vote. She meant (but wanted me to figure out for myself) that we shouldn't worry about who thought what or who would be mad or who would laugh about our choices. The purpose of an election is to vote the best person into an office. Period. And we realized that. We realized that the best people were already *in* the offices and we wanted to keep them there.

The laughter was fading, and Kristy straightened up in her chair. "What happened?" she asked us.

I raised my hand, heart pounding. I usually

122

don't speak up much in meetings, but I was pretty sure I had the right answer this time. "I think," I began, "that we realized the best people had already been elected to the offices. I mean, Dawn is organized, but Mary Anne is even more organized, and Dawn is better at keeping figures straight, so Dawn's the perfect treasurer and Mary Anne's the perfect secretary. It would be tough to name anyone but Claudia as vice-president, and Kristy, you really deserve to be president since the club *was* your idea."

Everyone was looking at me and nodding. I added one more thing. "Can you live with the results of the election?" I asked the four officers. "You were pretty fed up with your jobs a little while ago."

"I can do it," said Dawn quickly, and the others agreed. "There are parts of my job that I don't like, but I guess I know I'm best at this job. And it would really mess up the club to start switching things around."

My friends were smiling again. Then Kristy's smile faded. "I have something to say," she began. "Okay, we realized we were in the right offices. But I have to admit that right office or not, I have been too bossy. Maybe I do come up with good ideas, but I shouldn't force them on you. It's — it's just this thing

123

with Charlie, I guess. You know something? I don't think he's acting like a big shot because he'll be in college. I think he's worried that he won't get into college, and he's taking his worries out by bossing me around. Then I take things out by bossing everyone else around. Jackie Rodowsky pointed that out to me. I mean, he pointed out that I was bossing him around. So I'm going to try to be better. No more forcing rules on you guys. When I get a new idea we'll vote on it, okay?"

"All *right!*" cried Claudia.

So the meeting ended happily. And when Kristy suggested again that we go over to the Mancusis', everyone wanted to see Misty. And Mal didn't mind. She was glad our club was a club again.

So was I.

CHAPTER 14

We arrived at the Mancusis' just before twelve-thirty. Mr. and Mrs. Mancusi wouldn't be home until later in the afternoon.

I unlocked the front door, feeling like a nervous grandmother. How was Misty doing? Had she had her babies yet? How long did a hamster take to have babies anyway?

"Follow me," I said. "Misty's in the kitchen." (For some reason I was whispering.)

I tiptoed into the kitchen, and Mal, Kristy, Claudia, Dawn, and Mary Anne tiptoed after me. I paused in the doorway, listening for unusual sounds, although what sounds a baby hamster might make I cannot imagine.

At last I looked into Misty's cage. There she was, a golden brown body. . . . And there were four tiny pink bodies! They looked like jelly beans. They had no hair at all and their eyes were closed.

I gasped. "She's had them!" I whispered. "Misty had four babies!"

Everyone crowded around the cage.

"Make that five," said Kristy softly.

"Oh, EW!" exclaimed Mary Anne, backing away. "That is disgusting."

"No, it isn't. It's beautiful," said Dawn.

"Five babies. I wonder what the Mancusis will name them," said Mal. "I wonder if there will be more than five."

"*I* wonder if they'll keep them," said Claudia. "Do you think they will, Jessi?"

I shrugged. "I don't think another cageful of hamsters would be much extra work."

"Is there anything we're supposed to be doing for Misty or her babies?" asked Mary Anne, even though she wouldn't look in the cage anymore.

"I don't think so," I replied. "Doctor West said to be sure not to touch the babies, even if I think one is dead. He said Misty will know what to do. He said the babies — actually he called them pups — will get scattered all around the cage, but that Misty will take care of them."

We watched for a few more minutes. Finally I said, "Maybe we should leave Misty alone. If I were in a cage giving birth to hamsters, I wouldn't want six faces staring at me."

"If you were in a cage giving birth to hamsters," said Mal, "you'd be a miracle of science."

"No, she'd be in a zoo!" said Kristy.

We left the kitchen and wandered into the living room.

"Aw," said Claudia, "who's this guy?"

"That's Powder. Hey, do you want to meet the rest of the Mancusis' animals? I mean, do all of you want to meet them?"

"Thanks, but I've already met Barney," Mary Anne replied drily.

"There are other animals here, though, and Kristy and Dawn haven't been over before. Also — "

"Where's the beef? Where's the beef?"

"Aughh!" shrieked Kristy. "Someone's in the house! We're not alone!"

Dawn began to laugh. "It's a bird, isn't it?"

I nodded.

"We used to have one," Dawn told us. "A long time ago. I think it was a parakeet. His name was Buzz. He could say a few words. But the funniest thing he ever did was fly into a bowl of mashed potatoes."

"Dawn!" I exclaimed. "Is that true?"

"Cross my heart," she replied.

It must have been true.

We were all laughing hysterically and couldn't calm down for awhile. When we finally did, we checked on Misty (six babies) and then I let Kristy and Dawn meet the animals.

"Hey, Mary Anne!" called Kristy as we were leaving the sun porch. "Where's the lid to Barney's cage?"

Mary Anne began screaming without even turning around to look at the cage. If she had turned around, she would have seen that the lid was on tightly. Kristy had to confess her joke in order to keep Mary Anne from running home.

At last I suggested that we take Cheryl, Jacques, and Pooh Bear on their afternoon walk. I thought my friends might enjoy that.

So we took the dogs on a long walk. When we returned I said, "Well, you guys, I hate to kick you out, but I have to feed the animals. And I should probably be the only one here when the Mancusis come home."

"Okay," Kristy answered. "We understand."

My friends left. I was alone in the house, although not for long. The Mancusis would return soon. Even so, I phoned my parents to tell them where I was and why I'd be late. Then I looked in on Misty. *Ten* pups! And they were all gathered around their mother in a big jumbly pile of legs and feet and ears. I guess

Misty had finished giving birth. Now she could tend to her babies.

While I waited for the Mancusis, I found a roll of crepe paper (out in the garage, with all the boxes) and tied a big red bow to each of the dogs' collars.

"You three look lovely," I told them. "You're doggie fashion plates."

"Rowf?" asked Jacques, cocking his head.

"Yes, you're very handsome."

I was about to make bows for the cats when I heard a car pull into the driveway. "Guess who's home!" I called to the dogs.

Of course, they had no idea, but when I ran to the front door, they followed me. I opened the inside door and waved to Mr. and Mrs. Mancusi as they unloaded their luggage from the car. They were surprised to see me, but they smiled and waved back. Then, their arms weighed down with suitcases, they walked to the front door, while I tried to open it for them and hold the dogs back at the same time. It wasn't easy, but we managed.

As soon as the Mancusis were safely inside, I cried, "Guess what! One of the hamsters had babies! . . . Oh, I hope you had a nice vacation."

"My heavens!" exclaimed Mrs. Mancusi.

"One of the hamsters had babies?! How could we have missed a pregnancy? Are the babies okay? Which hamster is it?"

"Everything's fine. Honest," I told them. "I knew something was wrong, well, I knew something was *unusual*, so my mom drove the hamster and me to your vet yesterday. Dr. West looked at her and he told me what to do."

"Oh. . . ." The Mancusis let out a sigh of relief.

"Do you want to see the babies?" I asked.

"Of course," said Mr. Mancusi. He and his wife put down their suitcases and followed me into the kitchen, the dogs bounding joyfully at our sides.

"It's this one," I said. "I moved the other hamsters to the aquarium on the table." I stood back so the Mancusis could look in at Misty.

"Ah, Snicklefritz." Mrs. Mancusi scratched her head. "How did we miss this? I really apologize, Jessi. But I have to congratulate you. You did a terrific job in a difficult situation. We're very grateful to you."

"I guess," added Mr. Mancusi, "that in the excitement when we were trying to get away — our pet-sitter canceling and all — we just didn't notice that Snicklefritz was pregnant."

"Well, everything worked out fine," I spoke

up. "Mis — I mean, Snicklefritz has ten babies."

The Mancusis watched them for a few moments. Then they turned to me. "Thank you again, Jessi," said Mr. Mancusi. "You've been very responsible." He handed me some money — much more than I've gotten paid for any other job.

"Wow!" I cried. "Thanks. . . . Are you sure this isn't too much?"

"Not at all."

"By the way," said Mrs. Mancusi, "do you have any friends who would like a hamster? We'll let the babies go to anyone who will give them good homes — in about three weeks, that is. After the pups are weaned."

"*Any*one?" I repeated. "Gosh, we've never had a pet. I'm sure my sister Becca would like one. *I'd* like one. And, well, I'll spread the word. I bet I can help you find lots of homes!"

I couldn't believe it. A pet! Would Mama and Daddy let us have one? I had no idea. Neither Becca nor I had ever asked for a pet.

I headed for the front door. The dogs followed me.

"Good-bye, Cheryl. Good-bye, Jacques. Good-bye, Pooh Bear," I said.

The Mancusis were right behind the dogs. "They really like you," Mr. Mancusi said. "Oh,

131

and *we* like their bows. Very spiffy."

I smiled. "Well, thanks again. If you ever need another pet-sitter, let me know. And I'll find out about homes for the baby hamsters. I promise."

The Mancusis and I called good-bye to each other and then I ran to my house. I was just about bursting with my news — Snicklefritz's babies and homes for them. Maybe one would become our first pet.

"Mama! Daddy!" I shouted as I burst through our front door.

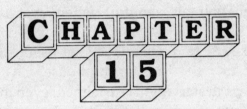

CHAPTER 15

The Braddocks were back. Ballet school was in session again. My life had returned to normal.

I missed the Mancusi animals, but I could probably visit them any time I wanted to. I'm sure I'd be allowed to walk the dogs from time to time.

Anyway, since my life was back to normal, I baby-sat for the Braddocks the next day, Monday, and then tore over to Claudia's house. I reached it a full five minutes before the meeting was supposed to start. I even beat Kristy, but of course she's at the mercy of Charlie, so she doesn't have a lot of control over when she arrives.

Claudia and Dawn were there, though.

"Hi, you guys!" I said as I entered Claud's room.

"Hello," they replied, smiling, and Dawn added, "You sound awfully happy."

"Glad to be back at the Braddocks'?" asked Claudia.

"Yes," I answered, "but it's more than that. I'll tell you all about it when everybody's here."

"Okay," said Claud. "Potato chips, anyone?"

"Oh, I'm starving!" I exclaimed, even though I sort of watch my diet because I have to stay in good shape for dance class.

"Um, can you help me find them?" asked Claud, looking puzzled. "They might be under the bed, but who knows?"

Claudia and Dawn and I dropped to our stomachs and crawled halfway under Claud's bed. A ton of junk had been stashed there — boxes of art supplies, folders of drawings and sketches, magazines for making collages, that sort of thing. And because Claudia is such a poor speller, they were labeled SKECHES or PANTINGS or BURSHES.

I found the potato chips in a box marked CALAGE SUPPLIES.

"Here they are!" I announced.

The three of us crawled out from under the bed, stood up, turned around, and found Kristy, Mallory, and Mary Anne staring at us. We began to laugh — all six of us.

"That was so attractive!" said Kristy. "I hope

I always come to a meeting just in time to see the three of you backing out from under a bed."

"My backside is my best side," replied Dawn, looking serious.

There was more laughter as the members of the Baby-sitters Club settled into their usual places. Kristy climbed into the director's chair. She put her visor on. She stuck a pencil over one ear.

And then she pulled a new checklist out of her pocket, smoothed the creases, and with big, showy sweeps of her arms, tacked it up on the bulletin board over the photos of Claudia and Stacey.

"There," she said with satisfaction.

Claudia, Mary Anne, Dawn, Mallory, and I just stared at her. I guess my mouth was hanging open. Everybody else's was.

"I don't believe it," muttered Claudia, but just when it looked like she might jump to her feet and strangle Kristy, Kristy jumped to *her* feet and ripped the checklist off the bulletin board.

"Now watch this, everyone," she announced. She scrunched up the checklist and threw it in the wastebasket. "'Bye-bye, checklist. That's the last of it. You won't see it or hear about it again."

At first the rest of us didn't know what to do. Then we began to smile.

"You mean that was a joke?" exclaimed Claudia. "Oh, my lord! *Kristy* . . . "

Kristy grinned at us. She looked like the Cheshire Cat reclining in his tree.

Dawn threw a potato chip at her. I think a potato chip war might have started if the phone hadn't rung.

"Oh, no! We haven't done any of our opening business!" cried Kristy. "Dawn hasn't collected dues, I haven't — "

Ring, ring.

Kristy stopped ranting and raving and answered the phone. "Hello, Baby-sitters Club."

We arranged a Saturday afternoon job for me with the Arnold twins. Then Kristy got down to business.

"Dawn?" she said. "Ms. Treasurer?"

"I need your dues," announced Dawn.

Dawn collected the dues while we groaned and complained. "I'll walk out with you after the meeting and pay Charlie," she told Kristy.

"Okay. Thanks. That'll be fine. Maybe that will improve Charlie's mood." Kristy paused. "All right," she continued, "any club business?"

"I have something to ask everyone," I said,

"but it can wait until after the real club business is over."

Kristy nodded. "Anything else?"

The rest of the girls shook their heads.

"Okay," said Kristy. "I'm done. Over to you, Jessi. Oh, by the way, did you all notice that I didn't ask whether you'd read the notebook?"

"Uh, yes," replied Dawn.

"Good. I'm not going to ask anymore. I'll trust you to read it. No questions, no checklists — "

"You'll actually trust us?" exclaimed Mary Anne.

"I'll actually trust you."

The phone rang again, and we arranged another job. When that was taken care of, I said, "Well, guess what. Misty's name turns out to be Snicklefritz and she had *ten* pups yesterday." (Mallory knew this already, since we tell each other everything. But the others hadn't heard.)

"Ten pups!" cried Mary Anne. "What will the Mancusis do with them?"

"Well, that's the rest of my news. The Mancusis are giving them away — to anyone who'll promise the babies a good home. *And* Mama and Daddy said Becca and I can have one! Our first pet! We decided to name our hamster Misty no matter what color it is, and whether it's a boy or a girl."

"Oh, that's great!" cried Mary Anne and Kristy at the same time. (They both have pets.)

"And," I went on, "I'm asking around, finding out if anyone else would like a hamster. How about one of you?"

Claudia shook her head. "They're cute, but I hate cleaning cages."

Mary Anne shook her head. "A hamster wouldn't last a second around Tigger."

Kristy shook her head. "We've got enough pets at our house already."

Dawn shook her head. "I like hamsters, but if I get a pet, I'd like a bigger one. A cat or a dog."

I looked at Mallory. She seemed thoughtful. "We've got ten people in our family," she said slowly, "but no pets. I don't see why we couldn't get one little pet. The younger kids would like a hamster. So would the boys. Well, so would all of us." Mallory dove for the phone. "Mom! Mom!" she cried.

(I could just imagine Mrs. Pike saying, "What on earth is the matter?")

"Mom, the Mancusis are going to give the hamster babies away. In about three weeks, I think." (I nodded.) "Could we have one? It would be a good experience for Claire and Margo. And I think Nicky would like a pet . . . Yeah? . . . I know . . . Okay . . . Okay, thanks! This is great! 'Bye, Mom." Mallory hung up. "We can have one!" she announced. "We'll be getting our first pet, too!"

I have never seen so much excitement.

Then the phone rang and we lined up three jobs.

When the phone rang a fourth time, Mary Anne opened the record book again, and we sat up eagerly. I picked up the receiver. "Hello, Baby-sitters Club," I said.

"Hi," answered a very small voice. "I —This is Jackie Rodowsky. Is Kristy there, please?"

"Sure, Jackie. Hold on," I told him.

I handed the phone to Kristy, whispering, "It's Jackie Rodowsky."

Kristy raised her eyebrows. "Hi, Jackie."

That was all she said, and Jackie burst into tears.

"What's wrong?" she asked him. "What happened? Is your mom home?"

"She's here," Jackie told her. "And I'm okay. I mean, I'm not hurt. But we had our class elections today."

"Oh," said Kristy. "Right. And what happened?"

"I lost. Adrienne beat me. I tried and tried

139

to show the kids that I could take care of Snowball. But I don't think they believed me." Jackie paused. When he started speaking again, his voice was trembling. "I just — just wanted a pet to take care of by myself. That's all."

"Jackie," said Kristy gently, "I'm sorry you lost. I'm sorry the kids wouldn't pay attention to you. Really I am. Sometimes things just work out that way. But listen, could I talk to your mom for a sec, please?" There was a pause while Kristy waited for Mrs. Rodowsky to get on the phone. Then she said, "Hi, Mrs. Rodowsky. This is Kristy Thomas. Jackie told me about the elections today and I was wondering — could he have a pet of his own? I think he wants one, and I know where he could get a free hamster. . . . Yes. . . . Really? Oh, terrific! Could I talk to Jackie again, please?"

So Kristy gave Jackie the good news about his hamster.

"My own? My own hamster?" Jackie shrieked. "Amazing! What will I name it? Is it a boy or a girl? What color is it?"

Kristy couldn't answer his questions, so we arranged for me to take him over to the Mancusis' in a couple of weeks. The hamsters wouldn't be ready to leave their mother yet, but Jackie could look at them and pet them and play with them in order to choose the one that would become his very own. Jackie liked the idea a lot. So he thanked Kristy eleven times and then they got off the phone.

"Well, all's well that ends well," said Kristy.

"Huh?" said Claudia.

"I mean, happy endings everywhere you look. We got our club problems straightened out. The sick hamster turned out to be pregnant, and then she had her babies and they were born without any trouble, and now Jessi and Mallory's families will have their first pets, and Jackie lost the election but he got a hamster. Happy endings."

"Yeah," I said, smiling.

The numbers on Claudia's digital clock turned from 5:59 to 6:00.

"Meeting adjourned," announced our president.

I walked out with Mal. "I wonder," I said, "if I could talk Becca into changing Misty's name to Mancusi."

"Darn!" said Mallory. "That's what I wanted to name our hamster."

"Really?"

"Nah."

We giggled.

"Call you tonight!" I shouted to Mal as we separated.

Best friends have to talk a lot.

About the Author

ANN M. MARTIN did *a lot* of baby-sitting when she was growing up in Princeton, New Jersey. Now her favorite baby-sitting charge is her cat, Mouse, who lives with her in her Manhattan apartment.

Ann Martin's Apple Paperbacks are *Bummer Summer*, *Inside Out*, *Stage Fright*, *Me and Katie (the Pest)*, and all the other books in the Baby-sitters Club series.

She is a former editor of books for children, and was graduated from Smith College. She likes ice cream, the beach, and *I Love Lucy*; and she hates to cook.

Look for #23

DAWN ON THE COAST

Since no phone calls were coming in for the We ♡ Kids Club, we just sat around chatting. Jill and Maggie talked some more about the kids I remembered in our class. Right then an idea began taking seed in my mind. I started to picture myself back in the class, and how easy it would be to slip right back in.

Sunny came back up with the food — guacamole dip and cut-up raw vegetables that she had made earlier in the afternoon.

"All *right*," Jill said, grabbing a carrot stick.

"No calls yet?" Sunny asked.

We shook our heads. The phone hadn't rung once.

Sunny chomped on a celery stick and looked at me.

"It'd be great if you can stay for dinner," she said.

I thought back to all the times in the past that I had had dinner over at Sunny's house.

143

How many times had it been? Probably a thousand. Well, at least a hundred. Sunny's mom and dad were great. When we were younger they always let us be excused from the table as soon as we had finished eating, just so we would have a longer time to play.

"I hope you can stay," Sunny said again, and suddenly something popped into my head.

Maybe I *could* stay. Maybe I could *really* stay. Maybe I didn't have to go back to Connecticut at all, or just go back to get my things. Maybe I could move back in with Dad and Jeff, have my old room back, my old friends, my old school.

It was a strange thought, scary and exciting at the same time. Until then, I had just been having a great time, a *fabulous* time, but it had never occurred to me that I could think about making it last forever (or at least for longer). Now that the thought occurred to me, what was I supposed to do?

Here's some news about other books in The Baby-sitters Club series by Ann M. Martin

#1 Kristy's Great Idea

Kristy thinks the Baby-sitters Club is a great idea. She and her friends Claudia, Stacey, and Mary Anne all love taking care of kids. But nobody counted on crank calls, wild pets, and uncontrollable two-year-olds! Having a Baby-sitters Club isn't easy, but Kristy and her friends won't give up till they get it right!

#2 Claudia and the Phantom Phone Calls

Claudia has been getting some mysterious phone calls when she's out baby-sitting. Could they be from the Phantom Jewel Thief who's operating in the area? Claudia has always liked *reading* mysteries, but she doesn't like it when they *happen* to her!

#3 The Truth About Stacey

The truth about Stacey is her parents want to find a miracle cure for her diabetes. They're making Stacey's life so hard! The other Baby-sitters are busy fighting the Baby-sitters Agency. How can they help Stacey and save the club, too?

#4 Mary Anne Saves the Day

Mary Anne's never been a leader of the Baby-sitters Club. Now there's a big fight among the four friends. It's bad enough when Mary Anne has to eat at the lunch table all alone. But when she has to baby-sit a sick child with no help from her friends — it's time to take charge!

#5 Dawn and the Impossible Three

Poor Dawn! It's not easy being the newest member of the Baby-sitters Club. She's got three impossible kids to take care of. And Kristy thinks things were better *without* Dawn around. It'll take a lot of work to make things run smoothly again, but Dawn's up to the challenge!

#6 Kristy's Big Day

It's a big day for Kristy, all right — she's a bridesmaid in her mother's wedding! And if that's not enough, she and the other Baby-sitters Club members have *fourteen* wedding-guest kids to take care of. Only the Baby-sitters Club could cope with this one!

#7 Claudia and Mean Janine

This summer the Baby-sitters Club is starting a play group in the neighborhood. Claudia can't wait for it to begin — it'll give her some time away from her mean big sister. But then her grandmother has a stroke . . . and the whole summer changes.

#8 Boy-Crazy Stacey

Who needs baby-sitting when there are boys around? Stacey and Mary Anne are mother's helpers at the Jersey shore, and Stacey's mind is on hunky lifeguard Scott. Mary Anne's doing the work of two baby-sitters . . . but how can she tell Stacey that Scott's too old, without breaking Stacey's heart?

#9 The Ghost at Dawn's House

Creaking stairs, noises behind the wall, a secret passage — there must be a ghost at Dawn's house! The Baby-sitters find themselves and one of their charges wrapped up in a mystery. Will they be able to solve it?

#10 Logan Likes Mary Anne!

Quiet, shy Mary Anne has been growing up lately . . . and the Baby-sitters aren't the only ones who've noticed. Logan Bruno likes Mary Anne! He has a dreamy southern accent, he's awfully cute — and he wants to join the Baby-sitters Club. Life in the club has never been this complicated — or this fun!

#11 Kristy and the Snobs

The kids in Kristy's new neighborhood aren't very friendly. In fact they're . . . well, snobs. They laugh at everything — even Kristy's poor old collie, Louie. Kristy's fighting mad. But if anyone can beat a Snob attack, it's the Baby-sitters club. And that's just what they're going to do!

#12 Claudia and the New Girl

Claudia really likes Ashley, the new girl at school. Ashley's the only one who takes Claudia seriously. Soon, Claudia's spending so much time with Ashley that she doesn't have time for baby-sitting — or her old friends. And they don't like it one bit!

148

#13 Good-bye Stacey, Good-bye

There are lots of tears when the Baby-sitters hear the news: Stacey and her family are moving back to New York. The club members can't think of a special enough way to send Stacey off. They want to give her much more than a party. But how do you say good-bye to your best friend?

#14 Hello, Mallory

Mallory Pike has always been good at baby-sitting her younger brothers and sisters. But is she good enough to join the Baby-sitters Club? The club members go overboard giving Mallory baby-sitting tests. Mallory's getting pretty fed up. . . . Maybe she'll just start a baby-sitting business of her own!

#15 Little Miss Stoneybrook . . . and Dawn

Mrs. Pike wants Dawn to help prepare Margo and Claire for the Little Miss Stoneybrook contest. And Dawn wants her charges to win! The only trouble is . . . Kristy, Mary Anne, and Claudia are helping Karen, Myriah, and Charlotte enter the contest, too. And nobody's sure where the competition is fiercer: at the pageant — or at the Baby-sitters Club!

#16 Jessi's Secret Language

Jessi had a hard time fitting in to Stoneybrook. But things got a lot better once she became a member of the Baby-sitters Club! Now Jessi has her biggest challenge yet — baby-sitting for a deaf boy. And in order to communicate with him, Jessi must learn his secret language.

#17 Mary Anne's Bad-Luck Mystery

Mary Anne finds a note in her mailbox. *"Wear this bad-luck charm,"* it says, *"OR ELSE."* Mary Anne's got to do what the note says. But who sent the charm? And why did they send it to Mary Anne? If the Baby-sitters don't solve this mystery soon, their bad luck might never stop!

#18 Stacey's Mistake

Stacey's so excited! She's invited her friends from the Baby-sitters Club down to New York City for a long weekend. But what a mistake! The Baby-sitters are *way* out of place in the big city. Does this mean Stacey can't be the Baby-sitters' friend anymore?

#19 Claudia and the Bad Joke

Claudia's not worried when she hears she has to baby-sit for Betsy, a great practical joker. How much trouble could a little girl cause? *Plenty* . . . and now Claudia might even quit the club. It's time for the Baby-sitters to teach Betsy a lesson. The joke war is on!

#20 Kristy and the Walking Disaster

Kristy's little brother and sister want to play on a softball team, so Kristy starts a ragtag team of her own. With Jackie Rodowsky, the Walking Disaster, playing for them, Kristy's Krushers aren't world champions. But nobody beats them when it comes to team spirit!

#21 Mallory and the Trouble With Twins

Mallory thinks baby-sitting for the Arnold twins will be easy money. They're so adorable! Marilyn and Carolyn may be cute . . . but they're also spoiled brats. It's a baby-sitting nightmare — and Mallory's not giving up!

Dawn's trip to California is better than she could ever imagine. And after one wonderful week, Dawn begins to wonder if she might want to . . . *stay* on the coast with her dad and her brother. Dawn's a California girl at heart — but could she really leave Stoney-brook for good?

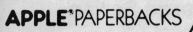

Dawn on the Coast

**Look for these and other books
in the Baby-sitters Club series:**

Dawn on the Coast

Ann M. Martin

AN
APPLE
PAPERBACK

SCHOLASTIC INC.
New York Toronto London Auckland Sydney

Cover art by Hodges Soileau

ISBN 0-590-43900-6

12 11 10 9 8 7 6 5 4 3 2 1   0 1 2 3 4 5/9

Printed in the U.S.A.   28

First Scholastic printing, April 1990

*The author
would like to thank
Jan Carr
for her help
in writing this book.*

CHAPTER 1

Dear Sunshine,

The countdown is on. Only a few days left until you get on that plane and land in beautiful, ~~sunny~~ California. I can't wait to see you, sweetie. And Jeff is so excited, you'd think it was Christmas morning. California, here you come! See you Sunday night at the airport.

Love and a big hug,
Dad

A trip to the West Coast. It was the highlight of my spring, that's for sure. When I got to California, I had an absolutely fantastic time. So how come I ended up feeling so confused? Believe me, there's a lot to tell. And I might as well start at the beginning.

First off, you're probably wondering who Sunshine is. Well, that's me. Of course nobody around here calls me Sunshine. Here in Connecticut they call me by my regular name, Dawn Schafer. But not my dad. He started calling me Sunshine when I was little and, unfortunately, it stuck. Maybe he gave me the name because of my long blonde hair. My hair is so light it's almost the color of cornsilk, and it reaches all the way past my waist. Or maybe Dad gave me the name because I love the sun so much. I really do. I love warm weather and the beach.

I guess I'm just a California girl at heart. After all, that's where I came from. And that Sunday, I was getting to go back for a visit!

I got the postcard from Dad when I came home from school that Thursday afternoon. I still had so much to do, so much to get ready. I dragged my suitcase out of the closet, threw it on the bed, and started to lay out my clothes. I decided to bring my white cotton skirt — I

2

could wear that with anything. And, of course, my bathing suit (a bikini) and my jeans and sneakers. I wasn't sure about my yellow cotton overalls. And would I really need *three* sundresses?

Maybe you're wondering why my dad lives in California and I live in Connecticut. Well, sometimes I wonder, too. Believe me, it's not the way I would've arranged it. But even so, things are working out okay. You see, about a year and a half ago, Mom and Dad got divorced. Dad stayed in our house in California and Mom moved me and my brother, Jeff, here to Stoneybrook, Connecticut. I think Mom wanted to come here because my grandparents live here and it's the town where she grew up. To tell the truth, at first I wasn't the happiest, but then I adjusted. I found myself a best friend, Mary Anne Spier, and I got invited to join the Baby-sitters Club, which is just about the most fun club in the whole wide world.

My brother, Jeff, though, didn't adjust so easily. In fact, he didn't adjust at all. He started getting kind of nasty with me and Mom, and he even started to get in fights at school. It was pretty bad. His teacher kept calling up Mom and I don't think Mom knew what to do. Finally we decided to let Jeff go back to California for awhile. He really just wanted to

3

be back with his friends and live with Dad. I don't think Mom was thrilled with the idea, but she figured she had to let Jeff try it for six months.

Me, I didn't like the idea at all. It was bad enough that Mom and Dad had to get divorced. Already our family was split. But when Jeff left Mom and me, too, it felt like Jeff was up and deserting us. And then another part of me thought, hey, why couldn't *I* be the one to get to move back to California?

Now I'm kind of used to the idea. In my head I understand all the reasons why things are the way they are. But sometimes it does seem strange the way the family has divided up. Boys against the girls. Or West Coast against the East Coast. I love Mom, and she and I get to stay together, but of course I love Dad and Jeff, and I miss them sometimes. And I know they miss us, too.

But Mom is the greatest. She and I have gotten a lot closer through all of this and we've made a whole new life for ourselves. We live in an old, old farmhouse that was built in 1795. No kidding. The rooms are really small and the doorways are so short that tall people have to stoop to get through them. Mom says people used to be shorter in the 1700s.

The best thing about our house, though, is

that it has a secret trapdoor in our barn that leads into a long, dark tunnel. You need a flashlight to walk through. The tunnel leads up into our house and comes out . . . right at the wall to my bedroom! The wall has a special latch that springs open to the touch. Talk about exciting. You should've seen the faces on my friends in the Baby-sitters Club when I showed them.

Maybe I should tell you a little bit about the club. There're six of us in it now, and we also have two associate members. What it is is just what it says, a club for baby-sitters. It was Kristy Thomas's great idea. She's our president. She figured that it would be great if there was a club that all the parents in the neighborhood could use whenever they needed a sitter. That way, they'd be pretty sure of getting someone for the job and they'd only have to make one call. Great for them, and great for us, too, since we're all super sitters and we love the work. Leave it to Kristy to come up with a good business idea. And leave it to Kristy to organize the whole thing.

What we do is this: Three times a week we have meetings in the afternoon. We meet at Claudia's house because she has a phone in her room . . . with her very own number! Claudia is Claudia Kishi and she's our vice-

5

president. Claudia is about as different from Kristy as you can get. Kristy is kind of small for her age and is a real tomboy. She always wears the same thing — jeans, a turtle neck, and sneakers. But not Claudia. You can always count on Claudia to be wearing some really unusual outfit, like a white jumpsuit with a wide purple belt and purple high-top sneakers. Claudia's Japanese-American and she's got beautiful, long, shiny black hair that she fixes differently practically every day. She loves art, too, so she has a really interesting sense of style.

After those two, there's Mary Anne Spier, our club secretary, and, as I said, she's my best friend in Stoneybrook. Mary Anne lives alone with her father because her mother died when she was a baby. Her father's been kind of strict with her and a lot of people think Mary Anne's quiet. It's true, she can be shy sometimes. But wouldn't you know it, she was the first one of us to get a boyfriend!

Speaking of boyfriends, when I first moved to Stoneybrook and became friends with Mary Anne, we found out something really exciting — my mom and Mary Anne's dad used to go out together in high school! Then, for a while, they even started going out together again! Imagine. My mom going with my best friend's dad. Mary Anne and I were in seventh heaven. We were hoping our parents might even get *married* to each other. That would've made Mary Anne and me sisters! Now things have cooled off a little, but as Mary Anne says, you never know. . . .

So that's part of the club. Kristy, Claudia, Mary Anne, and I are all in eighth grade, so we are *very* experienced sitters. We used to have another eighth-grade member, Stacey, but she moved back to New York City, which was really sad, so we had to get someone to fill Stacey's place in the club. That's where Mallory and Jessi come in. Mallory and Jessi are our sixth-grade members. They can't sit at nighttime, except for their own brothers and sisters, but both of them are really good. We know Mallory really well because we baby-sit for her family, the Pikes. The Pikes have eight kids, and since Mallory is the oldest, she used to help us out.

Jessi is Mallory's friend and she's a newcomer to Stoneybrook. Her family is one of the first black families in the neighborhood, so I think that in the beginning, Jessi felt a little strange. When she first moved here, she wasn't even sure she wanted to continue with her ballet lessons, and she is a really talented ballet dancer — long-legged and graceful.

Wow! When I think about it, I do have a nice bunch of friends in Stoneybrook. As I was packing that day, I also started thinking about my friends in California. Clover and Daffodil (those are the kids I used to baby-sit for) and, of course, Sunny, who had been my best friend in California since second grade. That reminded me — I'd better stick suntan lotion in my suitcase. Sunny and I would probably want to go to the beach one day. Then I started making a list of all the other cosmetics and things I would need.

Just then my mom came home. She usually doesn't get home from work until 5:45 or so, but that day she was early.

"Hi, Dawn!" she called up the stairs.

I could hear her kick off her shoes in the living room, drop her purse on the couch and her keys on the kitchen table. That's my mom, all right. I love her, but she is a little on the disorganized side. Mom padded up the stairs and plunked herself down on the one corner of my bed that wasn't covered with stuff.

"What's this?" she said, picking up my list. When she saw what it was, she laughed. "I guess you didn't learn that from your old mother," she said.

It's true. If Mom ever bothered to make a list, she'd probably just lose it.

"How was work today?" I asked her.

Mom sighed and looked vaguely across the bed at all my things.

"You're going to have such a good time," she said.

I suddenly realized that when I went off to California, Mom was going to be left all alone in Stoneybrook.

"Mom, are you going to be all right?" I asked. "I mean, all alone?"

She tucked her legs under her, like she had so many times lately when we found ourselves sitting in my room talking.

"Of course I am, sweetie," she said. "What? Are you worried about me? Don't worry. I've got Granny and Pop-Pop while you're gone. And Trip's already asked me out to dinner. . . ."

"The Trip-Man!" I groaned. Trip is a man who was dating my mother. I call him the Trip-Man. He's a real conservative type. Tortoise-shell glasses, you know what I mean. How could I leave Mom alone with *him*?

"Mom," I said, "I feel kind of funny going off to be with Dad and Jeff, and you having to stay here."

"It's only for your spring vacation," she said. "Besides, think of what an adventure I'm going to have without you. I'll probably mis-place my keys and not find them the whole time you're away. And when I go out with Trip, I'll probably end up wearing one brown shoe and one red."

I threw my arms around Mom and gave her a quick kiss.

"Oh, Mom," I said. "I'm so glad that you and I stuck together. What if you were here and I was there? What if the family was even more split up than it is now? I'll never leave you. Never."

Mom didn't answer me, she just stared across my bed at the suitcase and all my clothes. Her eyes got a little misty, but right away she turned to me and said, "You didn't start anything for dinner yet, did you?"

Weekday dinners are usually my job.

"Not yet," I said. "I was thinking maybe barley casserole . . ."

"Let's go out," Mom said suddenly. "What do you say? We'll go to Cabbages and Kings and have one of those wonderful tofu dinners."

"Or the avocado salad," I said.

"Aaaah, avocado . . ." My mother closed her eyes at the thought. "Think of all those wonderful California avocados you're going to be gobbling down soon. Come on. Let's go celebrate. Avocados, here we come."

I grabbed my sweater and Mom stood up,

puzzled, and glanced around the floor.

"Where're my shoes?" she said.

"Living room," I answered.

Mom fumbled in her pockets for her keys.

"Your keys are on the kitchen table," I said. "And your purse is on the couch."

Mom looked a little sheepish.

"What am I going to do without you?" she laughed. "You have to admit. We make a good team."

We walked down the stairs, gathered up Mom's things, and headed out the door. When I got home that night I would have to finish packing my things. But, for then, I left them strewn across my bed. It wasn't every night that Mom and I could decide to drop everything and go to Cabbages and Kings for a close, warm mother-daughter meal. And besides, on Sunday I'd be leaving Stoneybrook for two whole weeks.

CHAPTER 2

Friday

Dear Dad and Jeff,

Only two more days to C-Day! That's what I'm calling my trip to California now, and I can't, can't, CAN'T WAIT to see you. This'll have to be short and sweet because I'm rushing off to a slumber party at Kristy's house. All my Baby-sitters Club friends will be there, and I can't be late, since the whole thing is a good-bye party for...

Yours truly,
Dawn

What a party. I was the first one to get to Kristy's that night and, when I arrived, things were still a little quiet and calm. Kristy lives in a mansion. No kidding. But you practically need a mansion to hold all her family. There's Kristy and her mom and three brothers, and then there's Watson Brewer, Kristy's stepdad. He and Kristy's mom got married last summer and he has two kids of his own. (They come to stay every other weekend.) That would be plenty, but there's also Boo-Boo, the cat, and Shannon, the puppy.

I knocked on the big wooden door and Kristy let me in. She was wearing her usual — jeans, sneakers, a turtleneck. (What did I tell you?) She shut the door quickly behind me, so that Shannon wouldn't escape. Shannon jumped up on me and licked my arms. She really is a great puppy. She's still young, so her paws are too big for her body.

"Hi, Shann," I said. I petted her soft head and scratched behind her ears.

The doorbell rang again.

"Move it, Shannon," said Kristy. "It's probably Mary Anne."

The madness had started. When Kristy opened the door, it wasn't Mary Anne at all.

It was Karen and Andrew, Kristy's stepsister and stepbrother.

"We're here!" Karen shouted into the house. She dropped her overnight bag on the hallway floor. "Daddy! Everybody! Here we are!"

Karen is only six years old, but she's got lots of confidence and is never at a loss for words. Andrew looked up at me and smiled.

"Hi, Dawn," he said. "Are you baby-sitting us?"

Andrew's only four and sometimes I have baby-sat for him, although, of course, Kristy takes all the jobs in her own house if she can.

"Not this time, Andrew," I said. "But I think you are going to see lots of baby-sitters tonight."

"Hi, Karen. Hi, Andrew. Oh, hello, Dawn." Kristy's mother bustled into the room and gave Andrew and Karen each a warm hug and kiss. "Take your stuff up and stash it in your rooms," she said. "It's going to be a full house tonight. Kristy's expecting a few guests."

Karen bounded up the stairs with her suitcase and Andrew stumbled after her, trying to keep up.

Kristy put her hands over her ears. "Aughhh!" she cried. "It sounds like wild horses!"

The doorbell rang again. This time it *was* Mary Anne, and Claudia was right behind her.

"Come in, come in." Kristy opened the door a crack, then hustled them in, but Shannon was too quick for her. The frisky puppy darted between Claudia's legs and scampered right outside.

"Shannon!" Kristy called, and ran out to catch her.

While Kristy was chasing after Shannon, Mallory and Jessi arrived. Jessi saw what was happening and took a ballet leap into the yard, just as Shannon was about to run into the bushes.

"Gotcha!" she said as she grabbed Shannon's collar. We all started clapping and Jessi took a deep bow. *"Grand jeté,"* she smiled. "You just never know when one is going to come in handy."

Well, one crisis down, but another was on the way. While Kristy led Shannon back into the house, Karen came screaming down the stairs.

"Ben Brewer!" she shouted. "Ben Brewer! He's clanking his chains!"

For a six-year-old girl, Karen has one wild imagination. She's convinced there's a ghost in the house named Ben Brewer, and she tells stories about him all the time. As I looked up, Sam and Charlie were sneaking around the bend at the top of the steps. They're Kristy's older brothers. Sam is fifteen and Charlie's seventeen.

"Shhh," Sam whispered to Charlie. He slipped down the stairs after Karen, grabbed her up from behind, and lifted her over his head.

"Aughhh!" screamed Karen.

Mrs. Brewer stuck her head back into the room to see what was going on. David Michael, Kristy's brother who's seven, was right behind her.

"No horseplay on the stairs," said David Michael. (It was obviously a rule he had heard many times.)

"That's right," said Mrs. Brewer.

Just then, the front door opened behind us and bumped Claudia and Mary Anne on their backsides.

"Excuse me. Excuse me." Someone was pushing his way through the crowd. It was Watson Brewer, home from work. "Well," he said, as he took a look at the chaos that greeted him. "Five more daughters, huh? Where did I get them all? Hello, girls."

"Hi, Mr. Brewer," we chorused.

"All right. All right. That's enough," Kristy said suddenly. "Baby-sitters upstairs."

I'm surprised she didn't say, "Forward, march!" or "Single file!" (she did sound like General Kristy), but we all trooped up the stairs after her. We left Watson and Kristy's mom kissing hello in the hallway, with their kids and their animals chasing all around them.

"Phew!" Kristy said. She shut the door behind us. Mary Anne, Claudia, and I collapsed on the bed. Jessi and Mallory sat cross-legged on the floor. Kristy pulled up a chair. It looked just like a regular meeting of the Baby-sitters Club, only we were in Kristy's room, not Claudia's. Kristy picked up a clip-board and pencil and rapped on the arm of her chair.

"The meeting will now come to order," she said.

"Meeting!" Claudia cried. "Kristy, this isn't a meeting. It's a party."

I smiled at Mary Anne. Mary Anne is a good friend of Kristy's, but she knows how Kristy loves to be bossy.

"True," said Kristy. "It's not exactly a meeting. But we do have a few things to decide. Pizza, for instance. Do we want some? And, if so, what kind?"

"Pizza would be good," said Mary Anne. Mary Anne is always agreeable. "Does anyone else want pizza?"

"P-I-I-I-Z-Z-A-A!" said Claudia in a deep, rumbling voice. She sounded like Cookie Monster demanding cookies.

"That's three," said Kristy. "Dawn?"

"Do they have broccoli pizza?" I asked.

"Ew!" Kristy made a gagging face.

"It *is* Dawn's party," said Mary Anne. "I think we should do what she wants."

Claudia crinkled up her nose.

"If they do have broccoli, maybe they could put it on only *part* of the pizza," she said.

Claudia was more polite about it, but I think the idea of broccoli pizza was as weird-sounding to Claudia as it was to Kristy. I'm the only member of the club who really likes health food. Everybody else is happier with hamburgers and french fries. Especially Claudia. Claudia takes junk food to the extreme. She keeps her bedroom stocked with Ring Dings and Twinkies. In fact, right then she reached into the knapsack she had brought and pulled out . . . a handful of Tootsie Roll Pops.

"Tootsie Pops all around," she said, passing them out, "and a fruit roll for Dawn."

We all sucked on our treats while Kristy finished the pizza order. Half a pie with broccoli (if they had it), half plain, and one whole pie with the works — sausage, mushrooms, onions, peppers, and pepperoni.

"No anchovies!" everyone voted. For once we were all in agreement.

The rest of the party was just as crazy as the

start. When the pizza was delivered, Sam brought it up to Kristy's room. He knocked on the door. "Pizza man," he called in. Kristy let him in and tore open the boxes.

"What'd they give us? What'd they give us?" she said excitedly. "EW!!!!" Kristy jumped away from the boxes in disgust. We all crowded around to see. There, all over the tops of both pizzas, were worms! . . . Rubber worms. Sam's shoulders were shaking with laughter.

"SA-AM!" Kristy said hotly. We should've known Sam would pull something like that. Sam is one of the world's champion practical jokers. (By the way, underneath all the worms, the pizza place *had* sent my broccoli.)

After pizza we wheeled out the television and set up a movie on Kristy's VCR.

Kristy had picked out the spookiest movie she could find at the store, *Fright Night at Spook Lake.* It was all about a ghost who haunts an old lakeside resort house. When Karen heard the VCR on, she knocked on the door and asked if she could join us.

"Only if you don't get scared," said Kristy.

"Okay," Karen agreed. She climbed into Kristy's lap.

But when the ghost first came on the screen, Karen shrieked. "That's Ben!" she cried. "That's exactly what Ben Brewer looks like!"

"Karen!" Kristy said firmly. "There is *nothing* to be afraid of. Look at me. Am *I* afraid? Of course not. There's *nothing* to be afraid of."

Just then, in the movie, the resort house got strangely quiet. An eerie light filled the inn's reception room and a breeze rustled the curtains. A phone rang loudly — Riiiiing! — and at that moment, the real phone right outside Kristy's room rang, too! We all screamed and jumped a mile. Kristy gulped and looked at us. You could tell her heart was racing, and I think she didn't know whether to answer the phone or not, but she did.

"Oh," she said. "Hi, Nannie." She heaved a big sigh. "It's only my grandmother," she whispered to us. "Phew."

When the movie was finished, Kristy's mom came in to collect Karen and take her off to bed. We stayed up a long time after that. We pushed Kristy's bed out of the way and put our sleeping bags and bedding in a circle, so that all our heads met in the center. We just talked and laughed about school and about boys. Claudia got some pieces of paper from Kristy's desk and drew little caricatures of us all. When Jessi posed for hers, she sat on the floor, her legs stretched out on either side of her and her torso folded all the way over so her stomach was flat on the ground.

"Wow!" said Mary Anne.

I think by then we were all getting tired, but nobody wanted to admit it. We talked on, but one by one we started to drift off. Only Mary Anne lay wide awake beside me.

"In two days you'll be in California," she whispered to me.

"Yeah," I said. I didn't sound as excited as I thought I would. All of a sudden I was a little nervous about going. I looked around the room. Here I was, with all my best friends — especially Mary Anne.

It all felt so cozy and homey. It felt like . . . like a family.

"You'll be gone so *long*," Mary Anne whispered. "And you'll have so much fun you won't even *think* of us."

"Of course I will," I said. "You're my *friends*. Anyway, I'll be home before you know it."

"Well, call whenever you want," Mary Anne said. "And send me a postcard?" She took my hand and squeezed it.

"I'll send you a zillion." I squeezed her hand back.

My thoughts were all jumbled as we lay there in the dark. But the thoughts tumbled into dreams, and soon I was fast asleep.

CHAPTER 3

Sunday

Dear Mary Anne,

Well, I told you I'd send a postcard, but bet you never thought it'd be so soon. Here I am on the airplane and we've only been "in flight" for fifteen minutes. Not much to report, but I can tell you anything you want to know about oxygen masks, flotation devices, or exit doors. (The stewardess who did the safety demonstration reminds me of a Kewpie doll.) It's going to be a *long* flight.

Love,
Dawn

Long flight was right. Long morning, too. That morning I woke up really early, a half an hour before my alarm. My brain was racing with all the things I needed for my trip: toothbrush, toothpaste, swimsuit, airplane ticket. I even wondered if maybe I had gotten the ticket wrong. Maybe I was supposed to fly out tomorrow, not today. It surprised me that I was so jittery. I've flown plenty of times before. But that morning, when my alarm went off, believe me, I was wide awake.

I could hear Mom in the shower, so I went down to fix myself a quick breakfast. There was granola in the cupboard, but no milk in the refrigerator. I poured myself a bowl and wondered if maybe I could substitute orange juice for milk. I decided to eat it plain.

Getting Mom to an airport in time is no small task. She thinks you don't have to get there until five minutes before flight time.

"They're always late," she says. "We'll just have to sit there."

Me, I like to count on an extra forty-five minutes to an hour. What if there's a traffic jam? And airlines overbook all the time. I could hear Mom singing away in the shower. I decided to knock on the door.

"In a minute, honey," she said.

It seemed like forever to me, but finally we were both showered, dressed, and out of the house. Mom had had her coffee and we had found her keys and I double-checked the things I had stuck in my carry-on bag: a favorite collection of ghost stories (*Spirits, Spooks, and Ghostly Tales*), some magazines, and some cards to write my friends. Since this wasn't a night flight, and since I would be on the plane for practically six whole hours, I figured I'd better come aboard with a few things to do.

On the ride to the airport, Mom let me listen to my radio station and didn't even ask me to turn it down. She didn't say an awful lot during the drive. Every once in awhile, she'd pop in with, "You remembered your under-wear?" or, "Now don't forget your manners. 'Please, thank you.'. . . What am I saying? You know how to behave."

I think Mom was just nervous. I noticed that as she drove, her fingers kept kneading the steering wheel.

When we got to the airport, Mom found a spot in short-term parking. Then we went in, checked my suitcase, got me a seat (No Smok-ing/Window), and went to wait at the gate. I started to feel as choked up as Mom looked. I glanced at her, and she gave a half smile, and then her eyes welled up and over.

"Are you going to be okay, Mom?" I asked. Now I was beginning to cry.

"Oh, Dawn," she said. "I'm all right. I'm fine. You'd think I was sending you to Egypt or something."

When it came time for me to board, Mom walked me to the door and gave me a big hug.

"See you soon," I said.

She kissed my cheek. "Right," she said, awfully quickly.

I got on the plane and distracted myself with settling in. I wanted to make sure to get myself a pillow and a blanket. I wanted to check out the magazines that were on board — *Forbes, Business Week* . . . nothing for me. I guess I was starting to feel a little better because when the Kewpie doll stewardess gave her safety demonstration, I even found myself giggling. But when the plane started to taxi down the runway, I suddenly thought of Mom. I pictured her back in the parking lot trying to remember where she had parked the car.

"Row C," I thought, trying to send her the message. "Row C."

The plane took off and tears spilled down my cheeks. I was going to California. And Mom was going to be all alone.

Well, if it weren't for that stewardess, I might've cried the whole way out. I certainly wouldn't have had half as much to think about. See, this stewardess was a real strange one. First of all, she looked strange. Something about her hair . . . or her makeup. Her cheeks had a cakey look, and when she had put on her lipstick, she had drawn it above the natural line of her lips. Also, she painted on her eyelashes. You know, dark little lines painted on her eyelids. The whole effect was pretty weird. Even when you get a makeover at the Washington Mall, you don't come out looking *that* strange.

But worst of all, she was a total spacehead. Now most of the stewardesses I've met have been pretty down-to-earth. If you want a Coke, they give you a Coke. But this one I had to practically flag down anytime I wanted anything. The main trouble was, sitting next to me, in the aisle seat, was a very attractive guy. He was sandy-haired, good-looking, and had on a crisp white oxford shirt with the sleeves rolled up. Well, this stewardess practically drooled every time she walked by him.

"Can I get you anything, sir?" she asked.

When they came around with the beverage cart, he got an orange juice, and then she wheeled the cart right on! What about me?

"Excuse me," I said. "Excuse me."

"Excuse me," the man said. "This young girl didn't get a beverage."

"Oh, she didn't?" said the stewardess. She would've been blinking her eyelashes, only she couldn't. They were painted on.

"Tomato juice, please," I said. That was that.

Then she came around selling headsets for the music channels and the movie. Once again, the stewardess sold one to Mr. Handsome and ignored me. Once again, Mr. Handsome came to my rescue. When I finally got my headset, he winked at me.

"Now you know why I always get an aisle seat," he said.

Mr. Handsome's name was actually Tom and he turned out to be not a bad seatmate at all. He was a theater director, he said, and he was flying out to California to audition some actors. Wow! I thought. A theater director! I couldn't wait to tell Stacey. He and I had a little conversation about *Paris Magic* (which I hadn't even *seen*, just heard about from Stacey), and he wrote down the names of some other shows he thought I might enjoy.

"Gee, thanks," I said.

I tucked the slip of paper into the pocket of my cotton traveling jacket.

Well, Mr. Handsome (I mean Tom) had some scripts with him that he had to read, so I listened to the music on the headphones and paged through my book and magazines. But I was getting much too excited to do any real reading.

When it was time for lunch, Tom turned to me and said, "Do you think we'll have to go to battle for you again?" But lunch, I figured, would be no problem. I had ordered a vegetarian lunch ahead of time. You can do that on airlines if you don't want to eat the regular food they give you. I'm not a strict vegetarian, but the vegetarian meals on the planes are always much better.

Anyway, our stewardess had about half the plane to serve before she got to our row.

"Here you go," she smiled at Tom.

"And for the young lady?" he said.

"I get a vegetarian meal," I said.

"No you don't," she said flatly.

"Yes," I said. "I ordered it when I got my ticket."

"Name?" she asked briskly.

"Dawn Schafer."

The stewardess disappeared to the back of the plane and came back with a computer printout. She ran her finger down a list.

"Schafer, Schafer, Schafer . . . ," she said. "Oh. Here you are. Oh, dear."

"Is there a problem?" asked Tom.

"Well," said the stewardess. "I did have a meal for you, but I gave it away. To that gentleman three rows up. He asked for one and I thought it was his."

She handed me a tray with a regular meal. No apology. No question about whether or not I was a strict vegetarian. What if I *couldn't* eat meat?

"Oh, well," she said. "There's certainly no way we can get another meal *in flight.*"

Tom was looking faintly amused. I peeled back the tinfoil of my airplane lunch. Ew! It looked like the Friday lunch at Stoneybrook Middle School. There was some kind of meat with some kind of sauce on it. Mystery meat, I thought, and there was some soppy cole slaw and this disgusting rubbery Jell-O with globby things inside. There was also a salad (okay, I could eat that). And there was a piece of cornbread that *did* look more edible than the rest. What a lunch — cornbread and salad. I turned the meat over with my fork and thought about how Kristy would react if this were really a cafeteria lunch.

"Ew," she'd probably say. "Fried monkey

brains." (Or something even grosser.)

Tom offered me his cornbread to help fill me up.

The rest of the flight was, well . . . long. Think of it — how often do you have to sit in a cramped seat for six hours straight? The movie was a shoot-'em-up, which filled the time, but not much else.

The stewardess, though, had one last opportunity to bungle things. After lunch, when she came around with coffee and tea, I asked if I could have a little real milk to put in my tea. (All she had on the tray was packets of that white chemical stuff.)

"Sure thing," she smiled, with that too-red smile of hers.

Minutes passed, many minutes, and again I had to flag her down.

"My milk, please?" I said.

"Oh, right."

She disappeared, came back, and tossed two of the chemical packets on my tray.

"There you go," she said, and she was gone.

"Do you get the feeling we're characters in some play?" Tom smiled. "A comedy?"

But, really, what did I care about "coffee whitener" or mystery meat or even irritating stewardesses? When the flight was over, I'd never see her again. When the flight was over,

I'd be landing in my favorite place in the whole world . . . California!

The pilot's voice came over the intercom.

"We're preparing to land at the John Wayne/Orange County Airport," he said. (That's really what the airport's called. Honest.)

The wheels of the plane hit the runway, I felt the power of the plane pulling back, and there I was!

When I walked off the plane and into the waiting room, my heart was pounding. There were Dad and Jeff on the other side of the guide rope, waiting and waving, both of them with big, gigundo smiles. Behind Jeff another face squeezed through. Sunny! When I got through the crowd, Jeff took my carry-on, and Dad grabbed me up and swung me around.

"Sunshine!" he said.

"Oh, Daddy," I blushed. (I would have to tell him not to call me Sunshine when Sunny was around. It wasn't just embarrassing, it'd be *confusing*.)

While we waited for my suitcase, everyone chattered at once. I told them all about the stewardess. Jeff told me about all the fun they had planned. Dad kept beaming and ruffling my hair. He even started snapping his fingers and singing that old song, "California Girls." He sure was acting goony.

"That's what fathers are for," he laughed.

It hit me how much I'd missed him.

Before we left, we picked up some postcards of the big John Wayne statue that towers over the airport. (I was now in California, all right.) In the car on the way home, Sunny grinned at me and hinted that she had something to tell me.

"It's sort of a surprise," she said, but she wouldn't tell me any more than that. "Just come over to my house tomorrow night," she said. "Five o'clock."

Sunny always did love surprises. It sounded pretty mysterious to me. I wondered what she had up her sleeve.

CHAPTER 4

Dear Dawn,

    I'm writing this before you leave so you get it when you arrive. And anyway, I miss you already. As you read this, you're probably getting ready to go to the beach or to Disneyland, or you're probably lunching with movie stars. (Do they have movie stars in Anaheim?) Are the boys cute? Is everyone tan? Write me back!

           Your (best) friend,
           Mary Anne

When I woke up that Monday, my first morning back in California, at first I wasn't sure where I was. The sun was streaming in through the flowered curtains — the same curtains I had had when I lived here before. Maybe I had never left? From down the hall I heard silverware clinking and I also smelled something wonderful. Breakfast! I threw on my bathrobe and padded down the long, cool, tiled hall to the kitchen. There was Mrs. Bruen, the housekeeper Dad had hired. I'd never met her before, but we introduced ourselves.

Mrs. Bruen was busy organizing breakfast, so I sat at the table and took in the room. Everything seemed so spacious to me, compared to our little house in Connecticut. The rooms were so big, and the windows . . . Everything was wide open.

Our California house really is cool. It's all on one floor, but that one floor is long and wide and snakes around on two sides. The house is really shaped like a square, with only the top side missing. The floors are all tiled with terra cotta and there are slanted skylights in almost all the rooms. Now that Mrs. Bruen was taking care of it, the place was bright and sparkling.

Pretty soon Dad and Jeff stumbled into the

kitchen. I'd forgotten that I'd be up earlier than they would, with the time change and all. Since it was Monday, usually Dad would be going to work, but he'd arranged to take off the first week of my visit, and that day he was taking Jeff and me . . . to Disneyland!

"All riiight!" said Jeff.

Jeff and I have been to Disneyland lots of times before, since it's right in Anaheim and that's where our house is, but believe me, Disneyland is always a treat.

Mrs. Bruen brought our breakfast over to the table. She'd made fresh melon slices, cheese-and-egg puffs, fresh-squeezed orange juice, and wheat crisps. Yum!

"Beats a bowl of dry granola," I said, thinking of my last meal in Connecticut. My mouth was full.

"What?" asked Dad.

"Not important," I smiled.

"So what do you kids want to see today at Disneyland?" Dad asked. "It'd be nice to have some idea before we hit those lines and crowds."

That's Dad. Mr. Organization.

"Star Tours!" cried Jeff. "Big Thunder Mountain Railroad! Jungle Cruise! Space Mountain!" He kept going. "Matterhorn! Pirates of the Caribbean! Davy Crockett's Explorer Canoes! Penny Arcade!"

"Whoa! Slow down," laughed Dad.

Disneyland is made up of seven theme areas, and Jeff had managed to name exhibits and rides in every single one. Dad grabbed a pad and a pen.

"I knew it would be a good idea to talk about this beforehand," he said. "Okay, let's narrow down what areas of the park we're going to."

Jeff named three choices (Tomorrowland, Bear Country, and Frontierland) and I named mine (Fantasyland, New Orleans Square, and Jungleland). You'll notice that none of our choices overlapped.

"Of course you don't agree," said Dad. "That would be too easy. How about if you each pick two? We could probably manage to squeeze in four altogether."

"Does that count Main Street?" I asked. (Main Street, U.S.A., is the area leading into the park.)

"I guess not," Dad smiled. "Four, plus Main Street."

"All riiight!" Jeff said loudly. Jeff was already starting to get what Dad calls "Disneyland Wild."

"So what'll it be?" Dad asked. "Two each."

"Tomorrowland and Frontierland!" said Jeff. "No, Tomorrowland and Bear Country! No! I mean, Tomorrowland and Frontierland! Yeah, that's my vote."

My choices were Fantasyland and New Orleans Square.

Then Dad asked us what rides we wanted to go on and what things we wanted see. By the time we got out of the house and on the freeway, we had the whole trip planned out.

Disneyland is really super. I'd forgotten how much I love it. Dad bought our "Passports" at the front gate. Those are the tickets that let you go all through the park and on all the rides. (Of course, you can't buy things, like food or souvenirs, with them, but I'd brought along plenty of baby-sitting money for extras.) Jeff had brought his camera with him and took my picture by the Mickey Mouse face as we walked in.

"Dawn! Dawn! Stand over here!" he called to me.

It's things like that that let me know just how much Jeff really likes me. That was only the first picture of many. He must've taken two whole rolls of me that day.

We entered the park and walked up Main Street, U.S.A., which is made up to look like a small American town at the turn of the last century. It has horse-drawn streetcars and an old-fashioned fire engine, and because our visit was in the spring, there were tulips blooming everywhere. All the shops that line the street look like old shops, but you can buy really cool things in them.

I dragged Dad and Jeff into three stores. One for postcards (I was going to have a lot of *those* to write), one for Mickey Mouse ears (I bought a pair for each member of the Baby-sitters Club), and in the last store I got a special present just for Mary Anne (a plush Minnie Mouse doll for her bed).

"What do you say, think we've had enough?" teased Dad.

"No!" cried Jeff.

We had just begun.

At the end of Main Street is Sleeping Beauty's Castle, and that's the entrance to Fantasyland. When I was a little kid, I thought that castle was the most beautiful thing I'd ever seen. I could picture myself moving right into it. It really is fantastic. When I walk over the moat and through the castle, I really feel like I'm in Disneyland.

In Fantasyland, Jeff and I went on the Mad Tea Party ride (you sit inside these oversized teacups and spin all around) and on the Matterhorn Bobsleds. (Dad let Jeff pick one roller coaster ride and that one was it.)

From there we went on to Tomorrowland (with Jeff running ahead all the way). Of course, Jeff wanted to go on Star Tours, which has a really cool flight simulator.

"Too bad, Dawn," Jeff teased as we waited in line. " 'Children under three not allowed.' "

Believe it or not, that's exactly the kind of talk you miss when you don't have a brother around.

After Star Tours, we headed to Captain Eo, which is a 3-D Michael Jackson video. When we came out, Jeff started moonwalking. Brothers! They drive you crazy, but I have to admit, they can be pretty funny.

"Onward!" said Dad.

We caught the train that circles the park and rode it all the way to Frontierland. That's where Jeff wanted to go on the Mark Twain Steamboat. "Ah, here we go," said Dad. "A ride for old fogies like me."

The steamboat circles an island and I like to pretend that I'm Mark Twain, navigating the Mississippi, thinking up the stories I'm going to write.

"So. We're finished," Dad said as we got off the boat. "We've done everything on our list."

There was a teasing twinkle in his eye.

"No way!" cried Jeff. "You forgot New Orleans Square!"

Jeff was still more than a little "Disneyland Wild."

Everybody was getting hungry, so we decided to stop in one of the New Orleans "buffeterias" . . . after one more ride.

"Pirates of the Caribbean!" shouted Jeff.

"No," I said. "Haunted Mansion. That was my whole reason for picking New Orleans Square."

"You could split up," Dad suggested.

That's exactly what we did.

Haunted Mansion is right up my (spooky, ghost-ridden) alley. On the outside it's an old New Orleans house. You know the kind. It has those wrought-iron, curlicue trellises bordering all the porches. Inside, though, it's a real spook house. To go through, you get in a Doom Buggy. Sound creepy? That's the least of it. Ghost Shadows are cast on all the walls, and eerie music plays in the background. Upstairs, in the attic, there's about an *inch* of dust on everything. I'm telling you, one trip through Haunted Mansion equals about *ten* good ghost stories. And I ought to know.

Jeff and I met Dad at the French Market restaurant, where he had already snared a table for us.

"Yum!" I said, as I looked at the menu. It

was hard to decide between Cajun-seasoned trout or spinach quiche.

"Want to split them?" Dad asked. It was the perfect solution.

Now that we were sitting down and eating, Jeff began to wind down. Well, a little bit. We finished our meals and watched the Mark Twain steamboat glide by beyond the restaurant porch.

"Hey, Dawn," Jeff said. "Watch this."

Jeff made one of his silly monkey faces.

"Glad to see your sister, huh?" Dad laughed.

"Yeah," Jeff said sheepishly. He smiled at me, an awkward, self-conscious smile. "Sometimes I miss you, Dawn," he said.

Dad ruffled my hair, as if I were a puppy or something.

"We *both* miss you," he said. "That much is for sure."

There I was, back in Disneyland, sitting with my dad and my brother, and both of them being gushy. It sure felt good.

Dad looked at his watch.

"What time do you have to be at Sunny's, Dawn?" he asked.

"Five o'clock," I said. Whatever her surprise was, I'd better be on time.

"I think we have time to do one last thing," said Dad.

"Jungle Cruise!" shouted Jeff. He was never at a loss for ideas.

"No, this one's for your old man," said Dad. "I spotted it right as we came in the park. Back to Main Street, guys. Let's go."

"Where are we going?" asked Jeff.

"You'll see," said Dad.

He had that glint in his eye.

When we got back to Main Street, Dad led us straight to the Main Street Cinema, an old movie house that plays silent cartoon classics, ones like *Steamboat Willie* and *Mickey's Polo Team*. It was really fun to see them.

"They sure don't look much like the cartoons we have today," I said.

"They're better," said Dad.

"No way!" said Jeff.

All in all, it had been a perfect day in Disneyland. And the day wasn't over yet, either. I couldn't wait to get home to see Sunny. I couldn't imagine what she might have for a surprise.

42

CHAPTER 5

Monday

Dear Everybody,
    Well, I just can't seem to get baby-sitting off the brain. I'm mailing this to Claudia's so you can all read it at your meeting and I've just came from a meeting of my own. No kidding! There's a California branch of the Baby-sitters Club. It's called the We ♥ Kids Club and my friend Sunny started it. Some of the things about the club are the same, but it's _very_ California. I'll tell all when I return.
                    Love,
                    Dawn

No wonder Sunny wanted to surprise me. When I got back from Disneyland, I ran over to her house. (She lives only a few houses down the block. I used to be there so often I could find it in my sleep.) I got there at five o'clock on the dot. Sunny's mom opened the door.

"Dawn," she smiled. "Look at you! Look how you've grown! Oh, I know I'm not supposed to say that. Come in. Come in."

Sunny clambered down the stairs. She was grinning from ear to ear. She had a bandana in her hands. Sunny and her surprises . . .

"Hold still," she said to me, "and close your eyes."

She tied the bandana on me like a blindfold.

"What . . .?" I said.

"I told you," she insisted. "It's a *surprise!*"

Sunny took my arm and led me up the stairs to her room. She swung open the door and undid my blindfold.

"Ta-da!" she said.

There, in the room, sat two other girls, Maggie Blume and Jill Henderson. I remembered them because I used to be in their class at school. Was this the surprise? I smiled faintly. I knew these girls, but I hadn't ever really been great friends with them.

44

"Sit down," said Sunny. "Make yourself at home. What are you waiting for? Haven't you ever been to a meeting of a baby-sitters club before?"

Sunny still had that wide, teasing grin stretched across her face.

"Baby-sitting club?" I said.

"Yup," said Sunny, proudly, "the We ♥ Kids Club." And she told me all about it.

"Remember all those letters you sent me?" asked Sunny. "With all the news about your club?"

"Sure," I said. (I must've sent her about a hundred.)

"Well," she said. "It sounded like a good idea. I'd been baby-sitting a lot around the neighborhood, and so had Maggie and Jill — "

"It sounded like a *great* idea," Jill broke in. "Before, we were all sitting, but we were just out there on our own."

"So we got together the club," said Maggie.

"And we named it the We ♥ Kids Club," said Jill.

"And it was all I could do to keep it a secret!" Sunny laughed.

To tell you the truth, I was shocked she'd been able to carry it off. Well, if there was a surprise involved, Sunny could do almost anything.

"How long have you been meeting?" I asked.

"Six months," Sunny grinned. "Six long, silent months."

Of course, I had lots of questions. I wanted to know exactly how they ran their club. Some things were the same as ours — Sunny had gotten a lot of ideas from my letters.

"Like advertising," she said. "When we first started, we made up flyers and stuck them in every mailbox for ten blocks."

"And of course we collect dues," said Jill.

"For Kid-Kits!" Sunny cried out. She was practically exploding from the excitement of finally getting to tell her secret.

"You have Kid-Kits, too?" I asked.

Kid-Kits are a great idea that Kristy thought up. They're boxes that we fill with all kinds of things for kids to play with — books, games, crayons, puzzles. We bring them to the houses we baby-sit at and, of course, the kids just love them. They're also good for business. They show we really are concerned and involved sitters.

Sunny pulled out her own Kid-Kit, and I took a look through. Play-Doh, cookie cutters, watercolors . . . and a cookbook!

" 'Kids Can Cook . . . Naturally,' " I read.

"It's a great book," said Sunny. "All the

recipes are easy for kids — none of them involve the oven or stove. And they all use natural foods."

"Wow," I said. Imagine if I tried to introduce that book to my club.

"Oh, yeah," said Sunny, "and we've got an appointment book."

She pulled out a thin notebook and opened it to the day's page.

Well, it certainly did look as if the clubs were a lot the same, but believe me, there were lots of differences, too.

After Sunny had told me about the club, I figured she would call the meeting to order. I almost expected her to pull out a director's chair, just like Kristy sits in, and call for order. Instead we just sort of sat around and talked some more. They told me all about Mr. Roberts, their science teacher, and asked me if Connecticut schools make you dissect a worm.

Then the phone rang. Maggie reached for it and took the call. She put her hand over the receiver and said, "Mrs. Peters. Thursday. Anybody take it?"

"I will," said Jill.

It was as simple as that.

"Don't you take the information and call

them back?" I asked. That's the way we did it.

"Why?" said Maggie.

I just shrugged my shoulders. Somehow it seemed too complicated to explain.

After the call, Sunny wandered off to the kitchen and brought us back a snack — apple slices with natural peanut butter.

It's true, I thought. I really am back in California. This was a far cry from Claudia's Ring Dings.

"So who are your officers?" I asked.

"Officers?" asked Sunny.

"You know, president, vice-president, secretary . . ."

"We don't have anything like that," said Sunny. "Everybody just does what they do."

"Oh," I said.

Another call came in. This time Sunny took the job.

Jill pulled a bottle of nail polish out of her purse and started working on her nails. I could just see Kristy if one of us tried that back in Stoneybrook.

I got up and looked at Sunny's bookshelves — two whole shelves of ghost stories. Sunny and I had fallen in love with ghost stories back in fourth grade, at just about the same time. When our class went to the school library, we used to race each other because we both wanted to get there first, to get whatever ghost books were in that week. (I can still hear Mrs. Wright, our teacher, now. "Girls! No running in the halls!") Sunny had a lot of new books on her shelves now, a lot of books I hadn't ever heard of, like *Ghost in Whitcomb's Briar* and *Seven Gothic Ghosts*.

"Have you read *Spirits, Spooks, and Ghostly Tales?*" asked Maggie.

"Maggie loves ghost stories, too," Sunny explained. "I got her into them."

"Phew, I have to sit down," I said. What had happened? Had I died and gone to Dawn heaven? It sure felt like it. I was in California, where the weather was warm and beautiful. I was staying with my wonderful, goony dad and I had my good ol' brother back, too. Next, I found out my best friend in California had started up a baby-sitting club. Where they served *apple slices* for snacks. And to top it off, my old friends liked ghost stories, too! Sunny was piling up books in my arms to take back to Dad's with me.

"Vacation reading," she said.

Just then, the third and last call came in. It was Mrs. Austin, Dad's next-door neighbor.

She needed someone Saturday during the day to sit for Clover and Daffodil. I'd been their sitter many times before when I'd lived in California.

"You want it?" Sunny smiled at me.

"You bet!" I said.

Jill handed me the notebook and I penciled myself in.

We still had a few minutes of the meeting to go, so Jill painted all our fingernails and we sat around, waving our hands back and forth to dry the shimmering gloss.

"I've got one more surprise for you," said Sunny, blowing on her nails.

Another surprise? Sunny's eyes were twinkling. She blurted out the news.

"Our school's on spring break these two weeks, too!"

"Perfect!" I squealed. It was.

When it was time to go home, I grabbed my stack of books, popped in to say good-bye to Sunny's mom, and practically skipped the whole way home. It was 5:30, but the sun was still bright. It warmed my shoulders and toasted my hair.

The We ♥ Kids Club might not be as busy or have as big a business as the Baby-sitters Club, but it sure was fun. I loved the way everything in California was so easy, so free. I swung my hair from side to side as I skipped into the house.

"Hey," said Dad. "You look happy. Anything special?"

I stumbled to the table and dropped my books all over its top.

"Everything!" I laughed.

CHAPTER 6

Dear Dawn,
    Having a wonderful time. Wish
you were here. Wait! That's what
you're supposed to write to us.
Actually, we do wish you were here.
We sure could've used you the other
night at the Newtons. The two of us
sat for the Newtons, the Feldmans,
and the Perkinses. That's eight kids!
(Count 'em.) We figured out a game
plan ahead of time -- we were
going to get the kids out of the
house -- but guess what? It
rained. Help! But rain wasn't
the only surprise. Tell you all
about it when we see you.
                        Bye,
                Mary Anne and Claudia

The Newtons, the Feldmans and the Perkinses. That's one big group, all right. And that group is a handful and a half.

Mrs. Newton had cleared everything ahead of time with Mary Anne and Claudia. All the parents were going out together for dinner and a concert, so it seemed natural to put the kids all together and get two sitters. The plan was that everyone would stay at the Newtons. Jamie Newton is four and his little sister Lucy is just a baby. They're real cute kids. By themselves they're a pleasure. Then there're the Perkins girls, Myriah, who's five and a half, Gabbie, who's two and a half, and Laura, the baby. (I hope you're counting babies. That makes *two*.) Baby-sitting for Myriah and Gabbie is usually as easy as baby-sitting for Jamie. Myriah's really smart and Gabbie is really cute. She calls everybody by their full names. "Hello, Dawn Schafer," she always says to me.

So far, so good. But when you put those kids together with the Feldmans, well, then you might have yourself a problem. The Feldman kids are Jamie and Lucy's cousins. There's Rob Feldman (he's ten), Brenda Feldman (she's six), and Rosie Feldman (she's four). Hmm, what can I say about the Feldmans? Well, to start, Rob is a girl-hater. He's got it in his head that girls are no good, and that goes double for girl baby-sitters. His sister Brenda is just a fussbudget. It's hard to get her to enjoy anything. And the little one, Rosie, well, she's a one-girl noise machine. (But the thing is, unlike a machine, you can't just turn her off. And she can really give a baby-sitter a headache.)

When I got to talk to Mary Anne about it, she told me that she and Claudia had tried to plan the whole thing out ahead of time. They were going to give the kids an early dinner, and then, while it was still light, they were going to put the babies in their carriages and march the whole group over to the school playground. Outside, Rosie could make as much noise as she wanted. Rob could even hate girls. He could show off on the monkey bars and feel as superior as he wanted. The other kids, of course, would be perfectly happy on the swing set or in the sandbox. And when they'd tired themselves out? Home to the Newtons' house and into pajamas.

Well, it sounded like a good plan. Mary Anne and Claudia were very pleased with themselves for having so much foresight. Except, of course, it rained. Early that evening, when the two of them arrived at the Newtons, the sky had turned a dark shade of purple and a few big, splotchy raindrops had already splattered the front walk.

Mary Anne looked at Claudia. Claudia looked at Mary Anne. Jamie answered the door.

"Hi-hi!" he said.

Gabbie was right behind.

"Hello, Mary Anne Spier. Hello, Claudia Kishi," she said.

Jamie and Gabbie, both with their characteristic welcomes. Mrs. Newton was right behind.

"Hi, girls. Great. You're a few minutes early. Everybody's here. The kids are in the playroom. I made a big pot of chili for dinner. The babies, of course, get their own food. Come in the kitchen, let me show you."

Mrs. Newton had organized everything as well as she could. Dinner was on the stove, cots and sleeping bags had been set out in the living room (this was going to be a *long* evening), and she had settled the kids in the playroom with coloring books and toys. (Rob was watching television.)

Mary Anne and Claudia went to the playroom and sat themselves among the group. Mrs. Perkins was there with the babies, who were playing on the floor with plush toys.

"They'll go to bed by seven, seven-thirty," she said.

The parents all gathered around their broods to say good-bye, then they were off. The crowd looked smaller after the six adults had left but, somehow, it did not look quite small enough. Big drops of rain were now pelting the windows. (It kept up the whole night long.)

"How about one of us takes the babies, and the other the kids?" Claudia suggested.

Two little babies or six growing (active) kids. Somehow, it didn't seem balanced. Mary Anne looked skeptical.

"Okay, how 'bout we do it that way, then trade off?" Claudia suggested.

Mary Anne took baby duty first and Claudia took the kids.

Now, when you're baby-sitting for a crew, you'd better place yourself so that you can keep an eye on everybody at the same time. That's one thing we learned when we ran a play group last summer. You can't afford to get so involved with any one kid that the whole group falls apart. Claudia pulled a chair up to the play table. Jamie and Gabbie were working at one end and Myriah, Brenda, and Rosie were working at the other. All the kids had fresh sheets of white paper and their own little box of crayons. (Thank you, Mrs. Newton.) Except for Rob's television blaring in the background, the room was surprisingly peaceful.

Brenda pressed hard on her crayon to color in the giraffe she was drawing. *Snap!* It broke in half.

"My brown!" she said. "My brown broke!"

She grabbed the brown crayon out of her sister's box.

"Gimme!" Rosie shouted back.

"It's mine!" shouted Brenda.

Rosie began banging on the table. She had probably been waiting for just such an opportunity to make a lot of noise.

Now, Claudia is really the only sitter who has a lot of experience with the Feldman kids. A lot of experience, in this case, really means only two times. The first time she encountered this kind of problem, she ignored it and, when they didn't get any attention, the Feldman kids calmed down. The second time she sat for them, Kristy was along. Kristy had let out a sharp, shrill whistle and called the whole scene to a halt. Claudia didn't know how to whistle like Kristy, so she quietly took the brown crayon out of Brenda's hand and gave it back to Rosie.

"You know that's Rosie's crayon," she said gently.

Just then Mary Anne stepped in and took Brenda's hand. That's baby-sitting teamwork. "I need some help with the babies," she said.

"Brenda, you're a good helper. You come over and work with me."

Surprisingly, Brenda got up from the table and went to join Mary Anne. Claudia quieted Rosie and got her interested again in her picture. Rob looked over from the sidelines.

"I'm the oldest," he muttered. "And I know most about babies."

Mary Anne looked at him curiously.

"Would you like to join us, too?" she asked.

Rob eyed the babies.

"I'm watching television," he said. He turned his attention back to the screen.

Mary Anne and Brenda started a little rolling game for the babies with a cloth ball, but when Brenda rolled it, the ball rolled over toward Rob and bumped his knee.

"Here you go, babies," he said. He rolled the ball gently back.

Mary Anne shot Claudia a look as if to say, "Did you just see what I saw? Is that really Rob Feldman, girl-hater, sitting over there?"

Claudia shrugged her shoulders in reply. Maybe Rob didn't consider babies to be girls yet. Or maybe he had just grown out of his nasty phase. (After all, it had been almost a full year since Claudia had sat for him.)

"Blast off!" he said suddenly, his eyes fixed on the screen. "Babies into space!" Since he was watching a cowboy movie, no one knew quite what he meant.

The kids colored for awhile. At one point, Rosie started up her noise, banging her fists on the table, her feet on the floor, and loudly chanting a song she knew, but she was silenced by, of all people, Gabbie. When Rosie started her tirade, Gabbie put her hands over her ears and stared Rosie straight in the eye.

"You be quiet, Rosie Feldman," she said, very precisely. "You are really hurting my ears."

Rosie was so surprised at getting a reprimand from Gabbie that she screwed up her face and went back to her picture.

When it was time for dinner, Mary Anne volunteered to take Brenda and Myriah (the two oldest girls) to the kitchen to serve up the plates.

"What about the babies?" Claudia asked.

"Hmmm," said Mary Anne. "Maybe I could take them up and get them set up in their high chairs and the girls could serve the chili."

Rob swung around from the television.

"Little babies can't coordinate their hands with their eyes," he said. Then he looked at his cousin. "But you can, can't you, Lucy?"

Mary Anne shot Claudia another look. Well, it was worth a try, she thought.

"Rob," she asked, "why don't you come help me with the babies in the kitchen. Can you carry Lucy?"

Rob picked Lucy up and followed Mary Anne and the kitchen crew out of the playroom. He set Lucy into her high chair and strapped her in.

"How do you know so much about babies?" Mary Anne asked as she set the other baby down.

"*Babies in Space*," Rob said tersely.

"Is that a TV show?" Mary Anne asked.

"No," he said, as if everyone knew. "A book."

"Oh," said Mary Anne.

As it turned out, the book was a science fiction story about some scientists who send babies in a rocket to another planet. First, of course, they have to know everything about babies that they can, so the book is filled with little bits and snatches of scientific information about babies and how they develop.

Mary Anne opened a jar of strained pears, stuck a spoon in it, and set it down on Lucy's high-chair tray. Rob picked up the jar and started to feed her.

"When babies are nursing, they get immunities from their mothers," he said. He spooned some of the strained pear and aimed it high at

Lucy's little mouth. "Ready! Aim! Fire!" He made rocket noises as he dipped the spoon into Lucy's waiting mouth.

Mary Anne told me later that she thought, Well, you just never know. Rob Feldman, girl-hater/baby-lover. Now he seemed more like future baby-sitter material. Who could figure it? Baby-sitting is always a surprise.

Dinner went fairly smoothly. Claudia maneuvered the seating so Brenda wasn't sitting next to Rosie. (Those two were just a *bad* combination.) And after dinner, Rob helped Claudia get the babies off to bed.

When the parents got home, all the kids were in their pajamas and *most* were asleep. (Brenda kept waking up confused. "Where am I?") The Perkinses and the Feldmans picked up their pajama-ed and sleepy-eyed kids, covered them with raincoats, and ran them out to their cars.

"Oh," said Mrs. Newton, as she shook out her umbrella. "What a refreshing evening. And how did it go for you girls?"

Mary Anne grinned at Claudia.

"*Surprisingly* well," said Mary Anne.

CHAPTER 7

Thursday

Dear Kristy,
   As I'm writing this I'm
wiggling my toes in the hot
sand and I just finished
slathering sun lotion all over
my legs. Oops! Got some on
the postcard. Too bad this
isn't a letter. I'd stick some
sand in the envelope for you.
As you can see, I'm happy
as a sand crab.
                See you (too!) soon,
                        Dawn

Well, Thursday was what I would call a perfect day. (Perfect except for the strange feelings that were brewing inside me.) Dad volunteered to take me and Jeff, plus the members of the We ♥ Kids Club, *plus* a friend of Jeff's . . . to the beach! (Brave Dad.) Everyone gathered at our house after breakfast in the morning, and it did take us awhile to get going.

I had to run back into the house to slip a cover-up over my bikini so I'd feel okay for the car ride. (What if we stopped at a store for drinks or something?) Sunny, Jill, and Maggie arrived in their bikinis and the sight was just too much for Jeff and his friend Luke. "Underwear!" they screamed. "The girls are going to the beach in their *underwear!*" (Ten-year-old boys will be ten-year-old boys, all right).

There we were, all dragging beach totes with suntan lotion and beach towels, and all wearing flip-flops. No question about where we were headed. I took a look at us as we gathered in the driveway and noticed that we were all blond. Jeff and I are white-blond, but everyone there was some kind of blond or other. Well, this really was a stereotypical California group.

We waited for Jeff to run back into the house (two times) for more comic books, I checked to see that I had stuck my Walkman in my bag and, finally, we were off.

In the car, Jeff and Luke insisted on singing "99 Bottles of Beer on the Wall."

"Dad," I said. "Make them stop."

"I think it would take a power greater than I," he said.

Luckily, the boys got bored after about 82 bottles.

When we got to the beach it really was not very crowded. People in California wait until it's really summer to go to the beach, and also, it was the middle of the week. Actually, it was beautiful beach weather. Not a cloud in that whole wide blue sky, and the sun was beating down, warming the sand, the ocean, and us!

I ran ahead and found us a big stretch of sand. (We *needed* a big space.) "Blonds over here!" I shouted and everyone ran to the spot and spread out their towels.

"You're right about blonds," said Dad. "We look like the Swedish delegation to the blond convention."

And the whole rest of the day, that's what he called us, "The Blond Convention." Of course, it didn't help when Jill and Maggie pulled out their Sun-Light and combed it through their hair.

"Blond and want to be blonder?" Dad teased. He was using a deep, announcer's voice, like a TV commercial. "Try our products. That's Products for Blonds. In the pale yellow packaging."

We arranged the beach towels so that Dad was on one side of me, and Sunny and the girls were on the other. Jeff and Luke spread their towels a little ways away. I think they were looking for a place that would give them the best aim — at us — because, as we lay there in the sun, all slathered up, Jeff and Luke tossed little bits of dried seaweed and tiny pieces of shells onto our oiled backs and bellies.

"Bull's-eye!" Jeff yelled, when he got a shell right on Dad's bellybutton.

"Why don't you guys take a shell hike?" Dad suggested. He handed them the red plastic beach pail we had brought along.

"BO-RING," said Jeff.

"How about digging for clams?" Dad suggested.

"Yeah!" said Luke and Jeff at the same time. They were off and running.

Sunny, Maggie, and Jill decided to head down to the edge of the ocean and wade in. I wasn't really warm enough yet, so I decided to stay put and let the sun do its work.

"So here you are, Sunshine," Dad said when we found ourselves alone. "Sunshine in the sunshine."

Dad can be a real cornball sometimes. He grinned at me, then squinted out at the ocean.

"I'm glad you could come for a visit," he said.

"Me too."

Somebody walked by us with a radio. I could tell Dad was going to start up a serious talk, and I wasn't sure if I was ready for it. Well, ready or not, a father-daughter chat was in the air. I waited for Dad to start.

"So how's it going in Connecticut?" he asked.

"It's okay," I said.

"School?"

"Fine."

"Friends?"

"Friends? Friends are great," I said. I sat up on my towel and started to push my fingers through the sand.

"How does Jeff seem to you?" Dad continued.

Jeff seemed fine, and I told Dad so. I told him again how unhappy Jeff had been in Connecticut and how much trouble he'd gotten into at school and all.

"I guess Jeff's the type who just needs to be home in California," Dad mused.

"Lucky him," I said, half under my breath. I was surprised at how sullen I sounded all of a sudden. Usually I'm about as even-tempered as they come.

Dad glanced at me and then stared out at the surf where my friends were playing.

"So how's your mother?" Dad asked after awhile.

"Oh, you know Mom," I said. "I have to check her every time she goes out of the house for — " I almost said, "for a date with the Trip-Man," but I caught myself just in time. I really didn't want to get into a discussion about the Trip-Man with Dad. I paused awkwardly, then said quickly, " — for work. Out of the house for work."

It felt silly to have something I couldn't talk to Dad about. Somehow, the whole conversation was feeling awkward to me. I didn't know what was the matter. I dug my fingers deeper into the sand.

"Is she, uh . . . doing okay?" Dad asked.

"Pretty good," I said. The truth was, Mom *was* doing okay. She might be scattered, but that was just Mom. She might be a little weepy every now and then, but that was natural —

her family had been split up. "She likes Connecticut," I said. "She sees Granny and Pop-Pop. She loves the farmhouse. . . ."

"I hear you have a secret passageway," Dad smiled. "Something right out of one of your ghost stories, huh?"

I told him all about the passageway, about how we had found it, and how Mallory's brother Nicky had discovered it before any of us.

"He still hides out in there sometimes," I said. "Sometimes when he just needs some solitude."

"In a family with eight kids?" Dad said. "I can see why."

"Well," I said glumly, "I don't have that problem." Again, the tone of my voice surprised me. What was the matter with me? I was in California, at the beach. . . . The *last* thing I should have been doing was complaining.

Dad knew right away that something was up. He waited awhile before he said anything. Dad's good that way. He gives you whatever time you need to think things through.

"A little lonely, are you?" he said.

I hadn't thought of it that way before, exactly. Maybe I was. I wasn't sure what I was feeling.

Just then Jeff and Luke ran up and dropped a little sand crab in my lap.

"Ew!" I screamed.

"Jeff. Luke," Dad said sternly.

All of a sudden I felt like running, moving, getting up, doing something. I popped up, brushed the sand crab back onto the sand, and took off for the ocean. Sunny and the others were now waist-deep in the water.

"Aughhh!" I cried as I ran toward them, into the surf. The water was cold and shocked my skin, but I plunged in, ducked under, and came up wet and dripping. I bounded out to where my friends stood. The waves crashed against us and we jumped them and laughed. I waved to Dad back on shore. Suddenly I thought how happy, how *ecstatic*, I was to be home.

When my friends and I came back in, we were blue-lipped and shivering. Dad bundled us up in towels and we let the sun do the rest.

I sat at the edge of my towel and built a little sand castle.

"Want to help?" I asked my friends. They didn't.

I stuck some shells in the castle for turrets. My emotions were beginning to calm. I thought, in passing, of Claudia. The sand castle looked like something she might make. If Claudia were with us, I thought with a smile, she'd probably be building castles all up and down the shore.

After awhile we had a wonderful lunch that Mrs. Bruen had packed us — avocado salad with shrimp and sprouts and an unusual potato salad made with fresh parsley and herbs.

Yum! My friends and I gobbled it up.

When the sun started to fade, we gathered up our things and straggled back to the car.

"Blond Convention, ho!" Dad called, leading the way.

That night, much later, Dad suggested that I call Mom, just to say hi.

I wasn't sure, but I think she sounded a little shaky-voiced when she answered the phone.

"Dawn!" she said. Her voice was surprised. "So how are you?" she asked. "Are you having a good time?"

I babbled on about the beach, the weather, the housekeeper, my friends.

"We already went to Disneyland, then today we went to the beach. . . . And, Mom, I don't even have to miss the Baby-sitters Club. Saturday I baby-sit for Clover and Daffodil, and Sunny runs her club just like ours, except it's much more relaxed. . . . I'm having a *great* time. Jeff is real happy, and Dad is just super. . . ."

I think I must've babbled on for quite awhile. Out of nervousness? Something about it felt wrong.

"I'm so glad, honey," Mom said, when I had finished. Jeff was calling me in the background, so I put Dad on the phone.

There we were in our busy, active household, a family, and there was Mom in the farmhouse all alone. I guess, at the time, I didn't think of it that way. I certainly didn't realize how much *I* was really missing Mom. I guess I wasn't sure *what* I was thinking.

CHAPTER 8

saturday

Dear Claudia,
   Sorry about that rain you and Mary Anne had when you baby-sat the other night. Here? It never rains. This afternoon I baby-sat for Clover and Daffodil -- you remember I told you-- they're my old neighbors? Well, it was one of my all-time great baby-sitting days. Let me put it this way-- I came home with a better tan than I started with. Ah, California. You know how I love the warm outdoors...
                    Dawn

My first job for the We ♥ Kids Club really was a great success. When I got to their house, Clover and Daffodil practically knocked each other over trying to say hello to me. Daffodil was a little more subdued — she's nine years old and more grown-up than Clover, who's only six. Clover was pulling at my sundress before I could even get through the door.

"Whoa!" I said. "It's only me."

"Dawn!" cried Clover. "My favorite baby-sitter in the whole wide world!"

I must admit, when one of the kids gives you a compliment like that, it's not very hard to love your job.

Mrs. Austin gave me a big hug hello. It was like I was a long-lost friend, returning from a great war or something.

"The kids have been so excited," she said. She drew me into the room.

I always loved the Austins' house, especially the living room. Mrs. Austin is a weaver. Dad said when they were young, she and her husband used to be "flower children." (I think he means hippies.) That's why Clover and Daffodil have such odd names. Now, though, Mrs. Austin weaves professionally for a few stores that carry expensive hand-crafted goods, and she has three different-sized looms in her living room. The looms sit on the polished wood floor underneath the big bay window. I love to take a look at what she's working on. She mostly makes pieces with deep, rich natural colors. Beautiful warm browns and earthy reds. And there's always something different on the looms.

"I never have to redecorate," she laughs. "Whenever I change projects, I change the whole visual effect of the room."

That day, Clover and Daffodil were each wearing hand-woven cotton vests that their mother had made for them. Clover pulled a small change purse out of her vest pocket and shook the money into her hand.

"Pieces of eight!" she cried. "I'm rich!"

I had forgotten about Clover's wild imagination.

"I gave each of the kids some money," Mrs. Austin explained. "There's a small carnival that's set up over in the field behind the mall. Since it's such a beautiful day, I thought you might want to walk the girls over and spend the afternoon there."

"Super," I said. The afternoon couldn't be shaping up better.

Mrs. Austin grabbed her shawl (hand-woven, of course) and headed out the door. She was going to a Craft Council meeting, so she'd be gone all afternoon.

Before we could go off to the fair, Clover and Daffodil had to drag me all over the house and show me everything that was new. It *had* been a long time since we'd seen each other.

"This is the kitchen and this is the refrigerator," said Clover in her excitement.

"She knows *that*, silly," said Daffodil. "Come on. Let me show you my science project."

We went all through Clover's and Daffodil's rooms. They showed me new clothes, new toys, new books, new school projects, report cards, you name it.

As they were winding down, I sat on Clover's bed and she got out her comb to comb through my long hair. (She always did love to do that.)

"I think somebody spun your hair into gold," she said. "Did you ever meet a little guy named Rumpelstiltskin?"

Of course I told her no, but I think Clover secretly went on believing her own imaginative version. Daffodil sat quietly by. Sometimes, even though she's older, she gets overshadowed by Clover's more outgoing nature. She's also at that gangly stage — her legs and arms seem a little too long for her body.

"Well," I said, standing up. "Shall we head for the carnival?"

Clover popped up beside me. "To see the gypsies!" she cried. She was down the stairs and out the door, with Daffodil and I trailing behind her.

The day was warm and dry and the bright blue sky was streaked with thin, wispy clouds. We had only a short hike to get to the fairgrounds. Just as Mrs. Austin had said, the fair was set up behind the mall. There were a couple of rides — a ferris wheel and an octopus ride with cages that looped up and over.

"A space creature!" shouted Clover.

There were also lots of midway games, plenty of food booths (Hmmm. Hot dogs and cotton candy. Not my idea of a healthy treat), and a fenced-off ring with pony rides.

Clover had me by one hand and I had Daffodil by the other. Clover dragged us from one booth to the next, trying to decide where we should start.

"How about the ring toss?" Daffodil asked in a smallish voice.

"Ring toss!" Clover boomed in echo.

No sooner had she spotted it than we were there. The girls plunked down their money and got their handful of rings. As you can imagine, Clover was an enthusiastic player. Enthusiastic, but not very skilled. Out of six rings she got . . . six misses.

"Oh, well," she shrugged. It was Daffodil's turn.

Clover had pitched her rings quickly, but Daffodil took her time. She eyed the hook that was the target. She scrunched her eyebrows in concentration. One hit! Two! Three! A miss. Four hits! Another miss.

"Wow!" I said. "Four out of six. That's not bad at all."

Daffodil smiled shyly. Something about her reminded me of Shannon — she was like a puppy who had not yet grown into its paws.

"Can I try again?" she asked quietly.

"Sure," I said.

Daffodil bought another round of rings. Again she scrunched up her eyebrows in concentration before she started. One hit. Two. Three. Four. A miss. Another miss.

"Oh," I groaned. "So close!"

Daffodil smiled and said nothing. Clover was already dragging us over to the pony ring.

"Want to ride?" I asked Daffodil.

Daffodil emptied her change purse into her hand and counted her quarters.

"Nah," she said. "I think I'll wait."

Clover ran through the gate and hopped on the pony.

"Giddy-up!" she cried. She nudged the pony's ribs with her heels, but the pony stood still. It was waiting for a command from the young woman in jeans and cowboy boots who would lead it around the ring.

"Charge!" cried Clover.

I looked at Daffodil and grinned.

"Who do you think Clover thinks she is?" I asked. "Teddy Roosevelt?"

"Annie Oakley, I betcha," said Daffodil.

As it turned out, Clover was thinking of herself more as an Indian brave. She explained that to us after the pony ride and before the ferris wheel. Then, after the ferris wheel, of course, she had to go on the octopus ride. When she was finished, we were all ready for a little refreshment.

"Cotton candy!" yelled Clover.

Well, what could I do? Clover bought her cotton candy, and Daffodil and I got some fruit juice and vegetable fritters. We found a patch of grass to sit on at the edge of the carnival and let the sights and sounds play around us as we ate our snack.

Daffodil counted her change again.

"I could play two more times," she said.

"Ring toss?" I asked.

She nodded her head. We waited for Clover to finish her cone of cotton candy (of course it got all over her face. She looked like some sort of sticky, pink elf), then we headed back to the booth. Daffodil looked determined. She may be a quiet one, I thought, but she's got a lot of resolve.

Her first game came in short of the others. Only three hits and three misses. Daffodil licked her lips as she bought the rings for her fourth and last game. One hit! Two! Three! Four! Five! . . . We all held our breath. . . . Six!

"Yippee!" yelled Clover. She jumped up and down and shook her sister by the arm.

Daffodil's face broke into a wide, bright smile.

"I knew it," she said. "I knew I could do it."

In the back of the booth was a shelf of stuffed animals, which were the prizes.

"The pink elephant, please," Daffodil said to the man running the booth.

It certainly was pink. It was as pink as the cotton candy that still stuck to Clover's cheeks.

"Come on," I said. "Let's go home while we're winners. And let's get you cleaned up." I ruffled Clover's hair. "Miss Teddy Roosevelt-Annie Oakley-Spotted Deer, or whoever you are."

When Mrs. Austin got home, she had the

same reaction I did to the stuffed elephant.

"It certainly is pink," she laughed. "Congratulations, sweetie."

I don't think Mrs. Austin was going to pick that color for her next weaving project.

The day had been so pleasant, so easy. I was thinking how I couldn't wait to tell Sunny and the others all about it. There was a knock on the door. It was Jeff.

"Mom's on the phone," he said. "Come on."

Mrs. Austin slipped me my pay and I ran home after Jeff.

" 'Bye, Dawn-Best-Baby-sitter," Clover called after me.

As I was running I found myself thinking not of Mom, but of the day, of Clover and Daffodil, of Mrs. Austin, the We ♥ Kids Club. . . . I got on the phone and Mom started right in talking. She told me about Granny and Pop-Pop and then she said she'd run into Kristy and her mother at the store. "Oh," she said, "and Mary Anne called."

Wow! Mom, Granny and Pop-Pop, Kristy, even Mary Anne. I hadn't thought of any of them all day long. What did that mean, I wondered. I suddenly felt wrenched out of one world and yanked into another.

CHAPTER 9

Dear Dawn,

Thought you might want to know that nothing has changed in Stoneybrook. Saturday I baby-sat at the Brewers, and you'll be interested to know that Ben Brewer, the old ghost, is alive and well and living on the third floor. At least that's what Karen says. Me, I think Sam has something to do with it. This time, anyway.

See ya,

Jessi

Well, some things never change. When you baby-sit for Karen Brewer, there's bound to be ghosts involved, or witches with magic spells, or some such spookiness. Jessi had taken a job at the Brewers' for Saturday afternoon. Kristy was going shopping with her mother, and Sam, Charlie, and Watson were out who knows where. That left the younger ones — David Michael, Karen, and Andrew — in need of a sitter, so Jessi filled the job.

Kristy's mom walked Jessi around the house, giving her all the usual information — showing her where the emergency numbers were, the snacks, etc. Of course, Kristy followed right behind. Sometimes you'd think Kristy was the Baby-sitting Police, not just the president of our club.

"Aren't you going to ask about the first-aid kit?" she prompted Jessi.

"Uh, yeah," Jessi stumbled.

"It's right in the medicine cabinet," Kristy's mom said, smiling.

Mrs. Brewer could hardly get Kristy away from Jessi and out the door.

"Shannon and Boo-Boo have been fed," Kristy called from the doorway, "and the plants have been watered, and the dishwasher's run through."

"And the lawn has been mowed," Kristy's mom teased, "and the house has been painted, and the telephone bill's been paid."

Kristy blushed furiously.

"Okay, 'bye," she called to Jessi.

Jessi picked up Andrew and together they waved good-bye.

"Well," Jessi said, when the door had closed. "Now it's just the four of us."

"Oh, no," Karen said firmly. "Five. Ben Brewer."

"Right," Jessi smiled.

"Come on," Karen said, grabbing Jessi's hand. "Time to play Let's All Come In."

"Oh, no," groaned David Michael.

Let's All Come In is a favorite game of Karen's, if you can call it a game. She gets everyone to pretend that they're different characters in a hotel lobby, checking in. What it really is, is an excuse to play dress-up. Karen dresses up in a long black dress and a hat, and the boys wear sailor caps. I think David Michael has played this game one time too many.

"Andrew and I were in the middle of building a Lego city," he said. "Weren't we, Andrew?"

"Yup," Andrew agreed.

"Looks like it's just you and me," Karen said to Jessi.

"You, me, and Ben Brewer," Jessi smiled.

Jessi got the boys settled back in David Michael's bedroom, where there really was a Lego city in progress.

"I'm the architect," David Michael said importantly, "and Andrew is the construction boss. Right, Andrew?"

"Right," Andrew smiled. Construction boss sounded pretty good to him.

Karen took Jessi to her room and began to root through the trunk she kept her dress-up clothes in.

"Hmm," she said, looking Jessi up and down. "Do you want to be a cocktail waitress or do you want to be coming from the society ball?"

"Society ball, of course," Jessi replied.

"I don't think I have anything here to fit you," Karen said slowly. "You know what that means?"

"What?" asked Jessi.

"That means" — there was an ominous tone in Karen's voice — "we have to go to the other clothes trunk. And it's on *the third floor*."

If this had been a movie, right at that moment scary music would have sounded. The third floor was, after all, where Karen believed Ben Brewer lived. As it was, the only sound was the nervous tapping of Karen's little foot. She twisted her fingers and bit her lip.

"I don't know," she said.

"We don't *have* to play Let's All Come In," said Jessi.

Well, that decided it for Karen.

"Oh, yes we do," she said with great conviction. "We can't let a *ghost* rule our lives."

Karen took Jessi's hand and squeezed it firmly but bravely.

"Come on," she said.

For her, I think, being scared is half the fun.

Karen led Jessi up the narrow staircase that leads to the third floor of the Brewer mansion. The third floor is seldom used. The house is so big that the first and second floors can comfortably house the whole family, large as it is. The third floor is really only used for storage. It's like one big attic, even though it's sectioned into rooms.

As they neared the top of the stairway, Karen began to creep.

"Aughhh!" she screamed suddenly.

"What is it?" Jessi asked.

Karen's eyes, big as saucers, focused on the top of the bannister. She didn't say anything, she just pointed.

There, in the dust that covered the wood

bannister, someone had etched the words "Turn Back!"

"Maybe we should," said Jessi. She didn't believe in the ghost, and yet . . .

"There's no turning back now," Karen said dramatically. She pressed ahead.

Karen crept down the hall to the room where the other trunk was stored. The door was closed, but not completely. It was open a small crack. Karen pushed the door slowly. *CRASH!* A can clattered on the floor in front of them and water splattered from the can all over their shoes and legs.

Of course, Karen screamed again. At this point, though, Jessi began to be skeptical. The door had obviously been booby-trapped. Why would a ghost booby-trap a door with a can full of water? It seemed to Jessi that the tricks a ghost would play would be, somehow, more ghostly. This seemed more like a practical joke. And if she had to name a practical joker in the house, she was pretty sure she knew who that might be.

Karen swung the door open wide and stomped loudly into the room.

"Ben Brewer!" she called out. "We're coming in. You can't stop us. We've made up our minds."

Karen marched over to the large dusty trunk,

unlatched it, and opened its lid. The smell of mothballs flooded the room. Karen lifted up a dark blue crushed velvet dress that lay across the top of the pile.

"How about this dre — " she started to say, but her eye caught a note that had been tucked underneath the gown. The note was written in a thick, dark red ink.

"Blood-red," Karen whispered.

She picked up the note and read it.

"Death to all who enter here," it said.

Karen stood frozen, fixed in one spot. Her face paled.

"I think we better go back downstairs," she said to Jessi. Her voice was small and shaking. She dropped the note. It fluttered to the floor. She walked out of the room, gliding, like a sleepwalker or a zombie.

Jessi picked up the note and looked it over. The paper had been torn off a notepad. On the other side was a printed logo.

"SHS," it said.

SHS. Stoneybrook High School.

Jessi folded the note and put it in her pocket. She followed Karen back downstairs.

When Kristy and her mom got home, Karen ran down to the front hallway, frantic to tell them all the latest evidence.

"It *proves*," she said, "that Ben Brewer is

living right up there on the third floor. How do we know he won't come down?" she asked. "How do we know he doesn't want to take over the second floor, too?"

As it happened, Sam and Charlie pulled in the driveway right after Kristy and their mom. When Sam came in, Karen was going on about the ghost.

"The note was written in blood," she said, then shuddered. "I wonder whose."

Sam smirked and nudged Charlie. Mrs. Brewer shot a look at Sam. He shrugged innocently.

"I wonder how another child would fit into all this," Mrs. Brewer wondered aloud.

"Another child?" Kristy asked. "What do you mean?" Mrs. Brewer shrugged distractedly. Kristy shook her head and followed her mom into the kitchen with Karen trailing behind. Jessi pulled the note out of her pocket and handed it to Sam.

"Lose something?" Jessi asked.

Sam grinned sheepishly and shoved the note quickly into his pocket.

Kristy came out of the kitchen.

"Of course this ghost incident will have to be written up in the club notebook," she said. "You realize that all the other club members should be aware of anything this important."

Jessi told me later she just smiled and nodded. Ben Brewer was living in the mansion, all right. It was Sam Brewer who'd made sure of that.

CHAPTER 10

Monday

Dear Stacey,
   There you are in New York
City and here I am in
California. Whatever happened
to good ol' Stoneybrook, Connecticut? I'm having the time
of my life. It almost seems
as if I never left in the first
place. The We ♥ Kids Club is
keeping me very busy. It's
a baby-sitters club with a
difference — NO RING-DINGS
ALLOWED!
                    Dawn

All that weekend I looked forward to the next meeting of the We ♥ Kids Club. I had had such a good time with Clover and Daffodil, and couldn't wait to tell Sunny and the other members of the club.

When I arrived that Monday afternoon, Sunny was sitting on the floor of her room, with newspapers spread out all around her. She had a bag of potting soil, a couple of small clay pots, and a few jars in which she had rooted some babies from her spider plant.

"Hi. Come in," she said. "If you can find a place. I'm just potting these."

I sprawled out on an empty stretch of Sunny's green shag rug. It was the usual relaxed, California atmosphere of the We ♥ Kids Club.

While we waited for Jill and Maggie, I told Sunny all about my afternoon at the Austins, about Clover's wild imagination, and about Daffodil's tries at the ring toss.

"I think Clover's going to be an actress," said Sunny. "Or a writer or something like that."

"And Daffodil is the real surprise," I said. "You think because she's quiet she's going to be shy, but she has a real determination to her."

"Did you notice how she's suddenly all leg?"

Sunny asked. "She's like a colt or a baby deer. . . . "

"Exactly," I laughed.

As we were talking, a warm, homey feeling spread through me. It occurred to me that what we were doing was sharing the exact same kind of information that Kristy has the members of the Baby-sitters Club write up in the official Club notebook. And here we were just talking. Simple as that. See, I thought, you *can* accomplish things informally.

Jill and Maggie arrived together, talking about some kids at school. Sunny finished up her potting.

"Do you remember Joe Luhan?" Jill asked me.

"Sure." He had been one of the boys in my class.

"Well, he and Tom Swanson are having a party on Sunday. Will you still be here or are you leaving before then?"

"The day before," I said. "I'm leaving Saturday."

Too bad. That sounded like fun. A party with Joe Luhan and Tom Swanson. I'd grown up with those guys. I knew them better than I knew most of the boys in Stoneybrook.

Sunny's mom poked her head in the door.

"Am I allowed in here?" she asked.

"*Mo-om*," Sunny moaned. "Of course. What do you think?"

Her mom looked over at me and smiled.

"It just occurred to me," she said. "Dawn, would you and the girls like to stay for dinner? We won't get many more chances to see you this visit. You're just here for another week, aren't you?"

I looked at Sunny. Sunny looked at me.

"Oh. Stay, stay, stay," Sunny pleaded.

"I'll have to check with Dad," I said. He was back at work that week and wouldn't be home for another half hour. "Can I let you know at the end of the meeting?" I asked Sunny's mom.

"Sure," she said. "If your dad says yes, we'd love to have you." She winked at me. "Spinach lasagna," she said, and she disappeared out the door.

"Yum," said Sunny. "That reminds me. I'm hungry."

"Me too," said Maggie. "Starving."

"Should I get us our snack?" Sunny asked.

"Yeah!" we all agreed.

Sunny stood up and dusted the potting soil off her hands.

"Ick! Wash your hands first," Maggie teased.

Sunny wiggled her muddy fingers in Maggie's face.

93

"No way!" she laughed, then bounded down the stairs.

Since no phone calls were coming in, we just sat around chatting. Jill and Maggie talked some more about the kids I remembered in our class. Right then an idea began taking seed in my mind. I started to picture myself back in the class, and how easy it would be to slip right back in.

Sunny came back up with the food — guacamole dip and cut-up raw vegetables that she had made earlier in the afternoon.

"All *right*," Jill said, grabbing a carrot stick.

"No calls yet?" Sunny asked.

We shook our heads. The phone hadn't rung once.

"Maybe we should work on the recipe file," Sunny suggested.

This was a project I hadn't heard about yet. Sunny pulled a yellow plastic file box off the top of her desk. On the front she had pasted a picture of a bright red apple. Inside were cards with recipes that kids could make and that they liked to eat.

"Healthy recipes," said Sunny. "It's an extension of that cookbook I showed you."

"Wow!" I said. "What a great idea."

Maggie and Jill fished into their purses and each pulled out a recipe she had found over the weekend. Jill's homemade lemonade was from a magazine. Maggie's "Raisin Surprise" was from the back of a raisin box. They set about copying the recipes onto the small yellow index cards.

Sunny chomped on a celery stick and looked at me. "It'd be great if you can stay for dinner," she said.

I thought back to all the times in the past that I had had dinner over at Sunny's house. How many times had it been? Probably a thousand. Well, at least a hundred. Sunny's mom and dad were great. When we were younger they always let us be excused from the table as soon as we had finished eating, just so we would have a longer time to play.

"I hope you can stay," Sunny said again, and suddenly something popped into my head.

Maybe I *could* stay. Maybe I could *really* stay. Maybe I didn't have to go back to Connecticut at all, or just go back to get my things. Maybe I could move back in with Dad and Jeff, have my old room back, my old friends, my old school.

It was a strange thought, scary and exciting at the same time. Until then, I had just been having a great time, a *fabulous* time, but it had never occurred to me that I could think about making it last forever (or at least for longer).

Now that the thought occurred to me, what was I supposed to do?

I was still sitting in the same room, but it felt like I was in another world. Around me, I could hear Sunny and Jill and Maggie chattering away. Jill rummaged around in her purse for her bottle of nail polish, a different color this time. The phone rang, a call came in. I think it was one of the neighbors down the street, and Maggie took the job.

"Earth to Dawn. Earth to Dawn," said Sunny. She had her hands cupped over her mouth like a megaphone.

"Oh, yeah," I said. "I'm here." (Just barely.)

"So what do you think?"

"About what?"

"About the *nail* polish."

"What about it?"

"Do you think Berry Pink is better on Jill or Lucious Blush?"

Hmm, I guess I had missed a part of the conversation. I took a look. Jill had half of the old polish on and half of the new.

"Which is which?" I asked.

"Forget it," Jill giggled. "They'll *discontinue* the colors before you decide."

"What time is it?" I asked suddenly.

"Five-thirty," said Sunny. "Hey, you can call your dad now."

Five-thirty. Time to leave.

"I don't think I can stay for dinner," I said abruptly. "I have to do something. I mean, I have to talk to Dad about something."

"But . . ." Sunny started.

The phone rang again.

"It's Mrs. Austin," she said. "She needs someone for Clover and Daffodil. Do you want it?" she asked me.

"Yeah," I said. "Of course. Thanks. Sign me up. But I gotta run."

Sunny and the others stared after me. I grabbed my purse and ran out the door. It must've all looked very strange. Well, what can I say? It felt strange for me, too. Suddenly it seemed like my whole world was changing.

CHAPTER 11

Monday

Dear Mom,
~~I'm writing to~~ talk about
I just ~~want to say~~ that
This is a very difficult
~~thing for me~~ to

Well, that was a card I never finished writing. How do you tell your mother that you want to move away from her? That you want, in fact, to move to the other side of the country?

When I came back from the We ♥ Kids meeting I ran right to my room. I thought it might help if I wrote a draft of a letter to Mom and figured out how I might approach this very delicate subject. As you see, I didn't get very far.

I decided, really, that it was too early to think about Mom. The first step was just to talk to Dad.

Jeff knocked on my door to call me to dinner.

"Hey, Sis," he said. "Get your bod to the table."

How could I get through life without my dopey brother, I wondered. I didn't *want* to leave Jeff. I didn't *want* to leave Dad.

Mrs. Bruen had made her usual terrific dinner (fish fillets baked with tomatoes and covered with cheese sauce), and we ate it in the beautiful, clean dining room at a table with a tablecloth and flowers. Everything was arranged nicely, everything was organized. No misplaced purses, no lost keys.

I poured myself some juice from the frosty cold pitcher.

99

"Broccoli?" Dad asked me.

"Yes, please."

How would I start?

"Dad," I began.

"Yes?"

"I was thinking. . . ."

"Yes?"

"Um . . . Um . . . Hmm. I forgot what I was going to say."

Call me chicken if you want. It was very difficult for me to bring up the subject. We ate awhile, and I let Jeff and Dad talk.

"Aw, come on," Jeff was saying. "All my friends get to watch more television than *that*."

"Not on school nights," Dad said firmly. "Enjoy this vacation schedule while you can."

"But, Dad . . . "

"You heard me," said Dad. "Subject closed."

That quieted Jeff. It also gave me space to try again.

"Dad," I said.

"Yeah?"

"I was thinking. . . ."

"Sounds familiar," Dad grinned.

"Yeah, well, I was thinking . . . I mean, it's just an idea, but I was wondering if . . . well, what I'm thinking is, maybe I want to consider, well, maybe I want to consider staying in California, moving here like Jeff did."

100

I paused. Nobody said anything.

"It's just that I like it so much here," I continued. "Everything is just my style. The weather, the kids. I mean, I just got this idea today, but actually maybe it's been brewing all along. I'm not even sure it's what I want. But I'm thinking about it, so I wanted to bring it up."

Dad was watching me closely. Jeff was watching Dad.

Dad let out a big breath. You'd have thought he was the one doing all the talking.

"Well," he said slowly. "It's certainly a possibility."

Jeff tossed his napkin in the air. He'd been waiting for Dad's response.

"Yippee!" he cried.

"Well," Dad sighed again. "There's a lot to think about here."

It suddenly occurred to me that maybe Dad didn't want me. He didn't seem too enthusiastic. But then he burst into a grin, the kind of grin that's unmistakably his.

"Oh, Sunshine," he said. "You know how happy I would be if you were out here?"

"Yippee!" Jeff yelled again.

"Of course," Dad added quickly, "there's a lot of things we have to consider here. There's your mother. . . . " There was a long pause.

"And the custody and your school. And, of course, what *you* really want."

"But it's possible?" I asked.

"Well, from a practical standpoint, yes," Dad said. "You've got your own room here. Mrs. Bruen is already here and working. . . . But from a legal standpoint, I don't know. Your mother has custody, but then, she still has custody of Jeff and here he is. I'd have to talk to her and see, uh, see what we could arrange. Do you want me to call her tonight, just to talk?"

"No!" I was surprised at the strength of my answer.

"Do *you* want to call her?" Dad asked.

"Not yet," I said. I wasn't ready for that at all. "The first thing is I have to figure things out, decide what I want."

"You're the only one who *can* decide that, Sunshine," said Dad. "Your mother and I have the legal proceedings to work out, but we've got to know that it's what you want."

"Right," I said.

Dad and I ate the rest of our dinner in relative silence. You wouldn't have noticed the quiet, though. Jeff did a good job of filling that in.

"If you stay here we can go to the beach all the time," he said enthusiastically. "You can come to my school if I'm in an assembly. I can borrow your Walkman, you can borrow my camera. . . . "

Jeff went on like that for the rest of the meal, but I hardly heard him. All the things I had to think about were swimming through my head.

When I finished dinner I went back to my room and closed the door. California, Connecticut. California, Connecticut. I couldn't keep my thoughts straight. I decided to write them down.

I tore a piece of paper off my notepad and drew a line down the middle. At the top of the left half I wrote PROS: CALIFORNIA. At the top of the right I wrote PROS: STONEYBROOK. When I finished my list, this is what I had:

PROS: CALIFORNIA	PROS: STONEYBROOK
Dad	Mom
Jeff	
the sun!	
We ♥ Kids Club	Baby-sitters Club
Sunny (and others)	Mary Anne (and others)
healthy foods	
the beach	
an organized household	
Clover and Daffodil	the kids in Stoneybrook

I thought about adding "Disneyland" under "California" but decided against it. It didn't seem like enough of a reason to move from one coast to the other, and besides, the California side already had plenty of entries.

Well then, it seemed pretty clear. California. I guess that's what I wanted. Somehow, though, it didn't seem resolved in my head. I needed to talk about it some more. I couldn't talk about it with Mom, and I'd already talked about it some with Dad. Maybe I should call Sunny? I decided against it. She'd just persuade me to stay. Maybe Mary Anne . . . Of course. She'd *said* to call.

I wandered out of my room.

"Dad," I called. "Can I call Mary Anne in Connecticut?"

"It's ten o'clock there," he said.

It was late, but it was vacation, so she should still be awake.

"Can I?" I asked again.

"Sure," he said.

The kitchen was now empty, so I set myself up in there. I opened my address book to the "S" page and ran my finger across. Mary Anne's name was the first. She had, after all, been my first Stoneybrook friend.

As I dialed her number, I could almost hear her voice answering the phone. She'd probably squeal when she heard it was me. Mary Anne was a good choice, I thought. She'd be perfect to talk to in a situation like this. She's the kind of friend who would help me figure out what *I* wanted. I mean, of course she'd be sad if I wanted to stay in California, but she'd understand.

On the other end, the phone was ringing. Three rings. Four. No one picked up. Maybe they're just pulling into the driveway, I thought. I let it ring more. No one answered. I laid the phone back in its cradle and dropped down in a kitchen chair.

Around me the light was getting softer. The kitchen took on a rosy hue. Ten o'clock in Connecticut. I pictured Mary Anne and her father coming home from wherever they were, turning the lights on in their darkened house. Then I pictured Mom. I wondered what she was doing. Probably she was reading in bed. Or maybe she was out with the Trip-Man. (Horrors!) I wondered what she would say when I told her what I was thinking about. What would she do in that funny old farmhouse all by herself? If only *she* could move back to California, too.

Of course, I knew that was impossible.

The hard thing was, I found myself realizing that the person I really wanted to be talking to about all this *was* Mom. I wanted the two of us to be sitting on my bed, having one of our heart-to-hearts. I wanted her to ask me questions, say wise things. I wanted her to help lead me through all this tangle I seemed to be tied up in.

I started to feel closed in from all the things I had to think about. I went out to the back patio and watched the golden sun fade.

CHAPTER 12

Dear Dawn,
   It's business as usual at the Pikes. The other morning I sat there with Mallory, and wouldn't you know it, the triplets were on Nicky's back. Nicky ran off to you-know-where and eventually I had to go get him. Sound familiar?
                              Love,
                                  Kristy

P.S. Nicky talked a lot about you, actually. I think he really misses you. Well, he doesn't have long to wait now.

I got the postcard from Kristy that Tuesday, when I still hadn't made up my mind what to do. I didn't find out the details until later, but I could picture the scene at the Pike household, where things are always a little wild.

The Pikes, you may remember, have eight kids. And that's just one family, not two combined or anything like that. Because it's such a crowd, Mrs. Pike always gets two sitters whenever she goes out. Now that Mallory, the oldest Pike, is eleven and in the Baby-sitters Club, Mrs. Pike usually uses Mallory plus one other sitter. That day it was Kristy.

Claire, the youngest Pike (she's all of five years old), let Kristy in. She was still in her pajamas.

"Moozie!" she cried. ("Moozie" is what she sometimes calls her mom.) "Moozie! Kristy's here."

Moozie didn't appear, but Mallory did.

"Mom'll be down in a minute," she said.

"Where's everybody else?" asked Kristy. (The house seemed strangely quiet.)

"The triplets and Nicky are in the backyard, and Vanessa and Margo are upstairs."

"Well," said Kristy. "Where should we start? How about with you, Claire? Let's get you out of those pajamas and into your play clothes."

"These *are* my play clothes, Kristy silly-billy-goo-goo," said Claire. "Today I'm wearing my pajamas *all day long*."

Kristy looked at Mallory. Mallory shrugged. That's another thing about the Pikes. Mr. and Mrs. Pike hardly have any rules. If Claire were going to school that day, of course she'd have to get dressed. But for staying at home? If pajamas was what she wanted, pajamas it was.

Claire streaked up the stairs, waggling her head and crying "Moo!" Was she calling her mother or making cow sounds? Did it matter? This was definitely going to be one of Claire's sillier days.

The back door swung open and the triplets appeared. They each grabbed a cookie from the jar on the kitchen counter and then raced back outside. The door swung open again. It was Nicky. He'd come for *his* cookie. (The triplets are ten and Nicky is eight. He sometimes has a hard time keeping up.) *BANG!* Nicky was back out the door, following his brothers.

"Kristy, hi!" It was Mrs. Pike. In her hurry, she grabbed a sweater out of the closet. "Oops, that's Vanessa's," she said. She grabbed another. "I should be back early afternoon. More library business. And if the meeting gets out on time, I'm going to squeeze in a haircut."

109

She gave the sitters last-minute instructions and reminded Mallory that there was canned ravioli and homemade cole slaw for lunch.

Ravioli and *cole slaw?* Well, I guess, when you're getting meals together for eight kids every day, you come up with some pretty unusual combinations.

Mrs. Pike called good-bye over her shoulder and hurried out the door.

"I'll go let Vanessa and Margo know I'm here," Kristy said to Mallory.

To keep all fronts covered, Mallory headed out to the yard.

Vanessa and Margo are two of the middle kids. Vanessa is nine and Margo is seven. You can pretty much trust them to play well by themselves, but you always have to check to see what they're up to. In this case that was a good idea. Claire had joined them and Vanessa was showing her sisters how to write a letter in "invisible ink." She had dragged a carton of milk upstairs and the three of them were dipping paintbrushes into the milk and using it as ink to write messages on white paper.

"Kristy!" Vanessa said when she walked in. "Read my message. Can you, please? It's invisible, like the seas." (Vanessa is a budding poet. She loves to rhyme and doesn't always

110

care so much about making sense.)

Kristy looked at the blank sheet of paper.

"A polar bear in a snowstorm?" she guessed.

"Silly-billy-goo-goo!" cried Claire.

"No, it's a message," said Vanessa. She held the paper flat and blew on it so the milk would dry. "You can't see it now," she said, "but watch this."

She strode out of the bedroom and into her parents' room, where there was an iron and an ironing board standing up in the corner.

"Heat," she said. "We'll iron the messages and the heat will make the milk letters turn brown."

"Wait a minute. Wait a minute," said Kristy. "I'll be the one to do the ironing."

"But I iron all the time," said Vanessa. "For Mom. I do practically a basket a week."

Kristy considered.

"Well," she said. "You can iron, but I'll supervise. Claire and Margo, you sit over here and watch."

Kristy sat on the edge of the bed and patted places next to her for the two younger girls.

Vanessa waited for the iron to heat up and then ran it lightly over the sheets of paper. As she predicted, the white letters darkened and the messages came clear.

Vanessa's message read:

> "Ships on the ocean,
> Ships at shore,
> Wipe your feet,
> And close the door."

Margo's said, "My teacher is a big baboon."

Claire's just said, "CAT HAT RAT FAT CLAIRE." (Well, when you're first learning to write, you don't have a lot of words to choose from.)

"Let's write some for the boys!" Vanessa cried suddenly. She started out the door.

"Hey! Iron off," Kristy reminded her. (When you're a baby-sitter you *do* have to be thinking about safety all the time.)

Vanessa ran back and unplugged the iron, and the girls ran back to their room to write more secret messages.

By the time lunch rolled around, the girls had a stack of paper a few inches high. Each of the pieces had a secret milk-message written on it. It had been a busy morning.

Mallory was in the kitchen heating up the ravioli. (She had opened a giant-sized can. It looked like it was meant for an army platoon.) Kristy started dishing up the cole slaw.

"Nicky's in a little bit of a funk," Mallory said, filling Kristy in on the backyard crew.

"The triplets wouldn't let him play with them."

"Again?" said Kristy. This was an ongoing problem.

"Well, they were playing Frisbee and all they'd let him do was fetch it when it went out of the yard."

Nicky banged through the door and into the kitchen. He slumped into a chair and began to kick his feet back and forth.

"Hi, Nicky," said Kristy.

"Hi," Nicky said glumly.

The triplets trooped in behind him.

"Ravioli?" said Byron. "Cole slaw? Ugh!" But he sat right down at the table, and Kristy noticed that when she put his plate in front of him, he gobbled the food right up.

"We've got secret messages for you," Margo said to the boys. She handed Jordan the stack of papers.

"Who cares?" he said. He pushed the papers aside.

"Look at them," Vanessa said. "They've got secret messages on them. Bet you can't read them."

"Don't want to," said Jordan.

Margo grabbed the papers up.

"Well, don't then," she said. "We don't care."

Adam had taken his spoon to his plate and

113

was mixing the ravioli in with the cole slaw.

"Ooh, gross," he said. "Snake guts."

Nicky grinned.

"Hey, that's what it does look like," he said. "The tomato sauce is the blood."

Unfortunately, when Nicky said that, he had a full mouth of ravioli himself, and some of it splurted out on the table.

"Yuk!" Adam cried. "Ooh, Nicky! Say it, don't spray it!"

Nicky sat there quietly for a moment. Kristy thought he might be about to burst into tears. Instead, he looked at her and said, "May I please be excused? I want to go to the hideout."

Now, there's an example of one of the few rules in the Pike house. Nicky is allowed to go to the hideout only if he tells whoever is in charge where he's going.

"Eat some more ravioli first," said Mallory.

Nicky did, and he was excused.

The hideout that he disappeared to was the secret passage I told you about, the one that's in my house. Nicky goes in through the trapdoor in our barn. He usually just sits in there, reads or whatever. It's his special place.

That day, a half hour passed, then forty-five minutes. Lunch was cleared and cleaned up and the kids all went outside together to play in the backyard. Kristy decided she'd go check on Nicky. He was right where he said he would be, sitting alone at the head of the tunnel. Kristy climbed down the ladder and joined him.

"Hey, Nick," she said.

"Hi."

"Whatcha doin'?"

"Nothin'."

It took Kristy awhile to get Nicky talking, but they did talk some about how hard it sometimes was to be a younger brother.

"This feels like when Dawn talked to me," Nicky said.

I was the one who first discovered Nicky's hiding place. And when I found him, we had had a pretty good heart-to-heart.

"You miss Dawn?" Kristy asked.

Nicky nodded. "Will she be back soon?"

"At the end of the week," Kristy said.

Nicky heaved a big sigh.

"I don't know if I can last," he said.

Kristy laughed and gave him a hug.

"Come on," she said. "We better get going."

Back at the Pikes' house, things were as hectic as before. The only difference was, Mrs. Pike had come home.

"There's my Nicholas," she smiled.

She gave her son a quick kiss on the cheek and kneaded his slumping shoulders.

"You didn't get a haircut," Kristy noticed.

"No time," said Mrs. Pike. "Guess I'll have to call you again."

She paid Kristy and Mallory and left to check the backyard.

Hearing about the Pikes and reading Kristy's postcard got me thinking about the Baby-sitters Club and all the other big jobs we take on. "No job too big, no job too crazy" — that should be our motto. A lot of times it even seems the more chaotic, the more fun. In a way, I'm kind of proud of that. Whenever a problem has cropped up, we've pulled a solution from somewhere, out of our hats if we had to.

Listen to me. I sound like a testimonial.

Of course, the P.S. on Kristy's card helped. So Nicky Pike missed me, huh? Well, what do you know. . . . The truth was, I sort of missed him, too.

CHAPTER 13

Dear Dawn,

Miss you so much, honey. The old house just isn't the same without you. You'll be pleased (?) to know that I've had date after date with Trip. We've gone to a chamber concert, and a wine tasting, and I'll see him again Friday night before you get home. This time we're off to a lecture on humor.

Dawn, the very thought of picking you up at the airport has me all in smiles. A big hug and kiss for my sweet firstborn girl.

Love,
Mom

A lecture on humor? Oh, give me a break. How could Mom be falling for Trip-Man? That was *exactly* the problem with him. He'd be just the type to go to a *lecture* about humor. That's because he has no sense of it himself. Compare him with Dad. Dad is fun and funny. The Trip-Man is a bore.

I got the postcard from Mom on Wednesday, and no, I still hadn't made up my mind what to do. That wasn't the only postcard that came for me in the mail. There was also one from Jessi.

Dear Dawn,
Last night my family and I went back to visit our old neighborhood. It was fun, but also strange. All the relatives and all the old friends ... It was great to see them, but in a way, it made me think -- where is home? I guess it's Stoneybrook now. This is pretty heavy - I hope you don't

mind my writing you.
It's just that I figured
you're sort of going
through the same thing,
too.

See you soon,
Jessi

Well, what a haul in the mail. You can see why it was hard for me to make up my mind. My mom's postcard got me all agitated, but that got me thinking. I certainly did feel involved in the whole Trip-Man thing. I wanted to run right back to Connecticut so I could keep my eye on the situation. Did I want the Trip-Man marrying my mother? Moving into *our* farmhouse? No way!

Then, of course, Jessi's postcard . . . I never thought of it before, but she and I really *were* in very similar situations. Of course, Jessi went back to a neighborhood where everyone is black, and I went back to one where everyone is . . . well, blond. I thought of all my friends in the Baby-sitters Club. We all *were* very different — our backgrounds, the way we look, our interests. There was something very nice about that. Maybe Mary Anne doesn't read all the ghost stories that I happen to like, but what did that matter? And Claudia — she does eat a lot of junk food, all right, but she draws beautifully. I remembered the slumber party they had given me before I left. I pictured Claudia sitting on her sleeping bag, sketching Jessi, whose legs were stretched long, like a real ballerina's. This sounds corny, but the scene was like an advertisement for the U.N. or something. Different kinds of people with different interests, all getting along beautifully. (Okay, getting along *most* of the time.)

I headed over to Sunny's to spend the afternoon. I decided to talk with her about my dilemma.

"Dawn!" she squealed when I told her. "You're going to stay in California!"

"I didn't say that," I said defensively. "I said I was *thinking* about it."

"What's there to think about?" said Sunny. She picked up the California/Connecticut list that I had brought along with me. "It's all right here on paper. The vote is in."

"It's not that simple," I said. "Different things on the list have different weights."

"Okay," she said, looking down the list. "Your dad and Jeff. They balance your mom."

Well, sort of. How could I ever rate something like that?

"And the We ♥ Kids Club balances the

Baby-sitters Club," Sunny went on.

"Maybe not," I said carefully.

"Dawn, you told me yourself that you love how relaxed the club is here."

"Yeah."

That's what I said, but what I thought was the We ♥ Kids Club is not really as busy or as involved or active somehow as the Baby-sitters Club. Of course, I couldn't say that to Sunny's face. Instead, I just sort of shrugged my shoulders.

"Okay, another item," said Sunny. "Sunny (and others) versus Mary Anne (and others). I guess that balances, right?"

"Right," I said, halfheartedly. Was Sunny really as good a friend now as Mary Anne was? And really, I had five other friends in the Baby-sitters Club. Six, counting Stacey. I was much closer with all of them than I was with Jill and Maggie. Same with the kids I baby-sat for. Did Clover and Daffodil balance out all the kids in Stoneybrook? The Pikes, Jamie and Lucy Newton, the Perkins girls, Kristy's brothers and sister . . .

"Okay," said Sunny. "Here we go. The sun. The beach. Healthy foods. An organized household."

One by one she ticked off all the pros for California.

"Dawn, it's obvious. You're a California girl," she said.

"I know."

"And a California girl *belongs* in California."

I felt my face tighten. All of a sudden I didn't feel like discussing the subject anymore.

"You know what?" I said. "Let's drop this. I think it's better if I think about this whole thing myself."

"Okay," said Sunny. She looked a little taken aback.

That evening, when I went home for dinner, Dad was waiting to talk to me.

"Well, Sunshine," he said. "Is the verdict in?"

"Oh, Dad, not yet," I moaned.

Dad wrinkled up his forehead in concern.

"I know it's a big decision," he said, "but you're scheduled to fly back on Saturday. If you're really thinking about staying, I'll have to talk with your mother, well, the latest by tomorrow. We'll have to cancel the plane reservation, make other arrangements."

"Can I let you know tomorrow?" I asked. "Just one more day?"

Dad paused a long time.

"Oh, Sunshine," he said. "I don't want to influence your decision. You know what I would love, but there're many considerations here. Take the night to decide, but I really do have to know by tomorrow."

"Oh, thanks, Daddy," I said. I gave him the biggest hug ever.

Dad threw his arm around me and we walked into the kitchen to sit down for yet another terrific meal. The sun was streaming in through the skylight and the terra cotta tiles were cool and sparkling under our feet. (Mrs. Bruen had just given them one of her good moppings.)

After dinner Jeff and I helped with the dishes and then Dad brought a deck of cards out back. The three of us sat down at the picnic table for a game of Crazy Eights.

From where I sat I could see Clover and Daffodil next door, running around their yard barefoot, playing tag. I could smell the smokey scent of grilled fish coming from the barbecue of our other neighbors. A soft breeze rustled the skirt of my sundress against my warm, bare legs.

It'd be nice if Mom were here, I found myself thinking. If she were a part of things, playing cards with me, puttering around the patio. And wouldn't it be great if the doorbell rang and it was Mary Anne, just dropping by for a visit. What I wanted was to be able to share all the *things* I loved with all the *people* I loved. I imagined Nicky Pike out here holing up in a new, California hiding place. Maybe in the crawl space between the bushes. Maybe in the cave down by the creek.

That night, as I lay in bed, I made my decision. I knew what I had to do, where I had to be. I fell asleep hugging my pillow. I slept the whole night soundly, undisturbed.

CHAPTER 14

Dear Dawn,
  Kristy says you will be back on Saturday. If you hear a noise in the secret passage, don't get scared. It'll just be me. Lately I have a lot of ghost-hunting to do there. It keeps me pretty busy.
          Your secret tunnel pal,
              Nicky
P.S. You think maybe Sunday
     we could search the tunnel
     for old coins?

Thursday I woke up after Dad had already gone to work. I spent the day riding bikes with Jeff and came home to Nicky's funny note. Of course, I knew what I was going to do and by that point I was bursting to tell.

When Dad came home from work I sat him down to prepare him for my decision.

"I've decided to leave California and go back to Connecticut," I said.

Phew! Was that ever a hard thing to get out.

"I like both places," I continued. "I like them a lot. But I've made my home at Mom's now. It's time for me to go back."

Dad's eyes were all misty as I was explaining.

"I know," he said. "I guess I knew it all along."

Jeff, who had been standing in the doorway, turned around and stomped down the hall. It would take him another day or two to adjust to the disappointment.

"Well," said Dad, "for such a young girl you've had a big decision to make. You've got two homes. Just remember — this is always your home, too. We'll always be in touch, you can always visit. Your room here is reserved. And so is your place in our hearts."

Oh, Dad! What a cornball. By the time he finished his speech, my eyes were all misty, too. Okay, they were more than misty. Tears were streaming down my cheeks like rain.

"Dad," I blubbered. "Can I call Mom?"

"Sure, Sunshine," he said.

He left the room so I could be alone.

I think Mom was surprised to hear my voice all shaken up.

"I was wondering," I asked her. "Could you bring Mary Anne along to the airport with you?"

"Of course," said Mom. "I'll call her up as soon as we hang up."

Mom stopped talking. So did I.

"Dawn, honey," she said. "Is everything all right?"

Well, I hadn't meant to tell Mom that I had been thinking about staying in California, but somehow it all came flooding out.

"You know how it is, Mom," I said. "Avocados, the beach . . ."

"Oh, Dawn," she said, "I knew when you went out there you'd start thinking about moving back."

How come everybody seemed to know more about me than *I* knew? Dad had known I was going to decide to go back to Stoneybrook. Mom knew I was going to think about staying in California in the first place. Parents!

"You know, Dawn," Mom continued, "if

you *do* want to stay in California, we could give it some thought. I know it's been difficult for you. I know you love it out there."

"I made my decision," I said. My voice was cracking. "I'm going to come home."

"Dawn," Mom blubbered. "I would've missed you so much."

We certainly were a weepy family that night. Yup, the four of us were a family, even though we were split up in two different houses and separated by thousands of miles. And as far as understanding goes, I sure got a lot of that from my parents. From both of them. My dad might be on one coast and my mom on the other but, parent-wise, I guess I'm pretty lucky.

Friday, my last full day in California, was a pretty busy day. That morning I baby-sat one last time for Clover and Daffodil. Daffodil asked if she could write me. And Clover (always Clover) told me she might come visit me by spaceship. When Mrs. Austin came home, she slipped a thin package into my hand along with my pay.

"What is it?" I asked.

"Open it and see," she smiled.

Inside was a hand-woven purse that Mrs. Austin had made and lined in silk. The threads were red and a deep golden color.

"Like sunshine," she said. I blushed. Had Dad told her my nickname?

After the job, I ran over to Sunny's house for one last meeting of the We ♥ Kids Club. Actually, it was more like a party, a good-bye party for me. Sunny, Jill, and Maggie had made all kinds of treats — fresh pineapple wedges, zucchini bread, carrot cake. They had a big tray of food that they set down in the center of our circle.

Sunny banged her hand on the floor, like a gavel.

"This party will now come to order," she teased.

Believe me, there was no need to call us to the food.

The party was interrupted only twice by job calls. Maggie took one and Jill took the other.

There really wasn't enough work here to go around, I thought. In a way, it was good I was leaving.

When the "meeting" adjourned, Sunny pulled two packages out from under her bed.

"Surprise!" she said. "You can't go without your presents."

I *knew* it. I knew Sunny couldn't say good-bye to me without *some* sort of surprise.

One package, the first, was a book, I could

feel it. I tore open the wrapping paper. *Kids Can Cook . . . Naturally.*

"Thanks, you guys," I said enthusiastically. "This is great!"

"Open the other," said Sunny.

The other was my very own recipe file. The three of them had made it for me. The file box itself was blue, and they had pasted a picture of a sun on front. Inside were all their recipes, copied in their three different handwritings.

"You guys!" I cried. "You guys!"

What I was trying to say was, I just loved it.

I said good-bye to everybody. Then it was time for me to head home, for my last dinner with the California branch of the Schafer family.

Dad and I had discussed it, and we'd decided that, for the last night, it would be fun to go out. Dad had suggested a Mexican restaurant, a big favorite of mine and usually a favorite of Jeff's, too. Jeff, though, was still a little upset. He was my last hurdle, the last peace I had left to make. As we drove to the restaurant, Jeff kept a pouty look on his face. He squinted his eyes and puckered his mouth.

"What're you going to order, Jeff?" Dad asked in an effort to draw him out.

"Dunno," said Jeff.

"How about chicken enchiladas? You always like those."

"Yuk," said Jeff.

Dad and I exchanged quick smiles.

When we got to the restaurant, Jeff began twisting his fingers into the hem of the tablecloth.

"Dawn," he said sullenly. "How come you're leaving? Is it because we're boys?"

"No," I laughed. Jeff looked hurt. I tried to look as solemn as I could. "You thought I was leaving because you and Dad are boys? Not at all. I just have to go back."

"Maybe you can visit Dawn this summer," Dad suggested.

"Maybe she could come back and visit again *here*," Jeff insisted.

Jeff would always be true to California.

"Anyway, I had a good time with you," he said grudgingly.

"So did I." I smiled back.

"I liked when I took your picture at Disneyland," he said. "And I liked when I dropped the crab in your lap at the beach."

The very thought perked Jeff right up. Despite himself, he started to smile.

"Hey, how come you and your friends all wear those bikinis, anyway?" he asked. "Those things are really gross."

I had to laugh. And so did Dad.

When the waiter came, Jeff didn't even bother to look at the menu.

"Chicken enchiladas," he said.

That's our Jeff.

The meals came and we all ate hungrily. Dad ordered coffee before we left.

"You really can come back any time you want, Sunshine," he said. "Anytime during the summer, any vacation."

He took a sip from his cup.

"And hey," he said, suddenly inspired. "Why not bring all those friends of yours? All your friends in the Baby-sitters Club. I've certainly heard enough about them."

"Really?" I asked.

"How many would that be?" he calculated. "Six?"

"Six girls!" Jeff choked. "No way!"

"And all of them baby-sitters," Dad laughed. "Jeff, they'd have you corralled in no time."

The Baby-sitters Club in California? It was a *great* idea.

"Could I really bring them?" I asked. "When?"

"When?" Dad smiled. "Whenever!"

CHAPTER 15

saturday

Dear Dad and Jeff,

Hello from me (and from John Wayne, too!). I'm curled up in my window seat, watching the West disappear beneath me. Well, as you said, Dad, it's only a plane-ride away. But how come it's such a long plane ride?

Jeff, I hope you write me. Keep me posted about school, Clover and Daffodil, and, of course, the most important thing -- what Mrs. Bruen makes for dinner! (Just so I can eat my heart out.)

I love you both. I'll miss you a lot. Thanks for a fabu-ful, wonder-ific time.

Dawn

Well, it was C-Day again, only this time "C" stood for Connecticut, not California. That morning we had to get up pretty early to get me to my flight — because of the time change, the plane east leaves much earlier than the one going west. The neighborhood was quiet when we woke up, and the three of us sat groggily at the breakfast table, slowly coming awake.

"Mmm, coffee," Dad said, sipping from his cup.

That's about all the conversation any of us could muster.

When we got to the airport and got me all checked in, Jeff didn't want us to go to the gate.

"Wait! Let me take your picture by the John Wayne statue," he said. "Wait! Don't you want to buy another postcard?"

I think he thought that if he stalled long enough, I would miss my flight and then I would just stay in California forever.

Dad rested his hands on Jeff's shoulders.

"We'd better get your sister to her plane," he said. "Flights don't wait for passengers buying postcards."

By the time we got through the metal detector (we got delayed there — Jeff had a "Super

Special" jackknife in his pocket) and to the gate, the flight was already boarding. Dad gave me a last big hug.

"You take care now, Sunshine," he said. "And don't go forgetting about your California family."

"Don't worry, Dad," I laughed.

Jeff was shifting from one foot to the other.

"Come on," he said. "The plane's gonna leave."

I think now that he knew I was really going to go, he just wanted to get the whole thing over with. But as I got in line and was waiting for the flight attendant to take my ticket, Jeff called after me.

"Hey, Dawn!" he said.

I turned around.

"Smile!" he called. Jeff took my picture one last time, then gave an awkward little wave.

I went through the door and boarded the plane.

Out of one world and back to another. I was a little choked up as I found my way to my seat. I had a window again, this time over the wing. Outside, on the runway, the heat was already shimmering off the asphalt. I wondered what the weather was like in Connecticut.

I dug my hands deep into the pockets of my

cotton jacket, just for comfort, I think. Inside one I felt a little slip of paper. I pulled it out.

"Cat Dancing,
Romeo in Joliet,
Scheherazade's Tales," it read.

Hmm. What was tha — ? Oh, yes, the list of plays that Tom, my seatmate, had written down for me exactly two weeks before.

I found myself wondering whether Tom might be on my same flight back also. It wasn't impossible. Maybe his auditions had taken two full weeks. I glanced around at the other passengers on the plane, looking for Tom's sandy hair and fair complexion. The flight was not very crowded. There were lots of empty seats. I didn't spot Tom, but as I glanced back toward the kitchen in the rear, I spotted . . . Oh, no! That stewardess! I crunched down in my seat and covered my eyes. I bet she was assigned to my area. It was fate! There was no escape!

Sure enough, when it was time for the safety demonstration, there was the Kewpie doll, right at the head of my row.

Well, there was only one thing to do. I waited until we had taxied to the runway, had taken off, and were safely in the air. When the "Fasten seat belt" sign clicked off, I gathered up my carry-on bag and the blanket I had tucked around my legs. I glanced behind me. The flight attendants were back in the rear, preparing beverage carts, or whatever they do back there. I made my way up the aisle and across, to the other side of the plane. Since there were lots of empty seats I plunked myself down at another window. I stowed my bag, tucked the blanket up around me, and started the postcard to Dad and Jeff. (I had saved one last John Wayne postcard and decided to use that. I knew it would make Jeff smile.)

When the beverage cart came around, I had a regular, nice stewardess, one who even gave me extra orange juice when I asked for it. I threw a glance back at my old row. My old friend was at work, all right. I could see a passenger trying to wave her down. She had passed that person just as, two weeks ago, she had passed me.

Me, I was safe on the other side of the plane. Two weeks older and two weeks wiser. I smiled and went back to my postcard.

As the plane droned on, I got kind of sleepy. I don't think I'd ever really woken up that morning. My eyes started to slip shut and I think I slept through a lot of the flight.

I did wake up for the movie, though. It was (can you believe it?) *Adventures in Baby-sitting.*

Hurray! That got me thinking about all my friends waiting for me at home. I couldn't *wait* to see Mary Anne and, of course, Claudia, Kristy, Jessi, and Mallory, too. And then there were all the kids I sat for. I wondered if Nicky Pike really would come over on Sunday to explore the tunnel with me. I wondered if Mary Anne might want to come, too.

Going home felt very exciting all of a sudden. It really was home I was going to, too. "One home out of two," as Dad had put it, but I sure did have a lot of ties there.

I started thinking about Mom and how glad I would be to see her. I had packed her some avocados in my luggage, the wrinkly, dark green California kind. I'd picked out ones that weren't yet ripe, so she could eat them all next week. A little piece of California for Mom, because I knew she missed it sometimes, too.

I looked at my watch and set it ahead to East Coast time. Right about then Mom would probably be darting around the house, looking for this and that. I hoped she would remember to pick up Mary Anne and bring her along, like she said she would. With Mom, you just never knew.

When we had watched the movie and eaten our meals, the pilot came over the loudspeaker and told us about the weather on the East Coast.

"A light rain is falling," he said. "But the sun is apparently trying to peek through."

Exactly, I thought with a smile. That's Connecticut. (The sun, of course, was me.)

As we started our descent, my stomach got butterflies. It always does for arrival. I don't know if it's the descent of the plane, or the anticipation of arriving somewhere, but I always feel it.

When we finally landed, I jumped into the aisle, ready to race out the door. The people in front of me were blocking my way. One was reaching into the overhead luggage compartment and handing each bag — slowly — down to the other. "Come on!" I thought impatiently. I was ready to *burst* off that plane!

"Dawn!" a voice called out to me as I came through the door. It was Mom. She broke through the crowd, ran to me, and threw her arms around me. I was so glad just to see her — that Mom face of hers, that funny smile, and that pretty, light, curly hair.

"Mom," I cried. Again I got choked up.

What was it with my emotions lately? I felt like a regular crying machine.

Mom picked up my tote bag and led me

through the crowd. It was only then that I noticed the big white banner stretched across the room.

"Welcome home, Dawn!" it said.

Mary Anne was holding up one end of the banner, Claudia was holding up the other, and Kristy, Mallory, and Jessi were gathered underneath. It was the whole club!

"Surprise!" they cried.

In an instant, the banner was dropped and everyone was crowded around me, firing questions at me and hugging me hello.

"You're so *tan!*" Mary Anne cried.

She grabbed my arm and held it up for the others to see.

"Did you have a good time?" asked Claudia.

"Did you miss us?" asked Kristy.

"Tell us about We ♥ Kids," said Mallory.

"What was Disneyland like?" asked Jessi.

Phew! I couldn't answer everything at once, so I just stood there grinning. I dug into my tote bag and pulled out the five pairs of Mickey Mouse ears I had bought my friends as presents. Everyone grabbed for them and put them on right there in the airport.

We made our way to the baggage claim area, giggling and talking in a tight cluster. I guess we looked pretty funny. The people walking by smiled at us as they passed.

"We've got you signed up for some jobs," Mary Anne told me. Throughout the chaos, Mary Anne had stuck right by my side. "Hope you don't mind."

"Mind? That's great!" I said. Home just a few minutes and already I was booked. That was the Baby-sitters Club, all right. Bustling and busy.

When my suitcase came around on the carousel, Mom grabbed it up and the rest of us followed her out the automatic airport doors. She strode right to the parking lot, directly to the row where she had left the car.

"Here we are," she smiled, very pleased with herself. "Bet you thought your old mom would forget where she parked. My memory's getting better. Really. I'm making an effort."

We all piled in and I squeezed next to Mom. She steered the car to the ticket window and stopped to pay the charge.

The ticket. Mom fished into the pocket of her blouse. She grabbed her purse off the floor and rummaged through the various compartments. She looked through her wallet.

"Dawn," she said. "Will you check the glove compartment?"

No ticket.

"Maybe you stuck it behind the sun visor," I said.

She flipped the visor down. There was the ticket, tucked into the visor's pocket.

Mom handed the attendant his money and we drove out of the airport, onto the highway. As we sped home, I couldn't help smiling. My friends were chattering, my mom was Mom, and I was snug in the middle. I was home, all right. And it felt super.

About the Author

ANN M. MARTIN did *a lot* of baby-sitting when she was growing up in Princeton, New Jersey. Now her favorite baby-sitting charge is her cat, Mouse, who lives with her in her Manhattan apartment.

Ann Martin's Apple Paperbacks are *Bummer Summer, Inside Out, Stage Fright, Me and Katie (the Pest)*, and all the other books in the Baby-sitters Club series.

She is a former editor of books for children, and was graduated from Smith College. She likes ice cream, the beach, and *I Love Lucy*; and she hates to cook.

Look for #24

KRISTY AND THE
MOTHER'S DAY SURPRISE

I glanced at Sam and Charlie again. They shrugged.

Suddenly Sam said, "Hey, Mom, you're not pregnant, are you?"

"No," Mom replied. "I'm not. . . . But how would you kids feel about another brother or sister?"

"Another brother or sister?" David Michael repeated dubiously.

"A *baby*?" squeaked Andrew and Karen.

"Terrific!" I added honestly. I love babies.

Sam and Charlie nodded.

No one seemed to know what to say then, but it didn't matter because Boo-Boo came into the dining room carrying a mole he'd caught. The poor mole was still alive, so we had to get it away from Boo-Boo and then put it back outside where it belonged.

That was the end of dinner.

* * *

144

Later that night, I lay in bed, thinking.

I thought of Mom wanting to have another baby. Even though she's kind of old for that, it made sense. I mean, she's married to Watson now, so I guessed that she and Watson wanted a baby of their own. Boy. Mom would have five kids and two stepkids then.

She would need an extra special Mother's Day present. What on earth could I give her? I slid over in bed so I could see the moon out my window.

The moon was pretty, but it was no help.

Jewelry? Nah. Mom likes to choose her own. Stockings? Boring. Candy or flowers? Let Watson do that. Something for her desk at the office? Maybe. Clothes? If I could afford anything.

I had a feeling I was missing the point, though. I wanted to say thank you to Mom for being such a wonderful mother. (She really is.) So I needed to give her something special, something that would tell her, "You're the best mom. Thanks." But what would say that?

I thought and thought. And then it came to me. It was another one of my ideas. Carrying it off might take some work, but my friends and I could do it.

I couldn't wait until the next meeting of the Baby-sitters Club.

**Here's some news about other books
in The Baby-sitters Club series
by Ann M. Martin**

#1 Kristy's Great Idea

Kristy thinks the Baby-sitters Club is a great
idea. She and her friends Claudia, Stacey, and
Mary Anne all love taking care of kids. But
nobody counted on crank calls, wild pets, and
uncontrollable two-year-olds! Having a Baby-
sitters Club isn't easy, but Kristy and her
friends won't give up till they get it right!

#2 Claudia and the Phantom Phone Calls

Claudia has been getting some mysterious
phone calls when she's out baby-sitting. Could
they be from the Phantom Jewel Thief who's
operating in the area? Claudia has always liked
reading mysteries, but she doesn't like it when
they *happen* to her!

#3 The Truth About Stacey

The truth about Stacey is her parents want to
find a miracle cure for her diabetes. They're
making Stacey's life so hard! The other Baby-
sitters are busy fighting the Baby-sitters Agency.
How can they help Stacey and save the club,
too?

#4 Mary Anne Saves the Day

Mary Anne's never been a leader of the Baby-sitters Club. Now there's a big fight among the four friends. It's bad enough when Mary Anne has to eat at the lunch table all alone. But when she has to baby-sit a sick child with no help from her friends — it's time to take charge!

#5 Dawn and the Impossible Three

Poor Dawn! It's not easy being the newest member of the Baby-sitters Club. She's got three impossible kids to take care of. And Kristy thinks things were better *without* Dawn around. It'll take a lot of work to make things run smoothly again, but Dawn's up to the challenge!

#6 Kristy's Big Day

It's a big day for Kristy, all right — she's a bridesmaid in her mother's wedding! And if that's not enough, she and the other Baby-sitters Club members have *fourteen* wedding-guest kids to take care of. Only the Baby-sitters Club could cope with this one!

#7 Claudia and Mean Janine

This summer the Baby-sitters Club is starting a play group in the neighborhood. Claudia can't wait for it to begin — it'll give her some time away from her mean big sister. But then her grandmother has a stroke . . . and the whole summer changes.

#8 Boy-Crazy Stacey

Who needs baby-sitting when there are boys around? Stacey and Mary Anne are mother's helpers at the Jersey shore, and Stacey's mind is on hunky lifeguard Scott. Mary Anne's doing the work of two baby-sitters . . . but how can she tell Stacey that Scott's too old, without breaking Stacey's heart?

#9 The Ghost at Dawn's House

Creaking stairs, noises behind the wall, a secret passage — there must be a ghost at Dawn's house! The Baby-sitters find themselves and one of their charges wrapped up in a mystery. Will they be able to solve it?

#10 *Logan Likes Mary Anne!*

Quiet, shy Mary Anne has been growing up lately . . . and the Baby-sitters aren't the only ones who've noticed. Logan Bruno likes Mary Anne! He has a dreamy southern accent, he's awfully cute — and he wants to join the Baby-sitters Club. Life in the club has never been this complicated — or this fun!

#11 *Kristy and the Snobs*

The kids in Kristy's new neighborhood aren't very friendly. In fact they're . . . well, snobs. They laugh at everything — even Kristy's poor old collie, Louie. Kristy's fighting mad. But if anyone can beat a Snob attack, it's the Baby-sitters club. And that's just what they're going to do!

#12 *Claudia and the New Girl*

Claudia really likes Ashley, the new girl at school. Ashley's the only one who takes Claudia seriously. Soon, Claudia's spending so much time with Ashley that she doesn't have time for baby-sitting — or her old friends. And they don't like it one bit!

#13 Good-bye Stacey, Good-bye

There are lots of tears when the Baby-sitters hear the news: Stacey and her family are moving back to New York. The club members can't think of a special enough way to send Stacey off. They want to give her much more than a party. But how do you say good-bye to your best friend?

#14 Hello, Mallory

Mallory Pike has always been good at baby-sitting her younger brothers and sisters. But is she good enough to join the Baby-sitters Club? The club members go overboard giving Mallory baby-sitting tests. Mallory's getting pretty fed up. . . . Maybe she'll just start a baby-sitting business of her own!

#15 Little Miss Stoneybrook . . . and Dawn

Mrs. Pike wants Dawn to help prepare Margo and Claire for the Little Miss Stoneybrook contest. And Dawn wants her charges to win! The only trouble is . . . Kristy, Mary Anne, and Claudia are helping Karen, Myriah, and Charlotte enter the contest, too. And nobody's sure where the competition is fiercer: at the pageant — or at the Baby-sitters Club!

#16 Jessi's Secret Language

Jessi had a hard time fitting in to Stoneybrook. But things got a lot better once she became a member of the Baby-sitters Club! Now Jessi has her biggest challenge yet — baby-sitting for a deaf boy. And in order to communicate with him, Jessi must learn his secret language.

#17 Mary Anne's Bad-Luck Mystery

Mary Anne finds a note in her mailbox. *"Wear this bad-luck charm,"* it says, *"OR ELSE."* Mary Anne's got to do what the note says. But who sent the charm? And why did they send it to Mary Anne? If the Baby-sitters don't solve this mystery soon, their bad luck might never stop!

#18 Stacey's Mistake

Stacey's so excited! She's invited her friends from the Baby-sitters Club down to New York City for a long weekend. But what a mistake! The Baby-sitters are *way* out of place in the big city. Does this mean Stacey can't be the Baby-sitters' friend anymore?

#19 *Claudia and the Bad Joke*

Claudia's not worried when she hears she has to baby-sit for Betsy, a great practical joker. How much trouble could a little girl cause? *Plenty* . . . and now Claudia might even quit the club. It's time for the Baby-sitters to teach Betsy a lesson. The joke war is on!

#20 *Kristy and the Walking Disaster*

Kristy's little brother and sister want to play on a softball team, so Kristy starts a ragtag team of her own. With Jackie Rodowsky, the Walking Disaster, playing for them, Kristy's Krushers aren't world champions. But nobody beats them when it comes to team spirit!

#21 *Mallory and the Trouble With Twins*

Mallory thinks baby-sitting for the Arnold twins will be easy money. They're so adorable! Marilyn and Carolyn may be cute . . . but they're also spoiled brats. It's a baby-sitting nightmare — and Mallory's not giving up!

#22 Jessi Ramsey, Pet-sitter

Jessi's always liked animals. So when the Mancusis need an emergency pet-sitter, she quickly takes the job. But what has Jessi gotten herself into? There are animals *all over* the Mancusis' house! This is going to be one sitting job Jessi will never forget!

#24 Kristy and the Mother's Day Surprise

The Baby-sitters don't know *what* to get their moms for Mother's Day this year. Then Kristy has another one of her great ideas. The girls can thank their mothers by giving them a day off — without any kids around. It's a Mother's Day surprise that can't be beat . . . until Kristy's mom reveals a very special surprise of her own.

Kristy and the Mother's Day Surprise

Look for these and other books
in the Baby-sitters Club series:

Kristy and the Mother's Day Surprise
Ann M. Martin

AN
APPLE
PAPERBACK

SCHOLASTIC INC.
New York Toronto London Auckland Sydney

Cover art by Hodges Soileau

ISBN 0-590-43506-X

12 11 10 9 8 7 6 5 4 3   0 1 2 3 4/9

Printed in the U.S.A.   28

For Amy Berkower

CHAPTER 1

I've been thinking about families lately, wondering what makes one. Is a family really a mother, a father, and a kid or two? I hope not, because if that's a family, then I haven't got one. And neither do a lot of other people I know. For instance, Nannie, Mom's mother, lives all by herself. But I still think of her as a family — a one-person family. And I think of my own family as a real family . . . I guess.

What I mean is, well, my family didn't start out the way it is now. It started out as two families that split up and came together as . . . Uh-oh. I know that's confusing. I'm a little ahead of myself. I better back up and begin at the beginning.

This is the beginning: Hi! I'm Kristy Thomas. I'm thirteen years old. I'm in eighth grade. I'm the president of the Baby-sitters Club (more about that later). I like sports, and I guess you could say I'm a tomboy. (Well, wouldn't you be one if you had a whole bunch of brothers?) I'm not the neatest person in the world. I don't care much about boys or clothes. I'm famous for coming up with big ideas.

Okay, enough about me. Let me tell you about —

Knock, knock.

Darn, I thought. Who could that be? It was a Friday evening and I didn't have any plans or even a baby-sitting job. I was in my bedroom, just messing around, enjoying my free time.

"Who's there?" I called.

"Oswald!" my little sister replied.

Oswald? *Oh*. . . . "Oswald who?" I asked.

"Help! Help! Oswald my gum!"

I was laughing as I opened the door and found a very giggly Karen in the hallway.

"Pretty funny," I said, as Karen ran into my room and threw herself on my bed. "Where'd you hear that one?"

"In school. Nancy told it to me. What are you doing with the door closed?"

"Just fooling around."

"But this is our first night here."

"I'm sorry, Karen. I didn't mean to shut you out. It's just that I had a rotten week at school and today was especially rotten, so I wanted to be by myself for awhile."

2

You're probably wondering why Karen said, "But this is our first night here." I think now would be a good time to explain my family to you. See, Karen isn't exactly my sister. She's my stepsister. Her little brother Andrew is my stepbrother, and her father is my stepfather. Karen and Andrew only live with us part-time. I like when they come over because then my family consists of Mom, Watson (he's my stepfather), Sam, Charlie, and David Michael (they're my brothers), and Karen and Andrew. Oh, and Shannon and Boo-Boo. They're our dog and cat, and they're part of the family, too.

How did I get this weird family? Well, you can probably imagine. My mom and dad were divorced. They got divorced right after David Michael was born. Then, a couple of years ago, Mom met Watson and started going out with him. Watson was divorced, too. And after awhile, Mom and Watson got married, and then Mom and my brothers and I moved into Watson's house. That's how I got my big family. The only unusual thing is that Watson is a millionaire. Honest. That's why we moved into his house. It's a lot bigger than our old one. It's huge. In fact, it's basically a mansion. Living in a mansion here in Stoneybrook,

Connecticut, is fun, but sometimes I miss my old house. It's on the other side of town, where all my friends are.

So now I'm part of a six-kid family. My brother Charlie is the oldest kid. He's seventeen, a senior in high school, and thinks he's a big shot. Sam is fifteen. He's a sophomore in high school. Then there's me, then David Michael, who's seven, and then Karen and Andrew, who are six and four. Usually, Karen and Andrew only live with us every other weekend and for two weeks during the summer. The rest of the time they live with their mother, who's not too far away — in a different neighborhood in Stoneybrook. But the night Karen bounced into my room with her knock-knock joke was the beginning of a much longer stay. Karen and Andrew were going to be with us for several weeks while their mother and stepfather went on a business trip.

"Knock, knock," said Karen again.

"Who's there?" I replied.

"Hey, Karen! Come here!" It was David Michael, yelling down the hall.

"What?" Karen yelled back.

"Come look at this bug!" (David Michael just loves bugs.)

Karen was off my bed and out of my room in a flash.

4

I smiled. I really like my family, especially when Karen and Andrew are here. The bigger, the better. Sometimes I think of my friends as family, too. Is that weird? I don't know. But my friends do feel like family. I guess I'm mostly talking about my friends in the Baby-sitters Club. That's a club I started myself. Actually, it's more of a business. My friends and I sit for families in Stoneybrook and we earn a lot of money.

Here's who's in the club: me, Claudia Kishi, Mary Anne Spier, Dawn Schafer, Mallory Pike, and Jessi Ramsey. We are six very different people, but we get along really well (most of the time). That's the way it is with families.

For instance, I'm pretty outgoing (some people say I have a big mouth), and as I mentioned before, I like sports and couldn't care less about clothes or boys. My best friend is Mary Anne Spier (she's our club secretary) and we are *so* different. Mary Anne is quiet and shy, hates sports, is becoming interested in clothes, has a boyfriend, and comes from a very small family. She lives with just her dad and her kitten, Tigger. Her mom died a long time ago. Mary Anne and I have always been different and have always been best friends. We lived next door to each other until Mom married Watson, so we practically grew up together.

One thing that's the same about us is our looks. We both have brown hair and brown eyes and are short for our age.

The vice-president of the Baby-sitters Club is Claudia Kishi. Claud lives across the street from Mary Anne. There is nothing, and I mean *nothing*, typical or average or ordinary about Claudia. To begin with, she's Japanese-American. Her hair is silky and long and jet-black. Her eyes are dark and almond-shaped and exotic. And her skin, well, I wish it were mine. I'm sure her skin doesn't even know what a pimple is. Which is interesting when you consider Claudia's eating habits. Claud is pretty much addicted to junk food. Her parents don't like her to eat much of it, though, so she has to resort to hiding it in her room. Everywhere you look, you find something: a package of red-hots in the pencil cup, a bag of Cheese Doodles under her bed, a box of Cracker Jacks in the closet. This makes for a crowded room because Claudia is a pack rat. She has to be. She's an artist and needs to collect things for her work, such as shells, leaves, and interesting pebbles. Plus, she has tons of supplies — paper, canvases, paints, pastels, charcoals — and most of them are stored under her bed. Claud likes Nancy Drew mysteries and is a terrible student (even though she's smart). She lives with her parents, her grandmother, Mimi, and her older sister, Janine. It's too bad that Claud is such a poor student, because Janine is a genius. One last thing about Claudia — her clothes. They are just . . . so cool. Well, I mean Claud is. She's the coolest kid in our grade. Her clothes are wild. Claud loves trying new things and she has an incredible imagination. She wears hats, weird jewelry (she makes some of it), bright colors — anything she can get away with!

Dawn Schafer is the club's treasurer. Now *she's* got an interesting family. Dawn used to live in California. She lived there with her parents and Jeff, her younger brother. Then her parents got divorced and Mrs. Schafer moved Dawn and Jeff all the way across country to Stoneybrook. The reason she chose Stoneybrook is she grew up here, and her parents (Dawn's grandparents) still live here. We got to know Dawn and she joined the Baby-sitters Club and everything seemed great. Except that Jeff missed his father and California — a lot. Finally, he moved back there. Now Dawn's family is split in half and separated by a continent. Dawn seems to be handling the changes well, though. She's pretty mature. And she's a real individual. She solves her own problems, makes her own decisions, and isn't too affected by what other people think of her or tell her. Plus, Dawn is neat and organized, which makes her a good treasurer. Although Dawn has been living in Connecticut for over a year now, she still looks sort of Californian. She's got long hair that is the blondest I've ever seen. It's almost white. And her eyes are sparkly and pale blue. In the summer she gets this amazing tan. (The rest of the year she just has freckles.) And her clothes are casual and as individualistic as she is. She likes to wear layers of things — a short tank top over a long tank top, or socks over tights. Dawn is pretty cool.

The two junior members of our club are Jessi Ramsey and Mallory Pike. They're junior members because they're younger than the rest of us eighth-graders. Mal and Jessi are in sixth grade. They haven't been club members as long as us older girls. Still, they're beginning to feel like family to me.

Mallory used to be someone our club sat *for*. Isn't that weird? Now she's a sitter herself. Mal is the oldest of eight kids. (Talk about big families.) The Baby-sitters Club still takes care of her younger brothers and sisters pretty often. Anyway, Mal is a great sitter. She's levelheaded and responsible — good in an emergency. And she's the most practical person I know. Mal is struggling to grow up. Being eleven can be very difficult, and Mal thinks her parents treat her like a baby. However, they're starting to let up. Recently, they allowed Mal to get her ears pierced and her hair cut. (She had to get braces, too, though, and her parents said she's too young for contact lenses.) Mal likes reading (especially books about horses), writing, and drawing. She thinks she might want to be an author of children's books when she grows up.

Jessi (short for Jessica) Ramsey is Mal's best friend. Like Dawn, she's a newcomer to Stoneybrook, Connecticut. In fact, she's a newer newcomer than Dawn is. Her family moved here from New Jersey at the beginning of the school year. They moved because Mr. Ramsey changed jobs. In many ways, Jessi and Mal are alike. Jessi also loves to read, she wears glasses (just for reading), and she thinks *her* parents treat her like a baby, although they did let her get her ears pierced when Mal had hers done. But there are some big differences between Jessi and Mal. I guess the biggest is that Jessi is black and Mal is white. This hasn't made a bit of difference to the girls, but the Ramseys sure had some trouble when they first moved here. Not many black families live in Stoneybrook, and some people gave the Ramseys a hard time. Jessi says things are settling down, though. Another difference between Mal and Jessi is that Mal likes to write and Jessi likes to dance. Jessi is a ballerina. She's very talented. I've seen her dance — *on stage.* I was really impressed. The third difference is that Mal's family is huge, while Jessi's is average — Jessi; her parents; her younger sister, Becca; and her baby brother, Squirt.

And that's it. Those are the people in my family. It's a big family, when you add the members of the Baby-sitters Club. I could add a few more, too, I thought later that night as I lay in bed. There's Nannie. There's Stacey McGill, who used to be a member of the club, but who had to move to New York City. There are Shannon and Logan, whom I'll tell you about later. And there's my real father. . . . But, no, he doesn't count. Somebody who never writes, never calls, never remembers your birthday, never says he loves you, doesn't count at all.

I was growing sleepy, and I forgot about my father. Instead, I thought of my gigantic family. I fell asleep smiling.

CHAPTER 2

As president of the Baby-sitters Club, I get to run the meetings. I adore being in charge. Club meetings are the best times of my week.

"Order! Order, you guys!" I said.

It was Monday afternoon at five-thirty, time for our meeting to begin. Everyone had arrived and was sitting (or sprawling) in her usual place. As president, I always sit in the director's chair and wear my visor. I stick a pencil over my ear. That way, I *look* like I'm in charge. Claudia, Dawn, and Mary Anne loll around on the bed, and Jessi and Mal sit on the floor.

We hold our meetings in Claudia's room. She has her own phone.

This is how our club works: Three times a week, on Mondays, Wednesdays, and Fridays from five-thirty until six, our club meets in Claudia's bedroom. People who need sitters call us during our meetings. They're practically guaranteed a sitter. With six club members, one of us is bound to be free. So we wind up with lots of jobs. Pretty neat, huh?

The idea for the club was mine. (That's how I got to be the president.) It came to me way back at the beginning of seventh grade, before Mom was really thinking about marrying Watson. We still lived in this neighborhood then. In fact, we lived right across the street from Claudia. Anyway, one day Mom needed a sitter for David Michael, who had just turned six. I wasn't free and neither was Sam nor Charlie. So Mom got on the phone and began making call after call, trying to find a sitter. I felt bad for my mother, and even worse for David Michael, who was watching everything. And that was when I got my great idea. Wouldn't it be wonderful if Mom could make just one call and reach a whole bunch of baby-sitters at once? She'd find a sitter much faster that way.

So I got together with Mary Anne and Claudia and told them about my idea. We decided to form the Baby-sitters Club. We also decided we'd need more than three members, so we asked Stacey McGill, a new friend of Claudia's, to join the club, too. Stacey had just moved to Stoneybrook from New York City because her father's job had changed. I could see right away why she and Claudia had

12

become friends so fast. Stacey awed Mary Anne and me. She seemed years older than twelve — very sophisticated with trendy clothes, pierced ears, and permed hair. But she was also very nice. Furthermore, she'd had plenty of baby-sitting experience in New York, so we knew she'd be a good addition to the club.

After Stacey agreed to join us, we sent around fliers and ran an ad in Stoneybrook's newspaper so people would know when to call us — and we were in business! The club was great. By the time Dawn moved to town, we needed another sitter, and later, when Stacey moved back to New York, we were doing so much business that we replaced her with both Jessi and Mal. And somewhere along the line we decided that we better have a couple of people lined up whom we could call on in case *none* of us could take a job. So we signed up two associate members, Shannon Kilbourne and Logan Bruno. Shannon lives across the street from me in my new neigh-borhood. We're friends, sort of. Logan is a *boy* — and he's Mary Anne's boyfriend! Shan-non and Logan don't come to the meetings. We just call them when we need them, so that we don't have to disappoint any of our clients by saying that no sitters are available.

I run our meetings in the most businesslike

way I can. As president, that's my job. Also, I come up with ideas for the club and generally just try to keep things going smoothly.

The job of the vice-president is, well . . . To be honest, Claudia Kishi is the vice-president because she has her own phone and personal, private phone number. The club uses her phone so we don't have to tie up some grown-up's phone three times a week. The only thing is, our clients sometimes forget when our meetings are and call at other times. Claudia has to deal with those job offers, and she handles things really well.

Mary Anne Spier, our secretary, has the biggest job of any of us. Our club has a notebook (I'll tell you about that soon) and a record book. Mary Anne is the one who keeps the record book in order and up-to-date. She writes down our clients' names, addresses, and phone numbers and is responsible for scheduling *all* our sitting jobs on the appointment pages. This is more difficult than it sounds, since she has to keep track of things like Jessi's ballet classes, Claud's art lessons, Mal's orthodontist appointments, and you name it. I don't think Mary Anne has ever made a mistake, though.

Our treasurer, Dawn Schafer, collects dues from us every Monday and keeps track of the money that's in our treasury. We use the money for three things. One, to pay Charlie to drive me to and from the meetings, since I live so far from Claudia now. Two, for club parties and sleepovers. Every now and then we like to give ourselves a treat. Three, to buy materials for Kid-Kits. What are Kid-Kits? Well, they're one of my ideas. A Kid-Kit is a box that we fill with our old toys, books, and games, and also some new things, like coloring books, crayons, or sticker books. Each of us has her own Kid-Kit, and we need money to replace the things that get used up. The children we sit for love the Kid-Kits. Bringing one along on a job is like bringing a toy store. It makes the kids happy. And when the kids are happy, their parents are happy. . . . And when their parents are happy, they call the Baby-sitters Club again!

Mallory and Jessi, our junior officers, don't have any special jobs. The junior officers simply aren't allowed to sit at night unless they're sitting for their own brothers and sisters, so when Mary Anne schedules jobs, she tries to give the after-school and weekend jobs to Jessi and Mallory first. That way the rest of us will be free to take the evening jobs.

And that's it. That's how our club — Oh, wait. One more thing. The club notebook. The notebook is different from the record book, but just as important. It's more of a diary than a notebook. Any time one of us club members goes on a baby-sitting job, she's responsible for writing up the job in the notebook. Then, once a week, each of us is supposed to read the notebook. This is really very helpful. We learn how our friends solve sitting problems, or if a kid that we're going to be taking care of has a new fear, a new hobby, etc. Some of the girls think that writing in the notebook is a boring chore, but I think it's valuable.

Okay. That really *is* it. Now you know how our club began and how it runs, so let's get back to business.

After I had said "Order!" for about the third time, everyone settled down. "Any business?" I asked.

"Dues day!" announced Dawn. She bounced off the bed, blonde hair flying. The treasury envelope was in her hands, and she opened it.

"*Oh*," groaned the rest of us. We earn a lot of money baby-sitting, but we don't like to part with it for dues, even though we know we have to.

"Aw, come on," said Dawn. "It isn't that bad. Besides, think of me. I have to listen to this moaning and complaining every Monday afternoon." Dawn collected the money, then handed some of it to me. "That's for Charlie," she said. "We have to pay him today."

I nodded. "Thanks, Dawn."

My friends settled down. Claudia leaned against one of her pillows and began braiding her hair. Mary Anne unwrapped a piece of gum. Dawn flipped through the pages of the notebook. On the floor, Mallory doodled in one of Claudia's sketchbooks, and Jessi absentmindedly lifted the cover of a shoe box labeled PASTILS AND CHARCAOLS (Claudia isn't a great speller), and exclaimed, "Hey, there's M and M's in here!"

"Oh, yeah," replied Claud. "I forgot about those. Hand them around, Jessi, okay?"

"Sure!" said Jessi. She took out the bag of candy, replaced the lid on the box, opened the bag, and sent it around Claud's bedroom.

Everyone took a handful of M & M's except for Dawn, who mostly eats health food — she won't even eat meat — and can't stand junk food, especially candy. Claudia remembered this and handed Dawn a package of wholewheat crackers. Dawn looked really grateful.

This is just one of the things I love about my club family. We really care about each other. We look out for each other and do nice things for each other. Of course, we fight, too — we've had some whoppers — but that's part of being a family.

"Well, any more club business?" I asked.

Nobody answered.

"Okay, then. We'll just wait for the phone to ring." I picked up the record book and began looking at the appointment calendar. "Gosh," I said, "I cannot believe it's already April. Where did the school year go? It feels like it was just September."

"I know," agreed Mary Anne. "Two more months and school will be over." She looked pretty pleased.

"Yeah," said Dawn happily. "Summer. Hot weather. I'll get to visit Dad and Jeff in California again."

"Whoa!" I cried. I was still looking at our calendar. "Guess what. I just realized that Mother's Day is coming up — soon. It's in less than three weeks."

"Oh, brother. Gift time," murmured Mallory. "I *never* know what to get Mom. None of us does. She always ends up with a bunch of stuff she doesn't want and doesn't know what to do with. Like every year, Margo" (Margo is Mal's seven-year-old sister) "makes her a handprint in clay and paints it green. What's Mom going to do with all those green hand sculptures? And the triplets" (ten-year-old boys) "always go to the dime store and get her really ugly plastic earrings or a horrible necklace or something."

"Once," said Jessi, "my sister gave our mother a bag of chocolate kisses and then ate them herself."

We began to laugh.

"This year," Claud began, "I am going to give my mother the perfect present."

"What?" I asked.

Claud shrugged. "I don't know yet."

"I never have to think of Mother's Day presents," said Mary Anne softly.

The talking and laughing stopped. How is it that I forget about Mary Anne's problem year after year? I never remember until some-body, usually the art teacher, is saying some-thing like, "All right, let's begin our Mother's Day cards," or "I know your mothers will just love these glass mosaics." Then I watch Mary Anne sink lower and lower in her seat. Why don't the teachers say, "If you want to make a Mother's Day gift, come over here. The rest of you may read." Or something like that. It would be a lot easier on the kids who don't need to make Mother's Day stuff.

Dawn looked at Mary Anne and awkwardly patted her shoulder.

Claud said, "Sorry, Mary Anne."

We feel bad for her but we don't quite know what to say. Sorry your mother died? Sorry the greeting card people invented Mother's Day and you have to feel bad once a year? Sorry we have moms and you don't?

I was relieved when the telephone rang. (We all were.) It gave us something to do. I answered the phone, and Mary Anne took over the record book.

"Hi, Mrs. Newton," I said. "Friday afternoon? . . . Yeah, it is short notice, I guess, but I'll check. I'll get right back to you." I hung up. "Check Friday after school," I told Mary Anne. "This Friday."

Mary Anne checked. "Claudia's free," she said. "She's the only one."

I glanced at Claud and she nodded.

So I called Mrs. Newton back. "Claudia will be there," I told her. We said good-bye and hung up. The Newtons are some of our oldest clients. They have two kids — Jamie, who's four, and Lucy, who's just a baby. We all love sitting at the Newtons', but Claudia especially loves it. I knew she was happy with her job.

The phone rang several more times after that. All job calls. Then, toward the end of the meeting, we began talking about Mother's Day again. We couldn't help it. We knew Mary Anne felt sad, but the rest of us really needed to think about what to give our moms.

"Flowers?" suggested Jessi.

We shook our heads.

"Chocolate-covered cherries?" suggested Claudia.

We shook our heads.

"Oh, well. It's six o'clock," I announced. "Meeting's over. Don't worry — we have plenty of time to think of presents. See you guys in school tomorrow."

CHAPTER 3

When I left Claudia's house, Charlie was waiting for me in the Kishis' driveway. He has been really good about remembering to drive me to and from the meetings of the Baby-sitters Club. We *are* paying him, but still . . . I keep thinking he might get tied up with an after-school activity and forget me sometime.

Moving across town was *so* inconvenient. I'm not near any of my closest friends, and I'm not near my school. Now I have to get rides all the time and take the bus to school. The other kids in my new neighborhood go to private schools. But I wanted to stick with my regular school (so did my brothers), so we're the only ones who go to public. We really stand out.

Charlie pulled into the drive, and Watson's huge house (well, *our* huge house) spread before us. I am amazed every time I see it. We parked, and my brother and I went inside.

We were greeted by Sam. "Boy, Kristy. I don't know how you do it," was the first thing he said.

"Do what?"

"Baby-sit so much without going looney tunes."

I grinned. Sam had been watching David Michael, Andrew, and Karen, since Mom and Watson were still at work. "Baby-sitting is easy," I replied. "It's a piece of cake. What happened?"

"What do you mean 'What happened?' Nothing *happened*. They're just kids. I'm worn out. I couldn't give another cannonball ride if my life depended on it."

"That's Charlie's fault for inventing cannon-balls," I told Sam.

At that moment, Andrew came barreling into the front hall, crying, "Sam! Sam! I need a cannonball ride!"

Without pausing, Sam picked Andrew up, Andrew curled himself into a ball, and Sam charged off toward the kitchen, shouting, "Ba-boom-ba-boom-ba-boom-ba-boom."

"I thought he couldn't give another cannon-ball ride," said Charlie.

"Andrew is hard to resist," I told him.

Dinner that night was noisy. It was one of

the few times when everyone was home. Andrew and Karen usually aren't with us, and when they are, they're almost always here on a weekend — when Charlie's out on a date or Sam is at a game at school, or *some*thing. But that night was different. We ate in the dining room. Watson sat at one end of the table, Mom at the other. David Michael, Karen, and I sat along one side of the table; Charlie, Sam, and Andrew sat across from us.

When everyone had been served, Mom said, "Isn't this nice?" She had been a little emotional lately.

"It's terrific," agreed Watson, who sounded *too* enthusiastic.

Mom and Watson get all worked up whenever we're together as a family, and I know why. I like my family and everything. I like us a lot. But sometimes I think we feel more like pieces of a family instead of a whole family. We're a shirt whose seams haven't all been stitched up. I mean, Mom and Watson got married, but I would only go to Mom if I needed to borrow money. And Andrew usually heads for Watson if he's hurt himself or doesn't feel well. *We're* Mom's kids and *they're* Watson's kids. Two teams on the same playing field.

Don't get me wrong. It isn't bad. Really.

Our family just needs to grow together — so Mom and Watson make a huge deal out of things like all of us sitting down at the dinner table.

Our dinners are usually not very quiet. That night, David Michael started things off by singing softly, *"They built the ship* Titanic *to sail the ocean blue. A sadder ship the waters never knew. She was on her maiden trip when an iceboard hit the ship —"*

"Cut it *out!*" cried Karen suddenly. "I hate that song. All the people die. Besides, it's 'ice*berg*,' not 'ice*board*.' "

"I know that," said David Michael. But he didn't. He had said 'iceboard' every time he had sung that song.

He stopped singing. He made a rhythm band out of his plate, glass, fork, and spoon.

Andrew joined him.

Chink-a-chink. Chinkety-chink, chink.

Mom beamed. Why did she look so happy? Usually dinnertime rhythm bands gave her a headache.

"Hey, Karen. Your epidermis is showing," said Sam from across the table.

"What? What?" Karen, flustered, began checking her clothes. Finally, she said haughtily, "Sam. I am not wearing a dress. How can my epipotomus be showing?"

25

We couldn't help it. Watson, Mom, Charlie, Sam, David Michael, and I began to laugh. Not rudely, just gently. Well, all right. David Michael laughed rudely — loudly, anyway.

"*What?*" Karen demanded.

"It's 'epidermis,' not 'epipotomus,' " said David Michael, glad to be able to correct *her*, "and it means 'skin.' "

Karen looked questioningly at Sam.

"He's right," said Sam. "It does mean 'skin.' "

"My *skin* is showing?" said Karen. "Oh, my *skin* is showing! That's funny! I'm going to say that to everyone in my class tomorrow."

"Now let's have a little eating," said Watson.

For a few moments, we ate. I was working on a mouthful of lima beans when I heard David Michael murmur, "*Beans, beans, they're good for your heart. The more you eat, the more —* "

I kicked him under the table. Not hard. Just enough to make him stop. Mom and Watson *hate* that song.

But soon my brother was singing, "*Beans, beans, the magical fruit. The more you eat —* "

I kicked him again. "Cut it *out*."

"It's a different song."

"Not different enough."

David Michael grew silent.

At her end of the table, Mom put down her

fork and looked lovingly at Watson. "We're so lucky," she said.

Watson smiled.

I glanced at Sam and Charlie. Mom had been acting weird lately.

"We've got six beautiful children — "

"I am not beautiful," said David Michael. "I'm a boy."

"We live in a lovely town," continued Mom, "we like our jobs, we have a gorgeous house . . . with plenty of rooms. Do you realize that we have three spare bedrooms?"

My mother was looking at us kids.

I glanced at Sam and Charlie again. They shrugged.

"It *is* a nice house, Mom," I agreed.

Mom nodded. "Plenty of extra space."

Suddenly Sam said, "Hey, Mom, you're not pregnant, are you?"

(My mother *could* have been pregnant. She's only in her late thirties. She had Charlie right after she graduated from college.)

"No," Mom replied. "I'm not. . . . But how would you kids feel about another brother or sister?"

Oh. So she was trying to *become* pregnant.

"Another brother or sister?" David Michael repeated dubiously.

"A *baby*?" squeaked Andrew and Karen.

"Great!" said Sam and Charlie.

"Terrific!" I added honestly. I love babies. Imagine having one right in my house, twenty-four hours a day.

But the little kids just couldn't be enthusiastic.

"Why do you want a baby?" asked Karen bluntly.

"Oh, we didn't say we want a *baby* — " Watson began.

But before he could finish, Andrew spoke up. "A baby," he said, "would be the youngest person in the family. But that's *me*. *I'm* the youngest. I don't want a baby."

"Babies smell," added Karen.

"They cry," said David Michael. "And burp and spit up and get baby food in their hair. And you have to *change their diapers*."

"Kids, kids," exclaimed Watson, holding his hands up. "Elizabeth just asked about another brother or sister, that's all."

Silence.

At last David Michael said, "Well, brothers and sisters start out as babies, don't they?"

And Andrew said, "I think we've got enough kids around here."

"Yeah," agreed Karen and David Michael.

But I couldn't help saying, "Another kid would be great. Really."

Sam and Charlie nodded.

No one seemed to know what to say then, but it didn't matter because Boo-Boo came into the dining room carrying a mole he'd caught, and we all jumped out of our chairs. The poor mole was still alive, so we had to get it away from Boo-Boo and then put it back outside where it belonged.

That was the end of dinner.

Later that night, I lay in bed, thinking. Sometimes I get in bed early just so I can do that. First I thought about Boo-Boo and the mole. Charlie and I had caught Boo-Boo and held him. And David Michael had gotten Boo-Boo to open his mouth, which had caused the mole to drop out and land in the oven mitts Mom was wearing. Then Mom, Karen, Andrew, and David Michael had taken the mole into the backyard and let it loose in some shrubbery. It had scampered off.

I thought of Mom wanting to have another baby. Even though she's kind of old for that, it made sense. I mean, she's married to Watson now, so I guessed that she and Watson wanted a baby of their own. Boy. Mom would have five kids and two stepkids then.

She would need an extra special Mother's Day present. What on earth could I give her? I slid over in bed so I could see the moon out my window.

The moon was pretty, but it was no help.

Jewelry? Nah. Mom likes to choose her own. Stockings? Boring. Candy or flowers? Let Watson do that. Something for her desk at the office? Maybe. Clothes? If I could afford anything.

I had a feeling I was missing the point, though. I wanted to say thank you to Mom for being such a wonderful mother. (She really is.) So I needed to give her something special, something that would tell her, "You're the best mom. Thanks." But what would say that?

I thought and thought. And then it came to me. It was another one of my ideas. Carrying it off might take some work, but my friends and I could do it.

I couldn't wait until the next meeting of the Baby-sitters Club.

CHAPTER 4

I don't know whether to describe myself as a patient person or not. I mean, when I'm baby-sitting, I can sit for fifteen minutes, waiting for a four-year-old who wants to tie his own shoelaces. But when I have a big idea, I want to get on with it right away. And I had a *huge* idea.

On Wednesday, I begged Charlie to leave early for the club meeting. I reached Claudia's at 5:15.

None of my friends was there, not even Claudia.

"She is baby-sitting," Mimi told me. "At Marshalls'. Back at . . . at five, no at thirty-five. No, um . . . back for meeting."

Mimi is Claudia's grandmother, and we all love her. She had a stroke last summer and it affected her speech. Also, she is getting a little slower, and . . . I don't know. She just seems older. I wish people didn't have to change.

31

But they do.

"Go on upstairs?" Mimi said to me, as if it were a question.

"Is that okay?" I replied.

Mimi nodded, so I kissed her cheek and ran to Claud's room. I found the notebook and record book and set them on the bed. Then I put on my visor. I stuck a pencil over my ear and sat in the director's chair. I was ready for the meeting. The only thing I needed was all the rest of the club members.

Claudia arrived first. The others trickled in after her. By 5:29, the six of us had gathered. I was so excited that I rushed through our opening business and then exclaimed, "I've got an idea!"

"This sounds like a big one," said Dawn.

"It's pretty big," I agreed.

"Bigger than the Kid-Kits?" Mary Anne wanted to know.

"Much."

"Bigger than the *club*?" asked Mallory, awed.

"Not quite. This is it: I was trying to come up with a Mother's Day present for my mom," I began. (I couldn't look at Mary Anne while I talked about Mother's Day. I just couldn't.) "And I was thinking that her present should be really special. That it should have something to do with saying thank you and with being a

32

mom. And I thought, what would a mom like more than anything else? Then the answer came to me — *not* to be a mom for awhile. You know, to have a break. And *then* I thought, maybe we could give this present to a lot of the moms whose kids we sit for."

"Huh?" said Claudia.

"I guess I'm a little ahead of myself," I replied. (I'm usually a little ahead of myself.)

My friends shifted position and I looked at them as I tried to figure out how to explain my great idea. Mallory, with her new short haircut, was sitting on the floor, leaning against Claud's bed. She was wearing jeans with zippers up the bottoms of the legs, and a sweat shirt that said STONEYBROOK MIDDLE SCHOOL across the front. In her newly pierced ears were tiny gold hoops.

Jessi was wearing matching hoops (I think she and Mal had gone shopping together), a purple dance leotard, and jeans. Over the leotard she was wearing a purple-and-white striped shirt, unbuttoned.

On the bed, in a row, sat Mary Anne, Dawn, and Claudia, watching me intently. Mary Anne's hair was pulled back in a ponytail and held in place with a black-and-white checkered bow that matched the short skirt she was wearing. Around her neck was a chain and dangling from it were gold letters that spelled out MARY ANNE.

Dawn was wearing a necklace, too, only hers said I'M AWESOME. Honest. Where had she gotten it? California, probably. And in her *double* pierced ears were hoops of different sizes. See what I mean about Dawn being an individual? Also she was wearing a fairly tame dress, but on her feet were plaid high-top sneakers.

Then there was Claudia. She was wearing a pretty tame dress, too — with a red necktie! Then, she had on these new, very cool roll socks. When she pushed them down just right, they fell into three rolls. The top roll was red, the middle one was peacock blue, and the bottom one was purple. She looked as if she were wearing ice-cream cones on her feet. In her hair was a braided band in red, blue, and purple, like her socks. And dangling from her ears were — get this — spiders in webs. Ew. (But they were pretty cool.)

And me? I was wearing what I always wear — jeans, a turtleneck, a sweater, and sneakers. Okay, so I'm not a creative dresser. I don't have pierced ears, either. I'm sorry. That sort of thing just doesn't interest me much.

"My idea," I began, "is to give mothers a

break in their routine. I thought that as a present to the mothers whose kids we sit for — you know, Mrs. Newton, Mrs. Perkins, Mrs. Barrett, some of our own mothers — we could take their kids off their hands for a day. We could do something really fun with the kids so they'd have a good time, and while they were gone, the mothers could enjoy some peace and quiet."

All around me, eyes were lighting up.

"Yeah!" said Claudia slowly.

"That's a great idea," agreed Jessi.

"Awesome," added Dawn.

Mal and Mary Anne were nodding their heads vigorously.

"Good idea?" I asked unnecessarily.

"The best," said Dawn.

I breathed a sigh of relief. Sometimes I get so carried away with my ideas that I can't tell whether they're good or stupid.

The phone rang then, and we stopped and arranged a sitting job for Jessi.

"I was thinking," I went on as Mary Anne put down the appointment book, "that we could take the kids on some kind of field trip. I mean, an outing. I don't know what kind exactly, but we'll come up with something. And maybe we could do this on the day before Mother's Day. That way, the present will be close to the actual holiday, but we'll still be able to spend Sunday with our own moth — "

I stopped abruptly. How could I be so thoughtless? I glanced at Mary Anne, who was looking down at her hands.

"With — with, um, our families," I finished up. I prayed for the phone to ring then, to save my neck and Mary Anne's feelings, but it didn't.

Instead, Jessi said, "If we're asking our little brothers and sisters on the outing, I *know* Becca would like to come. Especially if we invite Charlotte, too." (Charlotte Johanssen, one of our sitting charges, and Becca Ramsey are best friends.) "Becca might be shy, but she always likes a good field trip."

I smiled gratefully at Jessi. She meant what she'd just said, but I knew she'd only said it to take everyone's attention away from mothers and Mother's Day. Also, she got our discussion going again.

"My brothers and sisters would like a trip, too," spoke up Mal. "Well, most of them would. The triplets and Vanessa might think they're too old for this. But, well, what about money? If this really is a present to mo — to our clients, then I guess we're going to pay for everything, right?"

"We should talk about that," I replied. "I

really haven't worked out all the details."

Ordinarily, I might have come up with some solution and said, "Okay, this is what we're going to do." But I know that I can be bossy. Sometimes it gets me in trouble. Not long ago, it nearly caused our whole club to break up. Well, maybe I'm exaggerating. But it did cause a huge fight.

So all I said was, "I don't think the day has to be very expensive. Maybe we could use money that's in the treasury. We have pretty much right now, don't we, Dawn?"

Dawn nodded.

"Okay, then. *But* — everyone has to agree to this. This isn't usually how we spend the treasury money."

We were in the middle of taking a vote when the phone rang. And rang and rang. We stopped to schedule a few jobs. Then we returned to the vote. It was unanimous. We agreed to use our treasury money.

"Now," I went on, "what should the outing be? I mean, where should we go? It should be someplace that's fun, but easy to get to and cheap."

We all thought. No one came up with a single idea. There isn't a lot to do here in Stoneybrook. Not a lot that's within walking distance anyway.

Claudia cleared her throat and we looked at her expectantly. "I don't have an idea," she said. "I was just thinking that the way we could ask kids to come on the outing would be to send invitations to their mothers. I think the outing would seem more like a gift then. An invitation could say, 'Happy Mother's Day, Mrs. Rodowsky. As a special present, the Baby-sitters Club would like to give you a day to yourself. Therefore, Jackie, Archie, and Shea are invited to go' . . . wherever we decide to go. Something like that."

"Ooh, that's great, Claud," said Jessi.

"Yeah," agreed Dawn. "Would you design the invitations, Claud? We'll help you make them, but you do the best artwork."

"Thanks," replied Claudia. "Sure. I'll design something."

"Maybe the fathers could be involved," I said slowly. "I'm not sure how to get them to do this, but they should be the ones to drop the kids off and pick them up. Stuff like that. And of course we can't take babies on the outing. So, for instance, if we take Jamie Newton for the day, Lucy will still be at home. Maybe Mr. Newton will agree to watch her while Jamie's with us."

My friends nodded. We talked and talked.

We talked until it was after six o'clock. We worked out all the details, but not what our outing would be. Where could we take the kids?

"You know," said Jessi, as we were getting ready to leave Claud's room, "I think our Mother's Day surprise solves a problem for me."

"What?" asked the rest of us.

"I think it can be my present to Mama. It'll get Becca *and* me out of her hair for a whole day. And if Daddy will watch Squirt, then Mama will really have a vacation."

"Same here," said Mal. "The younger kids can come on the trip, and I'm sure I can convince the triplets and Vanessa to stay out of Mom's hair. Or maybe Dad can do something with them."

"And same with me," I added. "Andrew, Karen, and David Michael will come with us. Charlie and Sam are hardly ever around on Saturdays anyway. I *think* this will be my gift. I'll just have to see."

"I wish the outing helped me," said Dawn with a sigh, "but it doesn't."

"Me neither," added Claudia. "All I've decided is to *make* Mom's gift, whatever it will be."

"Maybe I'll make mine, too," said Dawn. "Would you help me, Claud?"

"Sure."

We were filing out of Claudia's room, tired but excited.

Mary Anne was being awfully quiet, but just as I was starting to worry about her, she gave me a little smile to let me know that she would handle Mother's Day somehow — just as she had handled it every year before.

CHAPTER 5

Friday

I babbysat for Jamie newton today guess waht. Thanks to jamie I think I discovred the place wher we can take the kids for there outing. Jamie was in the bake yard and he was printinding to be in a circos or something. He was printinding to walk on a thight rope and be a clone and stuff. Then I took him inside for a glas of water and guess waht I saw. It looked like the anser to our probelms.

Claudia's job at the Newtons' on Friday afternoon turned out to be profitable. Not only did she have fun and get paid, but she found something pretty interesting. It was a flier posted on their refrigerator.

Well, once again I'm ahead of myself. I bet you don't have any idea what I'm talking about. (I don't blame you.) Okay. Let me go back to when Claud arrived at the Newtons'.

She showed up on time, of course. (A good sitter is *always* on time.) But she didn't bring her Kid-Kit. It was a sunny afternoon and she knew that all Jamie would want to do was play outside.

Mrs. Newton greeted Claudia at the door.

"Hi, honey," she said. "Come on in."

"Thanks." Claudia stepped into the Newtons' hallway.

"How are you? How are the art classes?" asked Mrs. Newton. She and Claud are pretty close. Mrs. Newton is interested in whatever Claudia does.

"I'm fine. My classes are great. And look what I made." Claudia pulled her hair back to show Mrs. Newton the earrings she was wearing. They were painted sunbursts.

"You *made* those?"

"Yup," said Claudia proudly.

Mrs. Newton shook her head in amazement.

"Where are the kids?" asked Claud.

"Jamie's out in the yard, and Lucy's upstairs taking a nap. I just put her down, so she should sleep for awhile. You can go out with Jamie, but stick your head inside every now and then to listen for the baby."

Claudia nodded. "Okay. Anything else?"

"I don't think so. You know where the emergency numbers are. And I'll be at a meeting at Jamie's school. The number is on the refrigerator."

A few minutes later, Mrs. Newton called good-bye to Jamie and left. Claudia joined Jamie in the backyard. She found him tiptoeing around with his arms outstretched. He was singing "Home on the Range," but he was getting a lot of the words wrong.

"Oh, give me a comb," he sang loudly, *"where the buffaloes foam, and the deer and the antinope pay. Where seldom is heard a long-distance bird, and the sky is not crowded all day."*

Claudia smiled, but she managed not to laugh. "Hiya, Jamie," she said.

"Hi-hi!" Jamie replied happily. He didn't seem to mind having been interrupted at all.

"What are you doing?" Claud wanted to

know. (Jamie was still tiptoeing around.)

"I'm a tightrope walker. Now watch this. I'm going to be someone else."

Jamie walked a few steps. He tripped and fell. Then he picked himself up and fell again. When he stood up, he shook himself all over like a puppy dog.

Claudia wasn't sure what was going on, so she was relieved when Jamie began turning somersaults and making silly faces. "You're a clown!" she exclaimed.

"Right!" said Jamie. "And now I'm going to be another person."

He raised his arms in the air and ran back and forth across the yard. *"Oh, he fries food the air,"* he sang, *"with the greatest of vease!"*

"A trapeze artist," said Claud.

"Yup."

The Newtons must have gone to a circus, she thought. And she thought that until she took Jamie inside for a glass of water. His throat was dry from all his singing and running around. Claud went to the refrigerator to get out the bottle of cold water she knew was inside — and her eyes fell on a colorful flier posted next to the phone number of Jamie's school.

COME TO SUDSY'S CARNIVAL! it read. GAMES! RIDES! SIDESHOW ATTRACTIONS! REFRESHMENTS!

Carefully, Claudia read every word on the flier. The carnival would be in Stoneybrook on Mother's Day weekend. It would be set up in a large parking lot that was near a playground not far from Claud's house. It would have midway games, some rides, plenty of food (cotton candy, peanuts, ice cream, popcorn, lemonade), and even a sideshow. Claudia raised her eyebrows. Were there *really* bearded ladies and people who were half-man, half-woman or who could swallow fire or swords? She wasn't sure. But she didn't care. All she was interested in was finding out more about the carnival.

Jamie saw Claud looking at the flier. "The carnival," he said sadly.

"What's wrong?" asked Claud.

"I really really really really really want to go, but I can't. Mommy and Daddy can't take me."

"Too bad, Jamie," said Claudia.

"I know. I want to see that man. That one right there."

Jamie reached up to touch a picture of a clown carrying a bunch of helium balloons.

"The balloon-seller?" Claudia asked.

Jamie nodded. "I would buy a yellow balloon. Maybe after that I would buy a green balloon for Lucy."

"That would be very generous of you."

"And then I would play some games. I would win some prizes, like a whistle and a teddy bear. The bear would be for Lucy, too."

Claudia smiled.

"But," Jamie continued with a sigh, "I guess I can't go. No clowns. No balloons. No prizes."

Claudia gave Jamie a hug, and then poured him his glass of water.

"Thank you," he said politely.

"You're welcome. And Jamie, you never know."

"What?"

"You never know about things. You can't be too sure. I remember once when I was six, a big circus came to Stamford, and Mom and Dad said our whole family could go. Only — a week before we were going to the circus, I got the chicken pox."

"Yuck."

"I know. And when circus day came, I was much better but I still had spots, so I wasn't allowed to go. Mimi took care of me while Mom and Dad and Janine went to the circus. Guess what, though. People liked the circus so much that it stayed an extra week, and Mimi and I went to it the next Saturday."

"*Really?* Wow."

Claudia suddenly realized that she shouldn't get Jamie's hopes up *too* much. After all, the carnival was still sort of a long shot. So she said again, "You just never know, Jamie. I'm not saying you will go to the carnival. But it's several weeks away. A lot could happen, right? . . . Right?"

"*Oh, give me a comb . . .*"

Jamie wasn't listening. He and Claudia went back outside. Jamie played carnival again. Every now and then, Claudia tiptoed into the house and stood at the bottom of the stairs, listening for Lucy. The third time she did that, she heard baby sounds. Lucy almost always wakes up happy. She doesn't cry. She just sits in her crib and talks to herself in words only she can understand.

Claudia poked her head out the back door. "Jamie!" she called. "Come on inside. I have to get Lucy up."

Jamie came in and found *Sesame Street* on the television, while Claudia dashed upstairs. She opened the door to Lucy's room slowly.

"Hiya, Lucy-Goose," she said.

Lucy's face began to crumple.

"I know. I'm not your mommy or daddy. I'm sorry. But it's me, Luce. It's Claudee." (That's what Jamie sometimes calls Claudia.)

Claudia puttered around Lucy's room, not going too near her. She sang "The Eensy Weensy Spider" and "The Wheels on the Bus."

Lucy began to smile. Claudia tickled her and changed her diaper, and she seemed to be okay. So Claud carried her downstairs. She could smell Lucy's baby smell — powder and Pampers and soap and milk.

"Jamie, look who's here!" said Claudia.

Jamie turned away from the TV. When he and Lucy saw each other, their faces broke into grins.

What a change from when Lucy first came home from the hospital, thought Claudia. Jamie wanted to send his sister back.

Claudia, Jamie, and Lucy played on the floor of the family room until Mrs. Newton came home at five-fifteen. Then Claudia raced to her own house for our Friday meeting. She couldn't wait to get there. For once, she would be the one with a big idea, and if everyone liked it, she'd make a lot of people very happy — especially Jamie Newton, who just might get to go to the carnival and see the balloon-seller after all.

CHAPTER 6

For the second time in a row I arrived at our meeting early. There was a good reason for this. It was because I had begged Charlie to leave early. "Please, please, please take me over now," I'd said. My next step would have been to kneel down and plead, but Charlie agreed to go.

I don't know why I was so eager for the meeting. It wasn't as if I had any news. I just wanted to get on with the plans for our Mother's Day surprise.

Anyway, thanks to Charlie, I reached the Kishis' just before Claudia came running home from the Newtons'. I could hear her calling to me as she dashed along the sidewalk.

"Hi, Claud!" I replied. I stood on her steps and looked across the street at the house that used to be mine. I'd grown up there. I'd learned to walk and ride a bike and turn cartwheels there. I'd gone off to school and watched my

49

father walk out on us and seen Watson come into our lives. I'd been away from that house for less than a year, but it seemed like a decade.

Time is funny.

Claudia raced up her walk and let me into her house. "You're early again," she said. "Do you have news?"

I shook my head.

"Well, I do! But I guess it'll have to wait until the meeting starts, right?"

"Not necessarily," I replied, since I was dying of curiosity, "but I guess you might as well. Then you can tell us all at once."

Claudia and I were both a little disappointed, but at least we didn't have long to wait before the meeting started. Mary Anne, Jessi, Dawn, and Mallory arrived on time, and I brought us to order immediately.

"The first piece of business," I announced, "is that Claudia has some sort of big news. Claudia?" I said, turning to her.

"My big news," Claudia began, shifting position on the bed, "is that I think I've found a place where we can take the kids on their outing."

Five pairs of eyes widened. The room was absolutely silent.

Then I cried out, "Where, where, *where*?" I couldn't help it.

"To a carnival," Claud began. "See, I was sitting at the Newtons' this afternoon, and on their refrigerator was a flier advertising something called Sudsy's Carnival. It's going to be in Stoneybrook the weekend of Mother's Day. There'll be all sorts of things kids will like — games, rides, even a sideshow. But the best thing is, guess where the carnival will be set up?"

"Where?" asked all the rest of us club members.

"In the parking lot near Carle Playground."

"Oh, wow!" I exclaimed. "We can walk there easily!"

"Right," said Claud. "And it seems like a nice, small carnival. I mean, it wouldn't be overwhelming for the littlest kids, and we'd have an easy time keeping track of everyone."

"I wonder how expensive a carnival would be," said our treasurer. "Any idea what it would cost per kid?"

I looked at Claudia.

"It's hard to say," she replied slowly. "The flier didn't mention a fee to get in — you know, the way you pay one big price to get into Funland, and then you can go on the rides as often as you want. I guess one fee wouldn't make sense at a carnival anyway, since so much of it is games that you have to pay for separately." Claud paused. She drew in her breath. "I'm guessing the carnival wouldn't be too expensive per kid. There's an awful lot just to look at, and if we limit the kids to, say, three things each, that wouldn't be too bad."

We asked Claudia a few more questions, but everyone in the room was smiling. We knew we had the solution to our problem, and what a solution it was!

"Jamie is going to *faint*!" exclaimed Claudia. "He's dying to go to Sudsy's."

"I don't think David Michael has ever been to a carnival," I added.

"Becca has," said Jessi, "and when she gets to this one, she'll think she's died and gone to heaven."

"I wonder if the kids will be able to spend all day at a carnival," I said suddenly. "That just occurred to me."

"Hmm," said Mary Anne. "Maybe not. Especially if they can only do a few things each."

"I don't think *I* could spend all day at a carnival," spoke up Dawn. "I was just at one when I visited Dad and Jeff in California. It was fun, but . . ."

"All day at anything is too long for little kids," I pointed out. "They need to rest. They get bored."

"Maybe," began Mallory, but she was interrupted by the phone.

We arranged several sitting jobs. Then Mallory started again.

"Maybe we should just go to the carnival in the morning when everyone is fresh and awake," she said. "Then we could eat lunch somewhere else, like at the playground, since the kids are bringing their lunches anyway, and we'll be right next to the playground. There are tables and benches everywhere at Carle. Our family has taken a lot of picnic lunches there."

"That's a good idea," I said. "Really good. Then the kids could play in the park for awhile, and then we really should give them a chance to rest before they go home."

"Well," said Claudia, "they *could* come to my house. Remember last summer when we ran the play group in Stacey's backyard? We could do something like that here. It would probably be for just an hour or two. We could read stories and maybe do an art project. The kids could make Mother's Day cards or little gifts or something. It would be a nice way for them to unwind after all the excitement."

"Great!" I exclaimed. "I think we've got our Mother's Day surprise." Then I remembered about being bossy and added, "Everyone who thinks this is a good plan, raise her hand.''

Five hands shot up, including mine.

"Dawn? What's wrong? You didn't raise your hand.''

Dawn grinned. "I don't think it's a good plan,'' she said. "I think it's an awesome one.''

Everyone laughed, and Claudia threw a pillow at Dawn.

"Okay,'' I said, when we had quieted down, "I know we don't have much time left today, but I think we should make a list of kids to invite so we can get the invitations out soon. There really isn't *that* much time until Mother's Day.''

"I'll take notes,'' said our secretary. Mary Anne turned to a blank page in the back of the record book. "All right. I'm ready.''

"Let's start with our little brothers and sisters,'' I began. "Karen, Andrew, and David Michael will be invited. And Becca Ramsey. And . . . Mal, who in your family?''

"I guess everyone except the triplets. Claire, Margo, Nicky, and Vanessa. I'm really not sure Vanessa will come, though. She's funny about big group things sometimes. She'd rather stay in her room and write poetry.''

Mary Anne nodded. "Well, if she comes, that's eight so far.''

"Jamie Newton,'' said Claudia.

54

"The Barretts," said Dawn. "Buddy and Suzi, anyway. Marnie's too little."

"Myriah and Gabbie Perkins," added Mary Anne, writing furiously. "And, of course, Laura is much too little."

"The Rodowsky boys," spoke up Jessi. "Oh, and the Braddock kids. How could we forget them?"

"I hate to say this," said Mary Anne, "but Jenny Prezzioso. We just *have* to ask her if we ask the Barretts and Mal's brothers and sisters."

"Oh, ew!" I cried. "Ew, *EW*! Jenny is so spoiled." But I knew Mary Anne was right. So Jenny's name was added to the list.

We kept on thinking of kids to invite — Charlotte Johanssen, some kids in my new neighborhood. When we couldn't come up with another name, I said to Mary Anne, "What's the grand total?"

Mary Anne counted up. "Oh, my gosh! Twenty-nine!"

"Twenty-nine!" exclaimed Claudia. "We're good baby-sitters, but the six of us cannot take twenty-nine kids to a carnival."

There was a moment of silence. Then Jessi said, "Well, they won't *all* be able to come. Mal said Vanessa probably won't want to, and some people are bound to be away that day, or to have plans."

"True . . ." I replied slowly. "Even so. Let's say twenty kids want to go on the outing. There are six of us. Some of us would have to be in charge of four kids all day. That's pretty many. And what if we end up with more kids than we think?"

"Well, how about calling our associate members?" suggested Mary Anne, grinning. (You could tell she was just dying to call Logan.)

"Maybe we better." I handed the phone to Mary Anne. She called Logan. His family was going to be out of town that weekend.

Mary Anne handed the phone back to me. I called Shannon Kilbourne. *Her* family would be having weekend guests. Shannon was supposed to stick around and be polite.

"Uh-oh," I said when I'd hung up the phone.

"Wait a second!" cried Claudia. "Oh, my lord! I've got a great idea. Let's call Stacey and invite her to Stoneybrook for the weekend!"

As if you couldn't tell from Claudia's excitement, she and Stacey McGill used to be best friends. (Well, they still are but it's difficult with Claud living in Stoneybrook and Stacey living in New York City.) Anyway, I knew we all wanted to see Stacey, and she's a terrific baby-sitter.

Claudia made the call. "Stace? It's me," she said. A whole lot of screaming and laughing followed. Then Claudia explained about the Mother's Day surprise. "So could you come?" she asked. "We aren't getting paid or anything. It would just be fun. And you could stay for awhile on Sunday before we put you on the train back to the city."

Stacey had to check with her parents, but guess what — she got permission!

"You can come?" shrieked Claudia. She turned to us club members. "She's free! She can come! . . . Stace? We'll make the arrangements later. Oh, I'm *so glad!* This will be your first trip back to Stoneybrook."

Well, it had been your basic red-letter club meeting. By the time Claud got off the phone, it was just after six, so we had to leave, but all of us felt as if we were floating instead of walking. We agreed to return to Claudia's the next day, Saturday, to make the invitations.

CHAPTER 7

The arrangements for the Mother's Day surprise were falling into place. Claudia's parents had spoken to Stacey's parents, and the adults had decided that Stacey would take the train to Stoneybrook on Friday after school. With any luck, she'd reach the Kishis' in time for our club meeting that day! Then she would stay with Claud until Sunday afternoon — and help us out on Saturday, of course.

Also our invitations had been designed, made, and mailed out. They were pretty cute, if I do say so myself. Claud had drawn two pictures on them. In the upper lefthand corner was a totally dragged-out looking mom. She was holding a briefcase in one hand and a vacuum cleaner in the other, and a baby was strapped to her chest. Her hair looked frazzled and there were bags under her eyes. In the lower righthand corner was a rested mom. She was sitting in a lawn chair with a book in one hand and a glass of iced tea (or something) in the other. She was smiling, and the bags were gone.

In the middle of the page, we had written: "SURPRISE! Happy Mother's Day! The members of the Baby-sitters Club would like to give our special moms a special gift."

(I thought that part was corny, but no one agreed with me.)

Then the invitations went on to say who was invited, what we would do, where we would meet, and that sort of thing.

I was at home on the Saturday my own mom received her Mother's Day surprise. It was one of those gorgeous spring days when you look at the sky and think, Could it possibly get any bluer? It was also unusually warm, so David Michael, Andrew, Karen, and I were out in our yard with no jackets or sweaters.

"It's summer! It's just like summer!" exclaimed Karen.

We still had a good two months before vacation, but I didn't say anything.

The kids were doing the outdoor things they missed during the winter, like skipping rope, tossing a ball around, and turning somersaults. Mom and Watson were inside. They were on the phone. They'd been making an awful lot of phone calls lately. And Sam and Charlie, as usual, were off with their friends.

Sometimes I feel . . . I don't know . . . left out of my own family. I love everybody, but I'm too young to hang around with Sam and Charlie, and too old for Andrew, David Michael, and Karen. They're fun, but they *are* just kids.

Anyway, David Michael's game of catch with Andrew was beginning to get out of hand.

"David Michael," I said, "you don't have to throw it so hard. Andrew's not that far away from you."

"But he keeps missing the balls."

"Maybe he's afraid of them. They're coming at him like freight trains."

"I'm not afraid!" protested Andrew.

I sighed. Since I wasn't baby-sitting, I didn't feel like getting involved in this argument. "I think I'll take Shannon on a walk," I said.

Shannon was playing in the yard, but I knew she'd want to take a walk. Any change of scenery was fine with her. I clipped her leash to her collar and we set off. I chose one particular direction. It was the direction in which Bart Taylor's house lies.

Bart Taylor is nice. Oh, okay, he's gorgeous and wonderful and smart and athletic. We sort of like each other, even though we don't go to the same school. Bart coaches a softball team called Bart's Bashers, and I coach one called Kristy's Krushers. So Bart is my rival, too. We try not to think of that. But we hardly ever see each other anyway.

Which is why I walked Shannon by his house that day. I tried to glance at it casually every few steps, but I couldn't see a thing that way. So finally I just stared. The front door was closed, the shades were drawn, the garage door was pulled down.

No one was home.

I walked Shannon sadly back to my house, feeling lonely and a little depressed. But the warm weather and the thought of the weekend stretching before me cheered me up again.

"Hey, you guys!" I called when I reached our yard. "How about some batting practice? The Krushers have another game coming up!"

Andrew, David Michael, and Karen are on my softball team. That ought to give you some idea of what the team is like. It's a bunch of kids who are either too young for Little League or even T-ball, or who are too embarrassed to belong to one of those teams — but who really want to learn to play better. The first time the Krushers played Bart's Bashers we almost beat them. That's how much spirit we have.

"Batting practice?" echoed Karen. "Okay. Let's go."

We found several bats and two softballs.

"I'll be the pitcher," I said. "We're going to work on your technique. David Michael, show me your batting stance, okay?"

My brother demonstrated.

"Good!" I cried. "That's really terrific." No doubt about it, my brother had improved since I'd started coaching him. I don't mean to sound conceited, but it was true.

I tossed the ball — underhand, easy.

David Michael missed it by a mile.

I take it back. Maybe he was still a klutz.

"Karen?" I called. "Your turn."

Karen was testing the weights of the bats when Mom dashed into the backyard, waving a paper in her hand.

Oh, *darn*, I thought. Which one of us messed up? What was she waving? A math test with an E on the top? A report with the words "See me" in red ink? (I swear, those are the worst words teachers ever invented.)

"Kristy!" Mom called.

Yikes! It was *me*! I had messed up!

"Honey, thank you," said my mother breathlessly as she reached me.

Thank you? Well, I couldn't have done anything too bad. I dared to look at the paper. It was the Mother's Day surprise. *Whew.*

"You're welcome," I replied, smiling.

Mom put her arms around me.

"It's your Mother's Day surprise," I said unnecessarily.

Immediately, Mom began to cry. It wasn't that sobbing, unhappy crying that mothers do when they're watching something like *Love Story* or *Brian's Song* on TV. It was that teary kind of crying where the voice just goes all wavery. "Wha-at a lo-ovely invita-ation," she managed to squeak out. She wiped at her eyes. Then she found a tissue stuffed up her sleeve, so she blew her nose.

(Well, I knew the invitations were nice, but I hadn't expected this. I would have to call Jessi and Mallory to find out if their mothers had freaked out, too.)

"Um, Mom," I began, gathering my nerve to ask the question that so far only Sam had dared to ask, "are you pregnant?"

My mother shook her head. She blew her nose again. "No."

"Are you positive?"

"Positive. . . . But if you were to have a new brother or sister, how — "

"Well, you know how I feel about kids, Mom," I said. "It would be fine."

But suddenly it didn't seem quite as fine as

it had seemed in the past. I love babies. I really do. But what would it be like if Mom and Watson had a baby of their own? That would be different from Mrs. Newton or Mrs. Perkins having a baby. It might draw Mom and Watson closer together — and shut us kids out, just when us kids need to be drawn closer to everyone in the family. Why hadn't I thought about that before? But all I said was, "Fine, fine."

Mom smiled. The two of us sat down in the grass. "So tell me more about this invitation," said my mother. "Who planned the surprise?"

"Everyone in the Baby-sitters Club," I answered, "only, the basic idea was sort of mine. Well, it was all mine."

"I'm sure it was. You always did have big ideas."

"Remember when we lived in the old house, and I worked out the flashlight code so Mary Anne and I could talk to each other from our bedroom windows at night?"

"Of course. And your big idea to marry me to the mailman?"

"David Michael wanted a father," I reminded her. "I was only ten then."

Mom and I laughed. We watched Andrew, Karen, and David Michael practice their pitching and catching.

"Well, anyway," I said, "we sent out invitations to twenty-nine kids."

"Twenty-nine!" squawked Mom.

"Don't worry. They won't all be able to come. Besides, Stacey is going to be in town that weekend. She's going to help us. So there'll be seven sitters. If we wind up with, let's say, twenty kids, that's only about three kids per sitter. We can handle that."

"And you're taking the children to a carnival?"

"Yup. It's called Sudsy's. It's just a little one. It'll be set up in that big parking lot near Carle Playground. We'll spend the morning at Sudsy's, go to the playground for lunch and some exercise, then walk back to Claudia's house for stories and stuff, so the kids can rest. We figure we'll have the kids from about nine until four. That'll be a nice rest for you, won't it, Mom?"

"A wonderful one."

The phone rang then. We could hear it through the open kitchen window. A moment later, Watson called, "Elizabeth? This is an important one."

My mother leaped to her feet like an Olympic athlete and dashed inside.

I went back to my sister and brothers.

"How are you guys doing?" I asked. I asked

65

it before I saw the scowls on the kids' faces.

"He is a klutz," said David Michael with clenched teeth, pointing to Andrew.

"Am not."

"Are too, you little wimp. And you're Watson's favorite."

"No, he isn't," cried Karen indignantly. "Daddy loves us both the same."

"What about *me?*" David Michael threw his bat angrily to the ground.

Karen and Andrew did the same thing. Softballs, too.

"Well, I guess it figures," my brother went on. "Of course he loves you guys more than me. He's your real father. He's just my step."

"Your mom loves you more than us," spoke up Andrew, to my surprise. "She's *our* step."

"*Hey, hey, HEY!* What is this talk?" I cried. "Everybody loves everybody around here."

"No," said David Michael. "Sometimes Thomases love Thomases more, and Brewers love Brewers more."

Karen sighed. "I'm tired of this. Let's play ball again."

The kids picked up their bats. They forgot their argument for awhile.

But I didn't.

CHAPTER 8

"Well, it's finally happened!" I announced.

"What?" asked Claudia, Jessi, Dawn, Mary Anne, and Mallory.

We were holding a meeting of the Baby-sitters Club, and the last of the RSVPs for the Mother's Day surprise had just been phoned in. I gave the news to my friends.

"We can get a total count now," I said. "That was Mrs. Barrett. Buddy and Suzi can come on the outing. They were the last kids we needed to hear about. Mary Anne?"

Mary Anne had opened the record book to a page on which she was listing the kids who'd be coming to Sudsy's with us. "Ready for the total?" she asked.

The rest of us nodded nervously.

"Okay, just a sec." Mary Anne's pen moved down the page. Then, "It's twenty-one," she announced.

"Twenty-one! That's perfect!" I cried. "Seven

sitters including Stacey, so three kids each. We can manage that."

"Sure," said Dawn.

"We can help each other out," added Claudia.

"Read us the list, Mary Anne," I said. "Let's see exactly what we're dealing with here."

"Okay." Mary Anne began reading, running her finger along the list. "Claire, Margo, Nicky, and Vanessa Pike." (Vanessa had surprised everyone by immediately agreeing to come.) "Becca Ramsey; David Michael Thomas; Karen and Andrew Brewer; Jamie Newton; Jackie, Shea, and Archie Rodowsky; Jenny Prezzioso." (I tried not to choke.) "Myriah and Gabbie Perkins; Matt and Haley Braddock; Charlotte Johanssen; Nina Marshall; and Buddy and Suzi Barrett."

"And who couldn't come?" I asked.

"Let's see," said Mary Anne, turning to another page in the record book, "the Arnold twins, Betsy Sobak, the Papadakises, and the Delaneys."

I nodded. "Okay. I was just curious."

Ring, ring.

Dawn reached for the phone. "Hello, Babysitters Club," she said. "Yes, hi, Mrs. Arnold. . . . Oh, we're sorry, too. The twins would probably love Sudsy's. . . . Yeah. . . . Yeah. . . . Okay, on Tuesday? I'll check. I'll call you right back."

We arranged for Mal to sit for Marilyn and Carolyn Arnold (can you believe their names?) on Tuesday afternoon. Then we went back to our work.

"I guess we should make up groups of kids for the outing," said Claudia. "That worked well before."

Once, our club had sat for fourteen kids for a whole week. We kept the kids in groups according to their ages. It was really helpful. And we had done the same thing when Mary Anne, Dawn, Claudia, and I had visited Stacey in New York and taken a big group of kids to a museum and to Central Park.

"The only thing," spoke up Mary Anne, "is that I'm not sure we should group the kids by age. I think we should group them, but, well, Matt and Haley will have to be in the same group, even though Matt is seven and Haley's almost ten now. Haley understands Matt's signing better than anybody." (Matt is deaf and communicates using sign language.)

"And," I added, "I think Karen and Andrew should be in the same group, and David Michael should be in a different one. Andrew is really dependent on Karen, and lately the two of them have been having some problems with David Michael."

"And Charlotte and Becca *have* to be together," added Jessi. "Becca won't come if she can't be with Charlotte."

"Hmm," I said. "Anything else?"

"Keep Jenny away from the Braddocks," said Dawn.

"And Nicky away from Claire," added Mallory.

"Boy, is this complicated," commented Claudia.

"I know," I agreed. "But we can do it. Let's try to draw up some lists. Let's just see how far we get. Everyone, make up seven lists and then we'll compare them."

Mary Anne passed around paper and we set to work. We were interrupted four times by the telephone, but at last everyone said they had done the best they could.

I collected the papers. I looked over the groups my friends had come up with. I said things like, "No, that one won't work. Matt and Haley aren't together." Or, "Oh, that's good, that's good, that's — Nope. We've got Claire and Nicky together."

"I've got an idea," said Dawn after awhile. "Why don't you cut out all the groups, all forty-two of them, sort through them, and try to find the seven best?"

"Okay," I agreed. Claudia handed me a pair of scissors. "But I think I'll need some help."

Every single club member got down on her hands and knees. We spread the lists on the floor, examined them, and shuffled them around.

"This is a good one," said Jessi.

"This is a good one," said Claud.

Finally we had chosen seven good lists. We counted the kids. Twenty-one. We checked the kids against Mary Anne's list. Nina Marshall showed up twice; Shea Rodowsky was missing.

"*Darn* it!" I cried.

We started over. Finally, finally, finally we had seven lists that worked:

Kristy
Karen Brewer
Andrew Brewer
Shea Rodowsky

Mary Anne
Jenny Prezzioso
Claire Pike
Margo Pike

Claudia
Myriah Perkins
Gabbie Perkins
Jamie Newton

Dawn
Suzi Barrett
Nina Marshall
Archie Rodowsky

Jessi
Matt Braddock
Haley Braddock
Nicky Pike

Mallory
Buddy Barrett
D. M. Thomas
Jackie Rodowsky

Stacey
Charlotte Johanssen
Becca Ramsey
Vanessa Pike

"Well," I said, "we've got all the necessary combinations — Matt and his sister are together, so are Charlotte and Becca, Jenny is separated from the Braddocks, and that sort of thing. There are some good combinations here, too. Like, Jamie and the Perkins girls are together, and they're friends. And I think Jenny will work out okay with Claire and Margo, don't you, Mal?"

"Yeah, that should be all right."

"But," I went on, "there are some odd combinations here, too. Not bad, just odd. For instance, Shea Rodowsky is with Karen and Andrew. Shea is nine. He's a lot older than they are. But where else could we put him?"

The six of us leaned over to examine the lists.

"I don't really see any place," said Dawn after a moment. "Claudia's group, Mary Anne's, and mine are too young. Stacey's is all girls. Jessi's is perfect the way it is. Mallory's would be good because the kids are all boys, but they're younger than Shea, too. Besides, I wouldn't mind separating Shea and Jackie."

"Here's another odd list," said Claudia. "I'm not sure what Archie Rodowsky will think of Suzi and Nina. At least the three of them are about the same age."

"I think we've made good choices about the baby-sitter in charge of each group," Mary Anne pointed out. "Kristy, Andrew would want to be with you."

I nodded. "I know."

"And Claud, you're a good choice for Jamie and the Perkins girls. I think I'm the only one who will handle Jenny. Dawn knows Suzi Barrett really well. Jessi *has* to stick with Matt and Haley since she's the only one of us who knows sign language really well. Mallory will be good with the boys, and Charlotte Johanssen will just *die* to have her old sitter back. Remember how much she loved Stacey?"

"Boy, do I!" I said. I looked at the lists a few moments longer. "Okay," I said at last. "We know the groups are going to get all mixed up anyway, but they *will* be helpful. And I think these are the best we're going to do. Do you guys agree?"

"Yes!" It was unanimous.

"Gosh, this is so exciting!" cried Mary Anne.

"Yeah!" agreed Jessi. "It's the first big Baby-sitters Club project I've been part of."

"Me, too," said Mal.

"And I'll finally get to meet Stacey," Jessi went on. "It's so funny to think that I live in her old house — that I *sleep* in her old *bedroom* — and I've never even met her."

"Well, it won't be long now," said Claudia.

"How many of these big — I mean, really big — projects has the club worked on?" Mal wondered.

"Three, I think. Right, Kristy?" answered Dawn. "There was the week before your mom and Watson got married when we took care of the fourteen kids, and there was the play group in Stacey's backyard, and then there was New Yor — "

Ring, ring.

Mary Anne answered the phone while Dawn kept talking. But after about a minute we realized we were listening to Mary Anne instead of Dawn.

"You won't *believe* this!" Mary Anne was saying. (I guessed the caller was not a client.) "We were just talking about New York. Dawn was going to tell about when we took the kids to the museum."

"Is that Stacey?" Claudia cried suddenly. She scrambled off the bed.

I could feel excitement mounting. Stacey! Our old club member! Soon the club would be together again. Actually, when I thought about it, I realized the club would be together again for the first time — because the seven of us had never worked together. Jessi and Mal had joined the club after Stacey had left.

Claudia and Stacey talked to each other.

Then I got on the phone with Stace. "Hi! How *are* you? I can't wait till you get here. We are going to have such a great day. You won't believe how some of the kids have changed. Andrew is so much taller! Oh, and you can meet Matt and Haley Braddock and Becca Ramsey. And Jessi, of course."

"Same old Kristy," said Stacey, and I could tell she was smiling. "I'm fine. Mom and Dad have been arguing, arguing, arguing, but it's just a phase, I think. At least they aren't arguing about *me*."

Stacey has diabetes and her parents sometimes don't agree about the way Stacey manages her disease, even when she's following doctor's orders.

"What are they arguing about?" I asked.

"Oh, who cares? I can't wait to get back to Stoneybrook. Mom wishes she could come with me. She loves Connecticut. What's up with you?"

"Get this. *My* mom wants to have a baby."

"No!"

"Yeah. She and Watson want a baby. Can you imagine? I think they're too old," I said, which I knew wasn't true at all.

I changed the subject quickly, and Stacey and I talked a little longer. I told her about the day we'd planned, and about the groups we'd lined up. By the time we got off the phone, I was just as excited as Claudia about seeing our blonde-haired, blue-eyed, super-sophisticated former treasurer.

CHAPTER 9

" A ughh!"

"I don't believe it!"

"Oh, my gosh. She's here!"

"IT'S STACEY, YOU GUYS!"

It was 5:25 on the day before the Mother's Day surprise. Mary Anne, Dawn, and I had just entered Claudia's room for a club meeting — and found Claudia and Stacey there. Stacey was sitting on Claud's bed, as if she'd never left Stoneybrook. Claud was the one who'd shouted, "IT'S STACEY, YOU GUYS!"

Stacey leaped up, and she and I and Mary Anne and Dawn began hugging and jumping up and down — a group hug. And then we all began talking at once.

"You're here in time for the meeting!" I exclaimed.

"When did you get here?" Mary Anne wanted to know.

"Just a little while ago," replied Stace. "I caught an early train."

"You cut your hair!" Dawn cried.

"Yeah, a little. Do you like it? I went to this really punk place and told the guy not to make it too punk."

"We love it!" said Mary Anne, speaking for all of us.

We were finding places and settling down. I sat in the director's chair, of course. Dawn and Mary Anne squeezed onto the bed with Claudia and Stacey. We left room on the floor for Mal and Jessi.

"This is just so incredible," said Stacey. "Here I am, sitting in on a meeting of the Baby-sitters Club. A *real* meeting, not like the ones we had when you guys came to visit in New York. I feel like I never left here."

"I wish you never had," said Claud wistfully.

Stacey leaned over suddenly and put her arms around Claudia. Claud is not a big crier, but that hug was all it took for the tears to start to fall.

"I miss you so much," she said to Stace. And I knew what she *wasn't* saying: that Stacey was Claud's first and only best friend. And that she hadn't made a new best friend since Stacey had left.

It was while this was going on that I glanced

up and saw Jessi and Mallory hovering uncertainly in the doorway to club headquarters. Jessi looked confused, and Mallory looked bewildered.

"Come on in, you guys," I said loudly to our two junior officers. "This isn't going to be a cry-fest . . . is it, Claud?"

Claudia pulled herself together. She wiped her tears with a tissue and sat up as straight as she could.

And Stacey slid off the bed. "Mal!" she exclaimed. "I am *so* glad to see you! Congratulations on becoming a club member."

"Thanks, Stacey. Baby-sitting sure is more fun this way. It's nice to be official."

Stacey turned to Jessi. "I guess you're Jessi Ramsey," she said.

This comment was a little unnecessary. For one thing, Stacey knows that Jessi is black. I'm sorry to be so blunt, but that's the truth, and anyway I'm always blunt. Besides, who else would Jessi be? We don't bring guests to meetings.

"Yes," said Jessi. "Hi. I moved into your bedroom."

We laughed at that.

"Jessi is a terrific sitter," I said, as Stacey returned to the bed, and Jessi and Mal dropped to the floor. "She even learned sign language so she could communicate with a deaf boy."

"Matt Braddock," added Jessi, looking a little embarrassed by the attention she was getting. "You'll meet him tomorrow. And his sister, Haley."

"Great," replied Stacey. "I can't wait. I can't wait to see the other kids, either. I bet they've really changed."

I was about to say that she might not even recognize some of the youngest ones, when I realized that it was 5:35. "Oh! Order!" I cried. "Order! I cannot believe I forgot to bring the meeting to order, and we're five minutes late!"

"Kristy," said Claudia, "it isn't going to kill you."

I knew Claud sounded annoyed because she was still upset, but even so, I replied testily, "Well, I know *that*. But let's get going here. Hmm. No dues to collect. Any club business?"

To my surprise, Stacey said, "Can I ask a question?"

"Of course."

Ring, ring.

"Oops, the phone. Hold on just a sec, Stace."

I was reaching for the phone (so were Mary Anne and Jessi), when Stacey leaped up. "Can I answer it, please? It's been months and months since I've taken a — " *(Ring, ring.)* " — job call here with you guys."

"Sure," the rest of us replied at once.

Stace reached for the phone. "Hello, Baby-sitters Club," she said, sounding like she might either laugh or cry.

(This meeting was emotional for everyone.)

"Doctor Johanssen!" Stacey suddenly exclaimed. "Doctor Johanssen, it's me, Stacey! . . . No, you called Stoneybrook. I'm visiting. I'm here for the weekend. I'm going on the Mother's Day outing tomorrow." (Dr. Johanssen is Charlotte Johanssen's mother, and in case you can't tell, she and Stacey are pretty close. Stacey helped Charlotte through some rough times, and Dr. Johanssen helped Stacey through some rough times.) "Oh, don't tell Charlotte I'm here, okay?" Stacey was saying. "I'll surprise her when she gets to Claudia's tomorrow. . . . Yes. . . . Right. . . . Oh, a sitter for next Saturday? Boy, I wish it could be me. . . . No, I'm leaving the day after tomorrow. But we'll get you a sitter. I'll call right back, okay? . . . Okay. 'Bye."

Stacey's face went from excited to disappointed and back to excited while Mary Anne looked at our appointment pages. The Johanssen job was for the evening, and we signed Dawn up for it.

Stacey called Charlotte's mother back. While she did, Claud began searching the bedroom.

"What are you looking for?" asked Mal, as if we didn't know. (It must have been junk food.)

"Junk food," Claud replied. "I bought a bag of those licorice strings. I thought we could make jewelry out of them before we ate them. Oh, and Dawn and Stacey, I've got pretzels for you. I know that's not very interesting, but at least the pretzels look like little goldfish."

Claud handed around our snacks.

Then Stacey said, "Um, I had a question . . . ?"

"Oh, right!" I exclaimed. "Sorry, Stace." (If I'd been in a commercial, I would have hit myself on the head and said, "I coulda hadda V-8!")

"Well, I was just wondering. Could we run through tomorrow's schedule and all the details? I mean, like, who exactly is coming, and if we should expect any problems. I don't even know some of these kids. And you guys have talked about a carnival, but . . ."

"Oh, of course we'll run through everything," spoke up Mary Anne, who was playing with a licorice bracelet. "We didn't mean to leave you out. It's just that *we've* been making plans for so long."

"Anyway, it'll probably help *us* to run through the schedule," added Jessi.

I jumped right in. "I'll start," I said. I try hard not to be bossy, but after all, I *am* the president.

"The kids will come here at eight-thirty," I began. (I was trying to make licorice earrings.) "The fathers have been really cooperative, and they're doing all the stuff like dropping the kids off and picking them up. They're making the lunches, too, and watching any brothers and sisters who are too little — "

"Or too big," added Dawn.

" — to come on the outing. So the moms will really have a day off tomorrow."

"One exception," interrupted Mallory, as she braided together three strings of licorice. "The Barretts."

"Oh, yeah," said Stacey. "No Mr. Barrett."

"Right. So guess what?"

"What, Mal?"

"My dad is going to be Mr. Barrett for the day. He's going to bring Buddy and Suzi with my brother and sisters in the morning and pick them up at the end of the day. He's going to fix their lunches, and he's even going to baby-sit for Marnie all day."

"You are kidding!" cried Stacey.

"Nope. Dad loves little kids. Why do you think there are eight of us?"

We laughed, and I added, "Marnie ought to

spend the day with my mother. It would be, like, a dream come true for Mom."

At that point we almost got off the subject, but I went ahead and outlined the day for Stacey (in between a few job calls).

We were finishing up when Mimi wandered into Claudia's room, and I mean *wandered* in. She looked like someone who had gone for a walk without any destination in mind. She just sauntered in — and then she seemed surprised to find us club members there.

"Oh . . . oh, my," said Mimi vaguely.

Claudia leaped to her feet. "What are you looking for, Mimi?"

"The . . . cow."

The cow? My friends and I glanced at each other. But not one of us was tempted to laugh. This was not funny.

Claudia took her grandmother by the arm and led her gently toward the doorway. On the way, Mimi seemed to "wake up."

"Dinner is almost ready, my Claudia," she said. "To please help salad with me after meeting." (That was normal for Mimi.)

"Sure," agreed Claudia. "Just a few more minutes. Then Stacey and I will come help you."

Mimi left. An awkward silence followed. Jessi tried to make conversation. "I really like

84

your bedroom, Stacey," she began. "You should come over and see it, if you want. The wallpaper is so pretty that we left it up, and my furniture looks great . . ." She trailed off.

Claudia had tears in her eyes again.

Stacey said, "I decided I like it better than my room in New York."

Another awkward silence. Both Mallory and Jessi looked awfully uncomfortable. I wondered if they felt like the new kids on the block all over again.

"I wonder," I said, as if it were the only thing on my mind, "what my mom will look like when she's pregnant."

"Like she's going to tip over," replied Dawn, and we all cracked up. We became ourselves again. In the last few moments of the meeting we giggled and laughed and told school gossip to Stacey. Then the meeting was over. We left Claudia and Stacey, calling to each other, " 'Bye!" and "See you at eight!" and "Remember your lunches!"

That night, I could barely get to sleep. I was so, so excited about the Mother's Day surprise.

CHAPTER 10

Saturday

I can't believe it. I am actually writing in the Baby-Sitters Club notebook! I wasn't sure if this would ever happen again. Mom and Dad made all sorts of promises about letting me come back to Stoneybrook to visit but, well -- a club event is almost too good to be true.

Anyway, the morning of the Mother's Day surprise got off to a shaky start. It reminded me of the first day we took care of those fourteen kids at Kristy's. Even though the kids in today's group know each other (mostly) and know us baby-sitters, there are just some children who never like to be left in a new situation. And they let you know by crying....

Well, we did have some tears, but Stacey was right. The morning got off to a shaky start — but not a bad one.

However, the kids' tears came later in the morning. *Stacey* began her day much earlier, waking up in the cot that had been placed in Claudia's room. She yawned and stretched. She looked over at Claudia. Claudia was dead to the world. She could sleep through a tornado. No, a tornado and a hurricane. No, a tornado, a hurricane, a major earthquake, and a garbage truck. Luckily, when Claudia *does* wake up, she gets up fairly easily.

But Stacey didn't need to wake her up right away, which was fine because Stacey wanted to lie in bed and daydream. Actually, what she wanted to do was "rememberize," which was an old word of hers meaning "to remember something really well."

She rememberized the first time she ever met Claudia. It was the beginning of seventh grade — I think it might even have been the first day of school — and they ran into each other in the hallway. I mean, ran *right* into each other. Each of them was kind of mad because the other was dressed in such cool clothes — and each wanted to be *the* coolest.

But they calmed down and became very close friends.

Then Stacey rememberized the first time she baby-sat for Charlotte Johanssen. After that, she was about to begin a good daydream about Cam Geary, the gorgeous star, when she realized she really ought to wake up Claudia.

So she did. She leaned across Claud's bed and tapped her on the arm.

"Claud. Hey, Claud!"

"Mmm?"

"Time to get up."

"Why?"

"Mother's Day surprise. The kids'll be here in just a couple of hours."

"Oh!"

Claudia was up in a flash, and she and Stacey got dressed.

Now, here's a big difference between them and me. That morning, I dressed in my jeans and running shoes, a T-shirt with a picture of Beaver Cleaver on it, and my collie dog baseball cap. Then I added my SHS (Stoneybrook High School) sweat shirt that used to belong to Sam, since the weather would probably be chilly in the morning.

Stacey, however, put on a tight-fitting pink jumpsuit over a white T-shirt, lacy white socks,

and those plastic shoes. What are they called —
jellies? And Claudia wore a pale blue baggy
shirt over black-and-blue leopard-spotted pants
that tied in neat knots at her ankles. On her
feet she wore purple high-tops. And they both
wore all this jewelry and these accessories, like
big, big earrings, and headbands with rosettes
on them, and nail polish. Claudia even wore
her snake bracelet. Honestly, what did they
think we were going to do? Enter a fashion
show?

Oh, okay, I'll admit it. They looked great.
And I was a teeny bit jealous. I wouldn't even
know *how* to dress the way they do.

Anyway, Stacey and Claudia ate a quick
breakfast — they were both kind of nervous —
and then waited for the rest of us club members
to show up.

"You girls eat like hawks," said Mimi, while
they waited.

"She means 'birds,' " Claudia whispered to
Stacey.

Stacey nodded.

"What happen today?" Mimi wanted to
know.

Claud and the rest of the Kishis had only
explained this to Mimi about a million times
already, but Claudia tried again.

She was halfway finished when the bell rang. Stacey ran for the door. She opened it and found — me!

"Hi!" I cried.

"Hi!" replied Stacey. (We were both a little *too* excited.) "You're the first one . . . oh, but here come Jessi and Mallory."

We all arrived before eight o'clock.

"What needs to be done?" asked Stacey nervously.

"Divide up the group tags," I answered.

We had decided that we would color-code our groups. My group was red, Mary Anne's was yellow, Jessi's was green, and so on. It would help the kids to know who they were supposed to be with. It isn't a very good idea to let kids go out in public places wearing name tags, but we figured if, for instance, I was wearing a red tag around my neck, and so were Karen, Andrew, and Shea, at least they'd know the four of us were supposed to stick together.

So at our Wednesday club meeting that week, we'd cut twenty-eight circles out of construction paper and strung them on yarn. They looked like large necklaces. Now we each put one on.

Stacey and I looked at ourselves in a bathroom mirror.

"Ravishing," said Stacey.

I giggled.

"Kristy?" Mal called. "Claud wants you."

"Okay!" I replied.

Stacey and I ran downstairs and found the rest of the club members in the kitchen with Mr. Kishi and Mimi.

"Could you just tell Dad about the lunches again?" Claudia asked me.

"Oh, sure," I said. "All the kids are bringing bag lunches. We're going to leave the lunches here — if it's still okay with you — and then, if you don't mind, could you drive them to Carle Playground at twelve-thirty? We'll meet you there. That way, we won't have to carry the lunches around the carnival all morning. Is that okay with you? We'd really appreciate it."

Mr. Kishi smiled. "It's still just fine. Mimi is going to help me."

But all Mimi said then was, "I've got to get that box over to the planet." She was gazing out the window.

Ordinarily, any one of us club members might have burst into tears then. We were frustrated by not understanding how Mimi's mind was working these days. We wanted badly to understand.

But the doorbell rang.

"Someone's here!" cried Stacey, leaping to her feet. "The first kid is here!"

All seven of us sitters raced for the Kishis' front door.

Not one but six kids were crowded onto the stoop with their fathers: Jackie, Shea, and Archie with Mr. Rodowsky, Myriah and Gabbie with Mr. Perkins, and Jamie with Mr. Newton.

"Hi, you guys!" we greeted them.

Us baby-sitters stepped outside with the color tags, and the fathers left after kisses and hugs and good-byes. We thought the kids would feel more comfortable in the yard, where they could run around.

I was about to explain the tags to them when Jamie shrieked, "Stacey!" He ran to her and threw his arms around her legs. "You came back!"

"Just for a visit," she told him. "Boy, am I glad to see you! I think you've grown another foot."

Jamie looked down. "Nah. I've still got just two," he replied, but he was smiling.

"Okay," I said loudly, clapping my hands. "I have something special for each of you to wear today." I handed out the tags (Shea Rodowsky said he felt like a *gi-irl*) and then — Becca Ramsey and Charlotte Johanssen arrived.

They were wearing plastic charm bracelets

and were so busy comparing the charms that Charlotte didn't see Stacey.

Finally, as Mr. Ramsey was leaving, Stacey stepped up behind Char and tapped her on the shoulder. "Excuse me," she said. "Can you tell me where I could find a Charlotte Johanssen?"

"I'm — " Charlotte started to say. She turned around. She looked up. Her eyes began to widen. They grew and grew and grew. "Stacey!" she managed to say, gasping.

Becca grinned. She was in on the surprise.

"I'm back for the weekend," said Stacey in a wavery voice. Then she knelt down, held her arms open, and Charlotte practically dove into them. Stacey held Charlotte for a long time.

"Yuck," said David Michael, who was watching. He and Karen and Andrew had just arrived.

"Okay, kiddo," I heard Watson say to Andrew. "See you this afternoon. Have a great time at the carnival. I know you'll have fun with Kristy and Karen and David Michael."

Well, even with me there, Andrew was the first of our criers. The next crier was Suzi Barrett. She looked pretty confused as Mr. Pike dropped her off along with her brother and four of the Pike kids. Then Jenny Prezzioso began to wail. And finally Archie Rodowsky tuned up, even though he'd been fine before.

"Oh, boy," said Stacey.

Two of us took the criers aside and tried to quiet them. They had just calmed down (after all, they knew who we were, where they were, and where they were going), when Mr. Braddock brought Matt and Haley by.

Darn old Jenny Prezzioso let out a squawk. "Is *he* coming?" she exclaimed, pointing to Matt.

Mr. Braddock was leaving — so Haley made a beeline for Jenny.

"You wanna make something of it?" she asked fiercely. "You got a problem with that?" (Haley is a *really* nice kid, but she is super-protective of her brother.)

"No," said Jenny in a small voice. To her credit, she did not start to cry again.

"Kristy," said Stacey, "introduce me to Haley and Matt, okay? Oh, and to Becca. I don't know Jessi's sister."

I nodded. Then I spoke to Jessi. Jessi and Haley introduced Matt to Stacey, using sign language. Then Jessi introduced Becca to her.

"I think," I said, "that you know everyone else, Stace. It's pretty much the same crowd."

"Just older," she replied. She smiled ruefully.

"Well, let's get this show on the road!" I said brightly. "Are you kids ready for the carnival?"

"Yes!"

"Are you wearing your tags?"

"Yes!"

"Have you been to the bathroom?"

"Yes." . . . "No." . . . "I have to go again." . . . "Me too." . . . "I went at home." . . . "I don't *wanna* go."

It took nearly a half an hour for everyone to use the bathroom. When we were ready, we set out for Sudsy's Carnival.

CHAPTER 11

"We're really, really going to the carnival!" exclaimed Jamie Newton, as my friends and I led the twenty-one kids along the sidewalks of Stoneybrook. *"Oh, give me a comb,"* he sang.

I looked around and smiled. The groups were staying together. (So far.) And oddly enough, my funny little group was working out nicely. Because Andrew had cried earlier, Shea was very protective of him. And Karen seemed to have a crush on Shea. She hung onto every word he said, and gazed at him as if he were a superhero. Shea was playing the part of their big brother.

From the other children around me came excited comments:

"I'm going to ride the ferris wheel!"

"Oh, I hope there's a roller coaster!"

"I'm going to win a teddy bear for my sister." (That was Jamie.)

"I wonder what a sideshow is."

"Is there *really* such a thing as a bearded lady?"

"My daddy told me there used to be a circus man named P.T. Barnum, who said there's a sucker born every minute."

"What's that mean?"

A shrug. "Don't know . . . I hope there's cotton candy."

At that point, Stacey turned to me and said, "How are we going to pay for all this? The kids want rides and food and tickets to the sideshow. I don't blame them. I would, too, if I were their age, but . . . this morning is going to be expensive."

"Don't worry," I told her. "First of all, we decided no food at the carnival. We want the kids to eat their own lunches later. Second, we found out how much most of the rides and attractions at Sudsy's will cost and realized that we have enough money for each kid to do three things. And third," (I grinned) "every single kid came with extra money — either part of his allowance, or a little something from one of his parents, so we don't have to — "

"THERE IT IS!"

The shriek came from Jamie, who was at the head of the line with Claudia and the Perkins girls. We had rounded a corner, and in the huge parking lot behind Carle Playground was

Sudsy's Carnival. It spread out before us, a wonderful, confusing mess of rides and booths, colors and smells, people, and even a few animals.

The kids looked overwhelmed, so we walked in slowly, trying to see everything at once. There were a ferris wheel, a merry-go-round, a whip ride, a train, a funhouse, and a spook-house. At the midway were a penny pitch, a ring toss, a horserace game, a shooting gallery, and a fish pond for the littlest kids. The sideshow tent was set up at one end of the parking lot, and wandering among the crowds were a man selling oranges with candy straws in them, an organ-grinder with a monkey, and — Jamie's precious clown selling balloons.

"Oh, my gosh," whispered Shea Rodowsky, taking it all in.

Even he was impressed. I took that as a good sign.

Impressive as it was, though, the carnival wasn't all *that* big. I mean, it was just set up in a parking lot. Still, there was plenty to see and do. Us sitters wondered where to start.

The kids solved the problem for us. Karen had spotted the spook house.

"Please, please, please can we go in that haunted house?" she begged.

I hesitated. Would it be too scary? I glanced at my friends and they just shrugged.

What the heck? I thought. How bad could it be?

Sixteen of the kids wanted to walk through the haunted house. (Andrew, Archie Rodowsky, Suzi Barrett, and Gabbie Perkins were too young, and prissy Jenny announced that the house would probably be filthy dirty.) So Mary Anne stayed outside with them (she looked relieved), and the rest of us paid for our tickets and filed into the house.

"Where are the cars?" asked Karen. "What do we ride in?"

Not long ago, we had been to Disney World in Florida. We went on this incredible ride through a haunted mansion.

But that was Disney World, this was Sudsy's.

"You just walk through this house, Karen," I told her.

Karen looked disappointed, until we turned the first dark corner — and a ghost suddenly lit up before us. Shea, Buddy Barrett, Nicky Pike, and David Michael burst out laughing. A few kids gasped. Karen shrieked.

"It's all right," I told her, taking her hand.

We passed through the Death Chamber. "Cobwebs" swept over our faces. "Thunder" roared overhead. And a very realistic-looking bolt of lightning zigzagged to the floor with a crackle and a crash.

"Let me out!" cried Karen, as a headless ghost floated by. "Let me out!"

"Karen, I can't. We're in the middle of the spook house. We have to keep going. There's no other way out."

"Oh, yes there is," said an eerie voice.

I almost screamed myself before I realized that the voice sounded weird because it was coming from behind a mask.

"I work here," said a person dressed as a mummy. "There are exits all over the place. I can let you out if you want."

"Karen?" I asked.

"Yes, please," she replied, shivering.

I tapped Claudia, who happened to be standing right behind me, and told her that Karen and I were leaving. "The rest of you will have to watch the kids. Karen and I will meet you at that bench near Mary Anne."

"No problem," replied Claudia.

The groups were all mixed up, but it didn't seem to matter.

The mummy discreetly opened a door in a pitch-black wall, and Karen and I followed him into the bright sunshine.

"Whew," said Karen.

The mummy removed his mask. He was a she.

"Thank you so much," I said. "I guess we were a little panicky." I was trying not to lay all the blame on Karen.

Karen looked at her feet in embarrassment anyway.

The mummy smiled. "My name's Barbara," she said. "And don't feel bad. At least once a day, someone needs to use one of the special exit doors." She knelt in front of Karen. "I'll tell you some secrets," she said.

Tell Karen secrets? That was like telling secrets to the National Broadcasting Company.

"I'll tell you how they do the special effects," Barbara went on, "but you have to promise never to reveal the secrets."

Oh, brother, I thought. All of Stoneybrook would know within a week.

By the time we reached Mary Anne, the other kids were emerging from the haunted house. They were excited, and so was Karen, who was bursting with her precious knowledge.

"Rides! Rides! Let's go on rides!" chanted Vanessa Pike.

The chant was taken up by the other kids, so we set out across the parking lot. Before we were halfway there we were stopped by —

"The balloon-seller!" exclaimed Jamie.

Only he turned out to be a balloon-giver. The clown handed a free Sudsy's Carnival helium balloon to each kid. Then he walked away.

"What a nice man," said Suzi Barrett.

Us sitters began tying the balloons to the kids' wrists and our own. Just before Mallory could tackle Jackie Rodowsky's, it slipped out of his hand and floated away.

"Oh, Jackie," cried Mallory in dismay, even though he *is* our walking disaster. We know to expect these things.

But Jackie didn't look the least bit upset. "My balloon is on its way to the moon, you know," he said. "That's where these things go." He indicated the colorful garden of helium balloons around him.

"They go to the moon?" repeated Nina Marshall.

In a flash, the kids were slipping the balloons off their wrists.

"My balloon is going to the moon, too," said Claire Pike.

"Yeah," agreed Myriah Perkins.

"Not mine," said Jamie firmly. "Mine is for Lucy." He held out his wrist so Claudia could tie his balloon to it securely.

Balloonless (or almost balloonless) we reached

the rides. Suddenly, my friends and I could hear nothing but, "I'm going on the whip," or, "I hope we get stuck at the top of the ferris wheel," or, "Look, Gabbie, a train."

I smiled. I kept smiling until I heard a voice say, "*Please* let me go on the whip with you, Nicky."

"No way," he replied.

"No way is right, Margo." I looked around for Mallory. "Mal," I said urgently, running over to her and her purple group, "Margo wants to go on the whip."

"No. Oh, no."

Margo is famous for her motion sickness. She gets airsick, carsick, seasick, you name it. So you can see why the whip was not a good idea.

Mallory ran to her sister. "Margo," she said in a no-nonsense voice, "you can't go on any rides."

Margo's face puckered up. "But everyone else is going on something. Even the little kids are going to ride on the train."

The train was pretty lame. All it did was travel slowly around a track in a circle. The kids sat in the cars and rang bells.

"Hey," said Mallory, "you could go on the train, Margo. That wouldn't make you sick. At least, I don't think so."

"The train is for babies!" cried Margo, looking offended.

Mallory and her sister watched the rest of us kids and sitters line up for the rides we'd chosen. At last Mal said, "We-ell . . . maybe you could ride the merry-go-round, Margo. You can sit on one of those fancy benches. I don't want you on a horse that goes up and down."

"All right," agreed Margo, brightening.

Mallory accompanied her sister on the carousel. They sat on a red-and-gold bench. The music started. The ride began. It went faster and faster until —

"Mallory," said Margo suddenly, "I'm dizzy. I don't feel too good."

The words were barely out of her mouth before Margo's breakfast was all over the floor of the merry-go-round.

The Sudsy's people were not too happy. Neither was Stacey, who had seen the whole thing and can't stand the sight of barf.

It was time for quieter activities. We left the rides. Some of the kids played games and won prizes. Jamie tried desperately to win a teddy bear for Lucy, but all he could get was a squirt gun.

The younger kids had their faces made up. Mallory and Margo sat in the first-aid tent.

Jessi's group peeked into the sideshow tent and decided it looked like a rip-off.

By 12:15, half of the kids were begging for cotton candy and popcorn, so we left Sudsy's. It was on to Carle Playground for lunch.

CHAPTER 12

"But . . . but . . . box is not at planet. No, I mean *is* at planet, but where are my forks? And TV people. I try to watch *Wheel of Fortune,* and TV people are bother me. Will not leave alone."

I glanced at Claudia. My friends and I and the children had just reached Carle Playground, and there were Mr. Kishi, Mimi, and our lunches.

And as you must have guessed by now, Mimi was having some trouble again. I think it was because she wasn't quite sure why she was at a playground with her son-in-law, her granddaughter, her granddaughter's friends, twenty-one children, and twenty-eight lunches. It could confuse anybody.

I gave Mimi a kiss and told her not to worry about the TV people.

Mimi flashed me an odd look. "TV people? What TV people? We have lunch to hand out.

Better begin. Big job. Where is my Claudia?"

Mimi fades in and out.

I located Claudia. Then Mr. Kishi, Mimi, and my friends and I handed out the lunches. Very reluctantly, I put Margo's in her hands.

"How are you feeling?" I asked her, as she climbed onto a bench between her sisters.

"Hungry?" she replied, as if she didn't expect me to believe her.

"Really?"

"Honest."

"Okay," I said doubtfully. "But eat very, very slowly."

Margo nodded seriously. "I will."

Mr. Kishi and Mimi slid into the car then and drove back to their house.

The twenty-eight of us sat down and began eating right away. (We were starving.) We took up three entire picnic tables. I looked at my red group. Andrew, with a purple juice mustache, was munching away at his tuna-fish sandwich. Shea, a doughnut in one hand and an apple in the other, was watching Andrew fondly.

"I bet you're going to eat that whole sandwich, aren't you?" he said to Andrew. "That's really great. If you do, you might get muscles as big as Popeye's."

And Karen was just gazing adoringly at Shea.

At one point she said, "You know how they — " but she clapped her hand over her mouth. I knew she had almost given away one of the secrets she learned at the spook house. I'm sure she thought it would be a really terrific "gift" for Shea.

Up and down my table and even at the other tables, I could hear various comments and see various kinds of eating going on. For example:

Jenny Prezzioso is a slow, picky eater. She ate almost everything that was in her bag, but she did it in her own way. First she nibbled the crusts off of her sandwiches. "Okay. All tidy," she said to herself. Then she ate the insides of the sandwiches in rows. When she had two strips left, one from each sandwich half, she began playing with them. (I think she was getting full.) She played with them until they were dirty and had to be thrown out.

Jackie Rodowsky, our lovable walking disaster, dropped everything at least once. He was like a cartoon character. Accidentally (it's *always* an accident with Jackie), he flipped his fork to the ground. As he picked it up, he knocked his orange off the paper plate it was resting on. He returned the orange, knocked the fork off again, picked it up, spilled his Coke, and while trying to mop up the Coke in his lap, knocked his fork to the ground again.

Mary Anne, sitting across the table from him, nearly turned purple trying not to laugh.

Another kid I liked to watch was Buddy Barrett. He was the last person on earth I would have expected to be picky — but he was picky. He examined nearly every bite before putting it in his mouth.

"This has," he said, frowning, "a black speck. Look, right there." He leaned across the table to show it to Nicky Pike.

"So pick it off," said Nicky, who would probably eat something that had been rolling around in a mud puddle.

Buddy picked it off and gingerly ate the rest of the bite of sandwich.

Then there were Myriah and Gabbie, who were nibbling their sandwiches into shapes — a bunny, a cat face, a snowman, and a dinosaur.

Shea ate everything practically without chewing it. He just wolfed things down — an apple, a sandwich, a bag of Fritos. He finished his entire lunch before Margo Pike ate a quarter of her sandwich.

"Margo?" asked Mallory. "Are you feeling okay?"

Margo nodded. "I'm just eating slowly. Kristy said to."

I glanced at Mallory and shrugged. I hadn't

meant for Margo to eat like a snail, but I guessed it couldn't hurt an upset stomach.

Fwwwt. Nicky Pike blew a straw paper at Matt Braddock. Matt grinned, grabbed a straw from his sister, blew the paper at Nicky, then returned the opened straw to Haley.

Haley signed, "Very funny," to Matt.

Matt signed back, "I know."

Suddenly from the end of one table, I heard the beginnings of a song that I knew could lead to trouble — the hysterical kind of trouble in which a kid may laugh so hard he won't be able to finish his lunch. Or worse, he'll lose his lunch.

David Michael, my own brother, was singing. (I should have known.)

"The Addams Family started," he began.

Andrew giggled, knowing what was coming.

"When Uncle Fester farted."

Shea Rodowsky choked on his Twinkie, then laughed. And Haley Braddock laughed so hard she sprayed apple juice out of her nose.

"Oh, lord," said Claudia, looking at Haley. "What a mess."

We cleaned up Haley and her apple juice. Then we cleaned up straw papers and napkins and plastic forks.

"If you guys are done," I announced to the kids, "please put your thermoses and things back in your bags or lunch boxes. Anyone who's finished can go play. *Quietly*, since you just ate."

A sea of kids rose from the picnic tables. The only one left was Margo Pike. She was now eating the second quarter of her sandwich.

Stacey looked at her oddly. But before she could say a word, Margo said, "I'm eating slowly, *okay?*" She acted as if she'd been asked that question seventy-five times.

So while Margo ate, the rest of the kids explored the playground.

"Look! Horsies!" Nina Marshall called to Gabbie Perkins and Jamie Newton. She had found three of those horses on springs. They were painted like the horses we'd seen on the merry-go-round at the carnival.

"Go easy!" Claudia called to them.

The older boys found a much better activity. Shea started it. Our groups were completely mixed up again (which was okay, since everyone seemed to be getting along) and Shea, Jackie, David Michael, Buddy, Nicky, and Matt were gathered around two water fountains that were facing each other.

"Hey!" said Shea. "Look!" He turned the water on, then held his thumb over the stream of water, which sent it in an arc to the other fountain.

"Cool!" cried Nicky. He tried the trick with the second fountain and sent the water to the first one.

"Oh, I am so thirsty," signed Buddy to Matt. He stood by one fountain, opened his mouth, and Matt, catching on, sent a stream of water from the other fountain right into Buddy's mouth.

"Whoa, do I ever have an idea," said Nicky. "But I have to go get Claire. I'll be right back." Nicky went in search of his littlest sister.

He found Margo at the picnic table. "What are you doing?" he asked her.

"Still eating," she replied with clenched teeth. She took a teensy bite out of a plum.

"Well, where's Claire?"

Margo pointed to the slide, where Claire was whooshing down headfirst on her tummy. She stopped at the end and leapt to her feet like a gymnast.

"Hey, Claire! Come here!" called Nicky.

"Why?" asked Claire warily.

"Just come."

Claire followed him reluctantly to the water fountains.

"Stand here," Nicky directed her.

Claire stood between the fountains.

Nicky poised himself at one fountain. Buddy was at the other.

112

"Now!" cried Nicky.

Claire was hit by streams of cold water on both sides of her face.

Jessi went running to the water fountains. "Nicky! Buddy!" she began.

But before she could get any further, Claire burst out laughing. Water soaked her hair and dripped down her face, but she giggled and exclaimed, "Do it again!"

The boys, sure they were in trouble, looked at Jessi.

"Once," said Jessi. "You may do it once more. Then leave the water fountains alone."

The boys sprayed Claire, and she practically fainted from laughter. Jessi smiled but ushered everyone away.

Margo sat at the table, putting crumb-sized bites of graham cracker in her mouth.

Nina, Gabbie, and Jamie rocked on the horses.

By the swings, a small group of kids was gathering. Karen was at the center of them. They were very quiet — except for Karen. I glanced at Dawn. "I better see what Karen's up to," I said.

I crept toward the group until I could hear Karen say, "And they use masks to make the awful — "

Karen looked up and saw me. I raised my eyebrows at her.

"To — to, um, make the . . . Oh, it isn't impor — My gosh, look at that!" she exclaimed.

Eight faces turned to see a robin sitting in an ash tree.

"Big deal," said David Michael.

"I've seen a thousand robins," added Haley Braddock.

"Yeah!" called Margo, still at the picnic table. She took a tiny bite out of her plum, most of which was still uneaten.

"Boy, are you a slowpoke," said Jenny, running to Margo.

"She is not!" cried Claire, rushing to defend her sister. "She was sick."

"She's still slow."

"Is not!"

"Is too!"

Claire rushed at Jenny, but Mary Anne ran between them, just in time to ward off a fight.

At that moment, Andrew tripped, fell, and skinned both knees. He burst into tears.

"You guys!" I said to the other sitters. "I think it's time to go to Claudia's. We all need a rest."

CHAPTER 13

Saturday

Well, I think today went pretty well.
Really. I mean, so there were a few
scrapes and arguments. We were taking
care of twenty-one children. What did we
expect? (With seven brothers and sisters,
you learn to "go with the flow," as my
mom would say.) I think one upset
stomach, one set of skinned knees, one
argument, and a practical joke are pretty
good.

Anyway, after Andrew fell, and Jenny and
Claire had been separated, we left the
playground. My group -- Buddy, David
Michael, and Jackie -- was in fine shape.
They'd had a great day so far. They'd
been to the carnival, walked through a

spook house, flown balloons to the moon, ridden the whip, won some prizes, and discovered the greatest water fountains of all time.

A few other kids weren't quite so happy, though.

That's true. Mallory's group was in fine shape, while a few others weren't, but it wasn't any big deal. Everything was under control.

Us baby-sitters helped the kids collect their things — lunch boxes and thermoses, plus souvenirs from the carnival. Jamie tucked his squirt gun into his lunch box. Suzi was wearing a hat that made her look like the Statue of Liberty. Myriah was wearing a plastic necklace, and Gabbie was wearing a red bracelet that said *Sudsy's* on it.

"WAHHH!" cried Andrew as we walked away from the playgound. We'd washed his knees at the water fountain, using clean napkins, but they did look a little painful.

"We can get some Band-Aids at Claudia's," Mallory said to me.

Andrew wasn't the only one crying.

"WAHHH!" wailed Jenny and Claire.

"Keep them apart," Mallory whispered to Mary Anne. "I'm not kidding. They get along okay most of the time, but when they're mad, well . . ."

I almost expected Mal to say, "It's not a pretty sight."

Anyway, poor Mary Anne had her hands full between trying to separate Claire and Jenny, and keeping her eye on Margo and her touchy stomach.

Mallory saved the day, though. We'd just reached the edge of the playground and our criers were still crying. Jamie was starting to get mad about not having won a teddy bear for Lucy (even though he had a balloon for her), and Nicky and Buddy were walking behind Vanessa, trying to see if they could touch her hair without her noticing.

Trouble was brewing.

So suddenly Mallory let loose with, *"The ants go marching one by one — "*

"Hurrah! Hurrah!" chimed in Nicky and Mal's sisters.

"The ants go marching one by one — "

"Hurrah! Hurrah!"

"The ants go marching one by one," sang Mal, *"the little one stops to suck his thumb, and they all go marching down . . . beneath . . . the earth."*

Most of the kids were looking at the Pikes with interest. The criers had stopped crying. The complainers had stopped complaining. The teasers had stopped teasing.

So the song continued. The kids didn't know it, but they chimed in when they could. They always had to stop singing to find out what the little one did, though. (Two by two, he has to stop to tie his shoe. Three by three, he falls and skins his knee.) The song occupied the kids all the way to Claudia's house, by which time we were pretty glad to hear it end. Mallory knew only twelve verses, and we heard each of them a number of times.

"Just be glad it wasn't 'Ninety-Nine Bottles of Beer on the Wall,' " said Stacey, looking pale.

"Shh!" I hissed. "One of the kids might hear you."

At Claudia's, us sitters went into action.

I took Andrew into the Kishis' bathroom, washed his knees again, put some first aid cream on them, and then applied a fat Band-Aid to each one. Andrew liked the Band-Aids a lot.

"I feel better already!" he announced.

By the time we were outside again, things were going so smoothly I was amazed. The kids — all of them — were gathered under a tree with Mallory, Stacey, and Jessi, who were singing with them while the rest of us sitters got organized.

I kept hearing snatches of song, most of them sung by Mallory.

I heard: *"I've got sixpence, jolly, jolly sixpence. I've got sixpence to last me all my life . . ."*

Then I heard: *"Oh, we ain't got a barrel of money. Maybe we're ragged and funny . . ."*

And then: *"Won't you come home, Bill Bailey? Won't you come home?"*

(Where does Mal learn all this stuff?)

Finally I heard Jessi and Stacey teach the kids a round: *"Heigh-ho, nobody at home. Meat nor drink nor money have I none. Yet will I be me-e-e-e-erry. Heigh-ho, nobody at home."*

The round sort of got lost because the kids were saying things like, *"Heigh-ho, no one's at my house."* But you could get the gist of it.

Anyway, while the kids were singing, Dawn, the world's most organized person, took their bags, thermoses, lunch boxes, prizes, and extra sweaters, and organized them under a tree. When the fathers arrived to pick up their kids, nothing would be missing or hard to locate. Meanwhile, Claudia had found her art materials and was setting them out on the Kishis' picnic tables. And Mary Anne had found the stack of books we'd borrowed from the library.

"Okay!" I called as another round of "Heigh-Ho" came to an end. "Who wants to make a Mother's Day card?"

"Me!" cried all twenty-one kids.

"Great," I replied. "Everyone will get a turn, but half of you will read stories with Mallory and Jessi and me first. Then we'll switch."

Well, *that* was not the way to present things, because all the kids wanted to go first, but at last we got the problem sorted out. Live and learn.

Mal and I read *Where the Wild Things Are* and *One Morning in Maine* and *The Cat in the Hat* to the younger children, while Jessi read *If I Ran the Circus* and a chapter from a Paddington book to the older kids.

Then it was time for the children to trade places. The ones who had just made cards brought them over to Mal and Jessi and me. They were very proud of them.

"Look," said Claire. "Look at my card."

I looked. It said, "HAPY MOTH'S DAY LOVE CLAIRE."

Shea held his out shyly. On the front was written, "Dear Mom, you are . . . " and inside was written:

```
Marvelous
Outstanding
Tops
Honored
Excellent
Renowned
```

Jackie's was covered with smudges and drops of glue, with splotches and mistakes. It read: "Daer Mom, I love you. Love, Your sun, Jackie Rodowsky."

"Beautiful, Jackie," I told him, and he beamed.

The stories began again. The card-making began again. And before we knew it, Myriah Perkins was calling, "Hey, there's Daddy!"

And there he was. He was followed by Mr. Pike and Mr. Prezzioso. The kids started to gather their things. The littlest ones ran to their fathers and threw their arms around them.

Our day was over. The Mother's Day surprise was over. I felt sort of sad. But glad, too, because it had gone so well. I listened to the kids chattering away: "Daddy! I went on a ride. Let's tell Mommy!" said Jenny. And, "I have to tell Mommy about the balloon man," said Jamie. And, "We found the neatest water fountains," exclaimed Nicky. And, "Daddy, I threw up on the merry-go-round," said you-know-who.

"Oh," replied Mr. Pike, "Mommy will love to hear that."

CHAPTER 14

"Well?" I said.

"Well what?" replied Claudia.

The children were gone. Except for Andrew, Karen, and David Michael. They and I were at the Kishis' waiting for Charlie to pick us up and take us home. The rest of the sitters were still at Claud's, too. We had cleaned up every last crayon and shred of paper, but we just couldn't bear to part. So while my little sister and brothers sat under a tree and looked at the library books, the members of the Baby-sitters Club lolled around on the Kishis' porch.

"Well what?" said Claudia again.

"Well, what did everyone decide about Mother's Day presents?" I asked, not daring even to glance at Mary Anne. "Was the Mother's Day surprise good enough?"

"I'll say," said Mal. "It turned out better than I'd hoped. I bet it was the best Mother's

Day present Mom ever got. Especially when Dad pitched in."

"Ditto," said Jessi.

"Ditto," I said. "Mom got to spend the day alone with Watson, since Sam and Charlie went to school to help at a car wash to raise money for the football team."

"And our homemade presents are finished," announced Dawn.

"Well, they are, except for mine," said Stacey. "But Claudia's helping me, so I'll be done tonight."

"What did you make?" I asked.

Claudia, Stacey, and Dawn exchanged grins.

"Personalized pins," replied Claud. "My idea," she added proudly.

"They're more like brooches, though," said Stace.

"What do you mean, personalized pins?" asked Jessi.

"See," said Claud, "we went to the miniatures store and bought things that are meaningful to our mothers. . . . Well, I had to get Stacey's things for her since she wasn't here."

"Yeah," agreed Stacey, "and she did a good job. Like, my mom can sew, and she likes to travel and read, and she likes dogs even though we don't have one. So Claudia bought a tiny

124

airplane, book, thimble, pair of scissors, and dog."

"And then," Dawn continued, "we mixed up the little charms with glass beads and colored flowers, and we glued everything to a metal piece with a pin attached — "

"You can get those things at the crafts store," added Claudia.

" — and, ta-dah! A brooch. Each one different. Just for our mothers."

"Great idea!" I exclaimed.

"I, um, made a decision. I mean about Mother's Day," said Mary Anne.

Six heads swiveled toward her.

"I'm giving my father a Mother's Day present. He's been a good father *and* a good mother to me, or at least he's tried to be, and I want to let him know it."

"Mary Anne! That's great!" I cried. "We never thought of giving your *dad* a *Mother's* Day present."

The others were smiling, so Mary Anne began to smile, too. "You don't think it's corny?" she asked.

"No way!" exclaimed Mallory.

"What did you get him?" asked Jessi.

"A book. It's not very original, but it's hard to know what to get men. And I have to give him stuff on his birthday and Christmas and of course Father's Day, too. So I can't always be original. Anyway, I know he wants this book."

Beep, beep!

Charlie had pulled into the Kishis' driveway. Sam was next to him in the front seat. The car was sparkling clean. I figured they'd taken it through the car wash. Mom and Watson would be happy. The money had gone to a good cause, *and* the station wagon was clean.

"Come on, you guys!" I called to Andrew, David Michael, and Karen.

I said good-bye to my friends. Then my sister and brothers and I squished into the backseat, and Charlie drove home.

The six of us entered our house (okay, our mansion), bursting with news and stories. But we stopped in our tracks when we reached the living room. No kidding. We came to a dead halt.

There were Mom and Watson standing next to each other, very formally, their arms linked. They looked nervous, happy, and surprised all at the same time.

Karen and my brothers and I glanced from our parents to each other, then back to our parents. Not one of us said a word.

After a few moments, Watson cleared his

throat. Then Mom cleared *her* throat. Mom was the one who finally spoke.

"Watson and I have some wonderful news," she said. "We just heard it this afternoon. Let's sit down."

So we did. I sat on the floor, leaning against a couch. Andrew sat in my lap. Karen sat beside me, her head resting on my shoulder. My brothers lined up on the couch behind us. We knew this was good news — but not like we'd just bought another VCR or something. This sounded like life-changing news.

(I was pretty sure Mom was finally pregnant.)

"Hey, Mom, are you pregnant?" asked Sam for the four-thousandth time.

"No," she replied, "but we've adopted a child."

Adopted a child! Well, that was a different story!

"You've *what?*" cried Charlie.

"We've adopted a little girl," said Watson. "She's two years old, she's Vietnamese, and her name will be Emily Michelle Thomas Brewer."

"We'll pick her up at the airport tomorrow," added Mom. "And then she'll be ours."

"We wanted to tell you about this before," said Watson. "It's been in the works for so long. But we didn't want to say a word until we knew something for sure. Things kept falling through. This is definite, though."

Andrew stirred in my lap, and I knew he didn't really understand what was happening.

"So," said my mother nervously, "what does everybody think?"

What did we think? What did *I* think?

"I think . . ." I said, "I think this is totally fantastic!"

Suddenly I was so excited I could barely contain myself. A baby (sort of). But it wasn't Mom's and Watson's. Furthermore, I was getting another sister! I'd always thought there weren't enough girls in my family. Before Mom married Watson, it was me against three brothers. After the wedding, it was Karen and me against four brothers. Emily Michelle Thomas Brewer would almost even things up.

But it was more than that, of course. Even more than the stuff about Mom and Watson. I love kids. And we were adopting a two-year-old girl. She would be somebody to dress and play with. She would be somebody to teach things to. Things like, a family is just a group of people who love each other, whether they're brothers and sisters and parents, or stepbrothers and stepsisters and stepparents. Or adopted kids.

128

Sam and Charlie were as excited as I was.

"This," said Sam, "is really cool." He grinned.

"I can't wait to teach her how to play baseball," added Charlie.

"Hey, that'll be my job!" I cried.

David Michael seemed less certain. "Do two-year-olds wear diapers?" he wanted to know.

"Some of them do," answered Mom.

"Well, I'm not touching those Huggies things. Dirty or clean. But I guess a little sister will be okay. I mean, I've already got one," he said, poking Karen's back with his toe. "And she hasn't killed me yet."

Karen turned around and stuck her tongue out at David Michael.

"Karen?" said Watson. "What about you?"

"What about me?" Karen knew what her father meant, but she was being difficult. After a pause she sighed and said, "I thought *I* was your little girl."

Watson looked thoughtful. "You're one of them. Kristy's my little girl, too."

I didn't complain about being called a little girl. I knew that Watson was trying to make a point.

"Think of it, Karen," I said. "She's only two. Practically a baby. You can help her with things. You'll be her big sister. You can show her how to play with toys, you can teach her to color, and you can dress her up. It'll be fun!"

Karen smiled, despite herself. "Yeah . . ." she said slowly.

"Andrew?" said Watson. "What do you think?"

"*Whose* baby is she?" asked Andrew. "Why is she coming to our house? Did her mommy and daddy give her away?"

Oops. I guess we had some explaining to do.

Watson took care of the explaining while Mom and the rest of us did other things.

Boy, was there a lot to do. "We have to get a room ready for Emily," said Mom. And suddenly I remembered my mother talking about our spare bedrooms.

"A room!" I said. "What about clothes? What about toys?"

"I think we have plenty of toys here for now," said Mom. "We can buy some things for a younger child later."

"Well, we don't have any clothes for two-year-olds," I pointed out.

"She'll have a few things of her own, honey," Mom said patiently. "I'll buy her more on Monday. I think the room is the most important project to tackle now. She needs a place of her own from the beginning."

130

"Wait a sec," I said. "You'll buy her clothes on Monday? On Monday you'll be at work. So will Watson. The rest of us will be in school. What are we going to do with Emily all day?"

Mom was bustling upstairs and I followed her. "Watson and I are taking some time off from our jobs to be with Emily," she said. "We're going to find a nanny while we're at it."

A nanny? Like Mary Poppins? Boy, were things changing. I wondered if a nanny would make my bed for me.

We started in on Emily's room, all eight of us. We chose a room that was near Mom and Watson's. Some furniture was in it already, but it looked like an old lady's room. We got toys and a crib out of the attic, and put some pictures on the wall. The room began to improve. A rocking chair helped. So did a white bookshelf and an old Mother Goose lamp.

"Not bad," I said. I still couldn't believe that the next day I would have a new sister.

Andrew looked up at me. We were alone in the room while everyone else was in the basement, searching for a particular dresser. I was supposed to be arranging some of David Michael's old picture books on the shelf.

"It is so bad," wailed Andrew, and he began to cry. His cry wasn't one of those Kristy-

I-skinned-my-knees-and-want-Band-Aids-the-size-of-dinosaur cries. It was a Kristy-I'm-very-confused-and-a-little-afraid cry.

I knelt down and drew him to me. "Whatever happens, you know," I told him, "you're still going to be our Andrew."

That night, I called every single member of the Baby-sitters Club to tell them the news. I was so excited, I didn't know how I was going to wait until the next day for Emily to arrive. But making five phone calls helped pass the time. I would say to each of my friends, "I'm going to have a new sister!"

And whomever I was talking to would say, "Oh, your mom's going to have a baby! That's great!"

And then I would tell my news. Each time I did, the person on the other end would have to shriek and scream for a few seconds. Then she would ask lots of questions. I was glad for that, because by the time I got into bed, I was exhausted and knew I would be able to sleep.

I slept okay that night, but I was up at six o'clock the next morning. I don't know the last time I voluntarily got up at that hour on a weekend. But who can sleep on the day her adopted sister is arriving? Not I.

I tiptoed downstairs and found that I wasn't the first one awake. Mom and Watson were sitting at the kitchen table, sipping coffee. A high chair had been placed at one end of the table.

"Morning, Watson," I said. Then, "Hi, Mom. Happy Mother's Day!" I kissed her cheek.

"Thanks, honey."

"I wish I had a present for you, but you got your gift yesterday."

"Oh, I know," replied Mom enthusiastically. "And it was great."

"Funny," I said. "We called yesterday's outing the Mother's Day surprise. But I think

Emily is the *real* Mother's Day surprise. At least she is to me."

"In a way she is to us, too," spoke up Watson, as I slid into my chair with a glass of orange juice. "We've been trying to adopt for quite awhile. It takes time. We feel lucky to have Emily at last."

"Mom? Watson?" I asked. "How come you adopted? You could have had a kid of your own, couldn't you?"

"Yes," said my mother, "we could have. But I've already given birth to four children."

"And I've got two," added Watson.

"So we decided not to create a seventh. We decided to find a child who's already here but who needs a home. And when we went looking, we finally found Emily."

I nodded. "I like that . . . Boy, is it weird to see all this baby stuff." The high chair was at the table, a stroller was parked by the back door, and a car seat was waiting to be taken into the garage.

Mom and Watson smiled, looking like proud new parents.

They left for the airport around noon.

When Sam, Charlie, and I told them we weren't going to leave the house — we wanted to be here for the very first glimpse of Emily —

us kids were left in charge of each other.

As soon as Watson's car left the garage, I looked at my sister and brothers. "What are we going to do now?" I asked them.

We made about a thousand suggestions — and turned them down. At last I said, "I know what we're going to do. Well, I know what *I'm* going to do."

"What?" asked Sam and Charlie.

"Invite the Baby-sitters Club over." That would be great. Even Stacey could come. She wasn't leaving for New York until much later in the afternoon.

"Oh, no, no. Please, no!" moaned Sam.

"All those *girls?*" added David Michael.

I made a face at him. "You know all those girls. You spent yesterday with them."

"*I* didn't," said Sam. "I don't want them here."

"I thought you liked girls so much."

"I like the girls in my class. If you invite your friends over, it's going to be like a slumber party here."

"Oh, it is not," I replied, reaching for the phone.

"Besides, what's wrong with girls?" asked Karen.

My friends showed up within an hour. Each

time the doorbell rang, Sam and David Michael pretended to faint. But I have to admit that Sam was pretty impressed when Stacey immediately suggested a good project for the afternoon.

"We should welcome Emily," she said. "We should bake her a cake or something."

"Make a sign," added Sam, brightening.

"How about cookies instead of a cake?" said Mal. "She's only two. She might like cookies better."

"Okay," I agreed.

"From scratch, or those slice-and-bake things?" asked Charlie.

"Scratch," I replied immediately. "That'll take longer, and we want to fill up the whole afternoon. If we need any ingredients, you can run to the store."

"Oh, thanks," said Charlie, but I could tell he didn't really mind, as long as he was here when Emily came home.

"How come I don't get cookies?" asked Andrew, clinging to my legs. "Did anyone bake cookies for me when I was born?"

"I don't know," I replied honestly. What I did know was that Andrew didn't really want answers to his questions. He wanted a hug. So I gave him one.

It turned out that we had all the ingredients

for chocolate chip cookies. We also had paper, scissors, string, and crayons for making a WELCOME EMILY sign. We divided up the jobs. Stacey, Claudia, Mary Anne, Jessi, Sam, and David Michael covered the dining room table with newspaper and went to work on the sign. The rest of us began making a triple batch of cookies. Except for Andrew. He wandered back and forth between the projects, occasionally whining. He couldn't seem to settle down.

I stood at the table next to Dawn, who was stirring the cookie batter. She was humming a vaguely familiar song under her breath.

"What *is* that song?" asked Charlie.

"It's — You know, it goes, '*Lucy in the sky-y with di-i-amonds*'."

"Oh," said, Charlie. "That old one."

Dawn nodded. She continued singing it softly. ". . . *the girl with colitis goes by*."

"What?" I said.

"*What?!*" cried Sam. He let out a guffaw.

Dawn looked puzzled.

"It's '*the girl with kaleidoscope eyes*'," he informed her.

Dawn and I glanced at each other and shrugged.

"Either way it's a weird song," I said.

We finished our cookies. The sign-makers finished their sign.

"Did someone make me a sign when I was born?" asked Andrew.

I hugged him again. Then I sat down and pulled him onto my lap. "I will always love you," I whispered into his ear. "No matter what. Even if we adopt sixteen more kids, I will always love you because you're Andrew. And so will Karen and your daddy and my mom and David Michael and Sam and Charlie and everyone else."

Andrew smiled a tiny smile. He looked relieved.

"Where should we put the sign?" asked Claudia.

We ended up stringing it across the kitchen. (We were pretty sure Mom and Watson would bring Emily in through the door from the garage to the kitchen.)

Then we piled the cookies into a neat mound on a platter and set the platter on the kitchen table.

"Well, now what?" asked Sam.

"Now," I began. I paused. "They're here! They're *here!*" I screeched. "I heard the car pull into the garage! I swear I did!"

"Oh, lord!" cried Claudia.

"What should we do? What should we *do?*" Mary Anne was wringing her hands.

"Let's stand under the sign," I suggested, "next to the cookies."

We posed ourselves — the six Thomas and Brewer kids in the front, and my friends in the back, even though Mary Anne didn't show up because she's short and was standing behind Charlie.

We were ready. Emily's first sight when she came into her new home, would be of her special sign, her welcome-home cookies, and her brothers and sisters and friends.

The door opened. Mom came in first. Watson was behind her. He was carrying Emily Michelle Thomas Brewer in his arms.

She was fast asleep.

Mom looked at the sign and the cookies and then at Emily. I could tell she felt bad for us. But *we* didn't feel *too* bad. Emily would see everything later.

Mom put her finger to her lips, and we all crowded silently around Emily. I knew we wanted to say things like, "Ooh, look!" Or, "She's so *cute!*" Or, "I can't believe she's my sister!" But we just stared.

Emily's hair is dark and shiny. It falls across her forehead in bangs. Her skin is smooth, and her mouth and nose are tiny, like any two-year-old's. I wished I could see her eyes.

You can tell a lot about a person by looking at her eyes.

Emily Michelle. She's my sister, and David Michael's and Sam's and Charlie's. She's Andrew's and Karen's. She's the one person in our family who isn't a Brewer or a Thomas. Her mother is Mom and her father is Watson, but she isn't *their* baby; if you know what I mean.

She's just *ours*. She belongs to Watson and Andrew and Karen, and she belongs to Mom and my brothers and me. She would bring us together. She would unite us. That was what Mom and Watson's wedding was supposed to have done. But it hadn't exactly worked. Emily just might do the trick.

Mom made motions to let us know that she and Watson were going to take Emily upstairs to her crib. I nodded. Charlie and I followed. The others stayed behind. They could see Emily later.

Charlie and I stood in the doorway to Emily's room. We watched Watson lay our new sister in her crib. We watched Mom take Emily's shoes off, then cover her with a blanket. Emily stirred and made a soft, sleepy noise but didn't wake up.

When Mom and Watson left, so did Charlie,

but I tiptoed over to Emily's crib and looked down at her.

Hello, there, I thought. You are a very special little girl. I guess you are lucky, too. You found a family. And we are lucky. We found you. Do you know how much we want you? No? Well, you will when you're older, because we will tell you.

You have a lot of brothers, by the way. You have two sisters, as well. And a mom and a dad and a cat and a dog. Someday you'll know all this.

I tiptoed out of Emily's room — my new sister's room. Emily, I decided, was the best Mother's Day present ever.

About the Author

ANN M. MARTIN did *a lot* of baby-sitting when she was growing up in Princeton, New Jersey. Now her favorite baby-sitting charge is her cat, Mouse, who lives with her in her Manhattan apartment.

Ann Martin's Apple Paperbacks are *Bummer Summer*, *Inside Out*, *Stage Fright*, *Me and Katie (the Pest)*, and all the other books in the Baby-sitters Club series.

She is a former editor of books for children, and was graduated from Smith College. She likes ice cream, the beach, and *I Love Lucy*; and she hates to cook.

Look for #25

MARY ANNE AND THE SEARCH
FOR TIGGER

"Tigger!" I called.

I opened the door. No Tigger.

Sometimes he climbs onto a high place, such as the mantelpiece over the fireplace, and then can't get down. I checked the mantelpiece. No Tigger.

Okay. It was time for a room-by-room search. In a room-by-room search, I look through each room thoroughly. If I don't find Tigger in one room, I close the door to the room (if it has a door) and go on to the next one.

I began upstairs. I searched the bedrooms and the bathrooms. I didn't see Tigger, so I closed the door at the head of the stairs and ran down to the first floor.

I was on my hands and knees looking under an armchair when I heard my father calling me.

"I'm here, Dad!" I replied. "In the living room."

143

I backed away from the chair and stood up.

"What's going on?" asked my father. He crossed the room and gave me a kiss. "There's water on the stove but the burner isn't on, and there are vegetables all over the table. It looks as if you stopped in the middle of making dinner."

"Sorry. I guess I did. I can't find Tigger. And I've looked everywhere for him. Well, everywhere inside. He's never missed dinner."

"I guess we better search for him outside then," said Dad.

I gave Dad a grateful look. "Right now? That would be terrific."

"I'll go get the torches."

The torches are these gigantic flashlights we have. Each is bright enough to light up New York City.

I put a jacket on and Dad found the torches. He handed one to me and we went outside.

"Ti-i-i-igger! Ti-i-i-igger!" we called. We walked all around our yard. We shone the lights under bushes, up trees, in shrubbery. The longer we looked, the worse I felt. There was this awful feeling in the pit of my stomach, like I had swallowed a pebble and it had grown into a rock. Now it was growing into a boulder.

**Here's some news about other books
in The Baby-sitters Club series
by Ann M. Martin**

#1 *Kristy's Great Idea*

Kristy thinks the Baby-sitters Club is a great idea. She and her friends Claudia, Stacey, and Mary Anne all love taking care of kids. But nobody counted on crank calls, wild pets, and uncontrollable two-year-olds! Having a Baby-sitters Club isn't easy, but Kristy and her friends won't give up till they get it right!

#2 *Claudia and the Phantom Phone Calls*

Claudia has been getting some mysterious phone calls when she's out baby-sitting. Could they be from the Phantom Jewel Thief who's operating in the area? Claudia has always liked *reading* mysteries, but she doesn't like it when they *happen* to her!

#3 *The Truth About Stacey*

The truth about Stacey is her parents want to find a miracle cure for her diabetes. They're making Stacey's life so hard! The other Baby-sitters are busy fighting the Baby-sitters Agency. How can they help Stacey and save the club, too?

145

#4 Mary Anne Saves the Day

Mary Anne's never been a leader of the Baby-sitters Club. Now there's a big fight among the four friends. It's bad enough when Mary Anne has to eat at the lunch table all alone. But when she has to baby-sit a sick child with no help from her friends — it's time to take charge!

#5 Dawn and the Impossible Three

Poor Dawn! It's not easy being the newest member of the Baby-sitters Club. She's got three impossible kids to take care of. And Kristy thinks things were better *without* Dawn around. It'll take a lot of work to make things run smoothly again, but Dawn's up to the challenge!

#6 Kristy's Big Day

It's a big day for Kristy, all right — she's a bridesmaid in her mother's wedding! And if that's not enough, she and the other Baby-sitters Club members have *fourteen* wedding-guest kids to take care of. Only the Baby-sitters Club could cope with this one!

#7 Claudia and Mean Janine

This summer the Baby-sitters Club is starting a play group in the neighborhood. Claudia can't wait for it to begin — it'll give her some time away from her mean big sister. But then her grandmother has a stroke . . . and the whole summer changes.

#8 Boy-Crazy Stacey

Who needs baby-sitting when there are boys around? Stacey and Mary Anne are mother's helpers at the Jersey shore, and Stacey's mind is on hunky lifeguard Scott. Mary Anne's doing the work of two baby-sitters . . . but how can she tell Stacey that Scott's too old, without breaking Stacey's heart?

#9 The Ghost at Dawn's House

Creaking stairs, noises behind the wall, a secret passage — there must be a ghost at Dawn's house! The Baby-sitters find themselves and one of their charges wrapped up in a mystery. Will they be able to solve it?

#10 Logan Likes Mary Anne!

Quiet, shy Mary Anne has been growing up lately . . . and the Baby-sitters aren't the only ones who've noticed. Logan Bruno likes Mary Anne! He has a dreamy southern accent, he's awfully cute — and he wants to join the Baby-sitters Club. Life in the club has never been this complicated — or this fun!

#11 Kristy and the Snobs

The kids in Kristy's new neighborhood aren't very friendly. In fact they're . . . well, snobs. They laugh at everything — even Kristy's poor old collie, Louie. Kristy's fighting mad. But if anyone can beat a Snob attack, it's the Baby-sitters club. And that's just what they're going to do!

#12 Claudia and the New Girl

Claudia really likes Ashley, the new girl at school. Ashley's the only one who takes Claudia seriously. Soon, Claudia's spending so much time with Ashley that she doesn't have time for baby-sitting — or her old friends. And they don't like it one bit!

148

#13 Good-bye Stacey, Good-bye

There are lots of tears when the Baby-sitters hear the news: Stacey and her family are moving back to New York. The club members can't think of a special enough way to send Stacey off. They want to give her much more than a party. But how do you say good-bye to your best friend?

#14 Hello, Mallory

Mallory Pike has always been good at baby-sitting her younger brothers and sisters. But is she good enough to join the Baby-sitters Club? The club members go overboard giving Mallory baby-sitting tests. Mallory's getting pretty fed up. . . . Maybe she'll just start a baby-sitting business of her own!

#15 Little Miss Stoneybrook . . . and Dawn

Mrs. Pike wants Dawn to help prepare Margo and Claire for the Little Miss Stoneybrook contest. And Dawn wants her charges to win! The only trouble is . . . Kristy, Mary Anne, and Claudia are helping Karen, Myriah, and Charlotte enter the contest, too. And nobody's sure where the competition is fiercer: at the pageant — or at the Baby-sitters Club!

#16 Jessi's Secret Language

Jessi had a hard time fitting in to Stoneybrook. But things got a lot better once she became a member of the Baby-sitters Club! Now Jessi has her biggest challenge yet — baby-sitting for a deaf boy. And in order to communicate with him, Jessi must learn his secret language.

#17 Mary Anne's Bad-Luck Mystery

Mary Anne finds a note in her mailbox. *"Wear this bad-luck charm,"* it says, *"OR ELSE."* Mary Anne's got to do what the note says. But who sent the charm? And why did they send it to Mary Anne? If the Baby-sitters don't solve this mystery soon, their bad luck might never stop!

#18 Stacey's Mistake

Stacey's so excited! She's invited her friends from the Baby-sitters Club down to New York City for a long weekend. But what a mistake! The Baby-sitters are *way* out of place in the big city. Does this mean Stacey can't be the Baby-sitters' friend anymore?

#19 Claudia and the Bad Joke

Claudia's not worried when she hears she has to baby-sit for Betsy, a great practical joker. How much trouble could a little girl cause? *Plenty* . . . and now Claudia might even quit the club. It's time for the Baby-sitters to teach Betsy a lesson. The joke war is on!

#20 Kristy and the Walking Disaster

Kristy's little brother and sister want to play on a softball team, so Kristy starts a ragtag team of her own. With Jackie Rodowsky, the Walking Disaster, playing for them, Kristy's Krushers aren't world champions. But nobody beats them when it comes to team spirit!

#21 Mallory and the Trouble With Twins

Mallory thinks baby-sitting for the Arnold twins will be easy money. They're so adorable! Marilyn and Carolyn may be cute . . . but they're also spoiled brats. It's a baby-sitting nightmare — and Mallory's not giving up!

#22 Jessi Ramsey, Pet-sitter

Jessi's always liked animals. So when the Mancusis need an emergency pet-sitter, she quickly takes the job. But what has Jessi gotten herself into? There are animals *all over* the Mancusis' house! This is going to be one sitting job Jessi will never forget!

#23 Dawn on the Coast

Dawn's trip to California is better than she could ever imagine. And after one wonderful week, Dawn begins to wonder if she might want to . . . *stay* on the coast with her dad and her brother. Dawn's a California girl at heart — but could she really leave Stoneybrook for good?

#25 Mary Anne and the Search for Tigger

Mary Anne's adorable kitten, Tigger, is *missing!* The Baby-sitters have looked everywhere for him, but no one can find him. Then Mary Anne receives a frightening letter in the mail. Someone has taken her kitten, and Mary Anne has to pay a hundred dollars to get him back. Is this some mean practical joke, or has Tigger really been *cat*-napped?

by Ann M. Martin

The Baby-sitters' business is booming! And that gets Stacey, Kristy, Claudia, and the rest of The Baby-sitters Club members in all kinds of adventures…at school, with boys, and, of course, baby-sitting!

Something new and exciting happens in every Baby-sitters Club book. Collect and read them all!

More titles… ▶

titles continued...

❑	MG42501-3	#28	**Welcome Back, Stacey!**	**$2.95**
❑	MG42500-5	#29	**Mallory and the Mystery Diary**	**$2.95**
❑	MG42498-X	#30	**Mary Anne and the Great Romance**	**$2.95**
❑	MG42497-1	#31	**Dawn's Wicked Stepsister**	**$2.95**
❑	MG42496-3	#32	**Kristy and the Secret of Susan**	**$2.95**
❑	MG42495-5	#33	**Claudia and the Great Search**	**$2.95**
❑	MG42494-7	#34	**Mary Anne and Too Many Boys**	**$2.95**
❑	MG42508-0	#35	**Stacey and the Mystery of Stoneybrook**	**$2.95**
❑	MG43565-5	#36	**Jessi's Baby-sitter**	**$2.95**
❑	MG43566-3	#37	**Dawn and the Older Boy**	**$2.95**
❑	MG43567-1	#38	**Kristy's Mystery Admirer**	**$2.95**
❑	MG41588-3		**Baby-sitters on Board!** **Super Special #1**	**$2.95**
❑	MG42419-X		**Baby-sitters' Summer Vacation** **Super Special #2**	**$2.95**
❑	MG42499-8		**Baby-sitters' Winter Vacation** **Super Special #3**	**$3.50**
❑	MG42493-9		**Baby-sitters' Island Adventure** **Super Special #4**	**$3.50**
❑	MG43745-3		**The Baby-sitters Club 1990-91 Student Planner and Date Book**	**$7.95**
❑	MG43744-5		**The Baby-sitters Club 1991 Calendar**	**$8.95**
❑	MG43803-4		**The Baby-sitters Club Notebook**	**$1.95**

Available wherever you buy books...or use this order form.

Scholastic Inc., P.O. Box 7502, 2931 E. McCarty Street, Jefferson City, MO 65102

Please send me the books I have checked above. I am enclosing $_____
(please add $2.00 to cover shipping and handling). Send check or money order — no cash or C.O.D.s please.

Name _____

Address _____

City _____ State/Zip _____

Please allow four to six weeks for delivery. Offer good in the U.S. only. Sorry, mail orders are not available to residents of Canada. Prices subject to change.

BSC390